Praise for

Maplecroft

"Cherie Priest is supremely gifted and *Maplecroft* is a remarkable novel, simultaneously beautiful and grotesque. It is at once a dark historical fantasy with r⌐ ⌐r mixing Victori⌐ ⌐wn."

⌐rk Times
⌐nowblind

"With *Maplecroft*, Cherie Priest delivers her most terrifying vision yet—a genuinely scary, deliciously claustrophobic, and dreadfully captivating historical thriller with both heart and cosmic horror. A mesmerizing, absolute must-read."
—Brian Keene, Bram Stoker Award–winning author of *The Rising* and *Ghoul*

Praise for Cherie Priest
and Her Novels

"Priest can write scenes that are jump-out-of-your-skin scary."
—Cory Doctorow, author of *Homeland*

"Fine writing, humor, thrills, real scares, the touch of the occult . . . had me from the first page."
—Heather Graham, *New York Times* bestselling author of *The Night Is Forever*

"Cherie Priest has created a chilling page-turner. Her voice is rich, earthy, soulful, and deliciously Southern as she weaves a disturbing yarn like a master! Awesome—gives you goose bumps!"
—L. A. Banks, author of the Vampire Huntress Legend series

"Wonderful. Enchanting. Amazing and original fiction that will satisfy that buttery Southern taste, as well as that biting aftertaste of the dark side. I loved it."   —Joe R. Lansdale, award-winning author of *The Thicket*

"Priest masterfully weaves a complex tapestry of interlocking plots, motivations, quests, character arcs, and background stories to produce an exquisitely written novel with a rich and lush atmosphere."   —*The Gazette* (Montreal)

continued . . .

"Priest has a knack for instantly creating quirky, likable, memorable characters."
                                                                    —*The Roanoke Times* (VA)

"Cherie Priest has crafted an intriguing yarn that is excellently paced, keeping the reader turning pages to discover where the story will lead."
                                                                    —San Francisco Book Review

"Priest's haunting lyricism and graceful narrative are complemented by the solemn, cynical thematic undercurrents with a tangible gravity and depth."
                                                                    —*Publishers Weekly*

"With each volume, Priest squeezes in several novels' worth of flabbergasting ideas, making each story expansive as hell while still keeping a tight control over the three-act structure."
                                                                    —The Chicago Center for Literature and Photography

"Cherie Priest has mastered the art of braiding atmosphere, suspense, and metaphysics."
                                                                    —Katherine Ramsland, bestselling author
                                                                    of *Ghost: Investigating the Other Side*

"Priest does an excellent job of building tension throughout the novel, in fact, up to and including the satisfying ending. Writing that can simultaneously set a mood, flesh out characters, and advance plot is a force to be reckoned with. With writing this good . . . I have no doubts that we will be hearing from Cherie Priest again and again."   —SF Signal

"[Priest] is already a strong voice in dark fantasy and could, with care, be a potent antidote for much of what is lacking elsewhere in the genre."   —Rambles

"Priest is amazing at detail, brilliant at transforming an imagined, impossible history in such a way that flying airships and a decades-long Yankee invasion seem not only plausible but simply neglected in our history books."
                                                                    —LitStack

"An engrossing and exciting adventure from its first sentence to its last. . . . Priest once again delivers a rousing adventure that demonstrates both her love of history and her definitive knack for playing with and bending it to fit the purpose of her captivating universe."   —Bitten by Books

maplecroft

THE BORDEN DISPATCHES

CHERIE PRIEST

A ROC BOOK

ROC
Published by the Penguin Group
Penguin Group (USA) LLC, 375 Hudson Street,
New York, New York 10014

USA | Canada | UK | Ireland | Australia | New Zealand | India | South Africa | China
penguin.com
A Penguin Random House Company

First published by Roc, an imprint of New American Library,
a division of Penguin Group (USA) LLC

First Printing, September 2014

LIBRARY OF CONGRESS CATALOGING-IN-PUBLICATION DATA:

Priest, Cherie.
  Maplecroft: the Borden dispatches / Cherie Priest.
    pages cm
  ISBN 978-0-451-46697-6 (paperback)
  1. Borden, Lizzie, 1860–1927—Fiction.   2. Fall River (Mass.)—Fiction.
3. Women murderers—Fiction.   4. Murder—Fiction.   I. Title.
  PS3616.R537M37 2014
  813'.6—dc23   2014011172

Printed in the United States of America
10 9 8 7 6 5 4 3 2 1

Set in Horley Old Style
Designed by Spring Hoteling

ACKNOWLEDGMENTS

There are always too many people to thank—and I always live in fear of leaving someone out, but books don't come together without a hell of a team and I'm very lucky to have such wonderful folks on my side. So I will take a crack at it, and hope for the best.

First and foremost, thanks go to my editor, Anne Sowards, and all the fine folks at Ace/Roc, for taking a chance on this peculiar project of mine. I know it's a little on the weird side, but I'm terribly proud of it—and I'm grateful beyond belief that Anne was willing to take a chance on it, and that all the great people at her office have done such a stellar job with the final product. Likewise (and along that same vein), thanks go to everyone at Donald Maass, particularly and especially my agent, Jennifer Jackson, for closing the deal and generally being a shoulder to cry on, a wall to bounce things off of, and a partner in storytelling crime.

And then, of course, thanks to the usual suspects: my husband, Aric, whose patience with these things knows no bounds; Warren Ellis and everyone in the secret clubhouse that serves the world; GRRM and the Consortium; Greg Wild-Smith for the long-term and long-suffering Web support; Team Capybara and all its affiliate members; the Nashville crew in all its awesomeness (dear Lees, Harveys, et al); the kindly souls at Woodthrush and Robin's

ACKNOWLEDGMENTS

Roost; Bill Schafer, Yanni Kuznia, and the other assorted Michigan Maniacs; Paul Goat Allen at B&N (and everywhere else); Derek Tatum and Carol Malcolm for all the gossip and encouragement; and *Maplecroft*'s Chief Cheerleader, Christopher Golden. He knows *why*.

maplecroft

THESE ARE THE THINGS AN EARTHQUAKE BRINGS

❧

Lizzie Andrew Borden

March 17, 1894

No one else is allowed in the cellar.

Emma has a second key, in case I am injured or trapped down there; but Emma also has instructions about how and when to use that key. When she knocks upon the cellar door, I must always reply, "Emma dear, I'm nearly finished." Even if I'm not working on anything at all. Even if I'm simply down there, writing in my journals. If I say anything else when she knocks, or if I do not respond—my elder sister knows what to do: She must summon Doctor Seabury, and then prevent him from descending into the cellar unarmed.

I wish there were someone closer she could send for, but no one else would come.

The good doctor, though . . . he could be persuaded to attend us, I believe. And he's a large man, sturdy, and in good health for a fellow of his age. Quite a commanding presence, very much the old soldier, which is no surprise. During the War Between the States, he served as a field surgeon—I know that much. He must've been quite young, but the military training has served him well through the years, even in such a provincial setting as Fall River.

Yes, I think all things being equal, he's the last and best chance either Emma or I would have, were either of us to meet with some accident. And between the two of us, I suppose it must be admitted—to myself, if no one else—that accidents are more likely to befall me than her.

Ah, well. I'd take up safer hobbies if I could.

I locked the cellar door behind myself, and proceeded down the narrow wood-slat stairs into the darkness of that half-finished pit, once intended for vegetables, roots, or wines. I've paid a pretty penny to refurbish the place so that the floor is stable and the walls are stacked with stone. During wet weather, those stones weep buckets and the floor creaks something awful, but by and large it's secure enough.

Secure and quiet. Dreadfully so, as I've learned on occasion. I could scream my head off down there and Emma could be reading peacefully by the fireplace. She'd never hear a thing.

Obviously this concerns me, but what can I do? My precautions are for the safety and well-being of us both.

Of us *all*.

I lit the gas fixtures as I went. All three came on with a turn of their switches, and by the time I reached the final stair I cast a huge, long shadow—as if I were a giant in my own laboratory.

My *laboratory*. That feels like the wrong word, but what else can I call it? This is the place where I've gathered my specimens, collected my tools, recorded my findings, and meticulously documented all experiments and tests. So the word must apply.

I cannot claim to have made any real progress, except I now know a thousand ways in which I have failed to save anyone, anywhere. From anything.

It would be easier, I think, if I knew there was some finite number of possibilities—an absolute threshold of events I could try in order to produce successful, repeatable results. If I knew there were only a million hypothetical trials, I would cheerfully, painstakingly navigate them all from first to last. Such a task might take the rest of my life, but it'd be a comfort to know I was forcing some definite evolution to a crisis.

But I don't know any such thing. And more likely, the possibilities measure in the billions—or are altogether endless. I shudder to consider it, but I'd be a fool if I didn't.

So I go on wishing. I wish for the prospect of a definite finale, and I wish I were not alone.

That would make things easier, too—if there were someone else to share the burden, apart from poor Emma. And though she appeared invulnerably strong when I was a child (due in part to the ten-year difference in age between us), in our middling years her health has failed her in a treacherous fashion. Often she's confined to a bed or a seat, and she coughs with such frequency that I only notice it anymore if she's stopped. Consumption, everyone supposes. Consumption, and possibly the shock of what befell our father and Mrs. Borden.

That's the rest of what everyone supposes, and that's probably true, in its way. It's true that Emma has never been herself since those last weeks when she fled the house, insisting that something was wrong and that she felt a hideous suffocation, and she needed to find some other air to breathe.

That's how she put it. Finding other air to breathe.

At the time we assumed she only wanted a change of scenery from the fighting, the bickering, and the sudden appearance of William—and all the difficulties he inspired.

True, true. All of it true, but incomplete.

We were both contaminated by something, by whatever took the other Bordens. It worked its way inside us, too— whether by breath, or through the skin, or through something we consumed, still I cannot say. All I can do is pray that we caught it in time, and that we have removed ourselves beyond its influence . . .

Alas.

I almost wrote, "before any permanent damage was done." But then I thought of Emma and her fragile lungs, and her bloodied handkerchiefs. And I thought also of my poisoned dreams and the awful visions that sometimes distract me even while waking. I often believe in retrospect that they're telling me something crucial . . . but doesn't every dreamer insist that every dream is meaningful at the time? However, in the retelling, the dreams (and my visions) are trite at best, disturbing at worst.

I will not burden Emma with them, for she is burdened enough with her own body's complaints. And I don't have anyone else to tell, not really. Not except for Nance, and I fear to the point of fretful, bowel-clenching sickness that I might chase her away even without the secrets that darken the space between us. Little though I see her lately, since her most recent job for that director, Peter Rasmussen . . . still I value beyond my life the time I spend with her beside me.

Nance has accused me, once or twice in teasing, of being a sentimental old fool. She's right, absolutely.

She's also young—very young. So young it's all the more inappropriate, how we carry on between ourselves. Carelessly, it's been said. Wantonly, it's been accused. Nance wouldn't argue with either one; she would laugh instead, and add her own descriptors with even less propriety. But women her age, barely out of their teens and with the whole world before them, they haven't yet had time to lose the things they love. Every affair is a fairy tale or a tragedy, and either one is fine so long as the story is good. Every love is all or nothing, and even their "nothings" are poetry. They don't yet know how the years fade and stretch the highs and the lows, wearing them thin, making them vulnerable. They haven't yet known much of death.

I don't think I'm talking about Nance anymore.

It doesn't matter. She won't come again for weeks, maybe months. And I won't hold that against her.

I can't. I'm the one who asked her to stay away.

Upon reaching the cellar's floor I turned on the two largest gaslights, and the bleak, cluttered space was flooded with a quivering white light that joined the illumination from the stairs. I blinked against it. I set one hand on the nearest table and leaned there while my eyes adjusted, and when they did, I took a very deep breath and considered the week's samples.

My laboratory is a large open room, undivided except by two rows of three tables each. Several of the tables are occupied by jars of assorted sizes, ranging from tubes as small as my thumb to bigger containers that could easily hold a loaf of bread. Floating within them in an alcohol solution are things I've collected over the last two years. Some are recognizable as varieties of ordinary ocean flora and fauna, and some are not. I've gathered plants, fish, sea jellies, crustaceans, and cephalopods by the score, and I've cataloged them all by their deformities. Some are laden with so many aberrations that it's impossible to tell what the original species might have been; some have minor exterior problems, though these malformations often mask more obvious internal ones.

For example, one of my larger jars holds a brown octopus (*octopus vulgaris*) with two distinct heads and three extra tentacles. Upon a cursory dissection of it, I discovered that it also had twice the usual complement of hearts—which is to say six of them. Two of these hearts were pitiably underdeveloped, but distinct and bafflingly present.

I've also found fish with too many sets of gills, grotesquely oversized fins, or no eyes whatsoever. I've retrieved lobsters with three claws, with one claw, with no tail, or no legs. The story is much the same for simpler creatures, though the abnormalities are sometimes harder to spot.

My conclusions, such as they are, sound like utter madness. But I believe they are borne out by the books that are stacked on the other desks, where I've had to establish the library. We couldn't put shelves along the wall or else the damp would ruin them, so two of the farthest tables are stacked with shorter bookcases. Each of these cases is piled with volumes too arcane and peculiar to display upstairs, despite the fact that we virtually never see visitors.

Upon reflection, I'm not entirely sure who I'm hiding them from. Not Emma. She's the one who ordered most of them, and regardless, she's read them already.

Nance? No, I don't think so. Nance is difficult to scandalize, and she's aware of my interests—though not aware of their extent, or their origins. If pressed, I'd have to say that I'm hiding the books from Nance's friends, who sometimes accompany her when she visits.

Or maybe I only do it out of optimism, from the eternal hope that someday we'll have friends of our own again.

It's ridiculous, I know. My infamy taints my sister, who declares her intent to stay by my side even as we both know she's too fragile for any other recourse. And it's furthermore ridiculous because our respective activities require a certain solitude. I must be left alone to pursue my experiments, and Emma could never continue her correspondences with eminent scientists and biologists if anyone knew that "E. A. Jackson" was a woman. Thank heavens none of her correspondents has ever dropped by for a spot of tea. I honestly don't know what she'd tell them.

It's a blessing, really, that no one will have anything to do with us.

3 picked up the nearest lantern and lit it. It's a special one, affixed with mirrors and foils, to direct the light wherever I wish to project it—and I wanted to brighten the back right table, beside the two oversized sinks and an assortment of hoses, hooks, tongs, knives, and scalpels. There, in one of my larger jars, a peculiar mass had sunk to the bottom, where it sizzled enough to muster a light froth that foamed throughout the container. It'd been sizzling that way for two days, while an acid solution nibbled away at the calcite. Within that mass, I have always sensed there was something important.

When I first discovered it, the object was approximately the size of a small melon, and it lacked any geometric shape to speak of. If I were to assign it any general description, I'd say that it looked like a very large hand grabbed a fistful of the ocean bottom and squeezed until the sediment became stone. It was roughly column-like, with bits of finny fluting. Primarily it was white, or the swirled browns and bleached hues of ocean detritus.

I found it on one of my evening walks on the beach, after dark with a lantern. And at the risk of sounding hysterical, I believe that I *felt* it. I believe that it called me, and I heard it.

So I retrieved it, setting my lantern on the sand and hefting the rock into my hands, holding it there. Though it was in no way shaped like a shell, I held it up to my ear and listened—for what, I cannot say.

But this draw, this *lure*. I've felt it before and I don't yet understand the full implications of what it means, but I know I should've taken more care with the sample. I should've wrapped it in my apron and carried it that way, without touching it barehanded, but I didn't. I cradled it in one naked arm and held my light aloft with the other, all the way back home.

There, I returned to my senses and dumped it into the jar full of acid to let science sort it out.

I forcibly tugged my attention away from the bubbling, hypnotic jar and turned instead to a box I keep buried beneath the floor.

With a quick pop of a pry bar at just the right spot, a row of boards slipped out of place. My floor is not as seamless and immutable as it appears; it is riddled with compartments such as this one.

Some people keep cupboards in a wall. I keep them in the ground.

Beneath this lid, which I'd disguised as flooring, a box

squatted—smelling of wet soil and worms, and moss, and lichen, and whatever else blackens the earth below my home. I could have pried it out and brought it up to the floor, but I chose not to. For some reason, I felt that the box was safest right there, underneath everything. Underneath my house, my basement, my floor.

I would bury it deeper if I could, but I need to keep it within reach, this little repository of evil. Soon, I might need to add to its contents—depending on what lies at the heart of that strange mass which dissolves by atoms on the back right table.

I'm not sure what made me reach into the hole and touch the iron-bound top of that box.

Yes, again, I'm mired in uncertainties and suspicions, but I have taken all the precautions I can. More than likely, at least half of them don't work. But when I don't know what works and what does *not* work, all I can do is throw it all in together, and trust that some measure of success will result, even if that success is diluted by imprecision.

So there is a box that is lined with lead and sealed with iron bands, and inscribed with unsettling symbols, and buried in the earth, beneath the rowan-wood boards that make up the floor of my basement.

I reached down into the hole and fumbled with the latches until it was unfastened all around, and then I lifted the lid for no good reason whatsoever. I'd like to say that the motion was dreamlike on my behalf, that I scarcely recall doing it; but this isn't quite true, because I remember watching my arm extend, and my fingers manipulate the fasteners, and then lift the lid. I recall every bit of this, and in my recollection, I was fully in control of myself.

Except that I *can't* have been.

Because now, with some distance from that box and that basement, I know full well that it was a dangerous, absurd thing to do—and that not all the gold in the world, nor all the threats or complaints, could ever persuade me to open it right now, with nothing to add to its treasure.

And I jot this down, all of it, in case—upon eventual review—some pattern is revealed. These journal entries are already helping, for now I can see, going back over last month's notes, that there's a proximal effect to the lure of the box. The farther I remove myself from its contents, the less they affect me.

If I had any sense, I'd relocate to the desert or the mountains, and be done with this whole business once and for all.

I gazed into the box, upon six bits of stone or glass, all varying in their respective radiance and greenness. They go from the sickly yellowish shade of a toad's belly to a rich seaweed that could nearly be described as emerald. The smallest is the size of a child's fingernail. The largest is as big as a plum. All of them are beautiful. Very beautiful. So beautiful it's all but impossible to take one's eyes away, even though they look like nothing more alarming than bits of sea glass, glittering weakly at the bottom of a reinforced box.

Of course, they are more than that. I know it good and well, just like I know better than to kneel over the box and listen to the odd hum they make. But it's a lovely hum, you see? It's a calming, drawing thing. When I hear it, as I stare at those scattered pieces of precious jetsam, it's as if I can hear my mother beside my cradle, and feel the rocking of her gentle hand as she sings me off to a nap.

No, not the recently late Mrs. Borden—but my *true* mother,

Sarah, who died when I was very small. I have no real remembrance of her, but sometimes I think I recall a perfume, or a very distant voice. The rustle of a skirt, perhaps. A step upon the stairs. Emma says she was a pretty woman, and that she often hummed to herself while she worked around the house.

I envy my sister's solid memories.

My father married Abigail when I was two, and Abigail raised me, albeit reluctantly and without any warmth. She'd wanted to be a society wife, not the live-in caretaker for two girls who were not her own.

She did not let us forget it often, or for long.

(I was instructed to call her "Mother" when I was tiny. This was insisted upon to great penalty if I failed, though Emma was old enough that she was never commanded to do the same. I finally began to refer to her as "Mrs. Borden" when I realized that I was an adult, and that no one could make me do otherwise. I did not owe that cold, interloping daughter of a pushcart peddler the respect of the more personal term.)

I'd left the box open longer than I should have.

I knew this even before Emma came knocking, but it's strange—I couldn't seem to care. I was fully aware that I was tempting fate or something worse, and I was all too certain that the buzzing, warm green noise could be heard by more ears than just my own. But the stones were beautiful, and they were near. They calmed me, nearly to the point of a stupor.

Emma had called twice from upstairs, and she'd been pounding upon the cellar door for half a minute before I was able to rouse myself enough to say in a choked, weird voice, "Emma dear, I'm nearly finished."

I thought I heard her sob. She cried, "Lizzie, you must

come, quickly. Something . . . something is trying to come inside. Lizzie, something is *here*."

I slammed the box lid back down and dropped the board atop it, cursing myself for my inattention and reflexively seeking the weapon I keep leaned against the bottom of the staircase.

There it was, yes.

I grabbed my axe.

A DOCTOR, A LAWYER, A MERCHANT, A CHIEF

Owen Seabury, M.D.

MARCH 15, 1894

The first thing I ever learned of my patients is that they lie, incessantly and to their own detriment. They mislead me regarding their injuries; they feign symptoms; they deny delicate but pressing problems out of modesty or embarrassment, or fear of repercussions.

In short, they are utterly untrustable. But they are also readable, to an experienced man like myself—and I can learn much from the things they leave unsaid.

But this was not always the case.

So let me recount the Borden deaths. I may as well. I do not see the benefit of avoiding and ignoring the truth. To the contrary, I'd much rather address the case outright, and shine a light upon it—regardless of what sins of mine may be revealed.

These are the facts.

Sometime late in June of 1892 the Borden family began to experience a prolonged, peculiar set of ailments. I was a close witness to their distress, for I was not merely their doctor but also a nearby neighbor. They lived directly across the street from me and my now-late wife, so I had ample opportunity to observe them over the weeks leading up to the murders on August 4 of that same year.

The first complaints came from Abigail Borden, second wife of Andrew Jackson Borden and stepmother to Andrew's grown children, Emma and her younger sister, Lizzie, both of whom lived on the premises. Mrs. Borden came to sit in my parlor, having visited for an informal consultation.

I didn't know her well, but I liked what I knew of her. She was younger than her husband by enough years to remark it, and agreeable in that comfortable way women sometimes achieve when they marry into money and can expect to be cared for.

But on that summer occasion she was out of sorts, restless and pale. As she spoke, she fidgeted constantly with a pendant that hung around her neck from a long silver chain. I remember it so vividly because of the way the light caught it, and though I did not see the item clearly, I could not help but notice how its glassy stone gleamed a rich, ocean green shade that cast bright reflections on the walls.

"Doctor Seabury, it's a digestive problem. It's a horrible feeling, at once cold and bubbling. I'm so nauseous, and so light-headed, at times, that I must sit and cover my eyes until the sensation passes."

"I see. And is anyone else in the family displaying symptoms like these?"

After a brief hesitation she said, "Andrew is, a bit."

"What are his complaints? Are they precisely like yours, or is there some variation to his discomfort?"

"I couldn't say." She shook her head. "He hasn't spoken about it. I've only . . . noticed. As his wife, who shares the same household. You understand."

"Of course," I replied. "And what of your stepdaughters?"

Her face darkened and for a moment she quit worrying the pendant. "I wouldn't know. I haven't spoken to either of them lately."

"Ah. Has there been any significant change in the family diet?"

She shook her head again and said, "No, I don't believe so."

I did not press her any further. I already knew what bothered her bowels, though I couldn't bring it up without prompting denials and offense. So rather than invite confrontation, I said, "Perhaps it's something seasonal, then. Dyspepsia can arise from almost anything—and rather than leap to alarming conclusions, I honestly think this can be handled with simple, common treatments."

I offered her some harmless prescriptions, chiefly carbonate of ammonia pills and white bismuth. It wouldn't hurt, and it might even help.

I did not doubt that she was suffering from indigestion. I only doubted my personal ability to address the root cause thereof.

It was no great secret that the Bordens had difficulties. Andrew's spinster daughters never developed any affection for

Abigail; and with the lot of them living under one roof, tensions could—and often did—overflow into arguments . . . the kind of arguments which nearby neighbors might hear, and pretend they hadn't.

Not long before Abigail Borden sought me out for this first of many complaints, things at home had escalated in an unexpected and unfortunate fashion.

As I said, Andrew was older than his wife. He'd lived a full lifetime before ever meeting her. Whether or not she loved him I cannot speculate; but she was content with him, and by all appearances their union was a "good match," as they say, even though he was widely regarded as a tight-fisted curmudgeon. Regardless, she was at ease with the decisions that had brought her to Andrew, an aged but still vital man—who had a fortune and a family, if few friends.

That said, I do not think she knew about his son. I'm not sure anyone did, until he appeared.

When William strolled into town claiming Andrew as his father, efforts were made to keep his existence quiet. I believe he stayed at the Borden home for a few days, though surely a hotel would have been a better choice. At any rate, I saw him coming and going repeatedly over a weekend once, and the timing was *deeply* suspicious: The elder patriarch was in the process of revising his will—a tense time in any moneyed family. But to a family so fractured already, and burdened with middle-aged daughters unlikely to marry? What added pressure would come with a shiftless bastard in search of an inheritance?

Little wonder Mrs. Borden was experiencing gastrointestinal distress. She'd hardly be human if she didn't.

That's why I gave her the harmless medicines to soothe her.

And that's why I looked no closer, not at that time. The situation was so clear to me! So obvious!

Yet the matters were so personal, I doubted she would speak of them; and I didn't think she'd tolerate my talking about them with any frankness. After all, this was a woman unwilling to converse aloud about her husband's flatulence. Dragging his past indiscretions into the conversation could only make things worse.

Or that's what I told myself when I sent her away, bottles in hand, her pendant clinking against one of them as she walked.

The next week she came to see me again, twice in quick succession. Still she complained of the troublesome stomach, though the pains were worse, she said. I suspected the beginnings of a peptic ulcer, but I didn't go so far as to suggest it. The treatments were similar anyway, with the added admonition to rest, avoid stressful engagements, and alter her diet.

Abigail was already resting more than might have been considered strictly healthful, and she was scarcely eating as it stood. I was afraid that any attempt to more closely restrict her intake would lead to emaciation.

There wasn't much I could do about her stressful engagements. They all lived in her house, or insisted they had a right to.

Before long, Andrew sought me out as well. His complaints were similar, though never quite as advanced as his wife's—for Abigail's digestive issues continued and she grew paler before my eyes. Had the circumstances surrounding her decline been any different, I might have noticed sooner that I'd made some egregious mistake in the diagnosis.

But in my slim defense, William's interference had crossed a threshold from nuisance to criminal mischief. The authorities were called on two separate occasions; and on one of these, to my serious concern, both Andrew and Abigail accused the wayward young man of trying to poison them.

Back then, I considered the accusation, turning it over in my mind. Given even what little I knew of William's character, I couldn't dismiss the possibility outright; and the Bordens *did* appear collectively weakened—even Emma and Lizzie were unusually wan. They too admitted feeling as if they'd eaten something tainted, though neither went so far as to accuse their half brother of any misdeed.

I offered my assistance, providing more bismuth, diluted nitrous acid, canella bark powders, and even charcoal in case they suspected poison in the future.

Over the summer, the situation deteriorated.

I was busy—I was distracted by other patients, and by the gossip of William's presence and behavior lingering over the place like a fog. The murky context of the Borden home life obscured the truth from me. It was not my place to cut through the word of mouth. I was a friend to them, yes, absolutely. Or I tried to be. But I was not family, and whatever was happening across the street was a family matter.

By the end of July the shouting had stopped. I know, because the weather was overly warm, even given the season. All of us left our windows open, but I barely heard a sound from my neighbors, though my wife said she'd heard strange noises—the kind that made her worry for their health. She had seen their shapes at the window, moving slowly past the wind-stirred curtains.

I told her she shouldn't watch or listen for such things, that it wasn't polite. She pointed out that it was difficult not to watch or listen, given that the house was scarcely twenty yards away from our own, and if they wished to keep their problems private, they could close the windows or leave the city for their negotiations.

Then she said that in fact, Emma Borden had done just that. She'd packed up her things and called a carriage, and that was the last anyone had seen of her. (Somehow, this had escaped my notice, too.)

For that matter, William had left town as well a week previously—not entirely of his own accord. Andrew's influence had persuaded the authorities to become more aggressively involved, and the young man had vanished without returning.

Assuming this was the case, only Andrew, Abigail, and the younger daughter were left in the house. No wonder things had quieted. I hoped this meant the end, and that their lives could return to normal.

Surely if left in peace, the remaining Bordens would sort out their differences and their health would be restored.

I'll never forget the night of August 3. I wish I could—but I've played it over in my head a thousand times, and it's burned there like a book of photographs, flipped together to make a moving scene.

It was late, but my wife and I were still up. We were turning down the wicks and extinguishing the gas lamps, settling in for the night when we heard a loud thump downstairs against our front door, followed by a gruesome wail that sounded part human, part drowning animal.

My wife was alarmed, but I told her not to panic and I lit another lantern to carry downstairs. "Stay here!" I commanded over my shoulder. It wasn't necessary. She'd already thrown herself into the water closet and locked the door.

Down the stairs I rushed, stumbling over my slippers and wincing with every pound upon the door. They weren't the ordinary knockings of a late-night visitor, or the frantic beating of a desperate patient—a noise I knew quite well, after a career of delivering babies and attending the dying.

Instead it was a low, dull thud repeated without rhythm, and the cry came with it again. I wanted to shut my ears against the bellowing yowl, but I forced myself down the corridor. And there, shadowed in the colored glass of the small-framed window, I saw a shape flinging itself heavily, repeatedly, against the front door.

I froze, reconsidering my decision to answer. Whatever struggled on the other side couldn't be human, could it? But then I heard one word and my resolve quickened.

"Help."

A woman's voice. Garbled, even in that single syllable. But recognizable.

"Help us," she tried again, and I rushed toward the door.

I flung it open and held up my lantern. There she was, Abigail Borden—for all that I scarcely recognized her. How long had it been since I'd seen her? This change could not have dropped upon her overnight. What kind of failure was I as a physician and neighbor that this ghastly transformation had eluded me?

Her skin looked like that of a waterlogged corpse, doughy and far too white. She seemed swollen, and her hair was wild around her shoulders, falling down her back in seaweed tangles.

I croaked at her, "Mrs. Borden!" though there was no good reason I shouldn't have used her first name. I'd known her as "Abigail" for years, but this did not seem like her, for all that I knew it must be. I wanted to impose some distance between myself and this woman. Something was wrong. Any fool could see it. Even me.

I stammered again, "Mrs. Borden—what on earth is the matter?"

Her eyes met mine and they were rheumy and too large for their sockets, with surprise or stress or horror. She said, "It's poison, I think." Every word was thick in her mouth, and I wondered if she hadn't been drinking. I struggled to convince myself of any new cause—alcohol? laudanum? Dependency could change a person terribly; this much I knew. I clung to this explanation of what stood swaying before me.

"Poison?"

She was unstable on her feet. I should've reached for her, taken her arm and steadied her.

In my career I've had my hands upon more revolting bodies than a layman is likely to encounter in a lifetime of trying. I've squeezed boils, soaked my hands in blood and pus, slipped in entrails, swaddled slippery stillborns, and pulled excrement from unwilling bowels by hand.

But I did not want to touch that woman. I couldn't stand the thought of it.

All my oaths were failed in that night.

I opened my mouth to tell her something. Anything. A consolation, a suggestion. I have no idea what might've spewed forth if I'd had the opportunity to speak, but I was interrupted by a voice from across the road.

A low voice, another woman. Steady and authoritative. Firm and reassuring.

It was the younger Borden daughter, Lizzie. She stood on the front porch watching her stepmother shudder and beg before me. With just enough subtle volume to carry the short distance between us, she commanded, "Mrs. Borden, come back inside."

Abigail's eyes widened yet further, until a seam of white showed all around her night-blackened pupils. Slowly she swiveled her head to look back at her house, at her stepdaughter.

The moon and the corner gaslight showed Lizzie in shades of gray, tinted yellow. She was motionless. She might have been an apparition, or a daguerreotype. I could not say that her face was blank, for that would be untrue; I should say instead that she did not appear conflicted. Even given the distance and darkness between us, I could see that she had come to some resolution.

(Though it's easy for me to speak that way in retrospect, and it's possible I did not perceive any of this. I may only be coloring the past with my knowledge of what was to come.)

I said, "Mrs. Borden?" and she pivoted to regard me once more, unblinking.

For a very short flash—only an instant—her features shifted, as if her old self had seized control in order to speak.

She told me then, in that narrow window between fright and madness, "We're done for, you know. Whatever happens now, we won't be saved."

Then she backed away, nearly tripping over the top porch stair but catching herself at the last moment. She retreated without unlocking her gaze from my face until she reached the street, at which point she trudged back up to her own home and let Lizzie usher her inside.

As Lizzie closed the door, she too met my eyes. I saw only her certainty, and the moon's cold reflection. And then nothing at all, as they both disappeared inside.

Confused and unaccountably afraid, I lingered, with the wind gusting into my own house, flapping the curtains and rattling the leaves on the young rubber plant that shivered in the hallway.

My wife called out, "Dearest?"

I didn't answer. I didn't know how.

I shut the door and locked it, then in a fit of lunatic whimsy, I pushed the potted plant in front of the door. It slid against it with the dragging, grating scrape of unfinished ceramics. And it did nothing to make me feel less afraid.

The next morning, Abigail and Andrew Jackson Borden were found hacked to death. It's a well-known story by now.

Lizzie was the closest thing to a witness, and she said almost nothing. She'd found them, yes. Her father downstairs on the couch, reclined as if he'd been napping and caught unawares. Her stepmother upstairs in the spare bedroom, sprawled facedown on the floor.

Before the house swarmed with police and investigators, reporters and curiosity seekers, I was summoned by the maid, who arrived in a firestorm of tears, wails, and blubbered protestations. She was an Irish girl; Maggie was her name—or that's all I ever heard them call her. She tugged on my arm when I opened the door, and she drew me across the street, telling me everything between gasps and gulps.

And I went, with all the dread of the previous evening foremost in my mind, weighing down my feet as I plodded the few scant yards over to my neighbors' bloody abode.

The day was bright and hot. The sun bleached out all the colors, and some of the details, almost as badly as the night had just a few hours previously. And there was Lizzie, standing on the front porch waiting for me. Her mouth was fixed in a grim line, and her eyes squinted against the brilliant light of morning.

Just above her feet I saw dark stains spreading in a violent red against the light brown shade of her dress. She would later say, before a judge and jury, that her hem had become bloody when she stood beside the corpses, attempting to examine or rouse them.

(And at that same trial, I would testify on her behalf. I would recall the brown dress, and I would swear that the blood on her clothes was consistent with a concerned, frightened woman who'd approached the Bordens with intent to assist them.)

As I approached she said, "Doctor Seabury, my father and Mrs. Borden are dead. Something has killed them."

Much difficulty followed.

I was called upon to testify, as were many others. I would speak again and again of her dress and the blood, and my neighbors bashed open with the thick, heavy blade.

Lizzie comported herself admirably. She remained ladylike and reasonable, and she answered the prosecutor's questions so long as he asked them—always presenting a picture of calm cooperation, and only becoming slightly scrambled under the barrage of confusing questions. He worked hard to trip her, to compel her to incriminate herself.

She stuck to her story, and neither the witnesses nor the lawyers were able to rattle her into guilty confessions.

It was just as well. No one really wanted to believe she'd done it.

Was she physically capable of committing the murders?

No doubt. She was only thirty-two, and sturdily built. Her father was in his seventies. Her stepmother, although younger, was taken from behind, presumably by surprise.

But there was no one to satisfactorily accuse Lizzie. Maggie refused to condemn her, and none of the other witnesses could convince the jury that she had a motive for such horrendous acts. The small things added up to only more small things. The daily, petty gripes of a mixed household and Lizzie's cold behavior toward her stepmother . . . they seemed to fall within the parameters of reasonableness, if not pleasantness.

Nothing emerged to make Lizzie appear to the court like a monster gone mad, and so she was not convicted. She collected her inheritance, after the much-discussed "will" failed to materialize; and shortly thereafter, she and her sister, Emma, relocated together to the other side of town.

They purchased a large, beautiful home and they named it Maplecroft.

Phillip Zollicoffer,
Professor of Biology, Miskatonic University

❦

It arrived yesterday, though I did not have the opportunity to open and examine it until this afternoon. The package came wrapped in brown paper and twine, directed to myself with a return address of Fall River, Massachusetts.

Immediately I knew it had originated in the office of my distant colleague, Dr. E. A. Jackson—a knowledgeable fellow biologist, though now retired (or so I believed).

We began our correspondence in 1890, after I published a paper on a new strain of nuisance seaweed that was clogging beaches and boat-screws up and down the eastern seaboard. (I argued that it was a previously unknown subspecies of a common aquatic varietal and was experiencing an outrageous bloom.)

Dr. Jackson sent me a letter telling me how much he appreciated my diagnosis of the situation, and how he was additionally impressed by the thoroughness of my research. I was flattered, as any man might be, and I responded with my thanks. He wrote again with a question regarding a particular crustacean he'd found at the ocean's edge—a creature I later deemed to be a grotesque lobster, dwarfed and otherwise congenitally deformed—and since then, the conversation has scarcely ceased. From time to time, we even send each other samples and articles.

This package was one such sample, I assumed; and when the time finally presented itself, I closed my door and sat at my desk, reaching for a small pair of scissors to snip the string.

Within the brown paper I found a box. Within this box I found a large mason jar sealed with a screw-on lid, which had been furthermore made airtight with a blue wax seal. The glass was large enough to hold a significant sample, something bigger than my own hand. But in the dim light of my stuffy, book-lined office, I could not at first tell what was hidden inside.

I rested the jar atop two of my research volumes, and went in search of a second lamp. Shortly I found one, though it was low on oil, and I brought it over to my seat in order to illuminate my workspace.

Lifting the jar up to the light, I noted first that it was quite heavy. The contents sloshed very slightly, indicating a high water percentage, and through the thick container gleamed a dull ivory color. The sample was too dark to be called off-white, and too light to be called brown—with seams of a sickly blue (or perhaps green) swirling through the whole.

As to its shape, I'd be hard-pressed to say. Crammed as it was inside the container, it had no shape at all except that which it borrowed from the jar. But it was lumpy and gelatinous, that much I could see. Could it be some odd representative of Cnidaria?

I turned it over in my hand.

Yes, possibly. Some sea-jelly, though nothing I'd seen before.

At the bottom of the box a folded letter lurked. I set the vial aside and retrieved the heavy-stock paper, and flapping it open, I read:

Dear Dr. Zollicoffer,

I trust this missive finds you well. I'm including with this message a strange . . . substance? Creature? Glob of fauna? Honestly, I'm at a loss. I found it along the Atlantic coast not a mile from my home, as I was on the shore with my sister—who was assisting me.

(My physician, Doctor Seabury, suggests that I should do my best to remain active despite my encroaching infirmity. He thinks that the ocean air will do me well, and I believe he's right. I always feel invigorated after these strolls. As to my sister's presence in the tale—she is ten years my junior, and in far better health than I. Thus I enlist her aid for these excursions.)

I must forewarn you, this item has an odious scent which will become apparent the moment you release the seal. The texture also is abhorrent, and I recommend that you handle it only with the sturdiest of gloves— preferably gloves you can afford to discard. I ruined a very fine pair manipulating this awful thing, and I wouldn't wish that upon you.

At any rate, because it is such a curiosity, I thought I might pass it along. I have not preserved it in any solution, only taking care to seal out the air. I hope it hasn't spoiled further during transit, though given how awful it smelled when fresh, I'm not entirely certain how one would know the difference.

To my own casual inspection, it strikes me as possibly some peculiar form of Anthomedusae—or a corrupted polyp-stage example of the same? I understand these medusas sometimes grow in colonies, so perhaps I've only passed along some decomposing cluster of ordinary sea-jellies. If this is the case, I do apologize.

But I could not help but feel that this is something different, and stranger. I hope that if nothing else, you find it an interesting puzzle.

(My sister says I'm mad, and that you will no doubt cease all correspondence with me immediately upon receiving this. I believe she's just unhappy about the odor that lingers in the kitchen.)

E.A.J.

I examined the jar, holding it carefully between my hands. With only the lamplight to judge it by, few details presented themselves.

By my right elbow I kept an oversized magnifying glass in a jointed frame. I seized it and drew it forward, adjusting its screws to aim the lens at the jar's contents. Here and there, bubbles bobbed back and forth as I turned it about. They moved with a weird, low *squish* that would have disinclined me to unscrew the top had I been any other kind of scientist.

But I located a letter opener—sharp but not dangerous, and perfect for cutting through the seal—and I set upon the container with great gusto, determined to liberate the contents despite Dr. Jackson's warnings.

In another five minutes I had a desk covered with pale, curled scrapings of wax, and the lid was ready to be twisted. I braced myself, rising up out of my chair for added leverage. With a bend of my elbow I threw my strength against the jar and the lid shifted a quarter of an inch, breaking the seal that preserved the contents within.

My colleague had not exaggerated the reek.

I was genuinely astonished. The scent oozed and drifted from the jar, crawling up into my eyes. They watered. My nose stung. I could feel the stench in the back of my throat.

But I'd come this far and I was determined to proceed, though at this point it occurred to me that I had no gloves handy and was proceeding with naked fingers.

Alas. Nothing to be done about it now.

I struggled onward, pivoting the lid with my wrist and yanking it away with a flourish that sent foul-smelling slime streaking across my desk and one of my bookshelves, but no matter! The moment was upon me!

Before I could stare too closely, I flailed for the handkerchief in my jacket pocket and thrust it up to my face, for all the good it did. I held the jar at arm's distance and peered through the glass, doing my best to detect the contents without bringing my nose too close to the source.

As a good biologist, I ought to catalog even that, I suppose—outrageously unpleasant though it proved.

The sample smelled like pickled death. It stank of rot and fire, as of something imperfectly fermented. The fumes were thick in my nostrils, and I bit my tongue fiercely to keep myself from sneezing. Almost as if the contents emitted some noxious, dizzying gas, my vision became light and my concentration waned.

Shaking my head, I tried to clear it, even as I felt my grip on the jar sliding—very slightly—as it slipped through my fingers, down to the top of my desk.

I came to my senses in time to prevent a crash; I squeezed my hand like a vise and set the item down. Before I could talk myself into some other course of action, I peered into the jar, at the oozing thing within—with the added advantage of the magnifier and the nearby lamp.

Immediately beneath my desk table top, there's a drawer. I reached inside it and retrieved a set of long steel pincers with the hand which wasn't holding the handkerchief to my nose, and I used these pincers to prod at the thing within the jar.

It sloshed, and when I made a general attempt to pierce it (in order to judge its consistency) I found the task more difficult than expected. The thing was fleshy and dense, approximately the same as a sea-jelly—a diagnosis which now seemed likely, if imprecise. I needed to see it spread out; I needed to prod at its appendages, if it had any, and take proper measurements.

I then did what I should've done in the first place: I relocated to the chemical sink against the far wall. (It'd been installed three years previously, after some disagreements between myself and two other faculty members regarding usage of the facilities down the corridor. I fancied that this new one was "mine," and I could do with it as I liked . . . even if what I liked stank up the place and stained everything I touched.)

After a bit of hunting, I tracked down the drain plug and affixed it, then in one fell swoop I upturned the jar and dumped its contents into the enamel basin. It dropped and slid in a slippery roll, rollicking to a halt and sprawling out into a truer approximation of its original shape.

I retrieved my lamp and dragged it over to the sink.

The sink became a veritable theater—brilliantly lit, and with me the sole audience member, gazing upon the single player plopped upon the stage.

How to describe such a thing? Let me attempt it.

I've already recorded the texture, dense and fleshy. Its color was akin to old bones, except for the aforementioned greenish blue streaks and blotches. The creature—for it was definitely a creature, and no plant—demonstrated radial symmetry, perhaps pentamerism. Difficult to say. One portion of the thing looked as if it'd been torn, perhaps grabbed by a predator or snagged upon a rock. Overall, it lacked the traditional cuplike shape of Scyphozoa and more closely resembled something from a "stalked" class of sea-jellies.

The thing is a true puzzle, and I am overjoyed to have made its acquaintance!

But a more formal analysis will have to be postponed until later. I have a classroom full of students awaiting at the other end of campus, and if I'm more than a few minutes late, the whole lot of them will accuse me of abandonment and walk out.

Lizzie Andrew Borden

MARCH 17, 1894

Emma was frantic, and can't be blamed for it. I hadn't responded in my usual timely fashion, having been mellowed or stunned or mesmerized by the stones, and she could hear something outside, sniffing around, nosing closer.

When I reached the top of the stairs I unlocked and flung open the cellar door. My sister fell against me, but there was no time to catch her properly or comfort her—not while I held the axe, and not while something struggled to breach our stronghold. Her eyes were wild as I lifted her with my free arm. She toppled against my breasts and rapped her cheek against my shoulder. Her strength had been all but spent to bring me 'round, and now she was wasted, exhausted, unable to even stand. A smudge of half-wiped blood streaked from the corner of her mouth, down her jawline, and into her hair.

Had I done this? Had I brought the uncanny intruder to Maplecroft with my reverie, my stupid fascination with the contents of that iron-capped box?

I suspected already that the bizarre sea glass and the strange fiends operated in some unholy conjunction, and I wished to know more about their connection, to better judge how closely they were aligned. But not then. Not at the expense of my sister's life or sanity.

"Emma, wait here," I said, and I let her lean on me as she slid to the floor, into a seated position. "I'll take care of this. I'll take care of everything."

"The *creature* . . . it's around back. I saw it, at the kitchen window. Its *hands* . . ."

"Shush, don't talk now. Stay here."

She seized my sleeve as I rose away from her. "Don't leave me alone, with nothing to defend myself!" She did not ask, "What if you fail? What then will I do?" But the questions were implied, and though I did not intend to fail her, I understood her terror.

I squeezed her hand and saw that her knuckles were bruised, flushed, and welling blood. I dropped her battered fingers and hastened around the corner to the parlor, to our father's old cabinet, which had once been stocked with his favorite spirits and crystal decanters. Now it was also stocked with a pair of pistols, likewise once his own.

I seized them both, knowing that both were loaded.

I ran back to the cellar door, shut it, and dropped the guns into Emma's lap. They looked so heavy in her hands when she lifted them and checked to see that they were ready. She knew how to shoot because I'd taught her, and I had to trust that she'd defend herself ably should the worst occur.

But I warned her, "Don't be an eager shot, dear—I'm not going outside yet. Stay quiet."

She nodded with understanding. She knew the routine. Silence and darkness.

Taking my axe along for the tour, I went from room to room on our first floor and extinguished the gas lamps until nothing but the streetlamps cast illumination into our space. It was feeble light, fractured and prismatic, sent through the leaded-glass trestle and the street-facing windows, but it was enough for me to orient myself, and to feel as if I now had the space to listen.

I closed my eyes and opened them again, letting the darkness adjust my vision. I stood in the center of the large front room, strange lines and shadows marking me like a nightmare's checkerboard. I could see the patterns on my dress, slashing dark lines and light grooves across my skirts and down my arms. The tattoos of brightness shifted when I shifted, raising the axe and feeling its heft settle across my shoulder as I waited, squinting at the night outside and wondering where the would-be intruder had gone off to.

Where was it?

Emma said the kitchen; she'd seen it at the window. It wouldn't be there still. It would've tried to follow her, circling, tracking her through sound or scent or whatever it is these things use to perceive the world.

Mostly they seem to be blind, or to see very poorly. But they *feel* . . . they pat the walls, they lunge at the boards, they trip and scuttle and scramble up our stairs when they stumble across them. They press their weird, webbed hands against the windows and leave prints on the glass in the shape of starfish.

I held as motionless as possible, hearing only the creak of my breath against my clothing, the bones of my undergarments giving and resisting, the cinch of my tied belt stretching, the small stitches in small seams straining to contain me. And then I heard it, against the south wall. It must've been standing in the long, narrow rose garden, as if a thing like that cared a whit about catching thorns or treading on blossoms.

It wheezed and hissed, feeling its way along the exterior. The timbre of its flailing slaps changed when it reached the small side porch, and when it smacked the steps, and then the foundation stones as it relentlessly sought an entrance. It moved widdershins like the devil himself, and it made no sound apart from the exploratory jabs with its hands and the susurrous whistles of its breath coming and going.

Having pinpointed the brute thusly, I steeled myself and crept to the front door. Silently, or nearly so, I slipped outside and shut the door behind me with only the faintest of clicks. I took my key and fastened the lock as well, sealing Emma within to the best of my ability.

(I shuddered to consider it, but there was always the possibility of more than one interloper. Only once have I seen them work in pairs, but once is enough. It introduces the possibility of a second time, and for that, I invest in very good bolts.)

I stepped carefully through the covered porch area, keeping my steps as light as I could manage. My boots had low heels, but even low heels can tap and warn—so I tiptoed to the secondary door and unlatched it. It was a flimsy portal, intended more for show than for protection. I let myself out and shut it anyway, and it slipped into the frame with a muffled scuffing that felt terribly loud in the nighttime quietude.

I crept down the half dozen short steps to the ground, where the grass was more forgiving than the sanded slats of the porch. I moved through it swiftly, the rustle of the tiny green leaves whispering no more loudly than the sway of my underskirts around my legs as I trotted to the left, to the corner, where I paused and readied myself.

I heard the slithering, damp coughs of the creature very close by. Its exhalations gusted with the smattering strikes of its hands as it sought entry.

If I did not stop this thing, it would find a way inside.

Eventually it would break a window and sense the space within, and come crawling through—just like its uncanny brethren had done when we lived across town. When my father and Mrs. Borden were alive. (Though they were not themselves anymore. Not by then.)

I raised the axe, holding it aloft over my shoulder but slightly to the side—ready to swing in a deadly arc, at the approximate head level of a person-shaped thing. I adjusted the trajectory, opting to aim lower. My trespasser might be smaller than I. Better to risk a strike too low than to swing too high and miss.

On an internal count of three, I stepped swiftly around the corner and charged forward, headlong, bringing the axe wide and throwing all my strength behind it.

The creature turned its face to me.

I cannot say that it looked at me. I cannot say that those film-covered eyes could see anything, though I detected the dark orbs of pupils twitching left to right beneath some silvery membrane.

Its skin did not glow. It would be more accurate to say that it gleamed dully in whatever shreds of cast-off light reached us from the streetlamps at the distant corner. But the dull gleam was very, very white without appearing clean—the wet-looking pallor of boiled eggs, or navy beans left too long in a pot.

The thing's stretched-tight skin was translucent enough to show the inner workings of organs wrestling for space, jostling together in that narrow torso cavity that scarcely looked large enough to hold a rolled-up newspaper.

I'm saying this wrong. I'm making it sound fragile, or ill.

It was not. They never are.

Their muscles are thin as laundry lines, strong as steel. Their teeth, when they brandish them, are jabbing spikes as fine and terrible as needles.

The swing of my axe caught this creature in those teeth. They shattered like glass.

I'd been right to aim low. The visitor was a full head shorter than I. Almost childlike, if you wished to compare something so malicious and inhuman to the size of something innocent and mortal.

I'd pushed the axe with enough momentum, enough weight, enough of my own not-inconsiderable strength, that it came very close to decapitating the brute in one blow. Broken teeth glittered as they flew through the air; they stuck onto the gore-covered axe-head when I retracted it and went to swing again.

But the creature wriggled and fell, ducking away from my second blow—which slammed into the house instead. Windows above me rattled, not breaking but shuddering. The axe stuck in the siding. I wrenched at it, and retrieved it.

My adversary lurched to its feet once more, and the top of its head flipped open and backward, clinging to the whole of its shape by nothing but gristle and tendons, but this did not stop it. Whether or not it could think, or feel, or see, or bite ... minus all the obvious faculties to do so . . . I have no idea.

But it could *attack*.

It rushed toward me, but I was ready. I'd seen this trick before, how they could function like the worst vermin, the most disgusting bugs that could eat and fornicate and lay eggs . . . though their brains have been smashed to bits.

This one came at me the same way, its fingers fanning to show the connective webbing between them, and to brandish the curved claws they all boasted. Its head swung down between its shoulder blades, dangling there and spewing the green and brown bile that serves for their fluids.

It ducked and I slashed with the heavy blade—and the creature leaned in for me. It tumbled forward and snared my skirt, which ripped as I pulled away and then, because there was no room for me to rear back for another swipe, I shifted the axe in my grip and brought it up again—from underneath, and to my left. I leaned backward, shifting my center like a pendulum and whipping the weapon forward.

I caught the damnable thing below the throat. The axe shattered its sternum, and hacked up through its neck. Its lower jaw flew away, scattering more sparkling teeth in the garden roses, and in the grass.

It staggered.

I finished it. I kicked out my boot and caught it in the chest, shoving it back to the ground, where it writhed, clutching all its injured parts and gushing those terrible, foul-smelling fluids. I stood over it, and I bashed it again and again with the axe, until the pulp of its chest caved inward and the throbbing organs ceased their gruesome pumping.

When at last it was still, I dropped the axe-head to the ground and leaned on the handle, catching my breath as I gazed down upon my handiwork and listened to the sound of my heart pounding in my ears.

Thank God, I heard nothing else.

No curious neighbors, no late-night passersby wondering what went on at Maplecroft, where the notorious spinsters hid themselves like fugitives, and rarely showed their faces.

But this did not mean I had any time to waste.

Collecting my thoughts and my strength once more, I drove the axe deep into what was left of the thing's chest and dragged it that way, around to the backyard, into the deeper shadows and well beyond any chance of being spotted from the street. I heaved it along to the cellar's exterior entrance and fished in my pocket for the rest of my keys. Although I was warm and flushed from exertion, my hands conspired against me, and were cold. My fingers shook. Every small sound startled me, setting me yet further on edge.

But the big locks on the great double doors did eventually click, and I lifted the right one up, tilting it on its hinges, revealing a set of stone stairs.

My axe was still lodged in the brute, buried in the wreckage of its ribs. I took hold of the handle and drew the creature to the edge of the precipice, then swung its body over the stairs. I snapped my wrist, shaking the axe hard and fast. The corpse ragdolled itself to the bottom.

I followed more slowly behind it, drawing the cellar door down behind me and fastening the interior locks. The exterior set would have to wait, for now. I could return to them later, when I was finished cleaning up.

The battered remains smelled disgusting. Whatever these things circulate for blood, it is more foul than anything I could imagine for comparison purposes. The liquid itself congeals quickly when exposed to air, forming a nasty jelly the color of coffee—which meant I'd be scrubbing the steps and wiping down the floors before bedtime, whether I liked it or not. There's only so much evidence I can stand to live with overnight.

Using the axe to keep the corpse at arm's distance, I shoved, nudged, and leveraged the squishy, crunchy sack of skin over to the largest trapdoor—the one next to the slot where I keep the dreaded green stones contained and concealed.

I opened this horizontal cabinet to reveal the most expensive appliance in Maplecroft. Truly, it's a work of art. It's almost a shame that no one ever sees it.

Privately I think of it as "the cooker," a perfectly gruesome description that no doubt says something awful about my mental state, or possibly my sense of humor. But I've learned the hard way that simply burying the inhuman little bodies is insufficient. As they decay, their odor becomes increasingly unbearable, even when smothered with several feet of earth. Worse yet, it attracts more of their loathsome kind. And then what? Do I kill every intruder, every strange, murderous invader of dubious origin? After a while, I'd surely run out of places to bury them. Our yard is not so large that I can afford the space for a cemetery of the weird.

No, the cooker is the only reasonable means of getting rid of them.

It cost a small fortune, and I had to bring in a man from out of state to set it up. I couldn't risk any of the locals gossiping about it. That's the last thing Emma and I need, especially now that we seem to be watched by more than just the usual neighbors, who remain convinced that I've somehow escaped justice.

(They wait for me to make a mistake, to reveal some telltale clue or make some offhanded incriminating statement. They think they know the truth, and to a certain extent, they *do*. But they do not know the whole of it, and I am careful. I must be, for my sake and Emma's. For the whole of Fall River's sake, too. I do not know if I can save us all, but I have to *try*.)

I reached down into the cabinet in my floor and gripped a metal latch. I turned it, and a small handle released with a pop. I cranked it, and the cooker's heavy lid ratcheted upward.

The cooker is essentially an oversized version of a cast-iron pressure device—thus my revolting shorthand for it. Made of steel rather than iron, it is heated by a complicated system of pipes that siphon gas from the same household system that powers our lights. These pipes work together to heat the cooker well beyond normal boiling temperatures, necessitating the ring of asbestos that lines the cabinet—thirteen inches deep, on all sides—lest I inadvertently set fire to the place. This lining cradles an oversized metal basin. The basin is filled with lye.

Using the axe like a rake, I scraped the corpse to the basin's edge and then lifted it, exhausting what felt like the last of my strength. I couldn't just drop the thing into the corrosive bath, not unless I wanted to splash myself with its awful contents, so I lowered the body carefully into the thick, strong-smelling solution.

With a shudder, I released the crank hook and the lid ratcheted quickly shut. I fastened a set of locking bands into position, and then I worked a round dial just beneath the pressure gauge. I turned up the heat as far as it would go, and set the timer to keep it at full temperature for the next three hours—which would certainly be time enough to dissolve the creature down to viscous syrup.

Then, in the morning, I'd make sure. And once I was satisfied that there was nothing left, I would pull a lever and let the oily residue drain down a refuse pipe which emptied out under the lot behind our house.

As I said, this was not a cheap thing to have designed, produced, and installed in our cellar, though I don't regret a single penny of the expense. I got the idea from one of Emma's biology periodicals, wherein various authorities were discussing the best way to dispose of dead farm animals; and every day I half expect to see some sensational news story with my name on it because my bribery of the workers who brought the machine was not enough to keep them from talking.

Any day now, the authorities will knock and the headlines will declare I've been murdering again, and this time destroying the evidence.

I stood up straight and leaned back. I gazed tiredly at the cabinet door and kicked it shut. It fell with a thunderous clank that Emma heard, all the way upstairs on the first floor, where I'd left her.

"Lizzie?" she cried out.

"Everything's all right. It's done now," I said with a sigh. Then I remembered and called, "Emma dear, I'm nearly finished."

"Thank God," she murmured. I barely heard it.

"I'm cleaning up, that's all."

My axe was on the floor beside the trapdoor. It was covered in the creature's bile, or mucus, or blood, or whatever fuels it—pumping through those sinewy lines and oily muscles. The slime was foaming very slightly, blossoming into a revolting brown fluff. I picked up the axe and held my breath as I brought it close to my face, so I could see it better.

Yes, just like before. Where the putrescent fluids met the

iron, the weapon sizzled like it was doused with acid. But not an acid eating away at the metal—more the opposite, I should say. It is as if the metal eats away at the blood.

Iron hurts them somehow, doing more damage than if I hit them with a bat or a mallet. Wood won't do it. Stone won't do it—as I learned on one occasion, having been cornered by the porch stairs and finding only a loose chunk of paving rock to defend myself. It pushes them away, of course. Any sufficient blow will rebuff them, but only iron will stop them.

I took a damp rag from a bucket full of water and soap, making a murky soup. I scrubbed the axe-head down. If it'd been made of shinier stuff, it would've gleamed when I was finished.

I moved along to the splatters on the floor, and to the murk on the stairs. On my hands and knees, I washed the steps one at a time. And when I was finished, I retrieved the now-clean axe and brought it with me as I made my exit, pausing briefly at one of the book stacks and selecting a volume.

The axe-head. The iron.

I was reminded of something, and I wanted to double-check my memory on the matter.

The steps groaned beneath my feet, and I groaned with them. My ribs ached from the exercise, from breathing so hard against the corset stays.

At the top, I unlocked the door and let myself out.

Emma was still seated by the landing. The guns rested on her lap, leaving heavy dents in the folds of her skirt. Her hands lay atop the guns. She looked frail, and old.

She sighed with relief at the sight of me.

I tried to smile. "I told you I'd be right up."

"Yes, and I'm glad. I was worried—I couldn't remember if you'd taken your keys."

"I always have my keys. Here, let's get you to your feet," I offered, setting aside both the axe and the book in order to slide my arm beneath and behind her.

"I don't need so much help," she chided me.

Sometimes, she did not. Tonight, she did. "Stop fussing, and let me get you upstairs. It's late. We're both tired. I'll get you ready for bed."

Together we walked with excruciating slowness. If I'd urged her any faster I would've had to carry her, and that would've been embarrassing and painful for us both. Instead we moved at the steady pace that made my aching arms ache all the more, and the bruising at my ribs protested with every step, all the way to my sister's room.

I drew out the stool at her vanity and lowered her onto it, and I stretched, cringing at the crackle of joints popping, and the dull warmth of strained muscles.

Emma stared quietly at herself in the mirror, and at me. She said, "We're quite the pair, you and I. The invalid and the murderess."

I turned away from the mirror and went to the switch on the wall. I pressed it, and the room came alight with the glow of the wall lamp. Its pretty shade was made of frosted glass, so the light was diffused and softened. It was kind to us, or so I saw when I returned to the vanity seat and began to undo Emma's hair.

One by one, I pulled the hairpins gently free and laid them on the table. "The scholar and the warrior?" I tried. "Let's say that instead. I like the sound of it better."

She laughed. I think it was genuine. It's hard to tell, with eyes like hers—too wise to find many things funny. "Another set of lies, sister. Nicer ones."

"But you *are* a scholar. And tonight I've slain a dragon. Of sorts."

"True and misleading. I'm not Professor Jackson, and you're no Saint George, nor an Amazon, either."

"Says *you*."

I tugged at the final hairpin, the veritable lynchpin of her coiffure's architecture. It slipped free, and her hair came down in a jagged cascade, unfurling and unfolding in a marbled mixture of brown and silver down her back. I took a brush and began to smooth it. I told her, "No one ever needs to know."

And likely, no one ever would.

Emma Borden, consumptive spinster . . . masquerading as Doctor E. A. Jackson—retired professor of biology and chemistry. The venerable mythical doctor had authored dozens of papers published in journals as far away as France, on everything from seaweed blooms and ocean temperatures to parasitic infections in crustaceans of the northeastern Atlantic.

Who would even believe it, if we announced it? We could put an advertisement in the newspaper, and no one would consider it possible.

She mused, "Someday, someone is bound to learn some secret or another. Yours, or maybe mine. Someone could come here, looking for me."

"Someone?" I knew her too well. She had someone in mind.

"There's a fellow upstate, at Miskatonic University."

"You've mentioned him. You think he might come here? Seeking you?" I moved on from her hair to her dress, which I unfastened one rounded glass button at a time, feeding them through the tiny loops that ran from the top of her neck to the small of her back.

"There's always the chance. I rather like him, and I suspect we'd enjoy one another's company. Maybe he feels the same way."

Only a few more buttons to go. I fumbled with one of them, released it, and moved on to the next. I did not ask her anything. I only said, "If he comes, we'll deal with it then. We can always claim that the good doctor died since last you wrote."

"I'll say no such thing. I have two more articles pending for publication."

Wearily, I told her, "Well, the secret is yours, Emma dear. Do with it what you wish."

I helped her dress for bed. I fluffed her pillows and gave her the day's mail—including two of her favorite periodicals. I kissed her on the forehead and wished her good night. I lit the candles on the bedside table and extinguished the lamps as I left.

In the parlor, my father's old clock gonged the hour. It was one o'clock, and therefore, morning. I was filthy and my dress was ruined. I traded it for a nightgown with slippers, and re-solved to burn it, as I'd burned other dresses before it.

I'd wait for dawn, if I could sleep that long. Or sleep at all.

I remembered that I'd left the axe and my book downstairs. I set out to retrieve them.

Come daylight, yes—I'd destroy the dress, and check to bolt the cellar's exterior doors, so that no one could come or go without my keys (or perhaps a stick of dynamite). When the sun was up, I'd check the cooker and empty its contents; I'd examine Maplecroft's exterior, and its lawns, to make sure that no trace of the creature had been left behind.

But first, I staggered up to bed, toting my book and my axe.

I left the axe leaning against my nightstand, a childish

gesture which made me feel silly, but more secure than if I'd left it elsewhere. I wanted to keep it within reach.

I lit my candles. I drew up my knees and let the book fall open across them.

The volume was heavy. It left creases on the quilt. Its pages smelled like dust and feathers, leather and wood, mildew and uncertainties.

A People's History and Guide to the Myths, Lore, and Habits of the Fey, by Alfred Hanstible Valant III. Paris, 1797. (Translation provided by Edmund Lowe, PhD International Metaphysical Studies. MUP—1829.)

It's a silly title.

And to be clear, these creatures which are infesting Fall River . . . I do not believe they are fairies. They are not ghosts, or elves, or gnomes, or demons. They are not brownies or bogies. But when I read about such mythic monsters, I detect a glimmer of some similar sentiment—an undercurrent of truth, a glimmering seam of gold buried in a worthless boulder. I read about peasants, priests, and alchemists in days of old who had codified their superstitions into wards, hexes, potions, prayers, chants, songs, and systematic protective behaviors in order to keep themselves safe from dastardly influences. They were testing the boundaries of unknown things, attempting by trial and error to manage the stuff which goes "bump" in the night.

They were the scientists of their times, these people. They experimented with dark forces and dark creatures by choice or by desperation, combining and recombining the things they knew with the things they suspected—fishing, always fishing, for a reliable inoculation against evil.

I skimmed a few pages, running my finger down the lines until I found what I'd dimly recalled from earlier readings.

> One thing and one thing alone is certain with regards to foul specimens of the dark court fey: They fear and loathe contact with any rusted item, be it tool, or lock, or ornament. They eschew the touch of this substance, recoiling as if burned or otherwise contaminated. In some rural counties, where the friendly assistance of nearby neighbors or peace officers is not readily at hand, nails are left in the rain to rust—then gathered, collected, and pounded into doorways and windowsills as a barrier against entry by any unwanted supernatural creatures. A barrier such as this is considered to be one hundred percent effective, and utterly foolproof.

I found the "foolproof" bit unlikely, but this small, overwrought paragraph gave me much to think about. The author proposed that the critical element is *rust*. Rust does not occur without the presence of iron. My axe was not at all rusty; I kept its edge ground fine and its surface well cleaned. Yet still, I noticed a reaction. A difference. A significant improvement in efficiency, as compared to other instruments.

"It's not the rust," I argued with the book, and its long-dead author—should his disapproving shade be present. "It's the iron itself."

I considered the implications, if there were any. My bedside candle flickered and steadied, along with my thoughts. When first I'd read Dr. Valant's mention of the nails, I'm sure I thought it was frivolous. A fallacy of the poor and uneducated, a superstition without merit.

Now . . . I was not so certain. The two things, iron and rust. One known to be effective, one claimed to be. Did it matter that I did not understand the mechanism by which it worked to prohibit monsters? Not if it worked regardless.

I slapped the book shut and swung my legs out from under the bedspread. When I put my feet on the floor, the cold of the boards shocked some of the sleepiness out of my bones—thank God—because I'd never be able to sleep now, not until I'd tried it.

I did not care what time it was.

I cared only a little that Emma was fast asleep when I reached her room with a hammer in one hand and a box of nails in the other. I turned on the lamp to rouse her, and she blinked, yawning herself awake.

"Lizzie?"

"My apologies, sister dear. I'm afraid this can't wait."

"What can't wait?" she asked, her words clogged and close together. "What time is it?"

"Close to two in the morning, I imagine. But if this should work, and if I fail to do it, I'll never forgive myself."

"Oh dear. You've found some new . . . some new trick, that you want to try?"

"I don't think it's a trick," I told her. I got down on my hands and knees. I positioned one nail at the far left, against the door-frame. "I don't know why, but I think it will keep them out, even if I'm not here."

I drove the nail hard. The bang of the hammer was louder than thunder in our night-quieted home, and I flinched, but I hit the tiny spike again until it went flush with the floor.

Emma propped herself up on the pillows to watch me. She was resigned to this. It was not as if she could stop me should she want to, and she knew she could not talk me out of it. We'd fought about it often in our first year at Maplecroft, and never once had she won.

When I find a thing that works, I will implement it.

If it is inconvenient, if it is ridiculous, if it is insane . . . I do not care and will not let that stop me. I will try everything, and if even *some* of it works, *some* of the time, that's a measure of protection we would have otherwise lacked. I will never let it be said that my sister died, or was turned, or taken, by those insidious fiends. Not on my watch, and not from my home.

First, I would pound a million nails into the house, and do it gladly. First, I would let the whole town think I'm a madwoman and a murderer, let it scorn and reject me, let its children compose hateful rhymes to be sung whilst jumping rope, let the entire Atlantic bubble and boil and storm against our shores—throwing up with the tides a thousand such inhuman, unholy creatures as the one I'd killed that night.

One by one I lined up the nails and beat them into place, and when I was finished with Emma's doorway I moved on to her windowsill. And when I was finished there, my hands were chapped and beginning to bleed, so I stopped.

I could save my own doorway for morning, like everything else.

BE SURE YOUR SINS WILL FIND YOU OUT

❧

Owen Seabury, M.D.

MARCH 17, 1894

Matthew Granger has been a patient of mine since the moment he was born. I delivered him on a Sunday night, late enough that we may as well call him a Monday's Child. What's the lore on that one? Monday's Child is fair of face, isn't that the way it goes? Nonsense, of course. Even if he'd been a good-looking boy, one shouldn't read too much into these things.

Young Mr. Granger was not particularly handsome, though he wasn't the sort to frighten horses with his homeliness, either. An ordinary lad, you could say. Neither large nor small, thin nor fat, smart nor dull.

His father died when he was very young and when he was

ten his mother passed away also. Following this, he was taken in by Ebenezer Hamilton and his wife, Felicity—the godparents, I believe. They keep a shop down at the waterfront, performing all sorts of odds-and-ends duties for the fishermen who work the waters. At Hamilton's Ocean Goods and Supplies one can pick up stray parts for navigational equipment, find new nets and get old ones mended, acquire bait for more casual fishing, and pay a penny a pound for stray bits of wave- and sand-tumbled glass and shells from a barrel by the front door. These bits end up in decorative ponds and small aquariums, in water closets, and sometimes in jewelry, hair sticks, or other baubles . . . most often marketed to the tourists who visit the shores when the season is right.

Among Matthew's many minor duties was this one: He was obligated to keep the barrel brimming with attractive sea detritus.

Often he could be spotted down on the rocks, either in bare feet or wearing soft, flat slippers. He moved between the boulders like a cat on a shelf, picking his way deftly, his eyes on the cracks where soaked sand had been washed by the tide, threading itself in thin white seams full of tiny treasures. To watch him, you'd swear he was a creature of the shore himself, moving from stone to sand to surf with such unwavering expertise.

Just a child still, really. Not a man yet, though nearing that cusp where people hesitated to call him "boy" but wouldn't yet call him "sir."

When his godmother summoned me, she did so without his knowledge. She asked it as a favor, offering to pay me in the freshest seafood she could barter. Dutifully I appeared in her shop, strung with its nets, its gleaming brass instruments both assembled and disassembled for restoration, and its barrels of salt, stones, shells, floaters, linen scraps for sail patches, and every other thing a coastal shop might carry.

Mrs. Hamilton, stout of frame and white of hair, was frowning worriedly when I arrived.

After greeting me she said, "He's out there now, like always." And she wrung her hands together.

"Filling the barrel?" I asked, and glanced toward the door.

There it was, and overflowing. Literally—its contents spilled into drifts and hillocks across the creaking wood floor. Mrs. Hamilton had deployed a bucket to address the surplus, but it too was brimming. Likewise the mugs and the saucers were piled to heaping. It looked for all the world like there must be some leak in the ceiling through which these button-sized sea notions dropped in an unending trickle.

She told me, "Yes, that's all he does now. It's always been his favorite, you know—something he does when he's bored, or taking a moment from working the till or stitching up nets."

I crooked my chin toward the water. "The whole town knows to look for him there, out on the bay."

"More now than ever. It's strange," she said, leaning forward and crossing her arms on the counter. "And I don't like it."

Uncertain of what, precisely, she did not like, I indicated the collection at the barrel by the door. "But he's doing a very fine job."

"Better than fine, or worse. I can scarcely get his attention for any other task. And I know," she said with a shake of her head, beating me to my instinctive argument. "He's a lad still, and lads behave oddly without any prompting. But this has gone on for some time, and it's becoming more and more of a problem by the day."

I sighed and set my bag down on the counter beside her. "Perhaps you'd better begin at the beginning. What exactly is he doing that worries you? Apart from overfilling the stock barrel, which I can see for myself."

She exhaled deeply and her chest sagged, squeezing an abundance of bosom forward, over her arms. "It began a month or two ago. First he was having a hard time with the nets—he wasn't paying attention, and he was dropping stitches, tying them into the wrong kinds of knots. When he was finished with a net, it wouldn't have held anything. It wouldn't even spread for the throwing. I watched him work, and I tell you, his mind was elsewhere."

"Again," I said, "a common complaint when it comes to young men."

"But you should've seen it—the look in his eyes: *There wasn't one.* Thought it was in my imagination, I did, but no . . . I'm sure of that now. Over time it's gone from a boyish lack of attention to something . . . something I can hardly bear. Sometimes when he looks at me, he looks right through me. He doesn't see me! He doesn't hear me."

"He isn't listening?"

"I know. This, too—it sounds like a boy being a boy, but—" She stopped herself, as if she'd meant to tell me one thing, and changed her mind, offering me another thought instead. "He's listening, but not to *me*. He's listening to something *else*."

I frowned, and she frowned, too. Then she heaved her torso up from the counter and came to stand beside me. She laid a hand on my elbow and guided me to the window beside the front door. Its glass was scummed by years of salted air, but I rubbed the back of my hand to shine one corner of a pane, and I could see all the way to the coastline beyond the edge of the road, perhaps a hundred yards away.

"Watch him," she murmured, standing very close beside

me. Her breath was low and rushed, as if she'd been running and was pretending otherwise. "Look at him, and you tell me what he's listening to."

I watched as she'd commanded. The details were unclear; I was too far away to see much more than a long-limbed fellow picking around on the rocks, his face pointed down and his dark, wild hair billowing in the ocean air that gusted off the inrushing tide. At first I saw nothing remarkable, merely the same lad I knew on sight, in his natural habitat, performing his usual task.

But the longer I looked, the odder it seemed—and it was nothing I could immediately pinpoint. I stared. And I thought I saw an unusual jerkiness to his movements. He lacked his usual grace, the ordinary leaping, climbing, and leaning that typically characterized his hunts. He moved more heavily, and slowly, too. He did not jump from rock to rock, but he slid down one and scaled the next. His hands hung from his arms like dead things, or like whole things without fingers. They were flat and immobile, like fish at a market stand.

"He's listening," his godmother breathed. "Look at him. He's listening."

Yes, he was. I could tell it from the tilt of his head; every time he turned or pivoted, every time he changed rocks or changed directions—dipping down to the same level and poking through the sand. No matter which way he turned, the crook of his neck aimed his head at the ocean.

"Perhaps," Mrs. Hamilton urged, "you could have a word with him. Talk to him, please, Doctor. I'd feel better knowing you'd looked him up and down, even if you decide there's nothing amiss, or nothing you can do."

As I stood there, peering through the small, clear square of windowpane with Felicity Hamilton's labored breathing puffing against the back of my neck, I would have rather done anything else than to go talk to young Matthew. I wanted to turn, wish the woman a good day, and make an excuse or apology regarding some fictional patient requiring my immediate services.

But I did not. I gathered up my scraps of inner fortitude and forced a smile upon Mrs. Hamilton as I said, "Very well. I'll do just that."

She opened the door and saw me out, and when I looked over my shoulder she was still there, watching through the spot I'd smudged to clarity on her window, her nervous eyes darting back and forth between me and her ward.

I took a deep breath.

This was a simple thing—likely the simplest task I'd be asked to perform all day—and it should not have repulsed me so. On countless brief, perfunctory, casual occasions through the years, I'd exchanged more than a handful of words with the fellow out there on the rocks. That lad over there, picking his way between the tide-washed boulders and always moving so that his head was cocked toward the Atlantic . . . he was no stranger. I'd always known him to be the pleasant sort, relatively eager to please and optimistic that any errand might earn him an extra penny for his trouble.

So why did I feel such dread as I slowly trudged toward him? *He's only a boy,* I told myself. A simple truth, and one so obvious that it scarcely needed any mention. What else would he be? What was I so afraid of?

I approached him, stepping along the walkway as long as I could, and then only tiptoeing off the planks and onto the sand. I made a show of wanting to keep my shoes clean. It was only a show, but it allowed me to keep some distance—and it kept me off the rocks. I'm not as young as I once was, and I no longer cared to scamper along the boulders like some schoolchild. And this was one more thing I told myself, for show.

"Matthew?" I called.

I stood facing him, my feet half in the wet-packed sand, my toes jostling against the polished pebbles that collected up against the spot where the ocean ended. The wind came up fierce, whipping my coat and nearly stealing my hat. I held the coat shut with one hand and held my hat in place with the other, and I called out again, in case the wind had carried away my first attempt.

"Matthew?" I said it more loudly this time.

He stopped scanning the cracks between the rocks and allowed himself to slide down the slippery, shining-dark slope of a boulder the size of a pony; but he didn't meet my eyes and he didn't approach. He only stood there, waiting for heaven knew what, swaying against the buffeting wind.

"Matthew," I tried again. "Dear lad, would you come over here for a moment, off the beach? I was wondering if . . . if I could talk to you. I wanted to . . . to ask you . . ."

He lifted his head to look at me, almost; but there was that tilt—that alarming, off-kilter tilt that kept his attention always to the open ocean beyond the rocks.

My brain scavenged frantically for logical, reasonable things to say about Matthew. I wondered if he didn't have some kind of ear problem. He might've had an infection, or a fluid buildup, or some other kind of ailment residing therein, that seemed to so harshly alter his equilibrium.

"Matthew?"

He nodded, which seemed an odd response—as if he were confirming that yes, he was in fact Matthew. Ridiculous. Of

course I knew that. And he knew I knew it. What peculiar behavior was this, between two citizens who'd been acquainted
for better than fifteen years?

"Matthew, could you come here, please?"

If someone had held me at gunpoint, I could not have explained why I was so reluctant to venture any farther onto the
sand. I wriggled my toes inside my shoes, and the pebbles
banked around the edges of the leather soles. But I couldn't
bring myself to do it, to venture any closer to the rushing, rumbling waves beyond the rocks.

Matthew only looked at me, or through me—past me, like
he was looking hard at something just behind me. So effective
was this gaze that I looked back to make sure I wasn't blocking
his view of something more interesting. But no. There was
nothing behind me but the usual piers, shopfronts, passersby,
and preening white gulls.

When I had finished double-checking and once I'd made
myself certain that Matthew was, more or less, looking at *me*—I
met his eyes again.

I shuddered. I took half a step's retreat that almost sent me
falling over the edge of the walkway planks, and I corrected myself in time to keep from harm. But I flailed. And when I had
restored my body's balance I clutched my coat more tightly
across my chest. I released my hat, trusting it to remain affixed—
or not caring if it abandoned me.

The young man was giving me that look, and it was a blink-
less look that stared but saw nothing, and I'd seen it before. I
knew that mindless set of the eyes and then, as the awkward
moment stretched itself out long between us, I knew the cast of
his skin. I thought of eggs, peeled and pickled in a pantry jar. I

imagined sourdough beginning to turn too sour; I pondered the waterlogged flesh of the drowned.

And I remembered Abigail Borden.

The similarity shocked me, though the boy was clearly in some stage of whatever had overcome Mrs. Borden. Or . . . well. It's hard to phrase what I mean. She died by an axe; but something had been draining her, or sickening her, prior to her death. I can admit that now. I *must* admit that now.

It took me a moment to realize I was holding my breath.

I let it out with a whistle and a gulp.

What could I say? I had nothing to suggest, offer, or declare. The unhinged set of the boy's jaw, the tone of his skin, the slack and loose look of his face . . . I'd seen it before, as certainly as I'd seen typhoid shared from person to person in a battle camp.

A word bubbled to the surface of my murky thoughts.

"Symptoms." I said it aloud, letting the syllables slip out past my chilled, unhappy lips. The boy was displaying *symptoms*—of that I was certain.

But my God, symptoms of *what*?

I tipped my hat in his general direction, which caused him to budge not in the slightest. So I turned on my heel and left, trying hard not to hurry—lest it look like I was running away.

When I reached my home I shut myself inside it, leaning my back against the door as if I could hold at bay any contagion that the boy might've breathed toward me. It was ridiculous—perfectly ridiculous, and I knew it. But I also knew it was not my imagination that the two Fall River residents, Abigail Borden and Matthew Granger, were somehow connected.

The skin. The eyes. The lumbering, clumsy look—as if they lacked full control of their faculties, or their senses were somehow dulled. Matthew's condition was not yet as severe as Abigail's had become, but I could see it in his face. I could see it in his shambling movements. A more severe case of the Borden problem was working its way into his body, into his blood.

I fastened the front door with more precision than was necessary, and dashed upstairs to my office, where I kept notes, files, paperwork. Things to remind myself of patient histories, and records that might assist authorities in case of a plague.

In Europe, physicians and civil servants have been tracking disease outbreaks for decades, beginning with the cholera epidemics in London. Records compiled by doctors, clergymen, postmen, and others have proven invaluable to the study of how sickness spreads, and my own interest in the subject had prompted me to collect such day-to-day details and write them down. I'd begun perhaps five years before, recording basic information and keeping it in files after reading about the efforts of a Dublin doctor to do the same in the slums of that city. I had no slums for the studying, but I had Fall River and I knew its population.

I didn't honestly believe that any of my short notations would ever be as important as London's Ghost Map. No, certainly not. But I liked to think that one day my notes might benefit some researcher, somewhere.

My drawers and files had fallen into disarray, relative to how neatly they were kept when my wife was alive. Such is the way of things, all order passing into chaos, given time enough. But even so, I soon found what I was looking for: a few sheets of paper stuffed into a folder, labeled "Ab. Bord."—to distinguish her from Andrew but to preserve some measure of anonymity for the families whose well-being I observed.

(Privately, I assumed that any serious researcher would have no difficulty teasing out the particulars of my patients; but I liked to think that my little abbreviations would at least give me some protection, if any of those patients were to learn of my notes and take objection to them.)

My notes frustrated me. They were incomplete, and woefully so—through no one's fault but my own.

Upon my first visits with Abigail Borden, I had recorded everything from her temperature to her breathing rate, but as her condition deteriorated . . . it's as I said before. I was paying less and less attention, for I was distracted by the family drama that played out across the street.

I was deeply annoyed because the notes revealed that I'd become complacent and lazy, and that I have not always performed my job to the best of my ability.

When did that begin? When did I go from the ideals and optimism, and the intent engagement of youth, to the apathy of age?

I'm not so old yet as to be feeble or infirm. I'm scarcely in my sixties, and though my hair goes whiter by the year, I still *feel* like a healthy man with a sturdy constitution.

Granted, men with sturdy constitutions and feelings of health drop dead every day, and this should sober me. But it sobers me less than the awareness that I'm slipping, in my way. Maybe not my strength of body, but strength of character—or professional responsibility.

Disgusted, I stuffed the notes back into their sleeve. They told me nothing, and they would never tell anyone anything. I'd done too poor a job. I'd done nothing more than waste my time, and the time of any future readers who might stumble across my pitiful recollections.

On second thought, I decided I could spare one of us, at least.

I reached into the drawer and pulled out everything I could carry, and then I opened the next drawer and retrieved its contents, too. Everything that would fit in my arms I hauled downstairs, over to the fireplace—which had burned down low due to inattention. But it blazed bright when the first loose leaves of paper went over the grate and into the coals.

I'd wasted enough, and I would waste no more. No more time, no more vainglorious scribbling for posterity, serving nothing and no one.

And while my collection of trifles burned, I sat at my writing desk and I began to record in earnest every single thing— every impression, every suspicion, and every half-recalled idea—I'd ever known about Abigail Borden and Matthew Granger.

I CROSS THE MAGPIE, THE MAGPIE CROSSES ME

☙❀❧

Phillip Zollicoffer,
Professor of Biology, Miskatonic University

SEPTEMBER 22, 1893

The question is not "What is wrong?"

A closer query would be "What is different?" or "What is changing?"

Something is changing. Something is shifting, or slipping. I want to ask if I'm losing my mind, but who would answer? How on earth can I step outside my brain and ask it to evaluate, with all fairness, its effectiveness as a body-governing device?

It might only lie to me. How would I know?

And I can't rely upon the opinions of my peers; this much is certain. They've been all too happy for all too many years, calling me daft. They'll be no help at all, now that the question has seriously reared itself.

Then again, I don't *want* any help.

I'm feeling quite well, if occasionally light-headed. I don't believe I'm suffering from any illness or cancerous complaint. Nothing more dire than a peculiar clarity at times, and a warm resonance at others.

The resonance is difficult to describe. It tugs at me, an intermittent sensation as if I'm being lured. No, invited. Or even more precisely, *welcomed*. I'm not yet certain what brings this on, though I'm considering a series of experiments. The resonance is not quite repeatable at my command, but it's consistent enough to call a symptom. I will prod at it like a soreness in a tooth, pinpointing the trouble with my tongue until I know where the problem lies.

But there I go again, calling it something it's not.

This is no *problem*. This is only a condition, and a not altogether unpleasant one. I mentioned the clarity, did I not? I'm remembering things with greater sharpness, more vividly, with more significant contrast around all the edges. Something unusual is at work. I'm confident of that if nothing else.

I've begun to track my dietary intake, writing down every bite I take in the back of this journal. If these new feelings and facts are the result of some change in my meals (as I suspect may be the case), then I intend to catch it. All I have to do is recognize the pattern, or the new introduction to my *usual* pattern. Then I'll find it.

Maybe I'll add a second set of pages to the end of this volume, wherein I record the symptoms of resonance. Do they happen most often when I am indoors, or out? When I'm at the university, or at my home? Where do they come from, these flashes of . . . of overwhelming desire . . . of *yearning*, as if for someone or something who yearns for me in return?

I'll describe it yet.

I suspect I'd better—my students are grumbling more than usual (and honestly, drat the ungrateful lot of them). They've been grousing to the dean that I'm becoming unresponsive, not making my office hours, and grading unfairly. Not a new complaint in the lot, but the volume has raised some interest. I don't care for it, but there's only so much I can do. I'll carry on, teach my courses, and evaluate the brats as fairly as possible.

𝔜esterday in one of the elementary biology classes, there was an incident.

Dr. Warner thinks the fault lies with me. He says that it's a matter of my pride, and my obvious disdain for the students. He chided me to be more patient with them, for they are first-years, and still learning their way around the university and their coursework. He asked me what had changed, and if anything was wrong.

It is as I have said. Nothing is wrong.

But I'm sick to death of being patient with them. I've always been patient with them, for years upon years—as long as I've been at Miskatonic—and the time has come for a raising of the bar. It's an utter waste of my abilities, dealing with the first-years and their inadequacies!

One outstandingly inadequate youth is named Theodore. He is a small weasel of a lad, intelligent without being wise—and very quick to spout whatever is on his mind. It's as if there's no one at all working the drawbridge between his brain and his mouth. He's been trouble since his first class, and he's trouble now, and he's trying to bring the trouble to me.

Should I have attacked him? A noble man might say "no," behave in a penitent fashion, and hope for the least of all possible reprimands. The question, then, is whether I am more noble or less for refusing to pretend I did not intend to harm him.

For I *did* intend to harm him. And why not? He intended to insult *me*. An eye for an eye, or so it's been said. I will not quibble here, in my own papers, over whether or not a moral injury and a physical one can suitably correspond. I was justified. We'll leave it at that.

Theodore Minton, youngest son of a haberdasher from someplace no one cares about, I'm certain, stood up in class and accused me of mortal sins. Even the least puritan left among us in the region can understand the offense I took. He attributed unto me *sloth*, saying he'd caught me sleepwalking in the halls between the chemistry lab and the biology department on Monday afternoon.

I was not present in these offices on Monday afternoon, and therefore could not possibly be guilty of this offense. I told him as much.

He insisted that he'd come to ask my help with regard to one of the upcoming assignments, and that I'd rebuffed him with violence—pushing him into a door, and sending him sprawling. Then, he asserted, he'd gone to seek the department head . . . to tell him what, I wonder? That he was a weakling and a coward, a feeble, frail, useless little twig of a not-quite-man who'd been bullied by a fellow almost old enough to be his father?

(Which of course, did not happen. As I have said. For I was not present.)

I haven't the slightest notion of what went through the whelp's mind when he made this claim in front of the classroom,

God, and everyone else within hearing distance, but I *will not tolerate disrespect.*

He came too close; that is what happened. He put his face too near to mine, and his eyes were earnest—What an actor he must be! Perhaps science is the wrong discipline for him—and he tried to say that I had not been this way in the previous semester, when he'd taken the first round of my introductory biology course. Babbling, he said that everyone knew it, and no one understood it, but that he was taking his concerns to the top of the university's administration if I did not resume my previous demeanor.

"What *previous demeanor?*" I demanded to know. Nothing has changed in my classrooms, except that each season the boys are stupider and the classes feel longer; those are the only differences.

Something insipid fell out of his mouth, some diatribe couched in terms of concern for my well-being, suggesting that in prior months (before the summer leave) I had been more patient, more perceptive, and more willing to assist the young men who were my charges. He then was so bold as to inquire after my health, and went on to make accusations about my pallor— for neither that, nor my demeanor, either, was satisfactory to this wretched snake of a character.

I do not remember the precise words that moved me from where I stood, listening angrily, to up against him, with my hands on his throat.

But his classmates intervened—treacherous idiots, the lot of them—and someone ran out into the hall, where the lumberjack-sized (and -brained) Dr. Greer was dragged into the altercation, effectively bringing it to a close.

I was sent home like a naughty schoolboy, ostensibly to rest and recover, and to consider my actions.

Fine, then. I consider them.

While I consider them, and consider how grand it felt to squeeze the boy's pulse in his throat, as he struggled against my grip, I consider what on earth could have prompted him to make his unfair, unfounded accusations. What have I ever done to him, prior to this afternoon? Nothing, and that's another fact which has gone overlooked altogether by my superiors. I've never shown him anything but the fondest feelings of paternal kindness, in my efforts to instruct him.

I too am an actor, and a good one in my own right.

But. As I replay the events, today's and those which remain alleged . . . I am forced to wonder. I struggle to recall. What *was* I doing on Monday afternoon? Where was I? What inane, ordinary set of tasks did I perform? They must have been ordinary indeed to have slipped so precipitously from my memory.

I'm sure I was reading essays, or otherwise considering the grades of the same ungrateful slugs who watched me warily as I made my exit.

The last thing I recall with any great certainty is mundane enough to imply that the rest of my day was equally so. I was at home, in the office I've made for myself on the second floor, where I keep my samples, my supplies, research volumes, my periodicals. I was reading, I believe.

I was reading, and the window was open, and I fancied that I could smell the ocean.

Nance O'Neil

∽❧∾

LETTER ADDRESSED TO LIZBETH A. BORDEN,

FALL RIVER, MASS., MARCH 29, 1894

You're wrong, you know: I don't need your parties, your money, or even your smile—keep all that to yourself, and it makes no difference to me. I've never asked you to put on a show; if you're unhappy, be unhappy and I'll be right there with you, doing my best to change the situation. I lie for a living—I don't need more lies cluttering up my leisure time. Even the gentle sort, offered with good intentions.

Your insistence that I should stay away from Fall River "for my own good" is nonsense. I'd like to say we both know that, but perhaps it's only me, after all. Perhaps you honestly feel you're doing me some favor, by sending me away like a nervous child to a boarding school, for my own protection and well-being.

Unfortunately for you (but of dear happiness to me!) I am

not a child, and I cannot be dismissed so summarily. Therefore, let this letter serve as formal notice that I am coming to visit!

Not in this next week or two, but surely by the end of April. You may expect that I'll stay a few days or more, and I won't hear any protests to the contrary. You miss me. I know you do! I couldn't *possibly* miss you so thoroughly as I do, if it's all for naught and unreciprocated. I refuse to believe in a God so cruel as that.

(He's plenty cruel enough as it is, don't you think?)

Oh, Lizbeth, if you had any idea, these last few months . . . it's been a nightmare. The whirlwind kind, where you're tossed about from place to place, and can't remember anyone's name, or any of your lines . . . and the curtain is about to rise. They're the worst nightmares of all, the kind you can't wake up from— when it's all too real, and I'm all too awake, and none of this is anyone's fault but my own.

I could've taken the winter off, you know. I could've stayed in my apartment and rested, or I might've even sneaked into town to see you. For just one party, perhaps? Just a few short nights, and then back to New York on the train. You could've come with me, if you liked. They're different about things, in the city. I could tell you I loved you, if I wanted, and not worry so much that someone might overhear.

But I *didn't* take the winter off. And you *didn't* come to New York. And now I'm stuck here by my own design. This season, all the blame can lie with me. I took the second play, when I should've thrown my hands into the air and pleaded exhaustion.

(It would've gotten me out of *The Wanderer*, anyway. I mostly took that one because the director wants to arrange *Sappho* sometime this summer, and I want him to be happy with me, so he'll keep me in mind; but it wasn't a project that was near or dear to my heart, and I would have happily skipped it otherwise.)

And now, when I'm almost too tired to hold a pen and write this note, I have all these second, third, and fourth thoughts about the matter.

I should've sent Peter to Cathy Francisco or Mabel Lee. Either one of them would've done a perfect job in the role he wanted. And by "perfect" I mean, neither of them is a better actress than I am, and he wouldn't prefer either of them over me.

But no. I'm too frightened of being without work. Acting is such a terrible business! If only I'd been bitten by some other bug . . . but it's too late for that now, isn't it?

It's a permanent worry, I swear. Never confident of the next year's employment, always in fear that the critics will hate you— and even more afraid they won't notice you at all. It's a system designed to tug and batter at one's vanity. That's why, I think, so many vain fools survive it.

Sometimes I worry that I'm not vain enough, and this is making me ill, or unnecessarily frantic. I don't want to be unnecessarily frantic. I want to be calm, and quiet, with you in that lovely little town that leaves you alone. At least for a few days. Well, however long it takes for me to recover from this terrible exhaustion that's settled so deep into my bones.

I know you said I'd find no respite from exhaustion with you, and I'm not sure if you're making a joke or being morbid. Sometimes in your letters, I simply can't tell.

This is why we must speak face-to-face, quietly, over drinks in that wonderful parlor. We can sip scotch or whichever wine you have on hand (you still haven't shown me that cellar, and I'm beginning to take offense). We'll turn the lights low, let the fire burn down—for I doubt it will be so cold, by the time I arrive. And I can tell you everything about these last two plays. And you can tell me everything that's bothering you. All the things that make you want to push me away. I *demand* to hear them, no matter how dark they might drive the conversation. I'll listen. I'll do nothing *but* listen. I feel like I always talk—for the benefit of others, as often as not. I don't even use my own words.

It's tiresome. I'd rather listen to yours.

I doubt your sister would care to join us, but you must invite her. I wish she liked me better. You love her and I love you, but therein lies the problem, doesn't it? At any rate, I'm sorry. I'll leave it alone. This is meant to be a happy letter, not a reproachful one.

I am looking forward—not backward!

Backward is a grim, unpleasant place. If there are worse gossips or backbiters than actresses, anywhere on the face of the earth . . . I'm not sure I'd believe it. Wicked fiends, the lot of them—surpassed only by directors, whose evil nature is exceeded only by the pen-fiddlers who write for the papers, and tell the world of our triumphs but describe them as the most dismal of failures.

I've just now reread what I've composed so far. If I had more paper at my immediate disposal, I'd throw these sheets away and begin again. I'm rambling, and doing so with embarrassing inconsistency.

I'm tired, Lizbeth. That's the root of it all.

The days are so long in the theater company. Twenty-four hours, and they want them all. Half the week I sleep atop a pile of costumes backstage, with a bottle in my hand (if I'm lucky) or your letters (if I'm luckier still). Then I awaken when the first hands arrive, or Mary and I often do—and sometimes Anne stays, too. They expect the most from us, more even than they want from their leading men.

And look, now I'm sulking.

Forgive me. I'll stop wasting ink, and wasting paper.

This is a happy letter, because it announces that soon, you and I will be together. And we will drink and sleep and make whatever sort of merry we please. It will be lovely, and it will last as long as we like.

Don't bother to write and tell me to stay. It won't work. I'm well past taking "no" for an answer. If you turn me away, it will kill me. Maybe that would please your sister, but I don't think it's what *you* want.

I wouldn't ask you to choose between us. There's no reason you ought to, and no reason you have to. We're grown women, she and I, and we will behave accordingly.

I will see you shortly! So shortly . . . another two weeks, and then however long it takes to pack and book the train tickets. I'll send a telegram in advance of my arrival, so you'll know when to pick me up.

> All my love, of course. Always.
> GL (though don't you dare address me so.)

THIS KNOT I KNIT, THIS KNOT I TIE

Emma L. Borden

APRIL 11, 1894

Here comes Gertrude.

Oh, she hates to be called that, I know—she's a proper actress now, with a proper actress name. Why Lizzie indulges her, I have no idea. Or I do. I have several ideas, and none of them are very polite.

Though it might seem nasty of me to suggest it, I daresay the situation is not wholly different from older men who marry down, and younger women who marry up. And there it is. We are spinsters with fat pockets and purses, and we are pariahs so far as the entire county is concerned. Meanwhile, "Nancy" is a pretty, popular girl with a small measure of fame, if no fortune to speak of. (She avoids the subject, but I have gathered that her origins are somewhat dubious.)

Actresses come in two types, as I hear it: fabulously wealthy, and pitifully destitute. The difference between them is alleged to be the quality of their suitors.

All things being equal, I suppose it's safer than a street corner.

But Lizzie loves her, and I tolerate her. The girl isn't often untoward, but she's routinely uncouth and so very, very *young*. Plenty young enough (and if I am to be fair, beautiful enough as well) to find a rich man to keep her.

So yes, I can make my guesses as to what keeps her coming 'round. They're better than guesses, and anyone who suggests that ladies don't do such things doesn't know much about ladies. Or anyone else, I expect.

Thank the good Lord above for thick walls and large, sturdy houses. Our rooms are adjacent, but without a measure of shouting, no one is likely to hear anyone else.

Under more ordinary circumstances, this slight distance is a source of distress to Lizzie . . . she wants me nearer, closer, more easily guarded and defended even at night. (Especially at night.) I appreciate her protective streak, and indeed, it's kept me alive this long; but there are times when I find the attention stifling.

My resentment is unfair, in every way. It does not reflect on her in the slightest. It's only my old longing for the easy independence I took for granted when I was Lizzie's age. I am jealous, and that's the extent of it.

I'll leave it there.

"Under more ordinary circumstances." That's what I wrote only a minute ago.

But in a way, these circumstances of ours have come to feel . . . not ordinary, but perhaps consistent in their peculiarity. A woman can get used to anything, I guess. It must be something like the adage about a frog in hot water: Drop him in, and he'll jump back out. Turn the heat up slowly, and he'll sit there and cook.

We cook ourselves in fear.

Fear is the routine that has come to feel ordinary. That, and Lizzie's search, her quest for understanding. Her struggle to find a solution before her investigations are found out—as they very well might be, someday. We use a great deal of gas power. We send and receive an inordinate amount of mail, and from strange places. Stranger people. No matter how much caution we exercise, the details may eventually betray us. Now our terror is not merely that we'll both be thought mad, and possibly criminal. No, it's worse than that. How much worse, I dare not speculate.

No. That isn't true, and I shouldn't lie here. When I lie to myself, I lie to everyone. Here's the truth: I speculate all the time.

The threat is great against the pair of us, if we are found out before we can explain ourselves fully. At best, we might find ourselves incarcerated at a sanatorium, and what would become of Maplecroft then? What of Fall River? Massachusetts? For yes, the threat extends to the entire region—that much has become appallingly clear.

And how much farther than that?

To the whole of the nation? To the world?

We are pulling at threads in the darkness, traversing a labyrinth of ancient and awful design. There are worse things than minotaurs at the center. That much, I can state with utmost confidence.

. . .

And now, here comes Gertrude.

Nancy with the fancy actress name. "Nance," Lizzie calls her with enough affection that it makes me ill. Tall and pretty and strong, in some sense Nance makes a better, more reliable companion than I do. But she's naive and quick to take offense, and quicker still to leap to judgment. Her moods are mercurial under the best of circumstances, and Lizzie has enough to manage without her.

This having been said, my sister's mood has been grim for years, and it remains grim almost always . . . except when Nance brings herself around. When she's in Nance's company, she's as happy as I've seen her since before Father passed.

So there's one point in Nance's favor.

Since I'm feeling generous, I'll offer another: It could be worse—the girl could be stupid. But she's only rash and inexperienced.

Lizzie is already beside herself with regard to Nance's impending visit, her heart torn in the two most obvious directions. She's glad for the opportunity to see her young friend, but horrified at the sheer extent of what must be hidden before she arrives.

Over the winter we've settled into these awful patterns, these anxious routines, and they're beginning to show outside the cellar laboratory. The laboratory itself is easy enough to hide: You shut and lock the door, and it's sorted.

But the usual books on our shelves upstairs are joined by tomes more directly alarming; and we've made changes to the house which cannot altogether be written off to winter modifications.

In the kitchen hang racks of drying herbs that cannot be used for cooking. Around the yard, small stakes and barriers have been installed, to say nothing of the alarms and traps at the outer reaches of the property. And then there's Liz's recent fascination with the nails. Scores of them, pounded unevenly into the doorways, along windowsills, and across every threshold.

I made her take some of them out, because some of the doors refused to open or close properly, courtesy of her inexpert attempts to wield a hammer. Of course, the moment my back was turned, she went and reapplied them all. More tidily, I'll grant you. But still.

It was almost a real embarrassment, for when Doctor Seabury came to call yesterday afternoon, I found myself at a loss as to explain the exposed nailheads, after he tripped over one, and therefore noticed them all. I made some excuse about the house's foundation shifting and settling during the last hard freeze, and he nodded politely.

I doubt he believed me.

The doctor had come on my behalf, as he's made a habit of visiting once per month or so, depending. Sometimes we see him more, sometimes less. It all depends on my health.

Really, I find his appointments to be quite pleasant. We see so few other people, except in passing; and though his visits are not social in nature, they are nonetheless appreciated. He is patient and kind. He is a thoughtful, clever man.

When Lizzie was on trial, he defended her. He told the jury again and again that the stains on her dress were consistent with her story, that she had only found our father and his wife, and fretted over them. He vowed on the Bible and on his life that she could have never killed them, and certainly the murders were the work of a stranger.

He lied, and lied, and lied. I know he did.

But whatever he believed then, or believes now, he's never treated us with disdain or suspicion. It speaks well of him, though I think his amiability comes partly because he is lonely, and that's why he indulges us. His wife passed a year ago. No? Eighteen months, at least. It was after the trial, but not long after it.

Obviously I have noticed that he is still a strong, handsome fellow. And he might be old enough to be Liz's father, but probably not *mine*.

Now I'm only being silly, and girlish. I'm only tired and alone, except for my sister.

Many days, I'm at peace with the lot we've received, or chosen, or the fate which has befallen us. It is a hard burden to carry, all the more so with a back as feeble as mine. But it is *ours*, and it is noble, what we're doing. What we're trying to do. What we *will* do, eventually—for these people who would not spit on us, were someone to light us on fire.

But Doctor Seabury.

He came, and I waited for him in the parlor. Lizzie helped pin my hair, and she dressed me in something nice. She took me down the stairs and fashioned me like a heavy old doll.

The doctor and I made small talk while my sister made tea. And here was one more piece in the mosaic of our routine . . . I only just noticed it, how he's become a familiar part of our time, marking its passage from month to month. This is a happy realization, and I wish we could make our appointments less formal. But to do so would incur the wrath of his other patients—who already express whispered concern for his well-being, given his involvement with the pair of us.

As if Maplecroft were some den of roaring lions, seeking whom we may devour.

I think the town still "permits" him to come our way because I've never been implicated in any wrongdoing. I am only an invalid, at the mercy of my sister. Her sins apparently do not stain me as thoroughly as they could.

These appointments might best be viewed as some charity, then, on his part. I do not care for that thought, and I hope it's not the case.

Regardless, he came, and we chatted, and Lizzie left us with the tea.

"Tell me about your lungs. How have they been feeling?" he asked, as he gently manipulated my wrist, all the better to feel the beat of my heart running through it, between the bones and back from the tips of my fingers.

"About the same. No worse, at any rate."

He finished with my wrists or perhaps he gave up on them, or finding any feeble pulse. Instead he chose the scope from his bag. "Then we'll count it a blessing, shall we?" He warmed the scope's amplifier between his hands, and then inserted the other end into his ear. "Could you lean forward for me? That's far enough, thank you."

He placed the scope on my back, and I felt its round hardness through the fabric of my dress.

"Now breathe deeply—as deeply as you find comfortable."

I did my best to comply, but any inhalation harder than a light wheeze was enough to make my throat close and my chest convulse. I strived to hold my body in check, to force my lungs to remain calm, and still, and refrain from seizing, or flinging bloody mucus into the air.

Indeed, my body betrayed me within twenty or thirty seconds—but the doctor's hand upon my shoulder gave me some steadiness, some of the calmness I could not manufacture on my own accord. I finished coughing and went quiet, except for the rasping tone of air wrestling in and out through my mouth and nose.

He added a gentle pat to the comforting gesture. "Are they always this bad?"

I rallied enough strength to respond, though I did so through my handkerchief. "No. But sometimes . . . it's worse."

When I withdrew the handkerchief, it was stained with pink, but not much red. I went to hide it away, to cram it quickly in some pocket or corner where he would not see it—and this was preposterous, I know. I should've held it up for display and scrutiny, but I couldn't bring myself to do so.

He saw it anyway, and waved his hand, urging me to pass it to him for inspection.

"See? Not so bad," I attempted with a note of cheer, but his expression of solemn contemplation did not bend.

He said, "Not so bad, but not so good." And then his demeanor became more quiet; he stared at the scrap of fabric as if it held an extra measure of meaning—or that was my first impression. But then I realized that he was looking through it, toward his knees, past the floor. Staring at nothing, and using the dirty cloth as an excuse to think.

"Doctor?"

"Miss Borden," he said quickly in response, as if catching himself half asleep. Then just as quickly he added, "Might I ask you something of a . . . related nature, perhaps? It might be relevant to your condition, but it's a delicate subject all the same."

"Of course."

He glanced about the room, checking to see that we were

alone, which piqued my curiosity. "It's about Matthew Granger," he began slowly, organizing his words with caution.

Whatever subject I'd expected, this was not it. "Young Matthew? Down at the shore?"

"Yes, that's him. His godmother asked me out to see him; she had some concerns about his behavior, and wondered if he might be falling ill."

"I certainly hope the poor boy's well," I said with a frown.

"As do I," he assured me. "But this is why the matter is delicate, and I do pray you'll take no offense that I broach it here: Matthew's behavior, his appearance, his demeanor ... it ... what I mean to say is, it reminds me of something. It reminds me of someone—your stepmother, if I'm to be honest. Shortly before she and your father ... died."

That last word hung in the air, lingering between us like the miasma from a cigarette.

I was stunned, but not quite to silence. And not for the reasons he must've assumed.

I stammered, "Doctor Seabury, that's ... that isn't ... I'm not quite certain what you mean." Which was not quite true. I could make an excellent estimation, but I didn't want to contaminate his story. That's how Lizzie would put it. And she was in another room, perhaps even down in that laboratory, doing her scientific work with her scientific processes. I would conduct those same processes upstairs, then, and report in such a fashion as to please her.

"I'm very sorry, I didn't intend any offense or concern, it's only that in those last days, before their deaths, I had seen little of Abigail and less of your father—but ... but when I crossed their paths, I ... I could only fear for their constitutions. They seemed terribly sick, if you don't mind my suggesting it." He was speaking too fast again, my stammers feeding his stammers, spiraling us into social worry and sensitive concerns.

"No, please. No offense taken. It's only that you've caught me by surprise. You'd think such a common subject of gossip would rear its head more often in this parlor, but"—and I paused to cough, not quite so hard, with not quite so much mucus—"our visitors are few and far between. Please, could you explain what you mean? We were all feeling . . . strange. Back in those dark days," I added. I might have concluded, "Before they became darker still," but that crept too close to the secret Lizzie and I hold close, so I did not utter it.

"You must understand, I cannot divulge too much of another patient's condition," he said by way of retreat.

"Naturally." I nodded, allowing him to withdraw as far as he felt he needed. "But share what you can, and I'll see if I can help."

He fidgeted with my handkerchief, and then it occurred to him to return it. As he did so, he said, "There's a faraway look to him, as if he's not quite present. A vacant appearance, combined with a certain . . . slowness of his motion. As if his motor skills are deteriorating, but he hasn't noticed, or doesn't care. I watched him . . . ," he said, his own gaze becoming far away, but he was looking for some way to explain himself. Hunting for the right words. "I watched him, and he moved clumsily, and at such a tedious pace. All the while, his head was cocked toward the ocean, like a child holding a shell to his ear. But there were no shells," he said, coming back to the moment. To me. "Nothing beyond him but the water."

I considered this, and recalled with some displeasure the

weeks leading up to my father's and stepmother's deaths. What the doctor described was not dissimilar from the changes that had overtaken them. "My father and Mrs. Borden had fallen ill, that's true," I said carefully. "We wondered about it ourselves, my sister and I—we worried that we might come down with the same affliction. It was a source of tension between us, toward the end."

Eagerly, if unhappily, he leaned forward. "So you know the changes I'm referring to? The blank eyes, the paleness, the doughy flesh?"

"Indeed, though at the time we would not have put it that way. It came upon us gradually, you know; and by the time we noticed something was amiss, it was all that we could see. And all we could do was wonder how we'd successfully ignored it up to that point." The words were tumbling out. I wanted to rein them in, but I nattered onward, haltingly, stopping myself when I feared I might go too far.

"Truly, and often—I have thought the same thing."

"At first we thought it might be a problem with the family diet. But the family was also . . . in distress over other matters. There were arguments, as I'm sure you know. The whole neighborhood must've heard them. So after a while, Lizzie and I took up residence in a separate part of the house. We had our own apartment, with its own washing room and kitchen, so we saw our parents less and less. Virtually never, for four people who lived in the same home. From then on, my condition—and Lizzie's—improved . . . even as our parents' worsened."

"You separated yourselves. Separate meals, separate living quarters, and that's when you recovered?"

"Insofar as I ever recovered, I'm afraid." I sighed. "Maybe I consumed too much of the tainted food, if tainted food was ever at fault. Maybe my constitution was weaker all along, and less able to resist."

Even as I spoke the words, I was growing tired. This was more than I typically spoke in a week, and the toll felt heavy in my chest.

Doctor Seabury noticed. "I apologize," he said, and wound his stethoscope around his hand, twisting it into a coil. "I've asked too much of you, for the afternoon."

"No," I objected.

"Yes, and we both know it. My apologies again; it was a tender subject, one that is no business of mine."

"Your business is the health of Fall River. I'd say the subject is well within your business. It's true," I said. I put my hand on his medical bag, so that he might not close it shut and usher himself out the door with quite so much nervous alacrity. "A lengthy discussion of the matter is hard for me. Which is why I think . . . that you should speak to Lizzie."

He flushed and shook his head. "No, Miss Borden—I couldn't. It would be unseemly, or impolite, or . . . I wouldn't want her to think I meant any accusation."

"Ask her," I pleaded, removing my hand and allowing him to resume packing his equipment.

He hesitated, then asked, "Is there any chance . . . that you could have a word with her, first?"

Oh, I had every intention of doing so. "Of course." I smiled at him with sincere, if morbid, pleasure. "And next time you come, we'll sit down together. All of us."

At the ring of the bell beside my seat, Lizzie appeared from the basement to show the doctor out.

And I fell asleep before the fire before I could tell her any of what had transpired, even though the conversation had frankly invigorated me. My strength is finite, even if my interest is not.

I dreamed of my father, bloated and white, and hungry. I dreamed of him in my room, staring out my window, listening to the ocean.

AND IF YOU HAVE A HORSE WITH
ONE WHITE LEG . . .

꧁

Phillip Zollicoffer,
Professor of Biology, Miskatonic University

OCTOBER 29, 1893

The university thinks it might be done with me, but I'm beyond the point of caring. Right now, their reprimand feels positively uninteresting—as if it's something I should be aware of, yes, but not a source of concern. They've put me on leave, and it's a vacation of sorts. I'm sick of the students, as I told them quite frankly.

(They requested frankness, and they received it in abundance.)

Dr. Greer suggested I'm sick with something other than the

tedium of teaching, but he's a fool. It's difficult to take his accusations personally.

The one concession I wrangled from their uniform displeasure with my performance was this: I am still allowed access to my office and the lab rooms, where my specimens and samples are stored. They are mine, and not property of the university in the first place; and in the second place, I'm working on an article for *Marine Biology Quarterly* with regard to the siphonophore specimen sent to me by Doctor Jackson earlier this year.

What little study I've had time to perform has raised fascinating questions about the nature of a single organism versus a colony that performs in a singular fashion, and where the line between those two might lie. A siphonophore by definition is just such a paradox: many small things that function as one large thing. But how paradoxical is it, after all? A collection of like-minded things, operating under the direction of a sole authority . . . or an individual, individually inclined. Just two ways of saying the same thing, perhaps. From a distance.

(Contrary to the president's opinion, my study has been minimal—pitiably insufficient, really, and it has not "eaten up all of my time for students, papers, or grades." Far from it. I still had time to attend their stupid little meeting to reprimand me, did I not? Well, then. I'm not so disconnected as they claim.)

Is the specimen a whole, or a portion of a larger whole? It's nothing so simple as a *Physalia physalis*, that's certain—and I'm beginning to wonder if I don't have, in my own personal possession, an instance of *Marrus orthocanna* . . . which isn't ordinarily seen anywhere near the shore. It's a deep-sea varietal, and all but mythical until the most recent years, when fishermen turned up portions of one within a net. But I think that's unlikely. No, I think we're looking at a whole new animal (or a portion of one, as above noted).

If so, this could be a boon for the school.

Alumni might be persuaded to open their pockets, or the billfolds of grant donors might become loosened were there to be a new species coined after the university. *Physalia miskatonis!* Or *Physalia zollicoffris*—I haven't decided yet.

Right now it's merely "the siphonophore," and it awaits its formal analysis and nomenclature. And no one is allowed to touch it but me.

I was a little surprised to get this slight concession on Greer's part, but in the midst of the meeting I was seized with a terror that the specimen might be taken from me, and I could not bear the thought of losing it. Immediately, and from the depths of whence I cannot say, I informed them that the siphonophore was my personal property and I would consider it outright theft if the school tried to lay any claim to it. A lawsuit would undoubtedly ensue, thereby stripping the school of any honor by association, should the creature be proven unique or new. It was donated to me, courtesy of Doctor E. A. Jackson of Fall River, Massachusetts, and there was a trail of paperwork to support the transfer. Doctor Jackson would no doubt lend his considerable aid if anyone, anywhere, were to try to commandeer my work—or my materials—as his own.

At the reference to Doctor Jackson, they capitulated on the spot.

His reputation as a scholar and researcher is well-known, even among relative laymen like those who populate the school's board of directors. They're only marginally informed of scientific advances; theirs is to administrate, not educate—but even men unschooled in the finer biological arts had heard of him and his work.

At first, there was some measure of disbelief, as if it simply were not possible that I was friendly with the mysterious scholar. But I stomped free of their proceedings, to their noisy dismay, and traipsed down to my office (still *my* office, yes) to retrieve the letter that had accompanied the package.

I produced it with a flourish, gave them adequate time to read it, and watched at least Greer go a bit green when he realized I was telling the truth. I think it surprised him, though I can't imagine why. When have I ever misled him, or made claims greater than those I could support? He has me confused with someone else, or he's been listening to the slanderous lies spread by students and faculty.

And that speaks volumes about his leadership, does it not? What kind of chancellor takes the concerns of his inferiors to heart, or uses them to guide his policy? If his underlings were of his own caliber, they would've matched his position by now. Since they are not, they ought to be disregarded until and unless they produce evidence that they are worthy of interest.

Such as myself.

But I gave them the letter, and there was a great chorus of hemming and hawing, and then I received permission that I should've never required: the permission to continue investigation and exploration into my own private property, with the blessing of the university, which would seek to profit from my discovery.

Damn the lot of them.

So here I sit, not in my office but in the laboratory where I first uncorked the specimen, the siphonophore, *Physalia zollicoffris* after all, my pet, my beloved, my savior and specimen. The other labs in this wing have complained about the odor, but I scarcely notice it anymore. If anything, it's become a welcome scent—a friendly signal that all is right with the world, and that I have come *home*.

It's funny, now that I think of it. I've scarcely been at my own home these last few days, or this last week—I'm not sure. What is there at home for me? Nothing, save a small gray cat who cares for me approximately as much as anyone else in the neighborhood who occasionally lets it come inside out of the cold. And I haven't seen even the cat since the specimen appeared.

Now that I think about it.

At home I have food I don't care to eat, and a bed that is no more comfortable than the cot at my office—where I've been more inclined to rest, these recent weeks.

Not that I rest too much, anymore. How can I rest, when greatness awaits? When my darling specimen calls my name, and upon it I shall build a career of wisdom and greatness?

I'm not sure how long it's been since last I slept. I should take better care, when it comes to these things. As I used to tell my students, when I cared enough to improve them: A rested mind is a productive mind.

 don't know how long I'll have the indulgence of these old fools who run the university. I don't know how long I'll have access to their equipment, their space, and their patience. I don't know when they'll decide I'm more trouble than I'm worth, and evict me with my specimen—turning us both out into the street.

Or sending me back into my house, that small brown hovel I call a home, which . . . now that it occurs to me . . . is on school property. No, they quite literally *can* turn me out onto the street. I live here at their indulgence, and I will go without a place to live at their whim.

The world is a cruel and unfair place.

I should sleep.

Maybe I'll drag the cot into the lab. There's more privacy here, and less interruption. Fewer curious stares, fewer impertinent questions about how long my suspension might last, and whether it might become permanent. Fewer whispers of gossip overheard through the walls, tittering about how the smell travels with me, now, how they can detect the siphonophore on my clothes, and in my skin. Wondering who will have my office when I'm gone.

Is it such a foregone conclusion already?

These flickers of despair will be the death of me. I really *do* need some rest.

THE WORST IS TO BE JUDGED WITHOUT HOPE

꙳

Owen Seabury, M.D.

APRIL 13, 1894

I spoke with Emma Borden, and I can't quite decide if I'm cheered or frightened by her response. She was eager—very eager—to talk about the death of her parents, to such an extent that I was frankly surprised. I would've thought the subject would prove too sensitive, given the circumstances of their demise—regardless of any illness leading up to that event.

Emma thinks I should speak further on the matter with Lizzie, but I'm not sure that I can bring myself to do so. I've spent two years convincing myself of her innocence; and if anything, I've been her champion in difficult times, albeit at a distance.

I hate confessing things to myself, but here it is: I kept my distance then, in case I was mistaken. And I keep my distance still, because there is a balance here—her freedom, her exoneration . . . weighed against the possibility of her guilt.

I wouldn't entertain the darker possibility at the time, even when others were all too happy to do so. I'm not sure why. I can't say why I defended her so; or, if I must choose my reason, then I'd say it was because of Abigail—that awful night before she was killed. Something was wrong. Something was *worse* than wrong, and at the bottom of my heart I felt that their murder might have been some kind of self-defense, instead.

Over and over, while I was on the stand, I thought of Abigail Borden and her cold, damp hands pounding upon my door. I remembered my terror, and then my revulsion as I recognized her, and saw how terribly she'd changed.

Worse than wrong. Yes. I suppose that's the crux of it.

I have been afraid all this time that Lizzie performed some act of self-defense that could never be defended in court—an act that I would have pardoned and justified, given how readily I'd wondered where my pistols had gone when I saw that slack, imbecile shape rocking back and forth on my stoop.

But that can't have been all of it. Andrew was murdered in his sleep. Abigail was taken by surprise, from behind. Can any such attack ever be construed as self-defense?

And so I twist myself around and around again, never certain if I made the right decision, but quite certain that I couldn't have made another one. Not if I wanted to live with myself.

Now, if I wish to speak of the matter to Lizzie, I may threaten this weird balance between us. Our polite deferral of the topic, and a mutually agreed-upon (yet never openly discussed) pact to avoid it. My knowledge of the night before they died. Her knowledge of everything that came before and after.

What if she were to make some slip, drop a few stray words by accident—words that incriminated her? What if I am forced to confront the possibility that I was wrong to stand by her side? Would I be compelled to report the matter? Would it mean anything if I did? I don't believe she could be tried again, but public opinion has long since had its way with her.

It might well be that I fret for nothing but exposed feelings, and unpleasant truths that reveal nothing and mean even less, given that the time for consequences has passed.

So it seems my only excuse for avoiding Miss Borden the younger . . . is a squeamishness on my part. For all I know, she has no such squeamishness; for all I know, she has no polite agreement with me—a gentleperson's imaginary agreement, assumed in order to avoid an unseemly topic. This might be entirely one-sided, and it might be entirely in my head.

I believe I'll have a word with her after all, at Emma's next appointment.

Because I went back to see Matthew Granger today.

And just look at how many inches of script I've dedicated to avoiding that subject! But this is what happened, and I will not be squeamish about it. I'm a doctor, for Christ's sake. I've seen the worst the human body has to offer. This should not bother me, deter me, or disgust me. This should be recorded.

I will record it.

In only a matter of days, the boy's condition has deteriorated. His shoulders are sloping more steeply. His face is becoming fuller. He moves his hands as if he's forgotten he has fingers, slapping at things as if his appendages are only paws or flippers.

His godparents are beside themselves. They can no longer pretend that his condition is youthful depravity—and now they've removed him from his duties gathering the sea glass and knitting the nets. They've locked him inside their home, in the back rooms of their shop, under the guise of giving him rest in order to recover. I'm not so stupid as that. They've hidden him away so that others won't see what's becoming of him.

Mrs. Granger is a prayerful woman, and she sings her petitions to God, day in and day out. She's given the boy a Bible, which he ignores. She's left small crosses and holy baubles about the boy's room, and he ignores those, too. If he even sees them.

I don't know how much of anything he sees. His eyes are filmy, almost that same blurry fog of an older man's cataracts, but this is something else—something overlaying the exterior structure of the eye, almost like the nictitating membrane of a sickly housecat. When I made some efforts to examine this membrane, Matthew did not object or resist. And finally I noticed that he didn't merely appear unblinking . . . he had stopped that unconscious behavior altogether. Not in the twenty minutes I kept his company did his upper lid so much as *twitch*.

But he covered his eyes with his hands, when I brought the light too close. It was dark in that room. Sickrooms often are, but whatever is sickly about him, the darkness and quiet aren't helping it.

They're incubating it.

I had thoughts of asking for blood or saliva samples, but twenty minutes was all the time with the boy I could bear. I left his family with suggestions for soup, tea, and continued prayer.

Who knows? The soup or tea might actually do him some good.

As for the prayers, I suppose they can't hurt. I've never found much good in them, I'll confess that here, though I keep such thoughts private when in public company. Who would confide in a physician who claimed no affiliation with God? I still must feed myself, and keep my house. I still need my patients. But too many people believe with too much conviction in what amounts to, at best, a superstition.

I've seen science change a patient's diagnosis, but I've never heard a prayer that changed God's mind about a damn thing.

Lizzie Andrew Borden

❧

APRIL 13, 1894

Emma bared a bit of her soul to the doctor, and I'm not sure how I feel about it.

I suppose if she must unburden herself to someone other than me, she's chosen wisely; better Seabury than the postman, or the grocer's delivery boy.

She insists she told him nothing that would give him any real insight into our research, and she only said that yes, our family had fallen ill before they fell to the axe. She told him this much, and furthermore suggested that he speak with me. Really, I suspect, her motives are twofold: one, she'd prefer to have him come around more frequently, even if it requires his involvement in our secret activities; and two, she thinks we may have information that could be of great help to one another.

She swears that the latter is her true desire. If I brought up the former, she'd deny it with such vehemence as to harm herself with the effort. So I restrain myself.

But she might have a point.

Apparently one of the boys in town has come down with something like our father and Mrs. Borden, and that's a troubling development indeed. I've seen hints of that sickness, here and there about town, but nothing so fully formed. A paleness in the face of a man on the street. A slowness in the speech of a woman at the store, on the rare occasions I venture out. It worries me deeply, but until the doctor mentioned this new case, I'd seen no progression like the one that so upended our lives two years ago. It was as if whatever poisoned us had stopped with us. Or else it was otherwise spread so thin that nothing truly tragic resulted from any further contact with . . . with whatever it was.

Whatever those green stones are. The ones in the leaded box under the house.

Matthew Granger, the sick boy. He collects ocean glass and sea baubles for a barrel inside the shop's main door. The connection is an obvious one, and easy to make. He's picked up something more dangerous than glass, and it's made him into . . . into whatever he's becoming.

Or however it works.

The stones cause change, but they also lure. Are they luring something *in* to those who touch them? What a hideous thought. But now that I've had it, I'll see what my library has to offer with regard to possession. And if mine won't suffice, I'll pack up a bag and make the trip to Providence.

Perhaps Emma could come; it's not even twenty miles. We could spend the night away from home, and it might do us good.

. . .

But I've distracted myself. Here is a note, to bring me back on course.

I will jot this down now, so I do not lose the train of thought and forget to return to it later: Is it possible that the creatures who haunt the grounds of Maplecroft from time to time . . . might actually be the *end result* of this weird malady? It's almost too awful to consider. They could have been people, once. I might have killed half a dozen of them now.

If so, then the transformation eradicates any indication of humanity, save for the general shape of two arms, two legs, and a head atop a torso.

I thought that my father's case, and Mrs. Borden's case, were the end progression of this infliction. I might have been wrong, but even knowing this, I regret nothing. I would not have seen either one of them . . . no, not even my stepmother . . . reduced to such a state. And besides, they would've taken steps to murder me long before they ever reached that point.

The signs had already begun—and as it was, I constantly feared for my life, and for Emma's as well. That's why I sent her away, in those last days. I know everyone thinks it was because of William, but he was the least of our problems. William was only a conniving bastard, greedy for an inheritance he hadn't earned or deserved. He would've tried to bring us all down with a scandal, but he wouldn't have sickened or murdered anyone.

I write this with reasonable certainty but not, upon reflection, the utmost confidence. The truth is I never knew him well—only well enough to know that I didn't wish to know him better.

. . .

The more that I think about it, the more I wonder if Emma's proposal wouldn't be a good idea . . . a little sit-down chat with Doctor Seabury. If anyone else in town has been suffering such ailments, he'd be the first to know; and the fact that he mentions Matthew Granger as a case resembling my stepmother's suggests that it's the most advanced manifestation he's seen so far.

(Apart from hers, I mean.)

Now that he's recognized that something so pernicious is afoot, he might be better primed to see earlier symptoms . . . things which would otherwise go unnoticed, or unrecognized as part of a larger pathology.

There's much we might learn from each other, but it's a terrible risk.

If he decides that I'm daft, or engaged in illegal activities, he could hand me over to the authorities. It could mean the end of Maplecroft, the end of my laboratory. The end of what slim progress I've made against the creeping threat.

If I am removed from my studies, then truly nothing would stand between Fall River and whatever evil thing insinuates itself into our midst.

Not even me and my axe.

(And certainly not even Emma, with her steady, intelligent force of will. Given her state of health, she might very well be sent away to a sanatorium and left to die in clean white sheets, surrounded by men and women who owe her only professional tending and politeness, without any love or interest. I couldn't live with myself, if it were to come to that.)

The question, then, is can I trust the good doctor?

I phrase it that way because I do not doubt his integrity, only his suspension of disbelief. A reasonable man might hear my tale and believe I've become a violent lunatic, if I wasn't one before.

But he *did* see Mrs. Borden. He *does* see a connection between her malady and the growing problem in town. It *isn't* just Matthew Granger, and it isn't just my father and stepmother. It's the blind, sticky-handed, many-toothed things that creep the streets when no one's looking. I've caught six. No, seven. Last week's was number seven.

How many have I missed?

I can only make guesses. I suspect that two still roam, in the evenings, surely. I don't know if there's any good reason they can't come and go during the day, but their instinct leads them to darkness. And it leads them to kill.

Three people have been found dead in the last six months. Two others have gone missing. I suspect two other deaths were related, though the persons in question were elderly, and might have succumbed to causes more natural than these.

This is not a large town. These are too many people, lost in the night, turning up again (if they do so at all) drowned and waterlogged, with strange cuts and punctures. With pieces of flesh removed from their bodies in great chunks.

The papers printed stories that only alluded to these particulars, leaving me with insufficient evidence of anything except a streak of bad luck befalling my hometown. I wish I could've studied the bodies firsthand, but can you imagine? Me, of all people? Expressing eager interest in the investigation of a mutilated corpse?

They'd put me away.

But Doctor Seabury has surely seen the bodies. Some of them, anyway—a pair of sailors were shipped back to their homes up north before he might've gotten a look at them, but yes, come to think of it . . . he would've certainly seen some of the victims.

I could ask him about them. What they looked like, what carnage had actually occurred.

Not yet, of course. Not yet.

But it feels like . . . it *might* be worth the risk to court his friendship and confidence. Gently. Slowly. Cautiously. If I approach it carefully, he could become our greatest ally.

Our only one, if I'm to be honest.

Another note, recorded here so I do not forget. (And I'll transfer these to my lab books downstairs later, when I've had time to think on them more thoroughly.)

Is it possible that the creatures are spreading the sickness? Could it be some strange ichor they leave in their wake, or share with their oozing skin? Is this how these creatures reproduce, by sickening a host until the host evolves into that final, disgusting state?

Maybe, but if so, you'd think that Emma or I would be well contaminated by now, unless my improvised defenses have worked better than I've known. All along I've wondered if I wasn't wasting my energy with the folklore, the charms, the nails, the lines and symbols . . . but so far, nothing insidious has found its way inside the house; and so far, neither Emma nor myself is any sicker than we ever were, back at the Borden homestead.

Then again, that might not be fully true of Emma. But I have no way of knowing if her state is the result of the creatures and their poison, or some unfortunate, unrelated ailment. Either way, our proximity to the first bad outbreak can't have helped her condition.

I wonder if she knows how closely I watch her, every day.

Every time I brush her hair, every time I bathe her . . . I check her skin inch by inch, and I watch her weight, her shape, her eyes, for some incremental change brought about by whatever foul agent has settled into our lives.

Thus far, I've seen nothing but an ordinary woman, sick in an ordinary way. Daily I pray it remains so.

J made some offhanded comment to her about this; I told her that of course, yes, absolutely, I pray for her condition to hold steady at worst, and improve at best. I am a loving sister, after all, and what else would I pray for?

She shook her head. "Who are you praying *to?*"

I was taken aback. "The Lord in Heaven, same as any other God-fearing Christian."

Wryly, she told me, "This isn't what our library would suggest."

"So I read about the faiths of others. Their beliefs pose no threat to my own."

"You're looking for magic, Lizzie. God doesn't give us magic, only science."

"Last century's magic is this year's science," I argued.

"Point taken, but by now I am forced to wonder who you think is listening, when you offer up these petitions. The Lord? Some papist saint? Some old goddess, left over from darker times, in darker corners of the earth?"

"I'm praying to anyone who listens," I told her. "The Divine has many names. I doubt He cares which one I call. Or She, for all we know. Doesn't the Bible say we were created in God's image, male and female?"

"You're treading on dangerous ground."

"We're living on dangerous ground. And we can't seem to

leave it, so I'll work on making it less dangerous—which, yes, is a dangerous effort in itself." Exasperated with both her and myself, I threw up my hands. "I'm not sure what you want from me, Emma. I am doing my best, and that's all that can be asked of me."

"No one is asking more. But I fear for you, out there, downstairs, fighting monsters. You touch these things, and they touch you back."

BUT NETTLE SHANT HAVE NOTHING

❧

Nance O'Neil

April 16, 1894

I arrived in Fall River around noon, having caught a ride from the train station with a nice young man who'd seen me in *Hamlet* last year. I could hardly believe he remembered me, much less recognized me now, but such is the power of theater, I suppose. There may not be any money in it, but there's a certain kind of renown for the right kind of girl. And once in a while, that renown translates to a free ride into town, and to a loved one's house.

The young man in question . . . oh, I've already forgotten his name. Francis? Frederick? Something like that. You'd think that someone who earns a living memorizing pages upon pages of other people's words would have an easier time remembering other people's names, but you'd be mistaken on that point. I've always been terrible about it. Likely, I always will be.

But this young man, "F," was so wide-eyed and scandalized when I told him where I was going. I couldn't decide whether to be offended or amused, so I settled on amused. Lizbeth is the kindest, wisest, most caring soul in the world, and I've never before cared about what the papers have to say. Why start now?

(Knowing what the papers say and caring about it . . . those are two different things.)

Emma I could live without, but I won't, because Lizbeth loves her. You have to love your sisters, and if that's not some kind of real law, it's one of those moral laws that my father went on and on about for years. I don't know if Lizbeth would choose to love Emma otherwise. I wouldn't, but that's just me.

She's a cold thing, that Emma. Strange, really. Her sister is so warm.

But warm or otherwise, my beloved is up to something. Strange matters are afoot here at Maplecroft, and I get the distinct impression that the sisters are hiding something from me, if not lying to me outright. I'm not an idiot; I can see that things have been rearranged, and there are nails all over the floor in the doorways, and plants growing in odd pots, in odder places. For some reason, some doors are locked which otherwise used to be open. In corners there linger strange charms, snow-white grains of salt, and the faint odor of burned sage.

I asked Lizbeth about the locked doors, since that seemed like the easiest place to begin an investigation. She laughed, and it was worse acting than I've ever seen, which is saying something; but then she compounded the lie by telling me, "The cellar door's always been locked. It scarcely opens, and so we leave it shut. Anyway, it keeps the damp downstairs, where it belongs."

"I wasn't talking about the cellar, though I know you have wine and a laboratory down there—which you steadfastly refuse to show me. But what about that room at the end of the hall? Isn't it a library, or an office of some sort?"

"Storage, is all. My father's old things. I keep meaning to go through it, sort out the whole mess, and donate his papers or belongings where appropriate . . . but I've been quite tired, and I didn't care to look at it any longer."

"So you're entombing his memories, locking him away in the afterlife. Like . . . like some hapless victim in a Poe story."

"My father is dead," she said flatly, no hint of the very false laugh left in her cheeks. "And some days, I can scarcely manage my own affairs—much less tend to the ones he left behind. The bills are paid, at least, and nothing else is pressing. It can stay where it is, for now. Let it gather dust and let the papers molder away. It'll save me the trouble of sorting them later, if I can just sweep them into the bin."

But I pushed onward. "What about the other door, on the first floor? The sunroom, wasn't it? Or something like that?"

Without so much as a pause, she said, "The other night we had a storm, and a pair of the old windows broke—and the frames with them. We've sent for a man to repair them, but he can't arrive until next month. So we've covered the holes as best we can, but rodents and birds have a knack for finding their way inside. The door is an extra measure, that's all."

I would've bet my soul she wasn't telling the truth. "And the attic stairs?"

"One of the chimneys needs work. We've been expressly told to leave it alone, until the mason arrives, along with the window man. Loose bricks. Bats and the like, you know. Squirrels."

"And *that* is the most ridiculous answer yet!" I struggled to keep from yelling at her, or crying at her, or generally being the dramatic idiot her sister imagines me. But of all the little oppressions I hate the most, being lied to is right at the top of the list. It's disrespectful. It suggests I can't be trusted with the truth, whether to bear it, understand it, or keep it to myself.

Lizbeth stepped close to me then, so very near that I could see her pupils contract when I looked down into her eyes. She's almost half a head shorter than I am, but slender and tough where I'm made of rounder curves. I put my arms around her and embraced her, pulling her lean shape against my softer one.

She leaned up to speak into my ear, and I felt her lips against my hair. "You know how I adore you, but I don't think you know the lengths to which . . ." She stopped herself, and placed her head on my shoulder—so that when she spoke again, her mouth brushed the nook where my throat and collarbone meet. "You are mine and I love you. And I'm sorry if you feel I'm being dishonest."

Her hand slipped to the small of my back, and we stood there together like a man and woman dancing slowly, to thoughtful music.

Somewhat mollified, I put my chin atop her head. "But I feel you're being . . . not wholly truthful. Something is bothering you, and you're keeping it from me."

"Many things are bothering me. It comes with the territory of being . . . me."

"That isn't what I mean. And if I thought that's all it was, I would leap with you into the nearest carriage and we could ride back to Boston or New York—and you could forget about this place, for as long as you wanted."

"I couldn't leave Emma," she mumbled, and I knew that already. Some fierce, bitter, tiny, hell-bound part of my soul wondered how much longer the invalid could possibly survive, with or without her sister's money and attention. One day Lizbeth would be free of her, surely? God would see to it, if no one else.

But I remained stalwart, and I hope I sounded kind when I said, "That's why I'd never do such a thing. What would become of her if I spirited you away?"

She lifted her head and now she was smiling. The smile reached her eyes, and it looked perfectly wicked. "You think you could spirit me away? As easy as that?"

"I'm quite confident." I grinned back, wondering whether this was some kind of dare, and immediately daydreaming about it. "I outweigh you by forty pounds, if by a single stone. And look at me, darling: sturdy Midwestern farmer's stock."

"I thought your father was a preacher."

"A man of many hats," I assured her, and cuddled her close again. Emma was upstairs napping, and would not interrupt us. "So there's one tiny thing he and I have in common, if you squint at it from the right angle."

"You do have some lovely hats," she murmured.

And then we heard a bell ringing upstairs, so I was wrong— and Emma could interrupt us after all.

I told Lizbeth I'd make us all some tea while she tended to her sister's needs. I'm a grown woman who can find her way around a kitchen. I don't need to be entertained every waking moment; I can absolutely contribute to the care and maintenance of a household.

With a kiss I sent her upstairs, and then I went to the kitchen. I located the tea and all its accoutrements just fine, enjoying the size and well-stocked condition of the large room, lined with cabinets and shelves, offering a space for everything. Even when I'm not sleeping behind the stage, my own household is markedly smaller, and I share it with three or four other girls as often as not. (And Marcus, but let's be honest—he almost counts as one of us. It's not as if we've allowed Peter to come set up a cot beside us.)

I waited for the kettle to boil, an interminable task that never seems half so short as it ought to. I tapped one foot and peered around the room, still confident that the two upstairs were hiding something from me, but I had no idea what it could possibly be.

A thought sprang through my head: Maybe she's being courted. Is there a suitor? And then the thought sprang right back out again, because if I'd let it stay, it might've made me jealous and angry.

Emma already thinks I'm jealous and angry. I won't give her the satisfaction of being right.

Besides, a suitor wouldn't fit all the puzzle pieces I've found lying about this stately home. I extended my foot and ran the toe of my shoe across the doorway that led onto the back porch. A dozen nails were pounded right into the wood, with such fervent enthusiasm that it's a wonder the door would open or close at all. Maybe that was the idea. Maybe they're trying to keep someone out. Better locks would seem like a stronger approach.

Though this does raise an interesting question. If not a suitor . . . perhaps it's someone more menacing. Is someone causing her grief, here in town or somewhere at large? Not everyone thought she should've been exonerated, but that's because not everyone knows her as I do. If someone has been harassing her, I won't stand for that nonsense. Not for a second. Didn't she have a wayward brother or some such? I'd swear she mentioned him once, and without a drop of fondness.

The kettle hadn't popped, so I let myself seethe and let my mind wander.

She could be receiving threats in letters, in telegrams. Or they might arrive in person, but wouldn't even a harasser have better manners than that? Most men are cowards, and they're happiest to do their badgering through some other medium. Otherwise, they wait until they can get you alone, and I guess that's one good thing about having Emma around. Lizbeth is never alone.

The theater has taught me so much. Not all of it about acting.

I took another look around the place—just the kitchen, and the corridor beyond it—and I saw yet more nails driven into the floor here and there, which didn't make a great deal of sense, but the smell of sage, and the little bundles tied up over the door-ways . . . they reminded me of something: a brief run off-Broadway (*very* off-Broadway) in New Orleans. That city is a superstitious place like none other, and all the actresses were in love with it. We're a superstitious lot ourselves, worse than any-body, I should think—so it's not as if I'm casting stones.

Speaking of stones, there was a small dish on the windowsill over the sink, and in it were three very shiny brown stones with clear marbling. Quartz, polished into gems, I think.

Yes, in New Orleans. I'd seen such things there.

My eyes rose to the entryway that separated the kitchen from the corridor leading to the house's interior. Another nail, this one above the frame, overhead—and hanging from that nail, I spotted a small bag made of what looked like red felt, no bigger than my thumb.

Beside the sink was a small step stool. I dragged it into pos-ition, stepped atop it, and reached up for the little red bag.

My arms are long, and when I combined them with my height, I reached it easily. I squeezed it between my fingers and whatever was inside felt crunchy and light. Herbs? Papers? More tiny stones?

I caught a faint trail of scent, caused when I disturbed the bag and pinched its contents. Because I could not sniff the strange object without pulling it down from its position, I sniffed at my fingers instead. They smelled like cinnamon and something green. Not absinthe, not quite. Perhaps straightforward old anise.

The kettle blew behind me, startling me almost off the stool. Maplecroft is such a funny house, such a big, empty, warm, drowsy place. Even when everyone is home.

I stepped down, kicked the step aside, and retrieved the kettle with a hand towel left beside the stove. I set everything to steep and waited again. Another two or three minutes by myself, and then I could carry the tray upstairs.

More time to wonder in the big house's spell of silence.

But then . . . was it silence, really? When I listened hard, I thought I could hear Lizbeth upstairs, a faint rumble of her voice sifting down through the ceiling. And maybe, just barely, the fussing response of Emma, needing heaven knew what this time. Probably needing for me to leave, but she can't have that. Not yet. All I'll give her is tea.

And I heard something else, too. Not Emma, I mean.

This was something else . . . a dull roar—a rumbling, rolling, washing sound that came with an added whisper. Not quite the ocean. Not quite a seashell, held up fast to my ear. Not that sound exactly, but something like it.

We were close to the seashore, but not that close. I couldn't have heard the tide from the kitchen, nor even the street outside. Something else, then? A distant railroad train? No, not that, either.

The longer I stood there, letting the tea steep . . . the more I thought it must be coming from the cellar. There it was. A rushing, swishing, soothing noise.

Coming from behind the door.

I remember putting down the hand towel, for I'd held it all this time that I stood there, letting my imagination run wild. I set it on the counter, I'm almost positive—though I later saw it on the floor, and wasn't sure how it'd gotten there. I went to the cellar door and held my ear against it, thinking again of a seashell and all its auditory gifts. I was listening for the ocean. For answers. For something, and it was *there*, and I heard it; I'd bet my life on it. I'd bet Lizbeth's life, and that's saying something more.

"Nance!"

She said my name loudly, and it startled me. I jumped, a feeling of childish guilt washing through my chest, though I'd done nothing wrong. "Lizbeth!" I said her name back, with mock drama. "You startled me! Why would you shout like that?"

Her eyes looked old, very old. One way or another, she was about to lie to me.

"I called your name two or three times, and you didn't hear me. What are you doing? I thought you were making tea, but look—" She tapped the kettle with the back of her hand, quickly—to judge the temperature. "It's gone cool."

"Don't be ridiculous. It couldn't possibly . . ." I'd only been standing there a minute, if that long. I stepped toward the counter and slipped on that damn towel, almost falling headlong into the sink. I felt dizzy, and drained. Like I'd misplaced something—something I couldn't remember having lost. "Lizbeth, what's in the cellar?" I asked, too dizzy to play whatever game she'd crafted in this place.

She put her arm around me and gave me a long squeeze.

"Nothing's in the cellar, darling. Nothing but cans, preserves, and a few jars. No true laboratory of any sort, regardless of what I might have blurted while drunk. There's some wine, obviously, but most of it's not any good, not anymore. It's all gone to vinegar by now." She emptied the kettle and refilled it from the pump at the sink. "I'll just throw a new batch of water on the stove, and we can settle in with sandwiches. Would you like some? I can make some . . ."

I knew what she was doing. She was babbling, distracting me, even as she moved with great deliberation—like the deception was something that forced her to concentrate, and to perform. I still felt off my balance, like the room might have tilted while I wasn't looking, and I hadn't felt the shift.

"Sandwiches would be nice," I told her. For all I knew, it was only hunger that made me so scattered. "But I still want you to show me the cellar."

"Not now, Nance." She said it firmly, but she didn't turn around so she could lie to my face, when she added, "Later, maybe." From the box on the counter, she withdrew some bread—and in the drawer beside her hip, she found a knife.

"Maybe tonight?"

"Oh, not tonight. It'll be cold down there, and damp. But if it's dry and warm, we could do it tomorrow."

"And if it's not?"

She shrugged. "Then some other time. The day after next, or after that. Or your next visit. You'll come again one day, won't you?" She faced me then, quickly—and with worry all over her lovely face.

I forced myself to smile. "Always. Whenever."

"That's a relief," she replied. "I should hope that something as small as a tour of the cellar wouldn't be enough to chase you off."

"Oh, it's not," I promised. "You'll never get rid of me *that* way."

After tea I took the tray downstairs so that Lizbeth could spend a few minutes getting Emma ready for work time at her desk. This is quite an undertaking, wherein Lizbeth moves books, journals, a week's worth of mail, and her sister into an office at the end of the hall. Why Emma won't just write in bed, I don't know. If I were feeling ungenerous, I'd suggest that she does it on purpose, to interrupt my visit in as many small ways as she can possibly contrive.

I'm rather frequently ungenerous, these days.

But this particular interruption gave me another opportunity to spend time alone in the kitchen, where the cellar door was still calling me. Did it call? Or did it only sing such a siren song because Lizbeth wanted me to stay away from it?

No, I think I said it right the first time. It was calling me.

I'm forced to assume she keeps something dangerous or embarrassing down there, but how dangerous could it be? How embarrassing? She's renowned throughout the world as a murderess who escaped justice, and she's taken up with a flamboyant young actress in a more or less public, and *suspiciously* romantic fashion; you'd think she'd be well past embarrassment by now.

Regardless, she doesn't need to protect me—from herself, or anyone else. So I approached the door once again, though this time I didn't hear the ocean-swell sound rising and falling behind it. I pressed the side of my face against it, and I closed my eyes, and I listened for all I was worth.

I heard nothing at all.

CUT THEM ON FRIDAY, YOU CUT THEM FOR SORROW

⁓✤⁓

Owen Seabury, M.D.

April 18, 1894

Shepherd Duffy rapped on my door before the sun came up—a hard, insistent knock of the kind I know all too well. Someone was in labor; someone was injured. Some surprise catastrophe had befallen somebody, someplace. I knew it as I gathered my wits and stumbled down the stairs; and I knew it was likely worse than I'd thought when I saw Shepherd's hat through the glass pane in the door. He was dressed smartly, as always: in a crisp brown suit that identified him on sight more quickly than the badge upon his chest. Only a slight rumpling of his collar betrayed that he too had been roused from bed and thrust into action at such an inconvenient hour.

I opened the door and adjusted my spectacles.

Without preamble, and before I could ask how I could be of service, he said, "You'd better come down to the courthouse. Ebenezer Hamilton is asking for you."

"I'll get my bag."

"You won't need it. He isn't hurt."

"Oh dear . . ." Then the matter was grave indeed. "Has something happened to Matthew?"

"Yes, but it's nothing you can fix. Please, come along. I have a cart waiting, if you would be so kind."

"Give me one moment to grab my coat, and I'll be right there."

I didn't mean to close him out of the house, but he was already on his way back to the cart anyway, and I needed another moment or two to collect myself. I was dressed decently, if not well—having pulled a pair of pants over my sleep shirt before I'd come downstairs; but the clock against the wall informed me that it was just before four in the morning. The world could forgive me a lack of presentability.

I more thoroughly tucked in my sleep shirt, tied my shoes, and threw on an overcoat. The spring evening (or morning, depending) was chilly enough that I could see my breath when I stepped onto the porch, though it'd likely be warm enough come midday that I'd regret the coat. But for that moment, that long, stiff-legged walk to the sheriff's apparently borrowed transportation, I was glad for it. I was shivering, and it wasn't entirely the weather.

I climbed up onto the seat beside Duffy, who apologized again, this time for the accommodations. "I would've ridden over in the official carriage, but it's in use just now. This was all I could muster on short notice." He snapped the reins and the big brown horse pulled us forward.

"Not to worry. This is better than walking, by far. I used to keep a horse for such occasions, but in my old age I find that riding disagrees with my bones." He didn't reply, and I felt a peculiar urgency about the silence, so I prattled on. "Besides, it won't be long before we're all rolling around in electrical carriages, if the periodicals can be believed. But won't you tell me what this is about? Without my bag, I'm at a loss. Am I being called as some kind of witness? What's become of Matthew?"

The sheriff cleared his throat. "He's been shot dead."

"By Ebenezer?" I guessed.

"He's confessed to it, yes. Says it was a matter of self-defense."

"And what of Felicity?" I asked after Mrs. Hamilton. "Is she all right?"

"No. Matthew has . . . done something to her," he said vaguely. "Ebenezer tried to stop him, tried to . . . I'm sorry, it's all a bit unclear right now. We're still sorting out the facts. Ebenezer swears he'll talk to you, and no one else . . . but I'm not so sure. The man's so shaken he can scarcely breathe, much less explain himself, to you or anybody."

"But Felicity . . . is she dead?"

"Very, yes."

It was a strange answer, and I didn't like it. I felt like it implied something more awful than it stated outright, and I was on the verge of demanding answers when we drew up to the courthouse. The sheriff told me he'd tend to the horse and cart, and meet me inside.

"Go to the consultation room on the first floor. They're waiting for you there."

The night was still and very, very dark—despite the gas lamps that burned softly on the town's square. They cast shadows too sharp to be pretty, and if the moon was out, I couldn't see it. The air was thick with frost and something else: a peculiar odor. I caught the barest whiff of something rotting. Something that came from the sea, and ought to have stayed there.

I stamped my feet and went up the steps, letting myself inside.

Inside the courthouse was warmer and brighter, but it bustled with young men in hastily donned uniforms, and a pair of narrow old men in cadaverous black suits. I recognized them as the brothers who own the funeral parlor—last name of Wann, which is so appropriate as to be almost inappropriate, or so I've always thought. They nodded at me, with their usual grim expressions of sorrow and fortitude. They are good men, and good professionals, but they always remind me of crows on a laundry line. Vultures atop a gate. It's the job, and what their presence implies, that's all. It can't be helped, and my morbid fancies should not reflect upon them.

I nodded back at them, and carried onward to the consultation room at the end of the hall. A heavyset woman with a large bag begged my pardon, and turned sideways to pass me; I leaned against the wall to let her proceed, wondering at all this commotion, and what it meant. Knowing that it could not be good.

Matthew was dead, and Felicity was "very" dead. That was all I knew, and it wasn't enough to explain the nervousness that permeated the building. The hall was clogged with it, the unhappy vibrations of fear, confusion, and doubt.

The consultation room was on my left. Inside it, I found Ebenezer Hamilton seated between two sturdy men who were either guarding him or comforting him, or performing a bit of both as necessary. Ebenezer was covered in gore, his hands quivering, his eyes red. He wiped his nose on the back of his sleeve—which belonged to a thick-knit sweater like the old mariners often wore. In this little gesture, he managed to smear blood across his face. More of it, I should say.

He looked up when I entered.

"Doctor Seabury," he said, his voice choked with tears and phlegm. "I thank you for coming, and I'm sorry, I'm so sorry about . . . about . . . the hour . . ."

"Never mind the clock, Mr. Hamilton. I'm happy to help. But please, wouldn't you . . . or wouldn't *someone* tell me what's happened?"

He released a wretched, racked sob and once more wiped at his nose. "I don't know how to tell it," he said, looking down, then up at me with a pleading, pitiful gaze. It was an entreaty, I knew—a silent petition that I should *please*, for the love of God, believe whatever he said next.

Gently, I told him, "You must *try*. And I will listen, and you can tell me the story however you think is best."

He nodded wildly, and it didn't mean "yes." It only meant that he was glad for permission to sound entirely outrageous, if the circumstances called for it. "Doctor, I asked for you to come on out, because you'd seen Matty a time or two. And . . . and you knew, better than anyone but us, how strange the whole thing'd got."

"I only wish I'd been able to help."

"No one could've helped, no one but the Lord above. No one." He repeated himself, alternating now between nodding his head and shaking it. "You couldn't have known. Nobody could. Nobody could explain it, neither. Nobody. I can't. I don't. I just . . ."

Again, very gently—as if I were speaking to a child distracted by a broken arm, I tried to direct his focus. "No one is asking you to explain the matter. The world is full of nonsensical events and bizarre occurrences, understood only to God Himself. But you must tell us simply what happened. Start only at the beginning, and share only what you can. Begin with Matthew," I prompted. "Last I saw him, he was desperately unwell, if you'll recall."

I made a point of meeting his eyes.

He and I were now the only two men living who knew exactly how bad Matthew's condition had become. They'd been right to hide him away. At the time, I'd had doubts . . . but those doubts were withering, the longer I sat in that small, damp, cold room. I wish they'd done more than hide him; I wish they'd sent him away, somewhere far from the ocean—far from Fall River . . . for all the good that wishing did me.

"The poor lad was confined to his bedroom," he said cautiously. He did not mention that they'd bound him to the bed, or say that they'd covered all the windows with black cloth because of the way he used to scream when the sunlight touched him, as I'd learned in one of my subsequent visits. "And he was in there still, this evening. Late this evening, a bit after midnight, I'd say."

He stalled. I prodded him further. "Very good. You and your wife were home, alive and well, and Matthew was in his bedroom, having taken to his bed. Then something changed. What was it?"

He swallowed hard and took a deep breath.

"We . . . we heard something, in his room."

"He cried out?"

"No, it wasn't a cry. It wasn't . . . it didn't sound like him. It wasn't a sound a boy could make, or I wouldn't've thought so." He shuddered, and clutched at his own arms, hugging himself and smearing more blood from the spattered, soaked-in pools that marred the sweater. I wondered why no one had brought him something else to wear, but maybe they had. Maybe he'd refused. He was so unbalanced, he might've demanded or rejected anything.

"What did it sound like, then—if it wasn't a cry?"

He released his arms, and his hands settled atop the table, where they shook, leaving short streaks of bloody fingerprints dampening the wood beneath them. "It sounded like . . . a wet machine," he said at last.

The officer to his right said, "I beg your pardon?" before I had a chance to say it myself.

Ebenezer tossed his hands in the air in a broad shrug, and let them flop back down atop the table once more. "It weren't a sound like any animal I ever heard! Or any person, that's for damn sure!" To emphasize his point, he pounded his fist against the wood. "It weren't a sound like a living thing *makes!*"

"Ebenezer, please, remain calm. I believe you; I just don't understand you."

"It sounded like a *grinding* thing, all right? Like . . . like . . . a big millstone, underwater—with its wheel clanking right along, muffled and soggy-like. And it came from Matty's room!" he insisted with all his might. "Neither me or Lissy could figure out what it might be, so we went to go look—you understand?"

"The pair of you? Together?" I asked, hoping to bring him back to the tale, away from the speculation.

"That's right, both of us. We opened the door and . . . and . . . and . . ." His eyes grew frantic, and his hands fluttered. I was afraid I was about to lose his attention—and he was on the cusp of losing his sanity.

I said to the two officers seated beside him, "Gentlemen, could you possibly give us a moment alone? I'm afraid the audience is a bit much for him. Please, if you could be so kind?"

They exchanged glances, and I knew they were considering their jobs, and the correct procedures in a case like this. But I had a very firm suspicion that there was no such thing as a "case like this," and I was furthermore confident that Ebenezer would speak more openly to me, and me alone.

"He's not been charged with a crime, has he?"

"No," one of them confirmed. "Not yet, and maybe not at all. But that ain't up to us."

But leaving us alone . . . that was an act within their authority, or so they concluded. They were kind enough to see themselves out, and I rose to quietly shut the door behind them. "They'll stay out there," I said to Ebenezer, as I joined him again at the table. "Watching the door, I'm sure—but if you're quiet enough, they'll never hear you speak."

He agreed, and leaned forward. His large, chapped hands were still pressed to the table between us. In the cracks of his knuckles, blood was drying to the color of rust.

Quickly, he spit out the rest: "We went to the door together, and I told her we should wait, we should call for you, or for the police, because dear God in Heaven, we was in over our heads, you see?"

"Yes, I see."

"But my wife, she said it was nonsense, and he was only a boy, and she pushed me aside. She was crying, so I think she was foolin' herself, and she knew it good and well, but what could I do? What could I say? And if I sent for help, how could I explain there's some . . . some *machine* holed up in the bedroom with the boy?"

He caught his breath, wiped his brow with the other sleeve. The cleaner one.

"So we didn't do none of them things, and she opened the

door . . . and then there was this stench, you hear? Something so awful, like nothing I'd ever smelled—or I'd never smelled something half so strong." His attention snapped, and he was clear-eyed for a moment. "And I'll have ye to know that *I* was one of the men who helped carve up that dead whale last summer, the one what beached up on the rocks. It'd been cooking in the sun, rotting in the water, and the smell was so bad, I thought I'd die—but I didn't." Then he said, "The smell in Matty's room, it was worse than *that*."

He paused, and for a moment he stared into space, at some indistinct spot just behind me. Then he found my eyes again, and corrected himself slightly. "When we opened that door, I thought of that whale's innards, when Abe Scanton's shovel pierced its stomach and everything the whale'd eaten for a week came splashing out, and it smelled like rot and belly acid, and Abe fainted dead away on the spot. Yeah," he said with a nod. "The smell wasn't quite the same, but it wasn't quite different, neither."

"Very good," I said, filing this away with no small measure of distaste. But you couldn't fault the man for his lack of precision, or his sense of understatement. "You've established the smell—now can you tell me what you *saw*?"

"I saw . . . ," he started, and then he tried again, closing his eyes as if trying to remember the scene better—or maybe to block it out. "Water," he breathed. "On the walls, on the windows. Pouring off the edge of the bed, pouring down the dresser drawers, and along the floor in little streams, little lines. Draining away between the floorboards. And I saw Matty, but he weren't . . . he wasn't . . ."

Quieter now, his voice dropped low, to a horrified whisper. "He was swimming. Not in the water, but the air, above his bed. Treading water in the middle of the room, his eyes rolled back in his head, nothing showing but the whites, and they weren't very white anymore. They were blue and brown. Marbled, like a dirty old egg. And his mouth . . ." Ebenezer licked at his lower lip, and swallowed again. "It moved like he was talking, but he wasn't . . . he was making that noise, that grinding underwater noise. Like a machine with wheels and chains, and soaked-wet wood, pulling against some kind of weight. Dredging something up. Hauling something out of the ocean."

That last word hung in the air between us.

It was my turn to swallow hard, and to lick my lips, and now to lean back—and wrap my own arms around myself. "So Matthew *did* make the sound you heard?"

"Yes. No. He was . . . it *looked* like he was making it. But it wasn't a sound a boy could make. No living thing, Doctor. No living thing makes a sound like that." He might've argued further, but then he waved his hand, changing his subject or finding it again, as the case may be. "Then Felicity, she screamed—and she ran to Matty, pulled on his leg, trying to draw him back down to the ground. But whatever held him in the air did a mighty good job of it, and he didn't budge, not at all. He just hung there, his arms moving around like he was keeping himself afloat, swimming in the air like it was the ocean, his hair all swaying back and forth like seaweed."

I tried unsuccessfully to keep from gasping, and the sound stuck in my throat. "She . . . your wife tried to pull him down? And he . . . he was held aloft, somehow? By wires, by . . . by the ropes? There were ropes, I recall. Holding him to the bed."

"There were ropes *on* the bed, untied and hanging by the posts. He was aloft, sir, yes. But nothing kept him there that I could see," he vowed, his eyes haunted but deadly earnest. "It was all so unnatural, you know? I reached for my wife and tried to draw her away from him, but she weren't having none of it. She fought me, and fought for him." He said the last part with a cough and a grimace.

He continued. "Then Matty, he . . . he put a hand down and grabbed her by the hair, and he pulled her up to meet him—and she was screaming and shouting, and I was screaming and shouting, and Matty was making that noise, that same awful noise. I'll never forget it. Never forget it. Couldn't stand to hear it." He shook his head again, trying to shake the sound out of it, like water from his ear.

My voice shook as hard as Ebenezer's hands. "He lifted her up?"

"He lifted her up." He was back to that whisper, rising and falling as the sharing became too much for him. "Picked her right up off her feet, and her hair started swaying, like Matthew's, like she was underwater. She was gasping, coughing, thrashing about—just like she would if you held her head in a tub, you see? So I ran—into the next room, and I fished around under the bed for my gun. It's a hunting gun, that's all. A fowler's gun," he clarified. "And I never shot nothing with it but birds for the table—I swear it to you.

"And I didn't think . . ." He folded and unfolded his fingers, lacing them together, pulling them apart. "I didn't think I was gonna shoot Matty, or nothing like that. I thought I'd threaten him, maybe, and that'd get through to him.

"But by the time I'd got the gun and come back, Felicity wasn't moving. She was hanging there limp beside him, his hands tangled up in her hair, holding her up, and her feet dangling above the sheets. So I hollered at him. I told him I'd shoot! I told him, Doctor! And he didn't do a thing. It was like he hadn't heard me at all, and I thought he'd hurt Felicity somehow, so I couldn't just stand there doing nothing. So I shot him. I shot him, and he let go of her hair, and she fell to the floor. And I shot him again, and he fell a little lower. Then I had to either reload or tend to Felicity."

"So you tended to your wife."

"I tried! I tried pulling her out of that room, where everything was sopping wet, and I didn't know where all the water came from, and it all smelled so bad, Doctor, you have to believe me . . ."

"I do," I assured him, and I was horrified to realize I was telling him the truth. "I *do* believe you."

"I dragged her back out of the room, into the hallway, and some of the water came with her, but most of it stayed in there with Matty. I pushed on her chest, you know—seeing if she was breathing, or if I could start her up again. I put my head on her chest and her heart wasn't beating, so I pushed some more, and I turned her head to the side, and out of her mouth there was . . . there was . . . all this *blood*. It came streaming right out of her, pouring and pouring, like the water down the walls in Matty's room."

He fell silent, and in this new state of quiet I could hear footsteps outside the room, coming toward us. I sensed our time was drawing to a close, so I asked one last question. "What about Matthew? What about the sound you heard?"

"I stood up, once I knew my wife was done. I went back into the room, and Matty was lying half on the bed, half off it. There wasn't any more sound. There wasn't any more water, but everything was still wet."

The sheriff's knock announced him, and he interrupted us curtly, if politely. "Doctor, I thank you for your time, but the Boston office has sent a telegram asking us to send Mr. Hamilton along to them. There'll be an investigator here in the morning. Later in the morning," he corrected himself with a sigh.

"I understand," I said, and I patted at Ebenezer's hand. He didn't react, either to the news or to my awkward ministrations.

Duffy added, "The investigator's asked for a doctor's company while he looks at the scene. Can we send him your way, when he arrives?"

"Yes, by all means. Send for me at my home. I'll . . . do my best, I suppose, to get another few hours of sleep." Though I knew good and well that I wouldn't.

I wished Ebenezer Hamilton well, and before I left, I leaned in close—putting a hand on his shoulder. Into his ear, I said, "I believe you, and I will do what I can to defend you, and support you."

"Thank you, sir," he said, but he was hardly present anymore. His mind was back in that room with his dead wife, and dead godson. And I'll never forget the last thing he murmured, as I left the room. Not to me, and maybe not to himself. Maybe it was a prayer, or an observation for the sheriff, I couldn't say—but it was that last sentiment that kept me from returning to my bed for any further rest.

"That sound . . . that sound, it came from his mouth. It was the song of something dying. Something that never did live."

Phillip Zollicoffer,
Professor of Biology, Miskatonic University

⚓

I've taken *Physalia zollicoffris* for myself, and none other.

I may have burned a bridge or two while I was at it.

At present, I am torn between horror and delight, outrageous hope and astonished despair; but this was how it has to be, isn't it? Everything has been leading up to this eventual outcome, every single step. From the moment I received the sample, sealed up tight in that jar . . . every motion, every gesture, every note, and every word have accumulated into a mighty force, culminating with the match I struck this evening.

What a day. How can I recall it, or reconcile it with my life? My sanity? Am I in danger of losing either one? Both? I fear there are none qualified to render judgment at this point. None but the siphonophore itself, and it tells me plenty.

It? No.

Them, perhaps—but at the risk of saying something preposterous, I almost feel like the specimen is a *she*. Ridiculous, when addressing a plural entity with no construct of binary gender such as humans ascribe . . . but then again, there's a three-person God in heaven, or so we are often reminded. And I've never heard Him referred to with any pronoun but the masculine.

He is God.

She is Siphonophore.

They both are One, but also Legion.

Which is either blasphemy or the utmost truth, and I'm ill-prepared to offer an opinion either way.

We follow the ones who call us, and She has given me greater direction than any invisible sky-ghost ever bothered or dared. So I know Whom I will obey.

I am not offloading my actions upon Her, though I do fervently believe that She has endorsed my behavior and gazed favorably upon it. Everything I've done these last few weeks has been for Her, in order to please and protect Her. She knows this, and She approves.

But I assume all responsibility for what I've done. These were my choices. My decisions. My courses of action. My bridges to render unto ash.

I stood in the lab, with *Physalia zollicoffris* in a jar on the counter. It was the same jar in which She'd arrived, though it'd since been cleaned and aired, sterilized and polished. She deserves no less.

I was thinking about how She seemed somewhat smaller

than when I'd first laid eyes upon Her, sprawled out and stinking, apparently dead and pickled. At that time, She'd appeared big enough to fill the whole chemistry sink, perhaps to overflowing, except that no, that can't be true. She arrived in this jar, a mason jar of the oversized variety—perhaps it holds half a gallon, at most. She cannot be any bigger than that.

But . . . whereas before She occupied every square inch of space . . . filling the glass like a liquid, seeping and spilling and filling the area with Her bulk . . . now I can see emptiness between the creases and folds. I've replaced the liquid with ordinary salt water, a brine that felt more appropriate somehow than whatever chemical had kept Her secured during transport; but that wouldn't have caused Her to shrink. No, if anything it should've made Her stronger, fed Her, made Her feel more at home.

I hope I haven't made a terrible mistake.

No, I haven't done any such thing. She reassures me.

That must sound strange. Well, it *is* strange.

She tells me things. She warms me.

But I was looking at the jar, and its precious contents. And outside in the hall I heard Dr. Greer mumbling something or another—I didn't quite catch it, but it was something about me, and my suspension. Maybe he was saying it ought to become permanent, or maybe he was saying I ought to be reinstated. Really, I have no idea. I heard my name, and a reference to my office, and an idly voiced question that might have been so simple as a casual wondering about where I was, right that moment.

I thought about opening the door and announcing myself, then changed my mind. I resolved instead to listen at the door, or I *must* have resolved that, because I found myself standing there, my cheek pressed to the wood, my ear flat against the crack where the panel and the jamb connect.

I felt a slight breeze on my skin, for the building is old and it has settled, here and there. Its angles are not always perpendicular, and its floors are not always straight. Its ceilings sometimes leak. Its windows sometimes crack with age, or the weight of a building becoming comfortable on its foundations.

The floor beneath me vibrated, as if the men on the other side were bouncing up and down like unruly children in bed. But they were not. I listened, and their voices were steady. I still could not understand them.

I pulled my head away and shook it, then repositioned myself and tried again.

But they were speaking another language, nattering on in words that were mere syllables hurled and punched, and it was nonsense, all of it. Once I heard my name. Twice I heard my name, and then a laugh.

I looked back toward my specimen, my Lady.

My laboratory had grown dark. A storm had coagulated overhead, or it must have been the case, because the clouds were shimmering gray out through the window. Or . . . no. I couldn't see the sky from there. It must have been a sheet of water, cascading where the gutters have rotted through, making the world outside look so much like a filthy aquarium.

The gaslight flickered and went out. Except that I hadn't turned it on, had I?

It was definitely off. And the office was definitely gloomy, so gloomy that I could hardly see Her, sitting in the jar, cradled there, but deserving better.

She glimmered, and what little light remained in the room winked against the glass, showing off Her sinuous, swimming shape, twisting in the jar, a very slow whirlpool, or a carousel, or the ethereal winding of a cotton candy machine. She pivoted to show me Her whole self. She unfurled, and I was transfixed.

I couldn't hear the men outside the door anymore.

I don't know who Greer was talking to. Hanson, maybe, or Applegate. If they were still present, they'd gone silent. If they were standing on the other side of the door, they said nothing. I said nothing. I watched *Physalia zollicoffris*.

I looked away.

I opened the door with my left hand. My right hand was holding something, and I could feel it, hard and cold, but I did not look down to see what it was. I did not care. I knew what to do, and I knew where to go.

Into the hall I stepped. I walked. I proceeded.

Down the hall, which was empty. No one whispered, and no chancellor hung about, spreading lies and gossip. No students walked past, shirking their responsibilities in favor of cigarettes behind the boiler room.

(This hallway was the quickest shortcut. They came and went like the tide, always leaving a trail of tobacco vapors in their wake. Like they accused me. Of leaving. What was it? The odor of the specimen. In my wake.)

Like my office the corridor was darkened, though it was midday, I was relatively confident. Midday, and not an ounce of sun to shine through at the ends of the hall, where a trio of great windows reached from almost-floor to almost-ceiling. They looked like the window in my office—no, in my laboratory, where the students come and go—covered in water, that drained down the glass in cascades. The whole building was submerged, as it ought to be.

To make Her more comfortable.

She was behind me, on the table, in the jar. I wished for Her but there was nothing to be done, not now, not yet. Work to do first. Then devotion.

There was no one in the hall with me, and I walked it forever.

My hand snatched out, the one holding the blade. It was a blade, not a scalpel, something larger. Smaller than a machete, larger than a pocketknife. Large enough, at any rate. I lashed and struck like a snake, at nothing, at no one. But there was blood on my hand when I looked down, and it wasn't mine. None of this was mine. But I was alone.

Somehow, this didn't confuse me. Somehow, She urged me on, and said that the answers would come, and She always speaks the truth, and never lies to me. It isn't Her way.

I proceeded to Greer's office because he was there. (I knew he was there. She told me he would be.) I did not knock on the door because I do not knock on doors, not anymore. I certainly do not ask permission of worms like that man with his name upon the brass plate, his letters etched into the metal, scratched there by some printer's claw.

I opened the door and the knob was chilly in my hand, so chilly that my skin stuck to it—the blood or the water on my skin, it froze, and I pulled myself free with a twist, after the twist of the knob. I did not like the metal. Wasn't sure what it was. Looked down, and saw it was the old-fashioned iron sort, a lever. Not a knob. I don't understand, because I thought I twisted it.

But it was cold, very cold. And it was lying on the floor

where I broke it off and dropped it, and the skin on my hand was torn, but it mended itself before my eyes.

Dr. Greer shouted at me. Some querulous complaint.

"Zollicoffer, what's happened? What have you done?"

Some series of meaningless question marks, cast at me like a spell. I understood his words again, and I understood that he was upset. He damned well ought to be upset. He'd offended Her with his treatment of me. He'd offended us both, Her in the glass throne I would carry with me always. Me in the flesh and blood, covered in flesh and blood, holding a blade, the kind scientists use to saw through bone. It came from the biology lab.

Did it? I couldn't recall having seen one like it there before. A fine steel thing, gleaming except where the gore had smudged off the shine. Its edges ragged and grasping, its teeth chewing on bits of skin and gristle that had snagged upon them.

I held it by the wooden handle. I held it with the blade point down, the way She told me. I held his neck. He stopped yelling at me, and that was a terrible relief. I couldn't stand the sound of his voice anymore. I couldn't bear the volume of it, the weight and the frequency of it, not until it faded into gurgles and bubbles, and his desk was awash with crimson.

The crimson was not as pretty as the water pouring down the windows outside.

She warned me not to watch the water too long. She warned me to move on to the next office, while there was time. Before anyone intervened.

I was unstoppable, but I mustn't stop.

Greer's office door banged open, and Dr. Madison stood there, his mouth hanging open like a wound. He began to shout, and his shouting was even worse than Greer's, which was truly saying something. His shouting took longer to stop. I had to drag him inside. He kept saying "No," as if he firmly believed this couldn't happen, and therefore it must not be happening.

But I was unstoppable, and I did not stop.

I left them lying together, their blood pooling into puddles, into deep enough puddles to drown in. Into ponds. Into lakes. And She told me not to watch it, that I had to keep going. I must not stop.

I was unstoppable.

HAPPY IS THE CORPSE THAT THE RAIN SHINES ON

❧

Owen Seabury, M.D.

April 19, 1894

The Boston inspector didn't arrive yesterday morning as I was promised, but he came this morning instead—bright and early, if not so early as the sheriff had the day before. The sun was up, I'd had my coffee and toast, and I was as prepared as one could hope for what we were bound to find in the Hamilton home, where two people had died, and now nobody lived.

The inspector's name was Simon Wolf, a fine name for a man who hunts wrongdoers—but aside from his peculiarly practical nomenclature, he wasn't at all what I expected. Rather short, somewhat wide, and thickly bespectacled, Wolf was nonetheless a sharp-witted man with an air of crisp professionalism about him. I knew immediately that I liked him, and that I could work with him.

Together we approached Hamilton's Ocean Goods and Supplies, the store which the Hamiltons had kept, and within which they'd lived (in the back rooms, apart from the business front).

The main entryway was closed off with rope, more for show than for restraint. A sign hung from the rope, announcing that the shop was "Closed Indefinitely," with the subsequent admonition, "Do Not Enter Without Police Approval."

But as Wolf put it, "My approval is somewhat more official than mere police permission. So I'll see to the knot."

"But you're a policeman, aren't you?"

"Something like that."

"I meant no offense, of course," I said, fearing I might have caused some all the same.

He waved away my concerns. "None taken. Our offices work in close conjunction. Fine men, the Boston police. But no, I'm not one of them. Good heavens, it's a devil of a knot."

I wasn't sure what he meant, but I did not inquire further. Instead I said, "I have a penknife, if you think it'd help . . ."

Before I could finish the offer, he'd released the informal barrier with a determined pinch of manual dexterity. "Thank you, but I've finally got it." He fished about in his pocket for a key, given to him by the sheriff, I assumed. Or maybe it came courtesy of some other authority, as he implied. He found the key, retrieved it, and inserted it into the lock. "You've been here before—is that correct?"

"Everyone in town has been here, at one time or another. It's a local institution. Or it *was*, I'm sorry to say."

The door unfastened, and he pushed it open. "There's

always a chance that someone will reopen it. Some family member or another. But the Hamiltons had no children . . ." It wasn't a question; he was merely recalling the facts as he'd heard them. I wondered who'd filled him in on all the peripheral details. "A brother, or cousin, perhaps."

"Ebenezer had a brother, but he was a mariner and I only met him once. He was older, too. For an old man who's spent his life upon the sea . . . it might be a good retirement, to operate a shop such as this," or so I thought aloud. "Then again, perhaps he's lost his taste for living on solid ground. Some of them do, you know. They take to the ocean, and never find comfort elsewhere."

"I'll ask Mr. Hamilton when I speak to him next. That poor man . . ." He might've said more, but we both stepped inside, where the store was dark and strangely cool. Both of us went quiet; we milled about in the entryway, beside the overflowing barrel of sea glass. It drew my eye, even when I consciously decided that I *must* look elsewhere.

Nervously, I said, "Bit of a chill in here."

"Bit of a smell, too. Did Mr. Hamilton mention it?"

"Yes, he did. Compared it to the stomach contents of a beached whale. And he ought to know—for he helped discard one. It was the talk of the shores last summer."

Wolf nodded. "The bowels of a rotting whale. That sounds about right." He flinched, like he'd prefer to pinch his nose, but it wouldn't be manly.

"It *is* terrible," I agreed, though it wasn't quite the veritable wall of stench I'd been guaranteed. It was more of an undercurrent in the chilly, damp air. Something riding the humidity, as if the very mist itself was the source of the odor.

It felt like some strange trespass, to visit the store under these circumstances. Closed for business, perhaps for good. Dark and quiet, with no Felicity Hamilton behind the counter, no Matthew to refill the odds-and-ends barrel. No Ebenezer on the pier just outside, spreading out nets and sails to dry in the sun, later to be repaired. I wondered sadly what would become of the stock, of the store, of the building itself.

"Can you imagine . . ." I murmured, scanning the room.

"I can imagine many things," he replied. "But what precisely do you have in mind?"

"Can you imagine buying a business or home like this, knowing what took place here? For generations, schoolchildren will accuse it of being haunted. You can rest assured of *that*."

"Children and adults alike—it's not as if we ever outgrow our darker fears. Let's not pretend we're all so reluctant to entertain the unknown."

"Do you?" I asked bluntly.

He faced me, and even in the low light I could see how quizzically he regarded me. He was thinking about his answer. He didn't know me well, and wasn't sure of what might turn my opinion, or so I gathered.

"Entertain the unknown? I constantly do so. It comes with my job. I entertain it, in order to solve it and make it *known*."

"That isn't what I mean." I went to the big bay windows that overlooked the water and the pier, and I drew back the canvas curtains. Light flooded in, and the place looked dusty and abandoned despite the added illumination.

"Are you asking if I believe in ghosts? Goblins? God?"

"There's no need to bring sacrilege to the conversation," I chided him.

"Indeed, no reason to bring religion into it at all. Given my preference, I'd skip the subject altogether. Now tell me, where are the living quarters?"

I accepted the shift in topic. It hadn't been polite for me to broach the other one, anyway. "In this direction. Behind the curtain at the end of the counter."

He brushed it aside, and recoiled, examining his hand. "It's wet."

"Everything feels wet in here, doesn't it?" I ran my fingers over the slimy counter.

I wiped my fingers on my pants, and Wolf wiped his on the hem of his jacket. "When did it rain last?"

"Oh, it's been a week or more. Last Tuesday, I believe. I can't imagine why it's so damp in here . . . but can't you feel it? Something abominable and atmospheric."

"Something unknown?" he asked with the lift of an eyebrow, and I wasn't sure if he was teasing me or not, so I gave him a self-deprecating smile.

"If so, then it falls well within your job description."

"Yours, too." He grinned back, revealing his picket-straight, shell-white teeth. I half expected to see canines every time he flashed them, but no, they were ordinary and I was an imaginative old fool. This much was established.

"Mine, too, yes. I agree. Down the hall," I directed, suddenly feeling odd about our lighthearted exchange. This wasn't the place for it. Or maybe it was the best place for it, a feeble, mortal attempt to offset the terrible and unfathomable.

Every moment, I turned Ebenezer's story over in the rear of my mind. Every moment, it played in the background of my everyday thoughts, my everyday actions. The sound he described, the floating boy, the stench . . .

That same stench rose as we slipped single file down the hall, toward Matthew's bedroom. Much stronger than near the front of the store. "Last door on the right," I said. I might not have bothered. He could've just followed the reek.

The floorboards creaked beneath our shoes, and they were spongy when we stepped on them, like they'd been waterlogged. But they had been, hadn't they? If I believed Ebenezer at all, there'd been a great tide, flowing from the walls themselves, draining into nowhere. Lifting and drowning and killing.

I'd told him that I *did* believe. At the time, I'd meant it. In retrospect, I wasn't so sure—but my heart went back and forth about it, seeking excuses and reasons, answers and logical explanations.

I found none. And I saw plenty of evidence to support the veracity of every frightful word he'd whispered in that courthouse room.

I followed Wolf down the dank hall, stinking of oceans and death; here we were, and this was the smell—just as Ebenezer described it—and the whole building was wet and cool, and the ceiling felt improbably low, and I could feel my heart hammering around in my chest because too much of it was true, too much already.

"Dear God Almighty," gagged Wolf. He surrendered and whipped a handkerchief out of his pocket, and held it up over his nose. "It's *infinitely* worse back here."

If I'd had a handkerchief, I would have done the same. Matthew's room was a wreck of soaked bedding, warped floors, peeling wallpaper, and moldering linens stained a bluish, greenish color.

I reached inside for a switch. There must be gas throughout the building—I was reasonably confident, for I knew there were lights in the store itself; but the place was too sodden, and the fixtures wouldn't spark. No comforting illumination came to warm us, and we were left with the dingy murk that showed us almost nothing.

"One moment." Wolf ducked past me, back into the store; he returned with a long stick. A cane? A tool of some variety? I didn't notice. He used it to push back the lank, sticky curtains and give us something to see by, not that the daylight could show us much of note. With the morning sun streaming inside, we saw more clearly than at first, but there wasn't anything new to encourage us.

We saw a room that looked like somehow, it'd been filled with a rancid tide. Oh, and there was blood, yes. A watered-down stain pooled along the bed, and along the floor—matching Ebenezer's statement that Matthew had fallen half on the bed, half off it. And when I stepped back to the darkened hall I realized there was more diluted blood on the floor. We'd walked right through it.

Now that I knew it was there, I tiptoed around it as much as possible. And while Wolf made his inspection, I made mine.

I knew from Ebenezer's testimony that the bloody stain left by Mrs. Hamilton was approximately thirty hours old. It was still half wet, like everything else—but unlike everything else, a gummy sputum was mixed with the froth that had surely spilled from her mouth. Quite a lot of it, really. It's a wonder we hadn't slipped and harmed ourselves.

I peered around the door's jamb and saw Wolf cutting buck-shot out of the far wall with a pocketknife, like a proper alienist. He dropped it into a glass vial and used a wad of cotton for a stopper. Then he pulled out a tape and measured the room—I offered to hold one end, for accuracy—and when he was finished recording the dimensions, he retrieved a sketch pad from his inner jacket pocket.

How he could stand to remain in that filthy, stinking room, I had no idea, but somehow the man had acclimated to breathing without his handkerchief. More power to him. I left him to sketch what he found important, and returned to the storefront area, which only felt grim and sad—rather than murderous and unsettling.

I stood in the middle of the room, staring down the two aisles of products and back again at the counter, and the register, and the faint tracks my fingers had left in the slime that coated everything. From a certain angle, I could even see our footprints on the floor, when the light hit them just right. The whole place was tainted with something, and I was seized with the impulse to dash home and run myself a bath.

But I could do that later.

I kept my breathing shallow, lest I suck in any more of the disgusting air than I absolutely had to . . . and I strolled about, trying to be an observant and useful partner to Wolf, but mostly just wanting to take off my clothes and fling myself into the nearest supply of clean water.

I wandered to the door, and to the window beside it. The glass was murky, like everything else, and when I ran the side of my thumb along the nearest edge of the pane, it came away black. Almost as if it were the stain of old soot, or the residue of a place where men too often smoked. But that was a silly thought, wasn't it? Smoke and fire, in a place all but destroyed with damp. It wasn't quite right, and I knew it.

I can only talk my way around these things. There is so little that can be precisely said. The room was chilly, perhaps sixty degrees. (I wished for a thermometer, but didn't have one handy and didn't see one in the store.) The bloodstains were approximately three square feet, and four square feet, respectively. Wolf's measuring tape would tell us more firmly.

(Edited to note—my guesses were good. I was only half a foot off in one case, and a quarter foot in the other.)

I am at such a loss, without numbers to enter and symptoms to record. Unless that's what I'm doing, in this roundabout way, as I keep these journals and record the day's proceedings. I might be thinking about the situation too broadly.

Wolf has his own notes, of course. I might ask to see them, in order to better flesh out my own research.

To return to my point, I stood by the door, by the window. And again I looked down into the barrel of odds and ends that Matthew so diligently filled, unto his last days. Same as before it was overflowing, with the excess deposited into buckets, jugs, and cups. No longer a barrel of goods—the goods had overtaken the space, and now acquired other spaces nearby in which to collect, and to spread.

The goods had become a veritable colony.

What a strange thing to write down. I'm not certain why I've done so, but there it is. That was what I thought, and how I felt. That's what I remember of it, and the rest is frankly foggy, but I need to stay on my toes and record it all to the best of my ability, so I don't forget it later.

I stood there, by the barrel, by the colony of glittery glass bits and shimmering shells, and I felt distinctly like I was forgetting something . . . forgetting everything, slowly. Like as I lingered, my attention was being drained from my body, a very slow leak, as from a balloon, and my awareness was sinking, dropping, falling.

Oddly, I was not particularly worried by this. I was only interested in the glint of the light on the pretty rocks, and the clicking sound they made when I put my hand into the barrel, gently so I wouldn't cut myself on any sharp edges. Clicking together, the pebbles and stones and glass. Clicking like crab claws, or beads on a necklace.

Clicking like a necklace.

But that doesn't make any sense, does it? Maybe not. Still, that was what sprang to mind, and something about the randomness of it all made me cling to it. It was too specific and weird to lack meaning.

I might've mulled this over further—or then again, I might've stood there all night, my fingers running through the barrel's contents, drawing little furrows, making tiny mounds and digging little holes—except that Wolf joined me once again, having finished his examination of Matthew's bedroom.

He said my name, loudly. He insisted that it was the third attempt to rouse my attention, and he asked if I was all right, but of course I was all right. Of course he didn't call my name thrice. I'm *confident* he must have been mistaken.

No, that's not so. I'm not confident of anything, and the thoughtful look on his face suggested that I would dismiss his concern at my peril.

"Of course I'm all right," I said in response, shoving my hands into my pockets, and clenching, unclenching my fists. My hands were cold from playing with the barrel's lifeless, brittle contents.

"I should hope so, because we've one stop left before I can return you to your routine, Doctor. I could've done this much of the trip myself, though I was happy for the company; no, sir, I need you for the funeral home. I want you to tell me about the bodies."

"Ah." It was all I could think to say.

My hesitation likewise gave him pause. "Ah? Is there . . . some reason you'd prefer to bow out?"

"No, no, that's not it," I said quickly. "I'm sorry—I only had a moment of moral confliction." I reached for the door and opened it, letting the real world, the real ocean air, breathe into the store.

"Moral confliction? Of what sort?"

"I'm terribly curious, that's all. I do indeed want to see them," I asserted, and this was true. "But it would be unseemly to get too excited about it, don't you think?"

"Not at all."

"Are you certain?"

He shut the door and locked it behind us. "We should always be excited about the pursuit of truth."

We stood there, taking in the sun, and together, I believe, we were both relieved at the normalcy of the morning on the shop's narrow stoop. With the door closed, there was no sign of what had gone on within.

None but the warning sign, that is.

It dangled from the rope, reminding me that I was wrong, and that I could pretend all I wanted that it was a beautiful day, and all was right with the world. But I was completely wrong.

The funeral home was only a few blocks to the north, so we walked the distance together. I led the way at Wolf's request, but I got the distinct impression that he knew the general location already. He was obviously a man who came to every situation prepared.

I wondered *how* prepared, and I frowned, but to parlay the act into something less vague I returned to his last comment. "You don't think it's strange at all?" I asked him. "You think it's well and good that we should grow giddy over the corpses of friends?"

"They're not *my* friends," he noted. "And I said nothing about 'giddy.' But I have no doubt that the deceased Hamiltons were fine, upstanding citizens, so yes, I am all the more interested in their remains, that we might find the justice they so richly deserve."

"But what justice is there, when a malady is at fault? One can hardly prosecute an infection." I scoffed at the very idea. "Matthew was ill—desperately so, and I can't speak as to the nature of his affliction. I did my best to treat him, but his condition was beyond my abilities."

"Beyond anyone's but God's?" Wolf asked. He looked up at me with a tiny gleam in his eye.

"Beyond anyone's," I said carefully.

"Filthy atheist," he replied.

It was meant to sound like a joke, so I laughed—but the laugh was awkward. "My beliefs have no part in this case. And you were the one who wished to abandon the topic of religion. If I recall."

"But if I'm to understand correctly, you *believe* that Matthew was sick, and that Ebenezer acted in self-defense when his godson threatened his wife's life. You have faith, is what you mean."

"That's . . . not the same thing."

"It might be. Look—is this the place?"

"Yes," I said, and I absolutely would not have described myself as "giddy." But I was indeed glad we'd arrived. I didn't want to talk about faith, because I don't have any. That having been said, I did not detect any judgment from the inspector, only curiosity. You never know. If I'd let the chatter run its course, I might have discovered a kindred spirit.

"Shall we, then?"

"After you."

I stood aside and he climbed the stairs first, and stepped inside before me—but held the door that I might join him.

The interior was a sadly familiar place. My own wife had been buried through that same establishment, as had a number of other friends and patients through the years. In a town so small, everyone is a friend, or a cousin, or a neighbor at the very least. When one person dies, it's likely that half of Fall River will turn out to pay respects—or watch others do so.

In the reception area we stood uncertainly. It was a warm place, without anywhere significant to sit; it was a place for exchanging condolences and news, and to ready oneself for the service as needed. The floors were covered in pretty, detailed rugs, and the windows were set with colored glass reminiscent of a church, in the area we all called the chapel.

A small white-haired woman poked her head around the corner, and I recognized her as Martha Wann, wife of the elder brother.

She recognized me in turn. "Doctor Seabury, hello. The sheriff said you'd be here this morning." She joined us in the foyer, and performed a little bow. To Wolf she said, "You must be the fellow from Boston."

"Inspector Wolf, yes." He returned her little bow. "A pleasure to meet you, though it's a pity the circumstances are so unfortunate. Please, could you take us to the Hamiltons?"

Solemnly she nodded. "Certainly, gentlemen. This way."

She led us back into the chapel, past the rows of simple wood chairs and through a door, beyond which we found a set of stairs. "The real work happens below, you understand," she delicately explained. "But the good doctor here, he knew that already."

"You've assisted with such things before?" Wolf asked me.

"A handful of times, when there's been uncertainty."

"About the cause of death?"

"Yes," I said. "But sometimes, I attempt to help identify an unknown body. They wash up from time to time, over at the rocks. Sailors and the like."

"And we return to the unknown, once again. That kind of identification must be tricky."

"Always. As often as not, all I can do is describe teeth, tattoos, and scars, or any bones that have broken and healed, in the case of a skeleton. Sometimes these things help a man's mortal remains find their way home, to the people who've missed him."

"But not always?"

I shook my head. "No, not always."

Mrs. Wann opened another door and held it for us, ushering us inside. "In here you'll find what you're looking for, but as a matter of kindness, I must warn you—it's not a pretty sight. Whatever became of them . . . I . . . I can't say. I've never seen its like. You really should prepare yourselves."

The inspector beat me to a response, though our sentiments were more or less the same. He said, "Mrs. Wann, I've seen all sorts, all kinds, in my line of work. Thank you for the warning, but we'll be well enough."

She nodded gently, not quite believing us—but her profession left her too ready to demur. "Very well, gentlemen. If I can be of any service to you, please let me know. I'll be right upstairs in the office."

Privately, I was thinking of Abigail Borden, and how her

body had looked lying on this same table beside her husband. They'd been hacked so badly, but still there was a swelling and, now that I considered it, a peculiar smell.

Not quite the same as the one from the shop. Not quite different from it.

We thanked Mrs. Wann, and when she discreetly closed the door behind herself, I drew Wolf toward a large table tilted at an angle, and covered with tin sheeting. (The genteel description of such a table is a "drying table.") Upon it rested two long shapes, covered in canvas cloths that were less like sheets, and more like the kind of drapes a painter might use. I think these cloths might have been waxed, to protect them somewhat against the damp of the dead . . . though ordinarily, the embalmers did not bother with such things in the privacy of their own laboratory.

It did not bode well that even the funereal folks couldn't bring themselves to look.

I took a deep breath to steel myself. I'd done this sort of thing before, yes—but this was different. I knew it was different, and I needed to see *how* it was different. And given the circumstances, I might need to prove how different this case truly was, in order to keep Ebenezer Hamilton a free man.

"The smell's not so bad in here," the inspector observed. "*Bad*, yes. But more ordinary bad than the shop itself, if that makes any sense."

There was that word again, "ordinary." As if we were trying to reassure ourselves.

I wasn't sure why the inspector needed any reassuring. He couldn't possibly know the truth, about either Ebenezer's experience, or the Bordens'. With regard to the latter, he would only know what he'd seen in the papers—and half of that was wrong.

"No, I believe you're right," I said of the odor. "Worse by far at the shop."

He mumbled, "Tell me, is there another light in here . . . ? Oh, wait, I see the switch."

At the touch of his hand, a very bright lamp sparked to life, illuminating the chilly place without adding any warmth.

I looked around the cool, utilitarian embalming room, and eyed the cabinets, jars, bottles, and needles in their stacks and baskets. I looked over the heaps of towels, the folded sheets, and the dirty cement floor beneath our feet, with its telltale drain.

"Shall we, Doctor?"

"I suppose there's no delaying it further."

Quickly, before I could make some excuse, I went to the nearest corner of the drape, and lifted it. I tossed it aside in one quick snap of my wrist—revealing the bodies of Felicity and Matthew Hamilton.

Inspector Wolf choked.

I almost did the same. I saved myself by turning quickly away, staring at the floor, and giving my mind a moment to adjust, and my stomach a moment to return to its usual position.

Mere gunshot wounds were bad enough, but the two people on that table had not died from anything half so normal.

Or . . . no.

That was not quite true, not exactly, because when I gathered the strength to look again at the table, I saw that yes, *technically* Matthew had expired due to an excess of buckshot from a fowler's gun. His torso was speckled and smashed with dozens of holes, and surely they would've killed him or anyone else at such close range. A chunk of his side had been blown free, leaving him with ribs exposed and shattered. He was missing most of one kidney.

I focused on these details because they were the ones I could write down in a report, and no one would question my sanity or my professional qualifications.

Inspector Wolf tamed his retching instinct, and once again having retrieved his handkerchief, he said what I was thinking (and wondering how to suggest it). "It's as if they were filled with water, until they burst."

"That's . . . not an unfair or inaccurate observation."

"If a disgusting one," he added, the words muffled by the scrap of fabric he was using to hide his mouth. "I mean, the lad there . . . shot, with two barrels of buck, at a very near distance. But the woman . . . ?"

"Mrs. Hamilton. Yes, she's . . . bloated," I said, finding the word I meant.

"Not a small woman in life, I shouldn't think."

"No, never the delicate sort. But she's taken on . . . what must be, I mean . . . I have to assume . . . a significant amount of water. And that *does* correspond with Ebenezer's report." I then realized with a fast jerk of guilt—that I didn't know what he'd ultimately told the police . . . or whatever higher authority in Boston the inspector represented. I knew I should watch my words more closely.

Wolf filled in a small bit of information. "About how Matthew tried to drown her?"

Ah. So that's what he'd heard. It was a reasonable thing for Ebenezer to say, when he did not wish to seem mad or unreasonable. What he'd shared with me, he'd shared in confidence. It would not do for me to betray it.

"Something like that," I said without confirming or denying anything.

Once again the Bordens leaped to the forefront of my mind. Their daughter's trial flashed through my brain, and yes, I reminded myself with terrific firmness: yes, I must be *very* careful with regard to what I said about Ebenezer's confession or behavior. Any little thing could be used, construed, or bent to whatever ends the authorities settled on when the time for formal inquiry came around.

But Wolf pressed on. "Something *like* a drowning? What do you mean?"

Still, I was cautious. "He was quite distraught. He talked in circles, and not all of it made sense."

The inspector eyed me warily, a moment longer than was comfortable. Then again, he might've only been trying to stare at something other than the corpses before us. My extensive experience with the dead had done precious little to ready me for the sight of these two, so I could hardly blame him if that was the reason. But surely a man who investigated murders would have experience comparable to mine in war, or *some* experience anyway. Unless he typically investigated something else. Really, I had no idea—and his evasive answers thus far suggested he wouldn't be too forthcoming, were I to ask.

I forced myself to look at the corpses again. No, even in war there was nothing to compare this to. War was only brutal. This was unnatural.

Beside the table was a shelf, with the implements of embalming ready at hand. How the Wann family planned to prepare the Hamiltons, I could scarcely imagine. The boy was in pieces, and his mother was . . .

Not herself.

I picked up a long metal probe and gingerly, with as much respect (and as little disgust) as I could muster, I prodded at Matthew's flesh. It oozed fluid—water? Some unusual decomposition?—and the probe left virtually no impression in the flesh. The texture reminded me of nothing half so much as a sea-jelly.

"What are you doing?" Wolf asked.

"Nothing useful. I'm at a loss. They've been dead two days or less, and they almost look like they washed up on the rocks after a week in the ocean. I've never seen anything like it."

He cleared his throat and reached into his pocket for a set of vials. "So might it be said, Doctor Seabury, that I have your permission to take some samples?"

"My permission? You don't need it. You'd be better served to ask the Wanns, but honestly, there's little they can do for these two. Other than close the casket."

He agreed, and selected a small scalpel from the table with the probes, tubes, and jars of foul-smelling fluids.

I averted my eyes while he worked, though I loathed myself for it, just a little. I ought to be stronger, better, more of a man— and a professional—than this. If I were to treat myself more kindly, I might've made the excuse that my specialty was the living body, and not the dead.

But in fact, I was a coward.

That night, I dreamed of the drying table, and the tubes, and the probes. But beneath the sheet lay Abigail and Andrew Borden, bloated and swollen. Waterlogged and yet living, their eyes watching me as I walked horrified around them, unable to leave the room. Unable to understand. Unable to look away.

Emma Borden was right. I needed a word with her sister.

A DWELLING PLACE OF JACKALS,
THE DESOLATION FOREVER

Emma L. Borden

APRIL 18, 1894

The Hamiltons have been murdered. Two of them, at least—
the wife and son. Nephew? Godson? I can't recall the particulars, but I believe he wasn't theirs by birth. Regardless, he's
dead now: shot by his father, or whatever the man of the house
was, in relation to him.

Ebenezer Hamilton has been taken into custody, and Fall
River whispers so loudly that even such shut-ins as my sister and
I have heard a number of details. The newspaper told us little
that the gardener or the milkman hadn't; we gleaned only one

new tidbit from the official report, which was very brief, likely due to the suddenness of it all.

Apparently the boy had been ill for some weeks. He'd been kept indoors before the tragedy, out of fear that he might be a danger to himself or others. There are rumors that he'd been physically restrained, tied to a bed.

None of these precautions were excessive, as it turns out. They were not even sufficient.

When young Tim Haines came to collect our newspaper fee, he added the salacious detail that Matthew (that's the boy's name—I'd forgotten it until just now) had drowned Mrs. Hamilton in a washtub, and Ebenezer tried to save her. That's where the gun came into it.

I have a terrible suspicion about this, and I know that Lizzie does as well. I know this, because she can hardly be persuaded to speak of it. She's hidden the papers from Nance, lest she be called upon to gossip about the situation, and it's entirely too near to the heart.

What an awful little place this town has come to be. Full of awful little people, and awful little creatures who make everything worse, exponentially. Daily.

And Nance hardly improves matters.

I honestly believe that Lizzie would throw that tall, noisy strumpet back onto the first train north for her own good, if she could—and it might yet come to that. I keep hoping there may be some catastrophic fight, instigated by my sister with the specific intent of sparing her beloved, even at the expense of the love itself.

If she were braver, that's what she'd do. Or if she were less lonely, I should say.

At least she's talked Nance out of a party. As always, that was the first thing the girl wanted upon her arrival, and the last thing we needed. So Lizzie is capable of putting her foot down on the big things, and thank God for *that*. I'd be happier about this development if I didn't know all too well how it's the little things that'll catch us in the end. They check the details for devils, you see.

Already, the poor girl has become fascinated with the cellar door, and we all know nothing good can come of it. Lizzie is almost out of excuses. And whatever's calling from down there . . . whatever it is . . . will undoubtedly win out over locks and prohibitions.

It's only a matter of time, I fear.

Hell, isn't everything?

Lizzie Andrew Borden

❧

APRIL 21, 1894

Doctor Seabury came today, and I hardly know what to make of his visit.

I am both invigorated and terrified, for he seems to be on the very edge of grasping how much there remains to be understood, and how far away is any mortal mind from understanding it. I hesitate to consider it, but we might well prove kindred spirits after all. My new optimism stems from the Hamilton murders, which occurred last week on the other side of town.

(Oh dear. I *really* shouldn't call it "optimism," considering.)

Regardless, my feelings are predominantly positive, tragedy aside. Some good may come of it yet, if the doctor and I can bring ourselves to trust one another enough. We came very close to naming a collaboration today, but not quite yet. We're both very afraid.

We have every right to be.

As for the Hamiltons, whose grisly end has brought us together . . . I never knew the family well, but I knew *of* them.

Everyone did, like everyone in Fall River knows everyone else, on sight if not in person. The Hamiltons owned a store down by the pier, catering mostly to mariners and those who like to pretend to such things, by way of keeping the trappings about their homes. The family unit consisted of a husband and wife a few years older than Emma, and a boy in his teens—their godson, otherwise orphaned some years previously.

It would seem that the boy attempted to drown his god-mother, and Mr. Hamilton intervened—and this intervention required a gun. Mr. Hamilton has been taken to Boston, but I don't think he's been arrested. I suspect they're evaluating him, considering whether or not to place him in an asylum.

That's the best ending he might expect, I'm afraid (assuming he's told the truth). His other option is likely prison, in the event that he's manufactured some cunning lie. And from what I recall of Mr. Hamilton, "cunning" wasn't the first descriptor that sprang to mind.

Kind, yes. Unlikely to go on a killing spree, certainly. But simple in his motives and actions.

And, I believe, quite innocent of murder.

Doctor Seabury came by to attend to Emma, as has become his custom. On this particular visit, she hovered excitedly, trying to urge us to talk—but her fluttering made nothing easier, since both he and I knew that she'd spoken to him, and that we were now intended to have a difficult conversation.

The whole thing was exquisitely awkward at the outset.

Finally, when Emma had exhausted all her heavy-handed tactics, she excused herself. Any fool could've seen that it was a ruse, and I'm certain that Nance wondered what was going on when my sister asked for *her* assistance, rather than mine. She couched it in the guise of Nance's height and strength, and hinted that I had some private matter to discuss with the physician.

It was true, but it made the whole thing sound dirty and weird, and I've put off explaining myself to my houseguest thus far . . . but my protestations won't work for much longer. I'll need a good story by this evening, or I'm afraid that Nance might become dramatic.

When the doctor and I were finally alone, we hemmed and hawed around the discomfort of our topic, until he surprised me by blurting out, "I saw the Hamiltons' bodies."

I wouldn't have been more stunned if he'd taken of his shirt and done a little dance.

"You . . . you *did?*"

The explanation tumbled out. He'd been keeping it bottled up tight, and once the seal was broken, there was no stopping him. "An investigator was sent from Boston, and he requested that I accompany him on his rounds. A fine man, name of 'Wolf,' if you can imagine anything more fitting . . . and he'd asked specifically to see the bodies."

He leaned forward in a conspiratorial manner, so I could scarcely stop myself from doing the same. "Given that the case is now a criminal one, or at least a *suspicious* one, I was pleased to have been included . . . I'll admit I was frankly curious and also . . . also, frankly frightened. Matthew had been unwell, you see, and I had worried for his . . ." He hesitated.

"For his safety?" I asked, somewhat boldly, in my own opinion. But the doctor seemed to require a prompt. While he considered how much to share, I added, "I should tell you, I've heard rumors. Gossip says he'd been tied to the bed."

Seabury's eyes met mine, and they were filled with turmoil. "For his own safety, yes. And his godparents' safety as well. He'd become restless, yet unresponsive. Something was wrong," he concluded with great conviction. "Wrong in a sense greater than any mere malady might explain. And it reminded me of nothing so much as your stepmother, Abigail."

He said that last part too quickly, so fast that the words ran together.

My mouth was hanging open. I closed it. "You saw her. The night *before*." I recalled it all too well, how she'd fled the house and run across the street. I'd been terrified that she'd go on a rampage herself, inflicting heaven-knew-what harm on whomever she encountered.

"Yes. I saw her. And whatever had gone . . . *wrong* . . ." He selected the same word again, and deployed it carefully. "It was not unlike the change that had overtaken Matthew. I did not know how to treat Abigail, and I did not know how to treat that young man, either." He held up his hands and looked at them, and looked at me again with that awful uncertainty radiating from his face. "I do not know what I am up against, and I do not think that it is natural. I do not think that it will stop with the Hamiltons."

A shiver ran up and down my spine, and I did my best to keep from breaking out into a wide, ridiculous smile. It was awful news! A terrifying prospect! An outrageous proposition, suggesting that the whole town was in danger of falling prey to this unnatural malaise!

A smile would've been grossly inappropriate, so I swallowed it down, and instead I reached for his hands. He didn't know what to do with them. They were flapping about, and I caught them in my own. In other circumstances, it would've been a forward gesture of something unseemly, but this was a unique case. I needed his attention, and we needed to trust one another—or at least *believe* one another.

His hands were large and dry, and they shook very slightly.

I met his eyes, and with all the calm I could muster, I asked, "Tell me, Doctor . . . did you speak with Ebenezer Hamilton, before they took him to Boston?"

He nodded. "I did."

"And did he tell you something impossible? Something that can't be remotely true?"

He nodded again. "Yet the corpses suggest that his explanation *must* be true. Or true enough, if you wish to believe that the trauma has unhinged his mind, and what he shared was only some distorted fraction of what really happened."

I took a long, slow breath through my nose, and sat back against the divan. I rubbed at my eyes, and again I tried to shake off the feeling of euphoria. This was nothing to be euphoric about, but my sensibilities betrayed me. I'd carried the knowledge around too long, and carried it all but alone. To clarify matters, I said, "You believe his impossible story, but in believing him, you risk your own sanity. Is this more or less the situation?"

Miserably, he bobbed his head. "I saw the shop, and the scene of the crime. I can't imagine an alternate theory with regard to what occurred, but the story is so outlandish that I don't dare admit that I've given it any credence at all."

"Did Matthew kill his godmother?"

"Yes," he confirmed.

"And Ebenezer killed Matthew, in an attempt to save his wife?"

"That is also correct. But I'm afraid they'll either commit him or hang him, depending on what he tells the authorities. I want to speak up for him. I want to defend him—"

"As you defended me?" I interjected. I didn't mean to.

He was silent, and then he said, "As I defended *you*."

I gathered my wits and my strength, and with all the courage I could muster I said bluntly, "You knew I was not innocent."

Just as bluntly in return, he replied, "I *feared* that you weren't, and I feared that no one would believe a plea of self-defense. But I *saw* her . . . ," he said, and his eyes went far away. "I saw what she'd become, or what she was becoming. That's what it is, isn't it? Some kind of . . . change. No one would've believed you."

My voice caught in my throat. I said, "Oh God . . . Doctor. All this time, and you . . . ?"

The heavy tread of Nance's feet on the stairs stopped me cold. I finished up by saying only, "Nance doesn't know. We mustn't speak of it in front of her. Not yet. Not now."

"But we will, won't we?"

"Later," I promised. I swore it again. "Later. Tomorrow afternoon? I'll find some errand for Nance and chase her out of the house."

I rose, and smiled primly, politely. He rose, too, and gathered his bags.

When Nance appeared in the parlor, the doctor was on his way out the door with a nod in her direction, and some murmured pleasantry about meeting her. She responded in kind, halfheartedly and without any real interest in the matter. She didn't care to pretend. She was interested in our conversation, and what it had entailed.

As soon as the door was shut behind him, the pantomime was over.

She demanded to know. "What the hell is going on, Lizbeth?"

"Nothing serious. Just a small question for the doctor. A private one, if you don't mind."

"You're lying. Not about the private bit, but you're keeping something from me—and I doubt it's a medical issue."

"I'm keeping a number of things from you," I said with attempted gaiety. It almost rang true, for I was still so charmed at the prospect of a helpful friend to share the burden of my research. I felt light-headed and all but delirious, stunned and yet energized.

From a practical standpoint, it was almost too much to hope for. Emma was helpful in her way, of course, but her condition prevented her from any firsthand investigation by my side; and her relation to me kept her from participating in the community, where the very best information was likely to be gleaned. Doctor Seabury, on the other hand, had no such difficulties—and he was an educated, informed, respected man whose profession gained him access to even the most closely guarded secrets.

But Nance didn't need to hear any of this.

"Lizbeth . . ." She nearly whined. The look I flashed in return suggested she should take a different approach. She did so, trying to mirror my lightness, the casualness of my dismissal. "So now we're keeping things from one another? Such as what?"

But just this once, I was the better actress between the two of us.

I didn't want to fight. I only wanted to distract her, and I knew precisely how to do so. "Such as . . . how the greens I ordered from McKamey's disagreed with me terribly, or how my eyes water at garlic, besides onions. And how my knees grow weak whenever you're present, my love."

"You've told me that one already," she replied sulkily, but it wasn't a pure sulk. A little flattery goes a long way with her, and I'm not above it.

"I'll likely say it again, at some point during your visit." I took her hands and gave her a quick kiss, an act which required me to stand on my tiptoes. "Now, how is Emma? Is she settled comfortably?"

"Took her own sweet time about getting that way, but yes, she's fine."

"You must be patient. Depending on the weather and her lungs, she finds it difficult to move as swiftly as you or I."

"I still can't imagine why she asked my help. *You're* the patient one," she said with a sigh.

A hasty lie sprang to mind, and I liked it, so I let it past my lips. "*I* suggested it. I thought you two ought to spend some time together once in a while. I truly believe that with a better acquaintance, you could become great friends."

"I don't know . . . ," she said dubiously. "We're terribly different."

"But you have some terribly wonderful things in common."

"Just you," she said with a wink. Then she took me by the hand and lured me back into the kitchen, and I thought I was in for a round of tea or perhaps something more engaging . . . and then I realized that I was wrong.

"Lizbeth, your sister is out of the way for now, and the doctor is gone . . . so there should be no visitors." Nance leaned against the cellar door, bouncing coquettishly against it with her bottom.

"Why don't you show me what's downstairs? There's privacy and darkness, and just you . . . and *me*."

The joy that had positively flooded my heart . . . now evaporated with her prettily phrased petition. I believe my face might've gone all but green. "Dearest, *no*," I said slowly. "There's nothing romantic about the cellar at all."

"Just dust and wine and bugs, or so you'd have me think. *Show me*," she insisted, and it wasn't just another whine. It bore all the hallmarks of a demand.

I was running out of ways to defer the exploration, and I knew it, and it was awful because every excuse was a lie—but a lie that might save her life, or her soul. "Darling, I'm not even sure where the key is right now. Off the top of my head . . . it might be in the odds-and-ends basket by the back door . . ."

"No," she said with steel in her eyes. "I already checked."

"You . . . you checked? You went looking for the key?"

"I found several keys, stashed here and there. In drawers, and atop tables. None of them fit this lock."

The key was safely around my neck, as always. But the fact that she'd gone looking for it chilled me to my core. "Why are you so determined to see it?"

"Because you're so determined to keep it from me. It must be terribly interesting, if you're so certain I shouldn't go anywhere near it."

"Rather the opposite," I said with a shrug, wandering to the sink and placing my hands along the cool enamel surface. I reached for the teakettle in order to have something to do, some meaningless task to distract myself—but she took it away and set it down on the counter.

"So it's a dull, safe, unremarkable place?"

"Entirely."

"Prove it."

"I don't have to," I said, digging in my heels. I'm at least as stubborn as she is, after all. "I don't like going down there. It's damp and cold, and all the wood is eaten up by rot. Every time I descend the stairs, I'm halfway convinced they'll shatter out from under me. Mildew and mold, all the way through."

"Doesn't sound very safe to me."

"Oh, stop it. You know what I mean." I moved away from her again, and she followed me again—staying very close to me, her eyes never leaving my face. I hated it, because it meant she'd been touched by the things down there, or called by them, and I was no longer dealing merely with a woman I adored but who could be a tad insistent.

I was confronted by a woman who'd acquired a compulsion.

And I hated it because she was looming over me, and I could not shake the feeling that it was deliberate. She was intimidating me, using her size against me. Using her height to tell me, without any words, that she could wrestle me into submission if she felt the need, and she was feeling all kinds of needs right now.

I didn't know if she could best me in a fight or not. I'm smaller, yes, but more compact. And in the previous two years, I'd learned a great deal about violence, and my capacity for it. "Nance," I whispered, and she was hovering so close that my breath tickled her eyelashes. "You're beginning to worry me."

"Worry you?" She cocked her head.

I swallowed, and leaned back away from her as far as the counter would allow. "I think you're trying to frighten me, and I don't like it."

My direct accusation broke the spell, or cracked it sufficiently that she withdrew, a look of honest horror on her face.

She blinked quickly, repeatedly, like someone awakening from an engrossing dream. "Frighten you? Lizbeth . . . whatever are you going on about? I'm doing no such thing."

I released a breath I hadn't noticed I was holding, and when I did so, my corset stays stretched against the fabric of my dress. Apparently it was a big breath. Apparently I'd held it hard.

"I'm sorry," I said, apologizing almost by reflex. "I didn't mean to imply . . . it's only that you've been so insistent, and I don't understand. You were so strange the other day, when I found you here and the tea was cold . . ."

It was easy to ramble and sound as if I fretted in earnest, when I stuck so close to the truth.

"It was only cold tea," she promised, but she kept her distance still. "Nothing more. I was distracted."

"I called your name, and you didn't hear me. Over and over I called it . . . and you were standing there, beside that stupid door," I spit out, directing my sorrow and anger at the cellar and its contents. It was either that or I must point it toward myself.

"It's only a *door*," she breathed, abashed and innocent once more. "And you won't let me past it, so I wonder, that's all. I want to see what you don't want to show me. I want you to trust me."

"It's nothing to do with trust," I assured her, though as I spoke the words I knew they were wrong. It did come down to trust, didn't it? I couldn't trust her to visit without snooping for keys, trying to circumvent me.

"Then *why*?" she pleaded, leaning against the counter and half sitting upon it.

"Can't I have a single secret? Just one?"

"But why do you *need* one?"

"I'll make you a deal," I said. "One small bargain between

lovers—people do it all the time; they ask that one thing be off-limits."

Quickly, as if she'd been waiting for such a moment, she snapped, "And in such a bargain, you wouldn't choose your parents?"

I was honestly stunned. What little discussion we'd entertained with regard to their deaths, it'd all come down to the easiest lie—they were killed by my half brother, or so I professed to believe. And she professed to believe that I was telling the truth.

Were we both lying? To ourselves, and each other at the same time?

"Is that . . . ," I began to ask, and then adjusted my approach. "Do I hear doubt in your voice? Or accusation?"

"Given the circumstances, you might as well conflate the two."

"All right then, I'll answer your question: No, I would not place my parents' death off-limits in any bargain between us. We've already had that conversation, and whatever else you'd like to hear, I'd be happy to share." I'd lied that lie enough. It had almost become the truth, or a fiction vastly better than the truth—because my half brother had vanished, and there was no proving anything with regard to his involvement. Or lack thereof.

Wherever he was, whatever he was doing . . . he sure as hell didn't care what I said about him.

"Then why the cellar?"

"If I told you that, we couldn't call it part of the bargain, could we? Now what would you like to place off-limits? What subject must I avoid at all costs, that you can withhold explanation until the day we die?"

She frowned. Puzzled, I think. She was thinking, considering, trying to figure out something she hadn't shared already. For the most part, she was an open book. If she had any secrets at all, she hid them well—behind a wall of information, chattered without apparent restraint, delivered at the slightest hint of permission or interest.

"I'll think of something," she decided.

"But you agree to the bargain? Leave me the cellar, and you'll stop hunting for keys?"

"I'll leave you the cellar. And stop looking for keys," she vowed.

I want to believe her. Desperately, painfully, with all my heart. But that's only what I want, and not what I think.

Nance O'Neil

I have the key.

Do I regret my trickery? Not at all. How can I regret the measures I've taken to protect and assist my beloved? I *know* she needs help. Whatever she's hiding down there, it's more than she can manage alone. I am confident of this. I am at peace with this. And I will do what needs to be done.

Now that I've begun, I must follow through to the end, mustn't I?

She might see it as a great betrayal. I don't know. For all her silly talk of "bargains" and promises, there's no good reason to believe that she doesn't secretly want me to push onward toward the truth. Some people can't bear to answer some questions, but that doesn't mean they don't want anyone to know the answers. I'm not sure what mechanism this is, or what drive; I don't know why some people just can't say what they mean, say what they want, and be done with it.

But I am here to help!

She needs me more than she knows. Whatever she's engaged in, or fighting against, or keeping so secret, she can't keep it that way all by herself. That might be the root of it all—she knows it's too big for her to handle alone, and Emma is no help at all, no matter what she says about the old woman's books and notes and letters.

To hell with books and notes and letters.

Sometimes you need a hand instead.

Something just dawned on me: Emma must think the doctor might prove helpful to Lizbeth, with this weird undertaking she hides beneath the house. Seabury, that's his name. Seems like a nice old gentleman, and he's kind enough to Lizbeth—which I appreciate, given how the rest of this wretched little town will have nothing to do with her.

He is kind, then. But he is not close.

I am close. And I will be the partner that she wants. The partner she *needs*.

Soon I'll know the truth for myself. Tonight, when everyone's asleep. I didn't have time this past evening, for a dose of Mrs. Winslow's sleeping draught didn't maintain quite enough hold over Lizbeth.

I've not found evidence that Lizbeth is prone to drinking such draughts, to the point of developing a tolerance for them—though of course Emma keeps some around in the drawers beside her bed. She also keeps a great, heavy handgun, but I assume that's for protection. One thing my lover has confessed easily enough, without wheedling, bribing, or bargains is this: After her trial, there were threats by the score and she chose to arm the household. The threats were not against Emma, no, but Emma lives here, too—and she's as dependent as a toddling child, I swear. No great surprise she keeps painkillers, sleeping draughts, and weapons, but I can't imagine that most days she has the strength to lift any of them unassisted.

So Lizbeth has access to such things. Some nights, I'm sure she's indulged in something stronger and more fortifying than anything she may pull from her dead father's liquor cabinet; otherwise, how can she sleep at all? The world has left her highstrung, wound tight. It's left her defensive, a one-woman fortress with an axe by the door. I've seen the axe. Or I've seen *an* axe, here and there around the house. A defensive measure, I'm certain—if a grisly one.

I don't care; I sleep just fine knowing it's here, and knowing she's here, and that she knows how to wield it. I don't believe she ever wielded it against her parents, but I admit, sometimes it gives me a strange tingle to see it, or touch it. Just in case I'm wrong.

So in summary, Lizbeth might well be prone to downing soothing syrups like Mrs. Winslow's on occasion. Maybe she helps herself to Emma's. Maybe she keeps a stash of her own, hidden away. Regardless, I know she takes them—because the drops I administered should've produced a longer result.

Maybe that's what's in the cellar?

Some people take great shame in confessing that their bodies need chemicals. She doesn't seem the sort, but she *does* keep secrets—so how can I say? How can I know?

Well, I can go take a look. That's how.

. . .

I checked all the obvious places where a woman might stash a key: all the drawers, cabinets, ledges, tables, and bookcases. (My God, Emma keeps some strange books. At least, I assume they're Emma's. She's the one with the fondness for biology journals, but how some of these things are related to biology, I'm not sure . . . The connection seems tenuous at best.) I checked under beds and under sinks, beneath flowerpots and inside the dead father's leftover shrine to distilled spirits. I wonder if they've restocked it since his death. Some of the bottles look old. None of them look like they've been lately opened. The wool felt that lines the shelves has gone light with a coating of dust.

I'm answering my own question, I think.

But I *did* find the key.

That's what I mean to say. I must quit talking around myself. I spend too much time talking around myself, and what I really mean—and to think, I only just complained about people who do that. Physician, heal thyself.

God, I've been so distracted lately. Not the kind of distracted that ought to worry Lizbeth (but does, or so it appears), but distracted enough to lose my train of thought. Especially when I stand in the kitchen. Especially when I stand near the door.

And I have a key to that door.

Whatever's down there *can't* be doing this to me. Whatever's down there is likely only some peculiar embarrassment that would mortify no one but her, and certainly wouldn't bother me. For that matter, even if she *did* hack up her parents, I'm not strictly certain it would put me off. I know her and love her well enough these days to believe that she does only what needs to be done, out of love for her beloved problem of a sister. Or me, if I flatter myself—and I might as well.

But I don't think she did it. Sometimes she gently hints that
it's always *possible* she's guilty after all, and that I should be more
cautious about where I place my trust. But it's nonsense. She's
only testing me.

𝕷i𝖟𝖇𝖊𝖙𝖍 doesn't know I found the key. She doesn't know I have it,
but she'll notice it's gone before long. How long? I don't know. I
don't know how long it will take for her to notice I've replaced the
proper key with another of similar size and shape. It depends entirely on how often she goes down to the cellar, or basement, or
whatever awaits down there. The first time she tries, she'll fail, and
she'll know. And we'll have some terrible fight, unless I can satisfy
my curiosity and return the correct key to its original position.
That might prove trickier than my initial theft, or then again,
maybe it won't.

I might get lucky.

𝕴 thought I'd have to seduce her out of the key, and I was right,
after a fashion.

Emma wished to stay downstairs, for it's become warm
very suddenly—and probably not permanently, given the way
seasons shift and startle around here. Next week, I'm sure it'll
be dastardly cold for another bad snap, and then come May,
things will level out. That's my prediction.

So Emma was downstairs, where it was cooler, still. Heat
rises, and thank heaven for that simple fact of nature, because
the bedrooms are all upstairs and that meant we'd have the
whole floor to ourselves at last.

It took forever and yet another day to get Emma settled on
the grand settee, enthroned like a queen in a fort of pillows,
which must've been almost as warm as the stuffy room she

wished to escape—but what's it to me? Let her smother herself with feathers, or sheets, or whatever else makes her happy. It makes me happy to have her out of the way.

After a protracted ritual of adjustments, she finally was comfortable enough for us to turn down the lights and draw tight the curtains, and all the while Lizbeth was a grouch about it—fussing about every little thing, checking all the locks on all the doors and windows, as if someone would try to come inside the moment her back was turned.

Nonsense, Lizbeth. Nobody cares but *you*.

But with Emma settled, and now equipped with bells to ring in case of difficulty, we retreated to Lizbeth's room. I had a guest suite, but I was sick of using it. I wasn't here to camp at the end of a hall. I was here to see Lizbeth, and I would see every inch of her before my visit was up. She knew it, I knew it, and Emma likely knew it, too; but Lizbeth was so funny about Emma hearing any slight *peep*.

Honestly, that woman would sleep through a thunderstorm without so much as a flinch, if she ever sampled even a fraction of what she kept beside the bed. And the bottles there (and the labels upon them) were newer than those with the bourbon downstairs, so I knew they saw more circulation. Besides, the walls in this place are as thick as a tomb.

But propriety still means something to Lizbeth for some reason, and really, at this point I can't imagine why. Let us throw open the windows and let the whole block hear how happy we are to touch one another. Who cares?

What are they going to do, talk about us? You'd think she'd be used to it by now.

Sometimes I fear I don't understand her, not at all. But I will fix that. I will let myself downstairs, and see what she has to hide from me.

We undressed one another, and I thought we might take our time, since Emma was well out of shouting distance and we had all night; but Lizbeth was impatient, hungry. She almost tore my chemise, and with her head buried in my neck she told me not to worry, she'd buy me another. A dozen others. Anything, just hurry up and finish with these stupid clothes.

She pulled a pin out of her hair, and it came cascading down, all the way to her waist, and that was all she was wearing, standing in the moonlight that came filtered in through the curtains. Anyone who looked hard enough at the right angle from outside could've seen her. All the curves and lines of her, none of them concave except the hollow at her waist. The rest of her rounded and nicely muscled, almost like a dancer. Her arms were taut and all but swelled with strength, and her thighs were sharply cut.

She took my breath away.

Not just for being naked; that was distraction enough, and I welcomed it. But she'd forgotten to remove her jewelry. And around her neck she wore a heavy key.

The key.

She remembered it at the last second before pouncing upon me, and with what was surely meant to appear a careless, casual gesture, she pulled the chain until it unfastened by force, and tossed it onto the bureau.

I made careful note of where it went, though not so careful that I think she noticed.

When we were finished with our merriment—and it was merry indeed, because God, I was starving for her . . . I offered to make some tea, but she said no. She'd make it. I think she just didn't want me in the kitchen, so fine, all right then. We were both being wary about one another. But she didn't retrieve the key, though—so she was not as cautious as I was opportunistic.

She must want a partner, and not just a lover. Whatever she's hiding, I can bear it. We can hide it together.

$he was still shaking a little when she arose and pulled on a robe, and wearing nothing else she headed downstairs. But who would see her except for Emma? And Emma was already asleep, almost certainly.

So while she was gone, I crept free of the sheets, unwound myself, and walked naked as quietly as possible. My dress was on the floor nearby. In its front right pocket, I had a small assortment of keys, collected from around the house. I hoped none of them were important, but I doubted it; I'm sure they were merely the keys of a household, some left behind by the previous owner, some to locks that no longer existed, on doors that had long since been removed.

I felt around for a key that more or less matched the one on the chain, and when I found as near a twin as possible, I switched them out—stashing the cellar door key in my empty dress pocket, and vowing that sooner or later, I'd replace them all where I'd found them. Not that I could remember them all, but I had a general enough idea that my small act of subterfuge would not become known anytime soon.

More likely, it'd serve the purpose of confusing the gardener, next time he needed entrance into the shed out back. Small price to pay, in my estimation.

Lizbeth came back to bed with tea, and when she wasn't looking, I added a few drops of the soothing syrup. If she noticed anything was different, she didn't mention it. She downed the tea quickly (surely scalding herself), but I didn't mind, because then we were free again to untangle from our robes and sheets, and retangle to our hearts' content.

Later, when I came tripping lightly downstairs wearing Lizbeth's robe, I saw a candle or two lit downstairs by Emma's sleeping place. She was up, damn her—reading or writing, and within full view of my only passageway into the kitchen, to the cellar door.

So I gave up temporarily, thinking that I could try again some night when the cool weather returned, and the elder Borden had returned to her spot upstairs.

Back in Lizbeth's room, she too was stirring. "Where were you, dear? Where did you go?" she asked.

"I only wanted some water," I purred at her, as I slipped back between the light covers, and pulled my skin up against hers. "Go back to sleep." I drew her into my arms. She felt very warm and soft, all drowsy kitten and velvet skin.

"I *am* very sleepy," she said, and of course she was. I'd have been astounded to hear otherwise. If I hadn't successfully worn her out, Mrs. Winslow should've done it.

"Close your eyes, then. I'll sing you to sleep."

"No, don't do that."

For a brief second, I took offense. "You don't want to hear me sing?"

She shook her head, rocking it against my bosom. "Of course I do. But I'd prefer to stay awake . . ." She yawned. "Rather than insult you by drifting off during the performance."

I squeezed her, and adjusted myself on the pillows, so that I was lying on my back with her head atop my chest, and my arms around her more comfortably. "You're a silly thing," I told her, but I loved her, and maybe all love is silly in its own way.

"You, too," she said in return, and then she was out again. Her breath was damp and sweet against my skin, and it was lovely, this evening alone in bed, with the butter-soft moonlight to keep us company and no one ringing a bell for attention.

I petted her hair and tried to enjoy the moment, but in the back of my head, I was wondering how much more I ought to give her in a dose—in order to keep her sleeping soundly while I explore.

This was all the night before last.

It's still warm enough now that Emma remains downstairs again, but the old familiar chill is creeping back into the air, and I think we'll reinstate her to her proper bed this afternoon. This will all be so much easier when I only have to sneak past one of them.

But I can't put it off too much longer.

Eventually Lizbeth is bound to notice that the key she wears isn't the one she thinks. Somewhere a clock is counting down, waiting to reveal my deception. But I don't know where it is, and the only way past it is downstairs, through a strange door, and into whatever mystery awaits me beyond it.

Emma L. Borden

I finished the article I was working on, the one about the mollusks, that I'd promised to send off to the editor of *Marine Life* last month. I was a little late, but as far out as their schedules run, I won't worry much about it. If it's that great a problem, they can refuse to run it, and I'll sell it to *Aquatic Quarterly*. The lead biologist they consult is still that fellow at the university, my long-distance friend Dr. Zollicoffer. (To the best of my knowledge, that is.) He'll see to it that the piece finds publication, one way or another.

Speaking of that great man . . . I haven't heard from him in months now. I hope he's well. Perhaps I should send him a letter, or scare up a sample that might entertain him. The samples I've sent thus far have been gruesome, but well received.

The last missive I received from him requested more specimens like that one sample . . . the strange and smelly piece I sent him last year. Lizzie was confident that it was a half-rotted version of something ordinary on the beach, but my scientist's eye told me otherwise. Alas, I haven't seen any others since. He'll have to content himself with the one I sent.

I'm glad I passed it along. He seemed to enjoy it, and Lizzie wouldn't let me keep it in the house. It'd be a pity for the thing to go to waste, unexamined.

It is late. I ought to be asleep, but I'm finding it difficult this evening. I'd blame the balmy weather, for it certainly hasn't helped; but no, the real problem is Nance—to no one's surprise.

Not to mine, anyway. Sometimes Lizzie is hard to read.

I know she loves the girl, but for heaven's sake. If she loves her that much, she needs to invent an excuse and send her packing. Now is really *not* the time for visitors, least of all rowdy visitors who snoop, badger, fight, and ultimately yowl like a cat in heat, as if I can't hear through the floors. I'm feeble. I'm not deaf.

I'm sure that she and Lizzie both felt like the opportunity to banish me downstairs was a good thing, and I don't even care about that. It was my idea, to give them some time alone. I appreciate their impetus to carry on behind my back rather than in front of my face—honestly, I do—but all the tiptoeing around was becoming tedious.

Just *go*, already.

Traipse upstairs like the scandalous fools you are, get it out of your blood, and then get that girl out of our house. We have real problems here, and a real solution in sight—or at the very least, we have a real chance at an ally, and a shared wealth of added information. We can't jeopardize it over a silly fluttering of the heart.

𝕴 pretended I didn't notice, but just now Nance came downstairs. I don't know what she wanted, and I didn't ask. She made a show of getting a glass from the kitchen, collecting some water, and retreating again.

But she's up to something.

She's drawn to that damn cellar door, and drawn to what's behind it. That part she can't help; I know that, and I can't even hold it against her. But we have to keep her out, and I am absolutely terrified that Lizzie is on the verge of some terrible decision, or terrible slip of her concentration, and we might all be lost.

What if Nance finds her way to the key, or to some other method of opening the door? It's reinforced, yes. The lock is sturdy and expensive, yes.

But whatever is in those stones, those shiny bits of tumbled ocean glass (or so they innocuously appear) . . . it has an intelligence. Whatever voice cries through them, it cries not with words—yet it cries instructions, suggestions, and changes to a person's ordinary behavior.

It commands.

That's the word I'm looking for.

It commands, and it commands so forcefully that I must assume anyone snared in its call will find a way around whatever restrictions are tossed in front of her.

𝕴 caught Nance rifling through drawers, and she said she was hunting a pair of scissors. I directed her to the sewing room. I spied her examining the contents of Father's old cabinet, and she said she was hoping for something hard to add to her tea. I said she should help herself. I found her fishing about under the settee, and she insisted she'd dropped an earring. I wished her the best of luck in its retrieval.

Really, she must think I'm a fool.

If she stays here much longer, she'll find her way downstairs, and what will become of us then? What if she sees the whole lot of equipment, never mind what we added from the upstairs— the most incriminating books, charms, devices, and whatnot that we wished to remove from her view?

From a certain slant, it would appear that my sister and I are the witches we're accused of being.

Oh, I don't know. Perhaps the whispers have merit. What else would you call it but witchcraft—these experiments my sister undertakes in the basement laboratory, and around the walls and windows of this home? She's turning it into a fortress of superstition, but if you ask her, she'll argue that it's all science . . . of a kind.

I understand her sentiments, but it's hard to agree whole-heartedly when she starts wondering aloud which herbs and prayers might protect us.

The distance between an honest Christian mystic and a fortune-teller is sometimes less than half a whisper. Less than a pot of tea or the space between two book covers.

Unless I'm the silly one now—and that's entirely possible.

It's very quiet upstairs. I'm almost surprised they wore themselves out so quickly, though given the noisy vigor of the whole affair, it might not be such a mystery. Lizzie often has trouble sleeping, but if rumor among married ladies can be believed, there's nothing quite like a good frolic to send one off to slumberland with haste.

And yet.

Lizzie's trouble sleeping has extended into Nance's visits, in the past. But tonight, she doesn't even snore. It's only Nance who's restless, wandering up and down the stairs, standing in the kitchen like a ghost, like she's forgotten something, like she's waiting for something. Like she's listening.

This is the second instance tonight that the girl's appeared, and this time she either didn't notice that I was still awake and writing, or didn't care. She stood before the cellar door again; I could just barely see her shadow, stretching out into the corridor between us. It was long, for she is tall; and it was half-gauzy with the moonlight and gas lamp glow through the windows, shining through the fabric of her nightdress.

I reached for the bell beside my makeshift bed, but before I could ring it and, it is to be fervently hoped, summon my sister . . . Nance changed her mind and returned to the upstairs.

Maybe she was warned away by my candle after all.

Well, these words—combined with the last of the article revisions—have eaten up an hour and a half. No, closer to two, I should think. And I'm still wide-awake.

Perhaps I'll begin that letter to Doctor Zollicoffer.

I would dearly love to hear from him again.

Owen Seabury, M.D.

❦

I've avoided the Borden sisters these recent days—not by choice, but by forced circumstance. The mysterious Inspector Wolf has occupied much of my time, and most of that has been too tedious to record in this informal, private journal. Regardless, I am sickened at heart to know what I now know, or believe what I now believe; and the scientific facts under consideration do little to soothe me. Whatever they are, they don't add up. Whatever they say, it answers no questions that a reasonable man might ask.

When did I stop being a reasonable man?

It must have happened slowly at first, with Abigail Borden. And then with great finality, across that cold wood table from

Ebenezer Hamilton. And now . . . now I am either much closer to the truth, or much further from my sanity.

I honestly could not say which.

𝔈𝔟𝔢𝔫𝔢𝔷𝔢𝔯 remains in Boston, and I haven't spoken to him since that awful night in the courthouse. I offered my continuing services as confidant, witness, and even friend, should he require one; but either the message was not passed along or the ensuing silence was his response.

Were we friends, really?

No. But he needs one, and I'm too close to . . . to whatever this is . . . to walk away now. If he were to summon me, I would respond.

Inspector Wolf finally returned to that city as well, with all his notes and flash-fired photographs of the corpses, the scene of the crime (Was it a crime? No one seems certain), and whatever else he deemed significant. We shook hands and I told him to call upon me anytime, if he required a partner with a steady hand and a cast-iron stomach. He agreed with a smile, but I'd be surprised to see him again.

He suspects something strange is afoot. But suspecting it and doing something about it are two different things, and *my* suspicions tell me this: If I tried to bring him in, to confide in him the things I have learned, and the theories I'm inexorably forming . . . his training and allegiance to law and order would prevent him from being any real aid. Besides, he wouldn't even offer any badge, or the title of any official organization as employer. Heaven only knew who he was really working for. At worst, he might have me carted off to join Ebenezer, that we may rot together, two madmen in our soft-walled cells.

It is best that I leave him out of this, despite my inclination to do otherwise.

Upon reflection, it's apparent that I wish for someone to help me bear the weight of it, though. Lizzie must feel the same way. For that matter, she must've felt the same way for years now.

I wonder how long she's known?

Before her parents' deaths, that is. I wonder how long she'd been aware that something was amiss, and how long she'd told herself that no, it couldn't possibly be anything so absurd as . . . as whatever this has turned out to be. I wonder how long she lied to herself, and maybe to her sister, before the situation forced itself to a climax, and there were no options left except to murder or be murdered.

I have a few patients this afternoon, but tomorrow morning I'll pay the ladies a visit. I don't know whether that friend of theirs will be present, and I don't know whether she's aware of the murders—the new murders, or new deaths, or . . . I don't know. Even when I compose my confessions to no one but myself, I can't seem to get my head straight.

Every minute, my thoughts are occupied by fear.

At first I thought it was merely the flush of chemicals that flood the human body at the prospect of danger, excitement, or imminent threat. At first I thought it was only some leftover shaking, unresolved from that night with Ebenezer and that first day with Wolf, when we saw the corpses.

But that was only at first.

And now . . . now that's not what I think. Too much other strangeness abounds, and not all of it is contained within my head. I haven't the mental scope or imagination to produce it, only to recognize it, when it presents itself in patterns.

I walk down the street and I peel my eyes for signs of the dangerous taint—the sickness, if I must call it something mundane.

I watch for signals and symptoms; I gaze from beneath the brim of my hat, observing those who pass me by. I watch the men and women in the cafes and restaurants, and I watch them on the pier. I watch them about their business, running their daily errands, lifting their babies from basinets and riding their bicycles, buying their groceries, greeting the milkman, ordering seeds for their gardens. I stare at them while they're measured by tailors, searching their bags for coins to hand to the paperboy, collecting their mail, hanging their laundry pin by pin upon the lines—that it might dry in the sun, when the sun peeks through this oddly weathered spring. I scan their faces and their gestures, their postures, the gait of their walks, the flush of their cheeks, the way they count on their fingers or use their toes to nudge the neighbor's cat off the stairs and out of their paths.

I count how many times they blink.

If I'm not careful, I'll go mad. If I'm not careful, worse things yet may occur. So I remain careful, and I take my notes when I take my tea, and I brew coffee strong enough to keep my eyes wide-open as I make my rounds.

And I will record the things that I've seen, even if they seem trivial and unrelated. I do not know what relates to what, so everything must be mentioned and cataloged. Everything must be seen and remembered.

It's all written down. Not here, but in the patient folders.

Mr. Wells has developed a strange pattern of moles on his back, veritably overnight. Not shingles, not pustules, but moles with a spreading pattern, not unlike a swirl, a whirlpool, a twist of water. At first he swore that it itched and ached, but his wife confided that he's getting worse, and he's begun talking to the pattern and listening for a response. At night she hears something, it sounds warm and wet, and it smells like brine and seaweed in the sun.

Miss Fox's parents insist she's been feverish for two days, but when I visited she was clammy and cold, and her eyes would scarcely focus. She insisted she's fine, and wants to go back to school. I suggested another two days of bed rest. Something is amiss. Her mother says she won't stay in bed, but wanders the house at night, tapping her hands against the windows as if blindly feeling her way around the rooms, and when she walks in her sleep she whispers, *"Out, out, out . . ."* until they force her back to bed.

They've forced her back to bed, and lashed her foot to the post like a hobbled horse. (Like Matthew, before he went mad and murderous.)

Mrs. Williams lives around the corner from the Hamiltons' store and she's called for the police twice in the last week, confident that there's someone moving around inside the shop, someone trying to break down the walls and come through the building itself, trying to get *out, out, out.* Last night she was found on her front lawn, beneath the big oak in the yard, covered in blood. She stood in her nightdress, muttering about how she'd opened everything, she'd broken the windows and it could get out now, couldn't it? It would quit asking her now, wouldn't it?

I treated her cuts, and when I cleaned them I saw they were sliced in patterns, not the ordinary patterns of a window's shattered shards, but in horizontal lines, back and forth, very deep. It didn't match her story, but what could I say? Still she spouted nonsense, unless it wasn't nonsense. I gave her an opiate and sent her to sleep at her sister's house, at the other side of town.

There's more.

Several more I ought to mention here, and they all feel like a pattern, or part of one. But someone is knocking at the door, and it's the kind of knock that says to come *now*.

Lizzie Andrew Borden

❦

APRIL 25, 1894

I should've known something untoward was going on when I started sleeping better. *Suspiciously* better. Ordinarily I snap awake in the morning, shortly after dawn, no matter how late the previous evening has kept me working; but these last few nights, I'd drop to sleep and stay that way until seven or eight, and most recently, all the way to nine o'clock.

It was foolish to pretend that nothing was afoot or amiss, and it was more foolish still of me to pretend that Nance had nothing to do with it. She's the only new variable in the household.

No, that's not quite true.

There's Doctor Seabury. His knowledge of what we do here—even if it was, at first, a rudimentary understanding of what we're up against—*that's* new, and it counts for something.

But up until this evening, I could not have asked him to drop everything and come sit beside me, and listen to my tales of woe as if he had nothing better to do.

Now I know.

I've been looking at this all wrong.

This *is* the highest priority, for me, for Emma, and for him—for anyone who has any inkling of what's going on. I know it is. It must be. But progress on the matter has been so slow, and escalation had appeared to plateau until recently. My God, I'd become almost complacent about it.

About *them*. The creatures with the shark-white skin and glass-needle teeth.

But there have only been a few, and no new visitations since that one I killed in the middle of March. No new visitations of any kind except . . . well, Nance, and that's not the same.

Yet it's not unrelated, either. She came, and *she* caused this new escalation, but that's my fault. Mine entirely. I should've sent her right back home on the same train she arrived in. I should've thrown her luggage out on the lawn and told her to make her way back to the city. I should've pushed her away, chased her away, *thrown* her away if it came to that.

I didn't. And look what it's gotten me.

Look where it's gotten *us*.

I awoke to Emma's bell, but I awoke slowly and unhappily. I wasn't ready. I was dreaming of Nance, and there was silk. Silk dresses? Sheets? Something soft and luxurious, something that flowed and billowed. Something dry and smooth, but soft as mist. I can't recall, but wherever it was, whatever the dream was about . . . I didn't want to leave it.

But the bell rang and rang and rang, with all of Emma's strength, and I was compelled to answer it.

I tried to rise out of the covers, and I stumbled, falling to all fours. My head was swimming. *I* was swimming, my arms and legs made of some slippery, uncertain substance. Still stuck in the dream, they were. That's where I was swimming, I guess, wherever the world was made of silk sheets and quiet.

I forced myself to climb up, using the bed itself for support. And I realized then what I should've noticed immediately: Nance wasn't there. Her side of the bed was empty, and when I placed a hand on the indentation her body had made in the comforter, I found no warmth to suggest she'd only just left me.

And then it all fell into place.

My wobbly brain, my sleep growing longer by the night. Her fixation with the cellar door, all talk of lovers' bargains aside. Lies, and treachery. She's been drugging me, testing the dose to see what would send me deepest to sleep, and keep me there longest. She's been waiting for us to move Emma back upstairs, so that Emma wouldn't catch her by accident, or see her as she slipped downstairs to the door.

Perhaps oddly, I understood all of these things even before I noticed that the key was gone.

Sometimes it's funny, the way the mind works. How it assembles the minor pieces before the major ones arrive, solving the mystery in reverse, before all the clues are provided. It could've been the drugs—whatever she'd used against me. Some syrup or serum. Something that hid the big things but let me see the little ones.

I slapped my hand against my chest, where the cellar key usually hung on its chain. No, it wouldn't be there. It'd be on the dresser. I stumbled to the dresser, my feet still refusing to cooperate with me, not fully. I felt a moment's jolt of relief, even as Emma's bell still rang, because there it was—the chain with the attendant key I always wore against my breasts.

Then I picked it up.

I examined it, squeezing it to reassure myself that all was well. But all was not well. Emma was still ringing. Her wrists must've been about to fall off. It must've been exhausting, the ringing all this time. But still I ignored it, not quite alert enough to attend to more than one thing at a time. The key in my fist. It didn't feel right. It wasn't right.

It wasn't the cellar key, but some clever replacement, originally fitting the lock to God knew what. God knew where she'd found it.

God knew what she'd done.

I went for my wardrobe—almost fell into it, if the truth be known. I bruised myself against it as I wrestled the door open and pulled out my axe, which I did not leave out in the open when Nance was around, not anymore. I'd started hiding it, like it was some secret. Like she hadn't seen it already. She liked it a little too much, that was all. It made me feel strange.

"Emma!" I shouted, having heard all I could stand of the bell. "Emma, I'm up! I'm coming!"

I ran down the hall, my knees still feeling like they weren't quite mine, and weren't quite connected to my body. It was a jerky stumble at best, but I stayed upright and dashed to Emma's room, where I looked in and saw at a glance that she was alive, and unharmed, and that Nance wasn't with her.

"Nance . . . ," she gasped.

"I'll get her," I swore, half out of breath already.

I didn't stay to hear her reply. I made for the stairs, where I tripped over my own toes and went face-first into the banister—and I caught myself, dragged myself to a stop before I'd gone down too terribly far, and shook the ringing out of my ears. It wasn't Emma's bell anymore. It was just the incessant hum of my head trying to force the rest of me more fully awake, because this was bad. Worse than bad. Worse than terrible, and worse than whatever is worse than that. I felt it in my bones, and my bones were still shaking—not yet ready to hold me up. My legs ached, and I wondered quite seriously if I hadn't fractured something.

(I turned out to be right, but it wasn't my leg after all; it was my nose when it slammed against the edge of a step, or one of the banister rods. I have no idea which. I didn't see the blood until later.)

I didn't know what Nance would do if she found the cellar. Would she see the equipment and investigate it? Destroy it? Demolish my research at the behest of whatever drew her down there? What if she found the cupboard in the floor?

What would that mean? What would it do?

I made it to the bottom of the stairs by the skin of my teeth, collected myself, and retrieved the axe. (It had fallen out of my grasp and toppled the rest of the way down without me.) I scrambled into the kitchen, and there, yes—the cellar door. Flung open. Swinging slowly on its hinge, and a soft rushing noise like wind in a cave escaping past it, up into the house.

Hoarsely I screamed Nance's name, and took a better grip on the axe, praying that I wouldn't need it. I didn't know if I could kill her, if it came to that. I didn't know what I'd do when I found her, or what she would've done to herself.

What was calling her?

It must've been the stones, yes. Sealed in their box, and sometimes that wasn't enough to keep even me from hearing them, and becoming enraptured. I'd learned the price of listening to them, and I knew how much I had to lose. Nance didn't. Nance didn't deserve to be in the middle of this.

The lights were on, down there. The glow seeped up from between the steps, which were only wood slat things—I'd never installed anything sturdier, feeling that it wasn't worth the trouble. The glow was yellow, not the vivid white of the gas lamps, and I told myself that it didn't mean anything. I mumbled as I descended, insisting that it could've been worse—it could've been green.

"Nance?" I called again, and my head still spun, for I was still half stuck in the dreams from which I'd been so rudely dragged. I forced myself to work against the drugs, planting my feet one in front of the other, going a tad more slowly, clutching the handrail as I went because I wasn't sure I could get back up again, should I take another spill. My body already ached all over from the first one.

I heard her voice.

She murmured something, and I couldn't hear it. One word, or one syllable anyway. It could've been anything, but it meant she was alive and that she was still capable of responding to me. My panic wasn't entirely soothed, but such was my joy at hearing her that I took the last steps two at a time and almost fell again, but caught myself—using the axe as a cane to steady my balance upon my arrival.

"Nance, where are you? What have you done?"

My eyes answered both questions.

She'd found the cupboard in the floor. The stones themselves had told her where they were, and how to find them, and what they wanted.

She'd retrieved the box they were kept in, and now they were scattered around the ground, except for the one set in a necklace. It'd been Mrs. Borden's. It was the necklace I'd taken, after she was dead. Now Nance wore it, and the sight filled me with misery.

She was lying beside the hole in the floor, cupboard opened and box exposed, emptied. Its contents scattered. Her breathing was shallow, too fast, not normal at all. Her eyes were glazed over, and she stared at the ceiling—where there was nothing to see.

I flung myself down at her side, dropping the axe and seizing her by the shoulders. I shook her, but she didn't respond. I dragged her as far as I could, or as far as I dared, then I left her, gathered the scattered stones, and threw them back into the box.

My safeguards hadn't worked, but they were all that remained in my arsenal.

I reached back to her and wrenched her fist open. I retrieved the stone she held there, too, and saw that it'd burned a weird shape into her skin, but what it meant (or if it meant anything at all), I didn't know and didn't have time to decide. I tore the necklace off her, shattering the clasp. I threw it into the box as well, closed the lid, fastened the bands, and dumped it down into the cupboard. I closed the cupboard door and dragged one of my desks over to it, as if the added weight would hold it down.

Ridiculous superstition, just as Emma would've called it, but Jesus, what else did I have to work with?

I returned again to Nance, who was lying as if catatonic, slack-jawed and lovely, there on the floor. She wasn't blinking. Just breathing a quick staccato in and out, her chest fluttering. Her burned hand opening and closing like a flower.

I slapped her cheek, gently at first. Then harder. Then I said her name as I did so, and I realized that I was crying and bleeding both—when the blood splashed down onto her nightdress. I wiped at my nose with the back of my hand, and left a trail of scarlet down my arm, but I did not care. I only cared about her, as inert as a doll except for that uncanny pace of breath.

I couldn't leave her there.

I had to move her. Could I move her? I looked up at the stairs that would take us to the first floor, and I considered it. I had to try.

I wedged myself under her shoulders, using my arm and my badly bruised legs to lift her, and haul her upright. She didn't fight me, but she didn't do much to help—though to her credit, when I made her stand, her knees locked and she remained upright, so long as I prevented her from falling over. I guided her through the cellar, around the repositioned table, past the damnable cupboard, over to the stairs, and I hauled her bodily up them. She cooperated only so much. Maybe she couldn't do any better. Maybe she didn't know how anymore. I can't say, and I shuddered to consider—all I could do was insist to myself that she was only stunned, and would surely awaken any minute now.

Any minute. That's what I told myself as she languidly moved her legs up and down, not really catching the steps in order to climb them, but going through the motions through the sheer memory of her muscles. (Any minute, she'll come to her senses. Any minute, she'll find her footing. Any minute, and I'll have her back.)

I slammed the cellar door, but didn't lock it yet. I still wasn't sure where the key was, and anyway, the damage was done.

Emma was calling for me, but I couldn't deal with her, not quite yet. Not when I had Nance out of the basement at long last, but sprawled now upon the kitchen floor and looking like a corpse.

I slapped her again, until I was afraid I'd harm her should I hit her any harder, but I received no response. Her breathing slowed somewhat, as if distance from the cupboard had allowed her body to return to something like normalcy; but still she didn't blink, didn't answer, didn't show any sign that she knew where she was or what she was doing there.

Upstairs, I heard Emma shake the bell one last time and then in frustration, she flung it into the hallway. "Lizzie!" she shrieked, though her voice was almost gone. It came out in a fierce whisper with an edge like a razor.

At a loss, I replied, "Coming!" and on the way up the stairs again, I realized I hadn't used our secret phrase—but then again, I'd been replying from the kitchen, not the cellar.

I dragged myself up the steps to the second floor, and by the time I reached Emma's room I could scarcely stand. I was drained and aching, and my brain wouldn't yet stop sloshing around in my skull. Whatever Nance had given me, it'd done its job well, and it wasn't quite finished working.

Emma was out of her bed, leaning against the tall wooden post at the foot. She asked me, "Well?"

"Nance got into the cellar," I replied, summing up the situation.

She closed her eyes and took a slow, deep breath. "And?"

"And I don't know!" I put my face in my hands, but when I covered my eyes the world still wavered, as if I were drunk. I changed my mind and ran my fingers through my night-tousled, unchecked hair instead. "She's on the floor in the kitchen, and she . . . she isn't responding," I said, trying to force myself to treat this like a scientist, as if this must be new data. But it wasn't new data. It was my lover, and she wasn't herself right now. For all I knew, she might never be herself again—she could twist and warp and transform into one of the monsters with the glass-needle teeth, and then I'd have to kill her, and put her body into the cooker, and pretend that the juices and stench that remained were never the soft flesh and warm hair of the woman I'd loved.

"Go get Seabury," she said, and even through the effort of speaking, and the exhaustion in her voice, I heard impatience and anger. "We need him. You're bleeding."

"He won't know what to do any better than we do," I argued.

"You don't have any better ideas, do you?"

I shook my head. "I'll . . . I'll send for him."

"Go get him yourself."

"And leave her here? Alone in the house with you? When we don't know what she'll do . . . or what she'll *be* . . . when she comes around again?" I didn't say the rest of what I feared, that of course, she might never come around again at all—and I didn't know if that'd be worse. I was too afraid of too many things at once. They all swirled together fighting for dominance. None of them won. Or they all did, however you chose to look at it.

"All right, then. Jacob, next door."

"Right," I said, perking up at the scent of a plan. "I'll go get him, right now. I'll be back as fast as I can."

The neighbor's boy was ten years old and constantly offering to do odd jobs for money. It was late, and he'd be in bed—but a light still burned in a window at the big white house next door to ours, and I had no qualms at all about declaring an emergency. I said it was my sister, and we needed the doctor, but I couldn't leave her. Emma's condition was well-known, and it was the easiest, nearest lie I could offer and expect to receive any help.

I offered his parents a fistful of coins, probably three or four times what he would've asked, even at that hour. The boy hopped on a horse, and was gone.

I went back inside, where Emma had successfully come downstairs by herself. I didn't take the time to be surprised; her energy came and went. Some days were better than others, and under different circumstances, we'd celebrate her vigor with a glass of port—but I could only work with the spirits at hand, so there'd be no port.

"Brandy, maybe," I said aloud, as I dropped to the floor beside Nance, who hadn't moved.

Emma, ever to her credit, recognized my train of thought—or at least predicted its destination. "I'll open Father's cabinet, and find a clean glass."

I didn't really expect it to work, but it gave us both something to do.

I man-hauled Nance to the parlor settee and deposited her there, and soon Emma arrived with a decanter and a small glass. My hands shook as I filled it, and as I lifted Nance's head in an effort to make her drink.

Much like her cooperative walking and stair climbing, she agreeably sipped the beverage and swallowed it. I hadn't expected it, but I was relieved at this one small thing at least—she could drink, and presumably eat, and wasn't quite so lost to the world that she might die of starvation.

And that's preposterous, isn't it? Starvation isn't any real concern. If Nance is to die from this, it will almost certainly be at my hand. Whatever this illness is—be it infection, or some other form of affliction—it does not kill. It transforms, and inspires the victim to kill instead. They must be put down like rabid dogs, for the safety of everyone around them.

So already, kneeling on the floor beside her, with her lovely neck resting against my forearm as I propped her head into a drinking position, I was thinking ahead and planning for the worst.

"It might be," Emma began softly, "she's only stunned. You've been there yourself, and you've come back around again."

"Not like this," I said, and I would've sobbed if I hadn't

been all cried out for the moment. My eyes were sore from it. "I've never been this far gone."

"She may need a little time, and that's all. Give her overnight, and she may surprise you. Look, even now her breathing is calmed. It's practically normal."

She was right, but I didn't dare believe that it was so simple as that. "Doctor Seabury may know of some treatment to help awaken her. He's been working with . . ." I stopped myself. The only patients I knew who'd suffered anything like this had murdered, and then been killed.

"He's a brilliant man, and he may have ideas. He may see patterns that have eluded us thus far."

Emma sounded unbearably weary. I'm sure I did, too, when I replied with what pitiful hope I could muster, "Between us, we may have collected enough details to see those patterns. If there are any."

"Lizzie?"

"Yes?"

"Your nose . . . it's bleeding again. Or still, I don't know."

I felt the trickle even as she pointed it out. I rubbed it with the back of my bare arm again, and a second streak of red joined the first, which now had flaked and faded. This time, I noticed the pain. I rose to my feet and went in search of a tea towel. Upon finding one, I held it to my face and remained standing in the space between the kitchen and the parlor.

"I must look a sight," I said, my voice muffled by the fabric. "God knows what the Wilsons thought, when I knocked so desperately on the door for Jacob. But they didn't say anything."

"They were too surprised, I'm sure."

I dropped onto the arm of the settee. It creaked beneath me.

But then the door rattled under the knock of a heavy hand, and I jumped to my feet once more.

"The doctor," Emma breathed.

I opened the door and almost dragged him inside, babbling as I drew him into the parlor.

"It's Nance, Doctor Seabury. She's stumbled into my research, and she's become infected, or afflicted, or I don't know what word you'd use—I'm sure there's a better one, something medical that applies, but I don't know it, and she's gone catatonic, and *please*," I begged. "Please, will you help her?"

In a moment, he was at her side and unfastening the latch on his bag. He was rumpled, in that way of a man who's been ready to settle in for the night—only to be rallied before bedtime. I was so overwhelmed with gratitude that I felt positively embarrassed.

"I'll do my best," he promised, and he proceeded to poke and prod her with the diligence of a seasoned professional. He checked her pulse and her pupils, frowning at the state of her eyes and their failure to blink. He felt at her throat, and her belly; he clapped his hands in front of her face and received no response whatsoever.

He sat back on his heels. "How long as she been like this?"

Wretchedly, I confessed, "I'm not sure. Half an hour?"

"Closer to a full one," Emma corrected me. "I heard her come downstairs. I heard her open the cellar door . . ." She stopped herself, unsure of how much she wanted to share. Then she continued, "I tried to summon Lizzie," and then to the doctor, "I have a bell, you know. But it took her quite some time to come around."

He turned his attention to me, understanding plenty at a glance, I'm sure. My pupils no doubt told him plenty in return.

"I won't insult you by being overly delicate: I assume the cause is an opiate? One you've made a recent habit."

I dabbed at my eyes with the bloodstained tea towel. "She's been drugging me, at night," I said, cocking my head toward Nance, though I hated to implicate her. "I don't know what she used. I can go upstairs and search her things and see, or maybe she took something from Emma's cabinet."

He raised a quizzical eyebrow at Emma. "But you're not inclined to taking the drops or syrups, are you?"

"Not routinely. But sometimes, when I absolutely *must* sleep—and the cough is more than I can bear."

"I appreciate that you're not the sort to become dependent on them. They fog the brain," he said, casting another appraising look at me. "And your studies must prohibit it." She nodded primly, and for a moment I nearly hated her. Always the teacher's pet, wasn't she? And she'd always disliked Nance, so here was one more thing to lay at Nance's feet.

I fought the feeling down like bile. It wasn't fair or kind, and we were all just trying to understand, after all. I swallowed so hard that I almost banished the great lump in my throat, and I said, "I'm not accustomed to these things, either. It's hit me awfully hard."

"As did something else, if I must judge by your nose."

"The banister. I fell down the stairs, coming to check after Nance. I . . . it was so very hard to wake up."

"Depending on what she used, it's a wonder you managed at all. What was she looking for, down there?" he asked, returning his attention to Nance, who never stirred. He took her wrist in his hand and as he listened to my words, he listened for her heart.

I collapsed into the seat across from Emma, to the doctor's

right. I was worn out, and telling the truth required my full attention. I couldn't speak clearly and stand up at the same time.

"She wanted to see inside the cellar. I wouldn't let her; that's why she began drugging me. She stole the key from around my neck, and she was trying to keep me asleep long enough to investigate without my interfering."

Calmly, more like a priest than a physician, he asked question after question—sometimes watching me, sometimes watching Nance.

"Why did you want to keep her from the cellar?"

"Because it called her. Or something inside the cellar called her; that's what I mean." I was so tired I could hardly keep my eyes open, now that the first flush of mortal panic was finished with me.

"What are you collecting in the basement, Miss Borden?"

I sighed. "By now, you should call me Lizbeth, propriety be damned."

"It usually is. What are you collecting in the basement, Lizbeth?"

"Evidence. Research. Samples. Nance was lured there by the contents of a box, which I'd sealed up as best I could—but it clearly wasn't enough."

"What was in the box?"

"Beach glass, to the casual eye. Tumbled rocks and gems."

His eyes went distant, then focused sharply. "Beach glass?"

"Pieces I've found, here and there. They call me, too," I admitted, though I hated to hear myself say it. "I've made efforts to study them, and determine—"

"Just . . . little pieces of glass, from the shore?" he interrupted.

"Green ones, usually. Sometimes I find them embedded in

sandstone or lime, or polished and set into jewelry. But they always speak the same way, call the same . . . well, it's not a song." I struggled for the words.

"I've seen them," he said softly, but suddenly—before I could continue. "In the barrel at Hamilton's, the odds and ends, bits and bobs. The ones Matthew collected for the shop."

The connection clicked, in both our heads. Our eyes met.

I said, "They called him, too."

"And your stepmother," he said sharply, and with wonder. Like it'd only just occurred to him. "She wore something. I saw it on her once or twice. A necklace . . ." On some instinct, or half-spied detail he'd only just recalled, his gaze jerked down to Nance's neck. A thin red line marked the spot where I'd pulled the necklace off, breaking it and leaving a narrow welt.

"Nance found it." I offered it up as a whisper. I couldn't bring myself to say it any louder. "She'd put it on. I took it away from her."

Excitedly, he shifted to face me. "But you knew—you *knew* it was the necklace. And in time, you learned it was the stones themselves, and there were others like it."

"Yes, but I don't know what they mean, or where they come from. I don't know how they call, or . . . or . . . Doctor, I've tried everything. That's what's in the cellar: my laboratory, where I've performed what experiments my limited knowledge and resources have contrived."

"I must see it. You must show it to me," he said eagerly, and I wasn't sure if I was thrilled or worried by the enthusiasm. I didn't have time to decide, for it was in that narrow space between the two that Nance began to speak.

I knelt down next to her and collected one of her hands, squeezing it between my own. Doctor Seabury stood aside so I could reach her more easily, I could stroke her face, I could kiss her forehead and breathe the smell of her hair.

"Nance, darling, what is it? Are you there? Can you hear me?"

One word she puffed softly, over and over. At first I didn't hear it, she said it with so little force, just half a breath and the puckering shape of her lips to send it along.

"Out . . . out . . . out . . ."

Doctor Seabury inhaled slowly, deeply, in the hard reverse of a sigh.

"What's she saying?" asked Emma, who was seated a little farther away.

"Out?" I replied uncertainly, for it almost sounded like a soft cry of pain instead. "Doctor, have you ever heard anything like it?"

He nodded, but I knew he would. I could see it in his face when the word first became loud enough to understand.

His obvious concern left me flustered. I floundered. "What does it mean? Does she want to go out? Or is she warning us that something . . . something's coming out? From the cellar?" I was grasping at straws.

His certainty was terrifying when he said calmly, "She *wants* out."

"We should, we could . . . turn her loose and see where she goes," Emma suggested, and for the second time that night, I would've dearly loved to slap her.

"We aren't turning her loose!" I snapped. "She's not even *standing* yet. She's not going anywhere."

But the doctor said grimly, "She will stand. She will rise, and find a way out."

"And then what?"

"Then . . . ?" He shrugged tiredly, with his hands up and his shoulders sagging. "Then she's gone, one way or another. I've seen it once before. Twice, I suppose. I witnessed it once myself, and heard that it was said of Matthew, but he never spoke in my presence, to cry 'out' or anything else. By the time I was summoned to check on him, whatever had him in its grip . . . it'd rendered him mute."

"Then she's not so far gone," I said to reassure myself. "Not beyond hope or help. There's time to investigate, still. Time to figure out what's wrong with her, and do something about it. Did you hear that, Nance? There's time," I said, crushing her fingers in my own.

"Lizzie." Emma called my name like a warning.

"Oh, hush," I spit back at her. "She'll be fine, soon enough. And even if she won't, let me say it out loud in case words mean something, and can make a thing true."

"Lizzie," she said again, and this time it was more dire. "Do you hear that?"

I sat up straight, and released Nance's limp fingers. I didn't hear anything, but Emma's ears were sometimes keener than mine. "Where? What?"

My sister's eyes tracked around the room, seeking to pinpoint whatever had snagged her attention. Her ears settled on a corner back on the other side of the kitchen, if I read her correctly, and assumed she wasn't hearing rats in the walls between here and there.

"What are we . . . ?" the doctor began, wondering what we were listening for, or to, or what on earth we were going on about. But he was kind enough to keep from saying so, at least not without leading in gently.

I spared him the trouble by cutting in. "There's something outside the house," I said quietly. "You must stay here."

He rose to his feet. "I'll do no such thing."

"Doctor, I really must ask you . . ." Now it was my turn to half finish a thought. I heard it. I was confident, yes—the scratching, scritching, fussing noise of something nasty feeling its way around the walls outside. "Stay right here," I commanded him, having no idea whether he'd obey or not. "I'll take care of this. Please, stay with Emma and Nance."

"*Out . . . out . . . out . . . ,*" whispered Nance, with something closer to urgency than idle directing.

"Miss O'Neil, wishing to go outside. And something outside, wanting to come in?" he guessed. "These two things must be related."

"Yes," I admitted. "But you *must* stay here!"

I decided to take the front door. I could surprise it, if I came around the far side of the house, for yes, my ears told me it was tracking to the east.

I raced back upstairs to the best of my ability. My legs were still wobbly beneath me—but the drugs were wearing off, burned out of my bloodstream by the terror of Nance's condition. And now we'd see how much terror I could muster anew, because something walked outside, and I needed to be at my sharpest.

I was not at my sharpest. But what could I do?

I grabbed my axe.

RIGHT CHEEK, LEFT CHEEK—WHY DO YOU BURN?

꘎

Owen Seabury, M.D.

APRIL 25, 1894

I now know something of the torment which has afflicted Lizbeth Borden Andrew or whatever she calls herself these days. I kept meaning to ask which name she prefers among friends— but now that I think about it, she told me to call her Lizbeth, but didn't offer one surname or the other.

I'm not beginning this entry well. It was a terrible night, and I'm not yet recovered. Perhaps I never will be, but I must compose myself and thereby compose this entry. I must organize my thoughts and lay them all out, while I still remember everything so freshly that it hurts.

My ribs ache. They are lined with bruises that look uncannily like the impressions of human fingers, but that's not what made them. And these bruises, they are flecked with something sharp and itchy, some residue left behind. It feels almost like spun glass, but what small sample I was able to retrieve dissolved between my tweezers, and was gone.

Whatever these creatures are, they leave no useful trace of themselves behind. Only questions and horror, and bruises shaped like fingers.

I say "these creatures" because the thing I saw this past night was not the only one of its kind. Lizbeth told me so, and she showed me how she's been managing them.

But I stumble ahead of myself.

Let me try again.

I received a knock on the door, and opened it to find Jacob Wilson, young neighbor to the sisters at Maplecroft. He'd been sent to bring me around. Something about Emma; he wasn't too clear on the specifics. So I made my way there with all haste, and upon being granted entrance, I learned that the difficulty was related to Nancy O'Neil, their houseguest. She'd fallen catatonic, having somehow gotten inside a locked cellar and contaminated herself with Lizbeth's experiments.

But I'll come back around to how that situation came to be.

Nancy, called "Nance" by her friends, was placed upon a settee—lying on her back, staring up at the ceiling with the same blank, unblinking stare that I'm coming to find familiar, damn it all to hell.

No, I don't think hell is far enough away. If there's some farther, more distant shore where these things might be banished, then I pray for that instead.

In the course of my examination, Nance began to chant

"*Out . . . out . . . out . . .*" as I'd noted with previous patient Miss Fox. Same rhythm to it, same pace, same message. And this time, something answered her.

It tried to come in.

Lizbeth ran outside, despite the fact that she must've been in great pain from a broken nose and a badly bruised body, courtesy of a slide down the stairs. Besides that, she was not up to her full strength and clarity, due to some draught Nance had slipped her before bed. (It turned out to be Mrs. Winslow's, so it could've been worse. Anything too much stronger than that, and she might not have awakened in time.)

But the younger Borden rallied, and I was impressed with her determination—though I had no intention of following her command, which amounted to, "Stay inside with Emma."

Something wanted inside Maplecroft. Lizbeth wanted to go handle it alone, but that was madness, and she needed my help. I followed her outside.

I kept her in my sights, though the night was very dark, and there was a fog hanging so heavy that the gas lamps were almost no help at all. What little light there was bounced back and forth between the mist in patches, so the whole world was hidden, and yet it moved.

She rushed ahead of me, a womanly shape wearing little more than a nightdress; I think she'd paused to throw a housecoat over herself, before I arrived. Her form billowed as the fabric spilled behind her, and every so often I caught a glimpse of light sparking off metal. Her axe. I'm not sure I'd noticed her picking it up.

(Where did she keep it? Was it the same one . . . ?)

She wielded it easily, lightly. She carried it swinging like a baseball bat, only with more poetry to it. It was a frightening thing to watch, this small shadow of billowing gray fabric and sprawling, wild hair splaying out behind her, the axe held at the ready with both hands, poised and prepared.

I could scarcely take my eyes off her, but then again, I could scarcely see anything except the motion of her running around the side of that magnificent house . . . and as I brought up the rear I felt like a noisy, stumbling brute in her wake. She moved so quietly, you see—so practiced. She so beautifully disturbed the darkness, all flapping shape in gray and white. Like an owl. With that kind of grace and silence.

But she did not outpace me. I could not let her, for without her, what would guide me? The moon offered no assistance, and I knew that behind the house, the cream and yellow fog that shifted and swirled would lose even the lamps that colored it.

I did not call her name. She must've known I was on her heels, for she must've heard me; and by then I wondered if her stealth wasn't imperiled by my noisily added presence, but it was too late then. I'd left the other two women in the house, neither one of them able to defend herself worth a damn—and there was always the chance that Nance might rise up and prove a danger to anyone in her vicinity.

I tried to eject the thought from my mind.

Lizbeth had done so, and I knew—I believed, and from the bottom of my heart—that she was better versed in this awful matter than I was. What smattering of a dilettante's investigation I'd performed would hardly stand up to the knowledge of a woman who apparently had built and kept a laboratory in her cellar.

My experience could not hold a candle to a woman who'd seen this long before I had, and who'd already been compelled to kill because of it.

She rounded the house's back corner, and a few seconds

later I did the same. And then I could hear it, though I'd not noticed any sounds from inside the house—for all that Lizbeth and Emma had clearly caught it. Yes, there it was . . . the slap, slap, slap of what sounded like hands. The exploratory clap of someone feeling about for entry.

I expected her to draw up to a halt when she reached the potential intruder, but I was wrong—and I didn't even see the intruder in question before she swung the axe. But I heard the weapon connect with something wet and solid, and then with another swing the arc of her arm went wide and high, and for a brief moment I thought of sword fighters waving much lighter things, but with the same sort of skill and speed.

This time the axe missed its target.

Lizbeth gasped, and I gasped too because by then I'd reached her. My hands were empty and naked, as if I'd expected fisticuffs with whoever I found. I had a gun, my army revolver. I always wore it on a holster except no, not then. I hadn't put it on when Jacob had demanded an audience at Maplecroft. I'd been almost ready for bed and I wasn't wearing it. I didn't think to don it.

So, yes, my hands were empty when I reached her, and reached the *thing* with which she grappled.

It had her by the wrist, I saw, and she was reaching past it— grabbing for the axe.

She resisted, and she swung again while I stood there, mouth agape. It mustn't have been agape long. Not for the span of half a dozen heartbeats, surely no longer than that. But surely I can be forgiven, for what I saw was unlike anything I'd ever seen or even heard of. Whatever I'd expected to find, when Lizbeth went bolting from the house . . . whatever trespasser or intruder, whatever masked raccoon or hungry dog seeking scraps . . . none of those possibilities had led me to ponder a creature like that *thing* with which she did battle.

I must compare it to a person, when I describe it.

That's the only jumping-off point of reference at my disposal, and there's always the chance it was *once* a human being—though that possibility feels remote and unlikely. (Regardless, Lizbeth believes it could be true, and at present, she's the expert on the matter. The prospect instills me with the deepest loathing and revulsion that a man is capable of carrying. But she's right. We must consider everything, for we have little idea of what can be ruled out.)

But the *thing*.

It was the shape of a human being, provided that the human being had been horribly emaciated, his bones stretched, his skin blanched, and his head both swollen and misshapen. I would use the word "encephalitic," but it doesn't feel quite right. I've never heard of an encephalitic with a forehead sloped and pinched, eyes that were covered with the same membrane I'd seen before on other corpses in Fall River (so there's one point in Lizbeth's favor, or in favor of her revolting theory).

The thing's eyes were also shaped strangely, oversized and elongated, drawn back to a point that aimed at the forehead, almost as if they'd been turned on their sides. No, that's not what I mean. It was more the shape of a raindrop, landing on the face and sliding downward. It was . . .

. . . I am no good at this.

Already my memory fails me, and my eyesight, too—for if only there'd been some lamp or other light to illuminate the thing before it was shattered to death. If only I'd gotten closer, before Lizbeth smashed its face to bits, and the darkness glittered with the tinkling dust of broken glass.

She caught it in the face, in the mouth, I think, not in the eyes—though we ruined those in time.

The axe crashed down, sharp side first, and then on the next swing she used it as a bludgeon. But her reflexes were slowed. The creature was fast. It grabbed her by the arm again.

And whatever spell of astonishment had held me captive . . . it was broken when I saw the violence returned against her. It was one thing for me to watch a woman assault a monster, but another thing entirely to see her attacked in return.

None of this is making as much sense as I'd like.

But if I stop now, I'll wish tomorrow that I'd had the courage to persevere while the horror was new in my mind, and still flickered in awful plays of light and shadow inside my eyelids when I closed them.

The creature stood taller than Lizbeth, but not so tall as myself. It moved jerkily, as though it wasn't wholly comfortable with its joints, and it had too many of them. It moved in sharp, stuttering, staggering lunges. It moved like it was in pain.

(Well, it would've been by then, wouldn't it? Lizbeth had struck it solidly, several times.)

It gushed some weird liquid that I assumed must be blood, or hemolymph—isn't that what powers the circulatory system of insects? Arthropods, at any rate. Whatever it was, it filled the monster's skin and performed a similar function. It sprayed from its wounds, and wherever it landed, I felt a stinging on my skin. Later I would realize that the blood-substance was not quite blood-colored; it was darker, more like brown or orange, when exposed to the air and given a bit of time to dry. Something about it made me think of rust.

It had Lizbeth by the arm, and I reached for it, seized it by the shoulder and flung it backward—or that's what I attempted, to only modest success. I was stunned by how little I was able to move it, how it jerked itself out of my grasp and remained, feet planted, a high-pitched howl whistling from its ruined mouth and leaking from what passed for its nostrils.

"No!" she cried, and bless the poor woman, she tried to put herself between us. "You don't understand . . ."

And that was an understatement, wasn't it? But I was in the fray already, and there was no time to pause or regroup, not when the monster slathered and grimaced, seizing me and wrestling with me—grappling with its iron-hard fingers, crushing at my ribs and my arms, pushing against my belly in blows that would've stunned a seasoned boxer—blows that stole my breath and left me winded.

I am growing older, a fact that I do not contest or bemoan—but I am still a large man, and a strong one, too. No seasoned boxer, but well able to withstand a beating should one be delivered, or so I've told myself all these years.

So I stood against the thing, though its hands wandered and hit with such astonishing rapidity that even in the bright light of day, its motions would have seemed a blur. I was shocked, but not incapable of blocking and protecting myself with my arms; all my thoughts of assault having folded back in upon themselves, collapsing into the more immediate task of defense.

"It's the iron," Lizbeth wheezed. "Our bodies won't stop them, but the iron . . ."

I did not see her, because I did not dare raise my head. I now bore the full brunt of the creature's attention, and I would've told my companion to run for safety—if it would've mattered in the slightest. I'd interrupted her, and perhaps complicated her plans; except that no, she'd faltered and missed with her axe. I must have been *some* help, surely?

But not in that moment.

No, it was all her . . . when I heard the slice of the axe splitting the fog as neatly as a razor, and when the weapon came striking down—a vicious blow that took the creature in the shoulder, cutting past the collarbone and down into the lungs, if the thing had lungs at all.

(There was no time to examine it more fully, but I'll come around to that. I feel like I'm saying this too much, about too many things at once, but what can I do? There are too many things to say, so I must say them here and now, or remind myself to say them later. This is all I can do, and in this way I hope I'll come around to everything, in time.)

The creature stumbled forward and released me even as it crashed into me, knocking me backward and to the ground, where it jerked atop me, clawing at me—or clawing for purchase on the ground, I can't say which. It flailed and seized, and I lifted one leg and used all my weight, and the weight of my boot, to leverage it away in a mighty kick.

The creature fell backward, and Lizbeth's axe caught it on the downswing, striking the base of its neck and almost completely decapitating it.

Its head lolled to the side, and back, and down to dangle against its chest. The creature fell to its knees, and Lizbeth struck it some more, again and again, well past the point at which it must have been dead.

. . .

(But . . . once I thought I knew of death. Now I'm not so sure. The line is finer than I would have ever guessed, and with these inhuman things? Are they mortal enough to die? And if so, do they die on the same terms as the rest of us?)

Finally the monster lay on the ground, looking like some bony pulp with a loosely humanesque structure. I climbed to my feet and stood over the mess, wishing for all the world that we had a light and I could see it better—for this whole battle had been fought in pitch-dark, save what slivers of ambient glow the small town afforded us. The whole thing took place in silhouette, in outline, in vague impressions like strokes of paint intended only to suggest an event, not portray it with any real accuracy.

Half of what I've composed here has likewise been conjecture, informed by those brushstrokes. Conjecture, combined with Lizbeth's account. Between us, I think we've recorded it with as much truth as we could muster.

We've done our best, and then some.

But the creature . . . it lay flat upon the earth, oozing onto the grass. I thought perhaps it twitched, but again, the light was so poor that I would not swear this was the case. Lizbeth was panting, leaning on the axe for support, and clutching at her stomach as if she could scarcely catch her breath.

"Lizbeth," I called her by the name she suggested, the one I always tried to remember, but didn't, And my own breath had hardly been corralled enough for even that lone word.

"Doctor?"

"Are . . . are you all right?"

Grimly she informed me, "Not yet." She straightened up, sniffled hard, took a deep breath, and brushed her hair out of her face—for all the good that did. "We have to get this thing inside."

I thought I had misheard her. "Inside?"

"Yes, inside. You wanted to see the laboratory, didn't you? No—" She gestured with the axe and shook her head. I'd been leaning down to touch the thing. "Don't touch it," she told me. "Not with your bare hands. It'll only hurt later. We'll . . . you and I, Doctor. We'll put this thing to rest for good."

"Is it dead?"

She sounded exhausted when she replied, "I have no idea."

Together we hauled the thing to the cellar doors, a little farther around the back side of Maplecroft. She mostly used the axe to drag it along, and I kicked at it with my boots when pieces appeared on the verge of falling off.

When the doors were unlocked, Lizzie asked me to wait with the thing, and said that she had an idea. So I stayed there alone in silence with the festering mess, and none of this might have ever happened, or so I could almost convince myself. That's how quiet the whole damn world had become.

Had no one heard us?

Had no one noticed that a life-or-death battle with an unnatural monster took place, right behind a grand old house where the Borden sisters lived? No? I find that incredible, and I'm not sure that I believe it at all. Though if anyone overheard, no one came to help. And no one brought a light, so I'm reasonably confident that no one saw anything. I was standing right there, part of the action myself, and I could barely see it.

Lizzie returned shortly, bearing an old sheet. We scooped the creature's remains into the sheet and rolled it up, which *did* make it easier to maneuver the sodden mass down the cellar steps.

I insisted on carrying it. It wasn't very heavy, a fact which surprised me; and my companion was so tired and injured that it spoke to her credit that she hadn't yet passed out from the pain and exhaustion.

"Here," she said, gesturing at a spot on the floor. "I'll show you what to do now."

She did not so much kneel as fall to all fours beside an open trapdoor embedded in the floor. Inside I saw a metal trunk about the size of a shoebox, and when I looked at the box, I thought I heard a strange humming noise. It was not entirely unpleasant, but it *was* entirely distracting.

She closed the trapdoor and sat on it, then turned to another place on the floor and manipulated a cunningly concealed latch. Another portion of the floor lifted away, and I wondered at the honeycombing she must've accomplished beneath this house, and what else might lie under our feet.

"I call this 'the cooker,'" she said simply.

The cooker was an industrial appliance, built into the floor. Its contents burbled and bubbled, and steam valves and gauges covered a panel on the top. "What's . . . where did you get such a thing?"

"They're more common than you think. Mostly you find them on farms, or in slaughterhouses."

"For disposing of large carcasses?"

"Very good. Yes, that's what it's for. Now here—" She pointed at the rolled-up thing in the sheet and waved me closer. "Put it inside. Within a few hours, there'll be nothing left but liquid, which drains out underneath the backyard. Please, help me lower it. It mustn't splash; the contents of the cooker are highly corrosive."

"They must be, indeed," I agreed as I did what she asked. Sheet and all, I placed it within and resisted the urge to stir it up like a repulsive stew.

{238}

She shut the lid, set some dials, and a low, murmuring clank announced the steam was flowing and the cooker was doing its job.

Just as she went to close the cabinet door, I thought to exclaim, "Oh! But I would've liked to examine it, before we destroyed it. I'm in shock, I suppose. I should've said something sooner."

"There wasn't much left of it to examine, even by the time we got it to the stairs. Their soft tissue disintegrates very quickly, beginning almost as soon as they've stopped moving. The flesh melts down to gelatin, and the bones crumble, until they feel like pebbles in your hands. Still, I am happier to see them boiled down to nothing. At any rate," she added wryly, "I doubt you'll be forced to take my word for it. The odds are perilously high that you'll meet another, if you continue to keep company here."

"This isn't the first?"

"No. This is the seventh, or eighth. I can't recall right now. It's been . . . such a day. Such a night, as the case may be."

"Your stepmother, and your father. Is this what they were becoming?"

Softly she said, "I wish I knew for certain, but I have never— not once, in these last few years—ever doubted the course of action I took that night. They were becoming *something* else . . . and it wasn't human."

"Is that your confession?"

"Of something, yes. This has become my life's work, Doctor Seabury—accidentally, unfortunately, but what else can I do? Surrender to what comes, and let the whole world burn?"

"Or drown," I said, and I'm not sure why. It was a silly sentiment that sprang to mind, and I aired it.

She took it amicably enough. "Or drown, yes. These things,

they have some connection with the ocean—that much is clear. The sea glass, the finned fingers and webbed toes . . ."

"Do they have such things? I didn't see. There wasn't time or light enough; thus I wished we'd taken a moment, before tossing it into the bath."

"I'll give you my notes, and you are welcome to every scrap of knowledge I've collected thus far. I'm afraid it isn't much."

"It must be more than I've accumulated," I admitted. "I've only been aware of the affliction for these last few weeks, and I haven't done a very good job of understanding it. I suspect I've failed in ways I've not yet imagined."

We sat together in silence, me on the edge of a table and her still on the floor, where the cooker vibrated and hummed beneath her. Finally she said, "It's awful, knowing just enough to know how bad this is."

"And yet not knowing how bad it might get. Or how to fix it."

"That's the worst part, yes. But I pray—in case that means anything—I *pray* that you and I can work together, and you'll help me with this. I've shouldered it alone, and I cannot bear it much further. I'm at the end of my reach, and I don't know what else to try. Who else to ask. How else I might proceed. You've always been so kind to us, and I've appreciated it more than you know. Even the little things, the acts of politeness, they've meant the world . . . and now, I hope you don't mind my saying so, but you give me . . . well . . . you give me *hope.*"

I was touched. "I'm honored that you would take me into your confidence. And left to my own devices, I do not pray; but I verily hope that I prove myself worthy of your trust."

She smiled. It was a feeble smile, but a genuine one, I think. "Thank you, sir. And now, if you'll excuse me briefly, I'll check on my sister and Nance. Feel free to look around the laboratory, though I'd caution you to avoid the box in the floor beside the cooker."

"The sea glass baubles?"

"Yes. You hear them?"

"I do. But now I know the call for what it is, and I can resist it, I think."

I should've said it with more confidence. She watched me for a few long seconds, and then said, "Then perhaps you'd better stay with me. Please join me upstairs, and then when all's secure, and everyone's as well as we can manage . . . I'll show you around the laboratory. I'll open my notes and my research books to you, and maybe you'll see something I've missed."

"I will be fine unsupervised," I promised her, but I knew I'd said it too quickly. I felt it even as I heard the humming, purring, warm, wet sound . . . I didn't hear it with my ears, but with my soul. And it frightened me.

"All the same . . . ," she said. She collected herself, and rose from the floor. "Until you have a better grasp on what we're dealing with here, I'd appreciate your immediate proximity."

I did as she asked. She was the expert, after all.

But what a terrifying thought, that the world's foremost expert knew only enough to live in horror.

Aaron B. Stewart, Fire Chief, Farthington, Mass.

◆

APRIL 26, 1894

INFORMAL REPORT SUBMITTED TO COUNTY SUPERVISOR

MARTIN HELLERMAN

Since you've pressed us for particulars outside the bounds of the standard report, I will cheerfully oblige you—for there's nothing I can give you but the truth, and I must trust that it proves sufficient to appease the adjusters, or whoever leans upon you to lean upon us.

The call came at approximately four forty-five a.m. via James Horner, who arrived at the main station on horseback. He was frantic, and all the way from the other side of town he'd been rousing the populace, a veritable Paul Revere shouting out that the fire was coming, the fire was coming. Or rather, the fire had *arrived*—in all its sky-high glory, and the entire block would shortly be consumed if nothing was done, and done promptly.

The block in question once housed the Franklin Cassock Cannery and Shipping Facility, which closed eight years ago, in the wake of some industrial accident which was never satisfactorily explained. Something about a belt snapping, a compression device failing, and to sum up a tragic and tedious tale: a dozen people were killed. Whichever Cassock son ran the operation at the time (and I can't remember the name off the top of my head, but it's a matter of public record, I should think) . . . he never recovered from the shock. He witnessed the catastrophe firsthand, and subsequently took leave of his senses. Truly, the matter was heartrending for all involved.

But I tell you all that to say this: The place had been abandoned since the late 1880s, and boarded up tight to keep out the daring youths and derelicts who might be drawn to it. Though, all things considered, it wasn't quite the problem you'd expect. The old cannery was rumored to be haunted—and not in the charming, romantic way that attracts curiosity seekers, but in the fashion that frightens off all but the most desperate or inebriated. The buildings have been listed for sale for quite some time, but to the best of my knowledge there have been no offers, and no interested parties in pursuit of redevelopment.

The site has not seen a great deal of trespassing. That's what I wish to convey.

But at four forty-five in the morning, Horner came around crying about a fire—warning that it would surely consume the entire block, and it might well spread farther than that if the whole community were not rallied on the spot.

I wanted to say he must've been mistaken or deliberately

inflating the stakes, but when I stepped outside to greet him, I could see the glow of the blaze over the tops of the trees, lighting him from behind. My heart sank down into my belly, and rested there like a lump of lead.

I asked Horner if he'd summoned the police force yet, and he nodded, turning his horse and telling me that I was nearly the last man to be roused, because I was sleeping at the station's quarters—and inconveniently enough, the station lies at the most distant end of town from where the blaze began. He said I should bring the cart and all my men, and he'd instigate a bucket brigade in advance of us.

To be honest, I've always found Horner a bit too eager to please, or eager to make himself valuable; and in my experience a man is either useful or he is not useful, and those who must convince you of their enduring worth . . . probably fall into the latter category. But on that night, I could not fault him, and I was glad to have such an informed busybody within the town's limits.

After he'd gone, I raised my own alarm—ringing the bell and cranking the siren, bringing out my two nearest lieutenants, whose aid I needed when it came to fastening the horses and preparing the hoses. (The tanks were already filled in accordance with regulation.)

We maintain three such tanks, each one holding four hundred gallons, mounted on a reinforced wagon of the traditional metropolitan type; though here I must point out that if we'd received the funds for a new steam-powered engine, there's a fair chance that we might've saved more of the cannery than we managed.

When we work with horses and leather, as opposed to steam

and rubber, you can only hold us accountable to a given extent. We do our best with the equipment at hand, but it's hardly the newest technology—and I'm aware that Commissioner Freeman is loath to part with funds for a town the size of ours, but progress shall catch us eventually, if we do not catch it first.

You may expect me to follow up further, on this point. Perhaps at a later date, when the insurance men are satisfied. If ever they are satisfied.

But with regard to the Franklin fire, we were fortunate, after a fashion. When we arrived with cart and ladders, we found the north end of the compound wholly engulfed, and I knew immediately that there was nothing to be done for the place. It would burn to the ground, and the only question was how much property and how many lives it would bring down with it.

The flames had burst through the roof at the cannery's tallest point: a four-story tower that once housed the family offices. The blaze appeared to have begun there, but given the scope of the situation, I could not swear to it in court. Not yet. Not before all the investigations are concluded, and all the evidence sorted from the ashes.

Just call it the gut feeling of a longtime fireman, and lend as much weight to that as you like.

But the fire had not stopped with the tower offices, alas. It'd spread in both directions, up and down the block, devouring a smaller segment of the plant (which had collapsed before we got there), and devastating a wing where the sorting of meats once occurred. This left approximately half of the remaining structures unscorched, but in the inevitable path of a blaze that was wholly outside our capacity to contain it.

With a steam engine, we might have cut the unburned

structure off with a water wall, and saved it. But with rows of buckets and heavy hoses, I regret to say that we emptied all three tanks into the inferno to absolutely no effect. In the end, we were forced to retreat—and to ask the stalwart brigade members to abandon their posts.

We reassigned them to the side streets, where they doused cinders and stomped upon embers that still glowed. We sent some to the nearby rooftops with all the water they could carry between them, pumped from wells or dragged from creeks, so that the structures might be preserved.

Containment, sir. That's the best we could hope for, and I am proud that we accomplished even that much.

If the insurance company is unsatisfied with this account, then I scarcely know what else to provide. This was the situation, and these were the conditions. We were powerless against a problem of that size, and nothing short of the most advanced equipment—and another dozen trained men—would've made the slightest difference in the outcome.

I am personally insulted that the adjuster has called our efforts into question, and if he has any further inquiries—or any accusations, for that matter—you may send him to me directly. I'll no doubt be at my post, at the station. He's welcome to wave his paperwork and spew his nonsense as he likes, and I'll let Thompson or Coy have a go at him. Or at any rate, I won't stop them if they do.

It's our honor and our ability he's taking to task, and I won't stand for it.

This having been established, I am frankly surprised that he's asked so little after the bodies we found within the wreckage, in the days after the ashes cooled. Our final tally was eight, with remains that might have constituted a ninth discovered in a nook beneath the floor, where the boards had fallen. It's diffi-cult to say.

Word has it that a man from Boston is coming to investigate, but I'm not sure what he'll make of the corpses. Each set of re-mains would fit in a drawer, so little is left. But if he wants them, he's more than welcome to them.

No one here has the faintest idea who they might've been. Drifters, that's our assumption. Perhaps even criminals in hid-ing, as such things are not unheard of. Regardless, we do not believe the dead men were local, for as I said above, the cannery was avoided by everyone within the vicinity; and besides that, no one is reported missing.

The cannery was a cold, wet place, and an uncomfortable one, too.

It's almost bizarre to me, the thought that it's somehow burned. I can't imagine finding a surface dry enough to strike a match in there, so there's great speculation as to how the fire began in the first place. We didn't pump enough water in to cause such a soaking, as heaven knows we simply didn't have it.

There were no storms, no strokes of lightning on that night. No one reported hearing any explosion, or seeing any suspicious characters lurking about. For that matter, no one had any idea that anyone lurked within, and that's one reason we pulled back so quickly—not only could we not save the buildings, but so far as we knew, there were no squatters to be rescued. There was nothing to be lost but the timber and equipment inside, and we couldn't see risking our brave firemen or volunteers to determine otherwise. By then, anyone who was getting out . . . was out al-ready. And no one who went inside could expect to leave.

Other than this, I'm not sure what you'd have me say.

The cannery burned. We found some corpses, charred beyond identification. The circumstances were strange, but there
was no sign that the dead men had any ill intent, or that they
were the source of the blaze.

Between us, there might be more I could share . . . if I could
share it firsthand. If the commissioner is so up in arms about the
insurance adjuster, maybe it's for the best that you come yourself, and we can quit passing one another notes like schoolboys.
Or if you won't come, I suppose the man from Boston will lend
you his reporting, when he's accumulated it.

I don't know him by name or reputation, but he's called
"Wolf," and his interest in the case is very keen. If you're the
man who sent for him, you ought to say so. The town sheriff
swears he didn't make the request, and if *he* didn't, and *I* didn't,
then I assume it must've been you—unless the adjuster has
some special interest in learning about the bones.

Maybe it's that simple after all. Do you think he's afraid
there might be a lawsuit?

Never mind. Come and see me, and I'll tell you the rest. Or
don't, and wait for the inspector's report. I'll accommodate the
man as best I'm able, but if there's anything in particular you'd
like me to convey or withhold, it'd be helpful to know about it before he arrives.

This case has left me with a terrible taste in my mouth.
Something is very strange about it, and something is untoward.
I'm confident of that. But whatever strangeness or failings may
be deduced from the matter, I'll not see my department's actions or officers thrown into the mud over it. We did the best we
could, with the tools we had at our disposal. Asking any more of
us is wholly unfair and unreasonable.

I hope that your previous correspondence came at the behest of the commissioner, and not from any private concerns. I thought you knew us better than that.

Yours,
Aaron S.

Emma L. Borden

❧

He knows.

I cannot say that he knows everything, for honestly, who *does*? But he knows enough to either help us or see us in jail. So now we must hope for the best.

I'd be lying if I swore it wasn't some kind of relief, as if whatever burden Lizzie and I have borne is now cut by a third. Three sets of shoulders to carry it will make the load lighter for all, won't it? Or maybe it's all in my head. From another angle, it's now three who suffer—rather than two. I don't care.

Is that awful? Fine, then. I'm awful.

But he knows, and I'm glad. He's confused, frightened, appalled, and outraged, which only means that he's a good, sane man. Any other reaction would've worried me.

He's seen the creatures now. Firsthand. He's even been injured by one, though slightly; and now he knows that we've constructed our falsehoods of pure motives, and have only sought to understand the nature of what we're up against, using the best tools we could arrange. So he's passed that first test and not gone mad.

He passed the second test as well, when we sat up late in the night with Nance. Lizzie had gone downstairs into the laboratory to finish the last of the cleaning up and locking down, leaving me and Doctor Seabury to entertain one another over the sleeping, drooling form of my sister's lover—who never much stirred, and never much whimpered . . . except to cry softly from time to time. And to repeat that unsettling mantra: *out . . . out . . . out . . .*

So the doctor and I kept each other company. He asked me questions, and I answered them as best I could. If my sister had been there with us, she might've slipped me sharp gazes, or cleared her throat pointedly, to keep me from sharing too much. She's so very careful, always, and I do not mean to diminish the necessity of this—I only admit that I find it tiring. More tiring than being ill. More tiring than ringing bells for minutes and minutes on end, my heart racing with terror that the bells may ring forever and not be answered. Not by her, at least.

And when I can't ring the bells any longer, and when I'm all out of bullets . . . what would become of me then?

Same as Father and Mrs. Borden, I guess. Same as the Hamiltons.

Except . . . there's this. I've wondered a terrible thing, a time or two—then quickly shoved it from my mind, like the decent human being I remain thus far. What if I were to become afflicted, or infected, or . . . *touched* . . . with whatever strange taint is creeping through the town? What then? Would I become like

Father, with the strength of five men and the temper of a mino-taur, angry and hungry, but full of power? Would I turn into Mrs. Borden, fast and heavy, with fists that could break down doors and a back that could overturn a cart? Or Matthew? Who . . . if the doctor's report is accurate, via Ebenezer Hamil-ton, was able to lift his mother aloft with one hand and hold her in midair.

Such strength. Like I've never known, or can't remember. I don't recall the last time I was able to walk unaided into town, or dash up and down a set of stairs. I can't remember what it feels like to run, and I doubt I ever shall feel that joy again. Not without some unnatural intervention.

But I didn't tell Doctor Seabury about any of that.

Instead, I told him about the house, and the laboratory downstairs. I told him how Lizzie had so cunningly arranged to have it built out when neighbors were absent or otherwise occu-pied, and when perfectly ordinary excuses could be made for the equipment. They know we're rich. They think we're strange. Why would it surprise anyone if we installed extensive plumb-ing to upgrade the home to modern conveniences? And what of it, should we import a heater for all the water and install it in the basement? And so forth, and so on.

I also told him, in a moment of weakness or brandy, about my masculine persona.

Maybe it was silly, but the moment felt right and I made my confession. I told him I was a man, or that I had a man's brain— if that thought suited him better. I had another life, one on paper and sometimes in print across the globe, in places where I would never likely travel.

I tried to slow myself down, to keep some of it to myself, and maybe if Lizzie hadn't been downstairs with a mop and some hydrochloric acid, she would've stopped me. It might have been a favor, or then again, I might have hated her for it.

It felt so good, that's all—to let someone else hear it. And, after a moment of astonishment, even *believe* it. I credit him that much, and credit him richly: He did not argue with me, or scoff and declare that I must surely be mistaken. He only asked after the subject matter I pursued, and I told him all about how I'd gone about creating this second person, through which I lived a whole different life. In my imagination, if nowhere else.

He gently told me that he put more stock in imagination than many medicinal men, as he'd seen firm (if irrational) hope change the course of disease in patients, at times. I almost laughed, but it came out in a choked little sound instead. He asked me what was wrong.

"Sir, I do not argue with regard to the healing powers of optimism, but if they could change every patient's world, then my own would be much greater in scope these days."

"But I did not mean—," he said hurriedly.

I did not let him finish. "No, I understand what you meant. I suppose I am only sad, because I *do* believe you're right—but you are not right about everyone, and sadly, I fall into the group for whom no amount of imagination will restore my health."

"You shouldn't assume it. Science moves onward, upward, and in a thousand directions at once. Every year we see greater progress in every field. One day, you will find yourself restored."

"Don't make promises, Doctor. I hate promises. I am all too aware how imprecise science can be. As imprecise as faith, at least."

"Well, then, everything is imprecise," he said almost crossly, or I might've read too much into it. "But if we believe in nothing for a starting point, from what can we move forward? Even an educated guess is a starting point."

"Even a superstition," I said, hearing Lizzie rattling around down in that damnable laboratory.

"I beg your pardon?"

"My sister. Her brand of science looks like mythology, but you're right—without some place to stand and place a lever, there's nowhere from which to move the world." Then, before he could ask for more, I waved my hand and said, "It's all she has, all that makes sense to her. There is lore, you see. And no science to speak of, save what she's managed to conjure."

"Lore? Fairy tales, and the like?"

"Just so."

He considered this, nodded slowly, and said, "When confronted with a problem that appears so . . . so vastly outside the reach of science, it's not an unreasonable way to proceed. The tales of old wives have much value hidden in them, even if doctors cannot explain it."

"I'm a bit surprised at that response," I told him. "I expected you to be more firmly on the side of reason."

"I do my best to remain on the side of reason, as you put it, yes. Absolutely. But the things I've noted as of late . . . the things I've seen, and heard, and recorded in my own notes, for my own reference—or as comparison with your experiences, and your sister's . . . they are not reasonable. And I must admit that and accept it, if I wish to find answers."

"You make it sound as if we struggle blindly, in the dark."

"We all struggle blindly, in the dark. I did so just now, behind your house. It ended well for your sister and me," he said, rubbing at a spot on his upper arm. "This time. Next time, we might not be so lucky. And then what should we do, when our luck runs out?"

He cleared his throat, and leaned back in the chair, casting one nervous eye at Nance, whose chest rose and fell with a mechanical jerk, and hitch, and settling, that looked like nothing so much as the mindless thrashing of a machine.

Floundering for some uplifting sentiment, I tried, "Then we find some light, and use it to guide ourselves out. Many monsters lose their power to frighten, when they're dragged out into the morning."

"But some don't," he said, too quickly in my opinion. "Some only reveal in full the awfulness of their true nature, and assure us that there is no hope."

"Doctor!"

His eyes went far away, and then went hard before they returned to me. "I'm sorry," he apologized, though not fast enough. "But if you'd seen a battlefield first thing, in the light of dawn . . . then you might not wish so wildly for illumination. However"—he adjusted the timbre of his voice, and his position on the seat—"we are not cannon fodder tonight, and thus far, the daytime hours have been kind to us. Our advantages are few. Let's appreciate the ones we can count."

Gerald Macintyre, Telegraph Clerk, Western Union

⟨❦⟩

April 28, 1894

TELEGRAM AND ACCOMPANYING NOTE
TO SHERIFF DANIEL HARDING, JETTING, MASS.

```
Dead found in hotel basement identified as family
of five named frenchly stop cut open in awful ways
stop signs of water damage everywhere stop bones
picked clean with the meat left behind stacked like
steaks stop manning has sent for boston inspector
stop details in post should arrive by friday if not
send word stop
```

Good God, Daniel—what the hell is going on out there?

I'm acutely aware of my role as a receiver of information, and that my duty is to relate the missives with discretion, not commentary; but for heaven's sake, I'm only human, and I can't very well transcribe without reading and absorbing much of what I catch. This is the third such incident in as many weeks! The fourth, if you count that thing at the cannery. Not sure if we ought to or not, considering . . . but it's impossible to rule it out, wouldn't you say?

Now, when Preston says he's sent for the Boston inspector, that must be Wolf—isn't that correct? I've seen his name bandied about with some regularity, as of late. Assuming I'm correct, and he's the expert upon whom these recent hopes have been pinned, will you send for him, too? If you do, might I be allowed to accompany him? Let's be honest, dear brother-in-law, I'm probably better briefed on the crimes than half your force. By the sounds of things, you're playing this all very close to the vest, and I certainly won't fault you for it—but perhaps you'd prefer having a non-police set of eyes on hand. I could report back to you, and tell you everything he says, everything he wants. Everything he sends back to Boston.

I could be of better use to you out about town, rather than serving behind a desk—that's what I'm saying. I'm not your secretary, and I only wish for the chance to prove it.

At the risk of talking out of turn, I may have additional details which aren't quite public. Say what you will about my job behind a desk, but this desk is covered day in and day out with rumor, flashed back and forth across the country at the speed of electricity. You'd do well to take advantage of my inadvertent eavesdropping.

For example, did you know that there is talk of an altar? You know, like the kind in church, only not intended to praise the God of Love, I can promise you that much. Apparently, at the Wakefield scene and the Campton scene both, there was evidence of unholy worship, and again, it's possible that a similar setup was in use at the Franklin cannery. The fire chief found something in the ashes, and he refused to identify it formally, but when drinking with friends, he confessed it looked like it could've been some kind of sacrificial table, or cabinet, or . . . well, he declined to use the word "altar" as if he deliberately shied away from it.

But we're fooling ourselves if we don't admit the obvious.

These evil acts are performed by a group of men, and maybe women as well—you can't count them out. A group that follows the devil, that's how all signs point. The ritualistic murders, the altars, the frantic quiet of law enforcement officials like yourself . . . You don't want to cause a panic, and that desire is indeed commendable. But if you plan to withhold the facts until the case is closed, then surely your obligation is to close it quickly, and through any means necessary?

I'm better means than you might expect.

You're wrong when you complain of my imagination. It's not a nuisance; it's a virtue. You're wrong also when you assume my skills are less worthy than yours; though our abilities may differ, they have commensurate value. To be blunt, people will talk to me before they'll talk to you. They suspect you of watching them, and waiting for some misstep that might incur a fine or a jail cell—and even the most innocent of men will balk if he thinks it a possibility. They second-guess their every move, and wonder what wrong turn they've taken today, that you darken their doors.

But me? I'm the friendly neighborhood gossip.

Whether that embarrasses you or not, you'd be foolish to deny that my sociable nature is useful. Should you think otherwise, then I offer you a small tidbit for future thought: Ask your Boston investigator what he makes of the tentacles.

Owen Seabury, M.D.

❧

I was stunned—and not at all displeased—to find Inspector Wolf on my doorstep this morning.

His stout shape and bespectacled face were a sight for sore eyes, not least of all because I might be able to tell him something. Anything, really. Any small measure of what I'd learned from the Borden sisters . . . any illicit tidbit would unburden me by just *that* much.

I knew it was a silly, perhaps dangerous idea. But it had become so much to carry—so much more to watch for, to wonder about. It was as if my whole world had been upended, yet I remained unmoved. And now I am forced to piece together a mystery from my upside-down space, my head gone light and my brain confused by all the new angles.

Really, I was almost embarrassed by how glad I was to see him.

And before long, I would learn that he must be brought into our confidence to some minimal degree. Whether the ladies liked it or not.

I invited the man inside, and he politely agreed—though only long enough for me to find my shoes, coat, and hat. I was missing all three, but I was within my own home, and I'd learned that some mundane procedures of civility must be allowed to simply fall by the wayside when larger projects presented themselves.

He removed his hat and stood in the foyer, though of course he was welcome to enter the parlor, or anywhere else that suited his fancy, as far as I cared.

He said to me, "I hope I haven't come at an inconvenient time."

And I said, "No, of course not." Then upon gazing at my surroundings—which I'd been neglecting, and having let the housekeeper go the week before . . . I hope he was not afraid that he'd interrupted some kind of personal tribulation.

So I added, "I beg your pardon, with regard to all the clutter. I'm finally going through the particulars of my late wife's estate, on behalf of her sister in Virginia. It's been a difficult upheaval." I was lying through my teeth, and surely he knew it. "But a necessary one, all the same. Given the intimate nature of this matter, I've relieved the housekeeper for a week or two, and I'm sorting through the archives of papers and property myself."

"My sympathies on your loss, Doctor."

"And I do appreciate them, but enough time has passed now . . ." I hesitated, not wanting to appear too cavalier. "It's been two years. The time has come, that's all, and there are some

obligations we cannot foist off on other people. Now, tell me . . . ,"
I said, changing the subject as I reached for my jacket and shuffled into it, "how can I be of service?"

"Ah, yes. Perhaps I could treat you to coffee, or brunch? We
can share a few words over something warm and filling."

Such a delicate suggestion, that we get the devil out of my
filthy house—and it was presented with such aplomb! I accepted
the offer immediately. We went to a dining room down by the
pier, where over a light meal of coffee and egg sandwiches, the inspector unveiled the particulars that prompted this recent visit.

"Since last we spoke, there have been a series of peculiar
crimes throughout the state. For that matter, now that I say so
out loud, it's entirely possible that the incident with the Hamilton family was not the first representative of the . . . spree, if I
dare call it such."

"A spree?" I asked, hoping my voice portrayed the strictest
innocence.

"I shouldn't leap to such conclusions, Doctor—but for lack
of a better term, I'm afraid it will have to do. Suffice it to say,
people are dying in very strange ways. With little evidence to
suggest a perpetrator, or indeed—in some cases—even so much
as a crime."

"I'm not sure I understand."

"That'd make two of us." He sounded weary. He removed
his spectacles and wiped them clean on his napkin. "But there
seems to be a certain . . . biological component to the mysteries.
Something pertaining to the ocean, and what strange things
might lurk in its unfathomed depths. A name has come up, and
it's possible that this person has some involvement in the matter.
But *personally*," he said with great emphasis, "I suspect it's more
a case of devoted envy. I think the biologist has a reader who's

enthralled with the man's work, and might be using it as a guide, or inspiration, or . . . something," he finished weakly.

A warm, sick feeling in my stomach told me I knew the answer to my question before I even asked it, but I asked it anyway. "And this biologist's name?"

"The initials E.A., and surname Jackson. I put it to you that way, because there's precious little information on the man. Anywhere. He professes a doctoral degree in the sciences from Princeton, but Princeton has never heard of him. Neither have the next tier of schools, and neither have any I searched upon casting a wider net. As far as I can tell, he doesn't exist—outside a frankly outstanding set of publication credits, here in the States and abroad."

"You believe that E. A. Jackson is a pseudonym."

"It must be. Or else the man is a phantasm."

I tapped my coffee spoon against the saucer, and attempted to home in on his point. "But you said there's some connection, between this mysterious Doctor Jackson and a series of strange crimes—maybe even the Hamiltons, or so you'd have me suspect. Since you've mentioned all these disparate elements in the same breath."

He looked at me strangely, and that was fair enough. A logical leap I'd made, but I'd made it too easily. I think we both knew it.

"That is correct, Doctor." He was weighing something. I could almost hear the gears grinding together in his brain. But he reached his decision, and he leaned forward, setting his napkin beside his plate. "And here is the nature of that connection, which I pray you will keep in the very strictest of confidence."

From his inside pocket, he removed an envelope; and from the envelope, he removed a sheet of paper. It was covered in handwriting, large and precise. "A copy," he informed me, straightening it out, and likewise adjusting his glasses. "Of a letter left behind at one of the murder scenes."

He slipped it across the table.

I removed my reading glasses from my vest pocket, applied them, and began to read, though there were places where I fumbled the words aloud, for they did not line up in my head . . . they did not make sense, they only made patterns and noise. But there was the name, right in the middle. Clear as day, and no mistaking it.

My heart climbed into my throat, and stuck there.

Physalia, E. University I Was Not Now

❧

MISSIVE IMPERATIVE A DATE WOULD SAY NOTHING

these are difficult times, exceptional times, changing times and I for one welcome them with open arms, but such is my way, such is the way of the ocean, the waters coming and going, moving with the moon, back and forth like the blood in our bodies and really I must thank you doctor. I must thank you and I must thank you in person, I will come to you and we will meet and you must explain to me as much as you can as much as anyone can what has become of the ocean not the ocean but that which lies in the ocean, from whence cometh the sample I have named *Physalia zollicoffris* I have named it after myself because it came before myself and now it is myself, we are the same now you see or you will see I will see to it I will see to you.

. . .

𝕴 would be together with you and we will talk together, doctor
E A Jackson I recall thus your packages came signed that way
and I always welcomed them I especially welcomed the last one
and then I heard from you no more. it is possible I know it is
possible that you have become like me like I have become, not
one but many. not self but legion in accordance with the Bible
which is not a good book not a very good book not a book at all
just a stack of paper compared to the sample Doctor jackson I
need to speak with you I will

DEPART, ALL ANIMALS WITHOUT BONES

Owen Seabury, M.D.

APRIL 28, 1894

I sat aghast, the note of a madman painstakingly scrawled before me. For what else could this fellow be, if not raving? If not utterly divorced from his senses? I stared at it in silence, the letters parading before my eyes . . . saying so much and so little all at once. Declaring and warning, threatening and announcing. But what? Beyond a general desire to meet E. A. Jackson? And furthermore, how had Inspector Wolf come to have it in his possession?

Wolf prodded me. "Well?"

"Well?" I replied helplessly. "It's lunacy—that much is clear. Though the handwriting seems steady enough . . ."

"A copy," he reminded me.

"Oh yes, that's right. The words themselves, that's the real kicker. Where did you find this, again?" It was worth asking, though I knew he'd be evasive.

"At a scene . . . ," he said vaguely, confirming my suspicion. He still wasn't interested in telling me more about who he worked for, or what they wanted, or why. But the police accepted his authority, didn't they? He obviously had some credentials, someplace, that proved his status.

I lifted my eyebrow. "What kind of scene?"

"A scene not entirely unlike that of the Hamiltons. The water damage, left over from some weird interior flood that damaged nothing else. The blood, the convoluted evidence and terrible smell. At first we even had a witness: a young woman who raved like Ebenezer, or maybe worse than that. I can't say with certainty, having met the man after the fact."

"But you spoke to this woman?"

"Only briefly. It'd be more accurate to say that she spoke to me. And I have to tell you"—he leaned forward, finger tapping on the paper that now lay between us—"she spoke like *this*. Her words, they flowed together this way, repeating, ebbing and surging."

"Do you think she wrote the note?"

He shook his head vigorously. "No. I'm quite confident she didn't, for a couple of reasons. For one thing, the handwriting on the original note . . . it's definitely a man's."

"And for another?"

He took a swallow of coffee, and then told me flatly, "And for another, her right hand—her dominant hand—had been destroyed, its fingers chewed down to the first knuckles."

I shuddered, and he continued.

"It's possible she might've written it before . . . whatever occurred, but it seems unlikely. I hope you'll pardon me, if I preserve some of the details, but even telling you this much is in breach of some very strict protocols. Suffice it to say, the woman didn't compose this strange missive, but I believe she knew who did. I believe she saw him."

"Is that what she spoke to you about?"

"Oh, no." He shook his head again, more slowly this time. "She droned on about the water and the blood, and she cried and cried—mostly about her baby."

"There was . . . there was a baby?"

"We found its remains scattered across several rooms. Listen, Doctor . . ." He shifted the conversation quickly, but the queasy feeling that arose in my stomach was not so swiftly appeased. "The moment she was left alone, she broke a window and used the glass to slice her wrists, and then her throat. She did such a thorough job that if a physician such as yourself had been on hand when she'd begun, you couldn't have saved her. No, she was *determined*. And no, I don't believe she wrote the missive. Whoever composed it . . . whoever he was . . ." He stared down at the sheet, as if his willpower could compel it to give him more information. "He wants to visit this E. A. Jackson. And I believe that the mysterious doctor is here, somewhere in Fall River."

Carefully, I said, "What leads you to that conclusion?"

"Miskatonic University leads me to that conclusion." He withdrew another set of papers from his internal pockets, and for one insane moment I fancied his vest to be a magician's hat. "For it is upon that campus where yet another incident occurred, and unless I miss my guess, it was the very first."

He laid out a newspaper article in front of me. I skimmed it, reading with a dull sense of horror that a professor had lost his mind and murdered half a dozen of his peers before vanishing. I checked the date: December 7, the previous year.

"Phillip Zollicoffer." I read the name aloud. "Went mad and went on a . . . a spree, to use the word we nearly avoided earlier."

"A madman, to be sure. A brilliant one, with traceable degrees and a career of genius to recommend him. But something snapped, and now I suppose the university will need to hire a few more heads to round out its classrooms," he said drolly. "And look, it's the name, you see—here in the note. *Zollicoffris*. That's what he calls his 'sample,' whatever on earth that might be. When I asked after him at the university, I received more details than I'd ever care to hear, to be frank, but it's my duty to hear them, and I did. Indeed, he'd been corresponding with Doctor Jackson, who it would seem is quite an authority to be respected, in those circles."

He sighed.

I said, "So this professor, Zollicoffer, he goes on a killing spree at his place of employment and disappears—only to continue the spree elsewhere?"

"That is my theory," he said, and now he produced a map pocked with red circles, connected by a line. The circles began at the far northwest corner of the state, and then trailed southward with minor deviations to the east and west. "These seven points, you see? Each one a crime so terrible that we're keeping the journalists from as many details as we can. Beginning first up here, at the university." He tapped the northernmost dot. "Then one after the other . . ."

"Coming south. Coming toward Fall River."

"I believe so. This last set of killings—the woman and her family—it was only forty miles north of here, and a final destination of Fall River is no guess: for this is where Dr. Jackson's packages have originated. Or so I learned when I received the remains of one, and checked the mark upon it—but even without the postal hints, you could simply follow the trajectory thus far and see that Fall River is in Zollicoffer's way, if not in his plans. And his note, you see . . . it says, right here: 'I know it is possible that you have become like me like I have become.' What if the mad professor is right? What if Doctor Jackson is as mad as Doctor Zollicoffer—though his spree has run shorter, consisting only of the Hamilton family?"

"It's a clever hypothesis," I granted.

"Then you understand why I must find this fellow, and find him soon—before he selects another family to eradicate by whatever strange means his correspondent has discovered. If he's mad like Zollicoffer, surely he will not stop."

I fell quiet, because I had no other course of action to save me.

Inspector Wolf was silent, too, the pair of us looking over the sheets that sprawled across the table between us, occupying all the tablecloth between our plates and cups. Wolf was a brilliant man himself, and for all that he spoke of these two mysterious professors and their terrible brains, I had no doubt that one way or another, this inspector would find his way to Maplecroft eventually.

I didn't dare risk him snooping about, gathering information on the ladies therein, and possibly falling prey to some creature like the one I'd seen. No, all my good sense said it'd be wiser by far to escort him, quietly inform him, and allow him to ask his questions of the "doctor" herself—if she felt up to the task.

I made up my mind to serve as a helpful go-between. He could either storm into Maplecroft on his own, like a very smart bull in a very prickly china shop; or I could gently guide him there, and thereby minimize any damage he might inadvertently inflict.

"Inspector," I said with great caution, "I believe I can help you, with regard to this Doctor Jackson. But it will require a measure of trust on your part, for the truth of the matter is peculiar beyond belief."

"Really? You know the man—or know where I might reach him? And please," he said, his eyes eager behind the round spectacles, "don't be so cruel as to direct me to the graveyard."

"Oh no, he's not dead." I glanced around, and seeing no one within earshot, I added quietly, "But the situation is not as you imagine. Doctor Jackson is a patient of mine—and is absolutely incapable of any violence at all."

"Is that so? Does he suffer some physical defect, or ailment?"

I avoided my pronouns for the moment. "Largely bedridden," I said simply. "With an advanced case of consumption, for the last several years. There's more to it, I must tell you—but first, I must swear you to a very serious sort of secrecy."

"By all means, though I'd hope that my own divulgence of police procedure ought to earn me some measure of faith. But if Doctor Jackson is incapable of murder . . . then I suppose you must fear for your patient—now that you can reasonably expect that Zollicoffer is coming."

"I'm deeply frightened, yes. Jackson is scarcely capable of self-defense with a gun in hand, and in the event that you're correct . . . Doctor Zollicoffer is in for a rude surprise. One that will certainly drive him to violence, or greater violence, since he is already so inclined."

"Doctor Seabury, I truly believe that discretion is the better part of valor, but I wish you'd speak plainly."

"You know, I think it might be easier to show you plainly. Come with me, if you would. I'll take you to Doctor Jackson, and you can see for yourself."

Emma L. Borden

❧

Every time I think we've found the worst of it, I'm mistaken. You'd think I'd quit making such assumptions—that surely, by now, nothing could surprise or appall me, at least nothing *new*. But here it comes. And here we go. And if I was at a loss before, I'm utterly drowning in confusion now.

Doctor Seabury came around again today, and he was not alone.

He was joined by a man called Inspector Wolf, a name both ludicrous and accurate. Ludicrous, because you never saw a man who looked less like a wolf: he's a short, fat thing with a squint, watching the world from behind a pair of spectacles that might not be strong enough for him. I'll grant you, he's a sharp dresser. Maybe that's true of all gentlemen from Boston. I don't know; I haven't seen a large enough sampling. But he wears black and white, and everything is pressed and shined to its appropriate degree. Cleanliness and godliness, and all that rot.

I would've preferred some warning, prior to meeting him. Then again, I would have preferred a great many things which are well outside my grasp, so there's no sense in sulking. The good doctor has done well by us—as best as he could, given the circumstances. I know he meant no harm, and likely meant only to protect us from further inquiry, but still. I found the whole thing stressful beyond belief.

(As if Nance weren't already problem enough. She's presently secured to a sturdy set of mahogany bedposts in the second guest room. Lizzie lingers by her at every spare opportunity, but I can't say there's been any real change since the other night. She moans and fusses. She struggles and whines. She chants, or asks, or whatever she's doing, to be let *out . . . out . . . out . . .* until I'm so sick of the word that I wish to stitch her lips shut and throw her into the ocean. Would that be far enough *out* for her?

God, look at me. I'm coming apart at the seams. We all are. We all must be civil, instead. I must throw away these pages, lest Lizzie should see them.

But I'll write them first.)

The doctor came by, knocking on the door around lunchtime— when I was down in the parlor and Lizzie was in the kitchen, making cucumber sandwiches. I'd made my way downstairs myself, much to my sister's irritation; now she complained she had to go up and down the stairs every time she need tend to one of us, or the other.

But I don't always need tending, and I never want it. Sometimes I want to finish dressing myself and with the help of my cane, descend the stairs like a more or less normal woman who'd care to read the newspaper in the parlor today. A woman who's sick of being sick, and can't bear the thought of lying down another goddamn moment.

So I was in the parlor, and not in my room. When the knock came, I mean.

Lizzie answered it, at first with a smile, and then with a frigid politeness that told me something was amiss. I listened for all I was worth, and before she even invited them in, I knew it was Doctor Seabury come to visit . . . and that he was not alone.

Coolly, she ushered the men inside, and that's when I was compelled to make the acquaintance of Inspector Wolf, the strangely named.

Everything about the doctor's demeanor suggested apology, and a begging of indulgence. He didn't want to do this. He didn't want to be here, he told us all, but the matter was outside his control and he had nothing but our best health and happiness in mind.

My face flushed warm, and my hands went cold. I had no idea how much Seabury had told this man, and I was not certain of the subject matter. We hide so many secrets here at Maplecroft—it was impossible to assume which one might have been transgressed.

The doctor sat on the chair opposite the settee where I rested. He fidgeted with his hat in his hand, and seemed very earnest when he leaned toward me and said, "I apologize from the bottom of my heart, Miss Borden, but it's a matter of exceptional importance that brings us unannounced."

I tried to keep from glaring when I replied, "It must be indeed, for you to surprise us like this."

He nodded hard, his eyes trying to convey something I couldn't quite grasp. I think he was trying to tell me to trust him, but that wasn't easy. Not when he knew so much, and could do such harm. "Yes, and I trust you'll forgive me if I'm direct: This is Inspector Wolf, from Boston. He wishes a word with Doctor E. A. Jackson."

I was stunned. It would have almost been easier to swallow had he offered up some greater—but less personal—secret for this out-of-towner to chew on.

"About what?" I was not quite ready to give up the game. I had my gender on my side, for once. Any man would believe the whole thing was an utter fabrication, if I swore it was so.

The inspector answered this stuttered question of mine before the doctor had a chance. "I believe that he's in terrible danger. A madman on a spree wishes to meet him, and thus far, everyone who crosses this madman's path has turned up dead."

I struggled to get a handle on the matter, all the possibilities rolling around in my brain like so many marbles. "Dead? The doctor is being hunted by a murderer?"

"A murderer many times over. We've tracked him since his first killing spree at a university, up at the northwestern end of the state, and—"

I interrupted. I couldn't stop myself. "His *first* killing spree?"

"The first of seven, all told. Perhaps more," he informed me calmly but firmly.

I didn't understand. I couldn't figure out what my publishing persona had to do with a murderer on a spree, as if we didn't have problems enough in this household. "Who *is* this murderer?" I demanded.

"Madam—" Wolf made a conciliatory stab at calming me, using less condescension in his tone than I had any right to expect, given my outburst. "He's a professor who's taken leave of his classes and his senses alike. And it's only just now dawned on me that I must be speaking to Doctor Jackson this very moment, a fact which gives me some measure of pain and pause. I made assumptions, and assumptions rarely take me anywhere useful."

I swallowed back whatever had bounced onto the tip of my tongue, and I cast Lizzie a glance. She was standing in the doorway to the kitchen, looking helpless and afraid.

(I felt a flash of sorrow, a dim flicker of memory from when we were children and she was so small when our mother was buried. She looked that way beside the coffin, except then she was holding my hand.)

For her, then. I could be brave and adult about this. The inspector was being polite, and there was always the chance he was an enlightened sort. He must've seen so much of the world; perhaps he would not be surprised by something as innocuous as a woman with a pen.

I straightened up in my seat, held my head high, and said, "Yes. I am Doctor E. A. Jackson. Or I might've been, in another time and place. For now, as you see, I am a woman confined by her own skin."

I wondered at my own strange choice of language, and he did, too—but he didn't mock it. He only said, "Women attend universities these days. They become doctors of all manner. Still, I can't blame you for preferring the secret. And . . ." He looked around the room. He took in the blankets, the canes, the extra rails on the stairs and the bloodied handkerchiefs I'd collected in a pile on the side table. "I can understand if it gives you some feeling of freedom, or escape. May I ask: What is your specialty?"

"Marine biology," I told him. "And if I had a fraction of the health I once possessed, I'd be one of those women in the university, right now. I fear little, when it comes to the gaze or scorn of men."

He was looking at Lizzie now. Recognizing her. Piecing together the rest—who we were, where Doctor Seabury had brought him. No, not a stupid man. A very quick one, and tactful when it suited him. (As for other occasions, I'm unable to say.)

"Jackson," he mused. "Not the name either one of you was born to."

Lizzie answered, "No. But beyond a certain point, names become accessories. We swap them out as needed, for the sake of peace. You understand?" she asked him, her voice calm and level. She really wasn't asking if he understood.

"I understand," he confirmed anyway. "Though I disagree. Names aren't hats to change a look, or a suit to be swapped at a whim. Words mean things."

"Then we must agree to disagree," she told him. "Now. Tell us about this man who's coming for Doctor Jackson."

"It's as I said—a teacher who's lost his mind. We found a scrap of note, left by the killer at a scene. Not as a warning or boast, but as an afterthought, I think. Maybe he simply forgot about it. It seems to have been written to the doctor."

"It only seems that way?" I asked.

"The note rambles excessively, and it makes sense only in fits and starts. Here," he said, withdrawing a folded sheet from his vest pocket. "Since I believe it was intended for you, in a roundabout way. You may as well have it."

And then he handed over the most astonishing document I'd ever set eyes on.

I read it start to finish; then I read it again . . . and a third time. All the while, my skull was boiling, cooking through the details and trying to figure out how they all fit together.

"Zollicoffris," I whispered, my attention snagging on the corruption of a name.

"Does it mean anything to you?" Wolf asked carefully.

I cleared my throat. "*Zollicoffer*," I said with more confidence. "Phillip Zollicoffer, at Miskatonic. We've been correspondents for some years, off and on."

He sat back in the chair, exhaling. "So you *do* know the man."

"I know the handwriting, and this isn't his."

"No, madam. A copy, produced by one of the Boston record keepers. But should I trust that the two of you have never met in person?"

"Trust and believe it. He has no idea who I am, or that I'm a woman."

"When was your last exchange of letters?" he wanted to know, and when I finally tore my eyes away from the paper, I saw that he was now holding a notebook and a pencil. Something told me he was always similarly prepared. For anything.

"Erm . . . I don't know. Last April, I suppose. It's been a while. My health has its ups and downs, but last April I was strong enough to roam along the shore, a little bit. With my sister's help." I cast a nod in her direction. "Sometimes Doctor Zollicoffer and I would exchange strange finds, fossils or seaweed samples. That sort of thing."

"Samples, yes. He refers to a 'sample' in the letter. Is there any light you can shed upon those particular ramblings?"

I remembered it was warm for April, the last time Lizzie and I went to the shore. It was windy but not uncomfortable, and we'd brought my wheeled chair, but I was walking a little, here and there, running my feet over the rocks in the rubber-soled slippers that help me keep my balance. I was holding Lizzie's hand, and there'd been a smell . . . some strange stink from a tide pool, and inside the tide pool I'd found the dead thing. A dead thing like nothing I'd ever seen before, nor have I seen since.

"The ugly specimen . . . ," I breathed, running my thumb along the paper. A stupid gesture. It wasn't a genie's lamp, and if I asked it for anything, it'd only give me more questions. "The one that smelled so awful. Lizzie, do you remember?"

"How could I forget?" She'd come up behind me, to read over my shoulder. I hadn't even noticed. "You made me go home and get a jar to hold it. I thought you'd gone crackers, wanting to keep that awful thing—and then when you told me you'd send it to a colleague . . . I wondered how much you must hate him."

"That's right, and I believe you said as much. But I'll have you to know that he *loved* it. He told me so, in a letter I received a few weeks later. He was fascinated with it, and he very much enjoyed inspecting and researching it. He'd come to suspect it was a rare kind of siphonophore, if I recall correctly."

"A colonial creature?" Wolf asked with a lift of an eyebrow.

Mine lifted right back at him. It wasn't a word I would've expected anyone unaffiliated with the field to know, off the top of the head. "That's right. A collection of organisms, operating as a single creature. It truly was extraordinary, even for such an extraordinary breed."

"It was disgusting," Lizzie argued. "For days afterward, I could smell it on my hands."

"It was science, and it was worth investigating." And if no one else had been present, I might've quipped about the irony of an axe murderess being squeamish about a tide pool, but we were not alone and I restrained myself.

Doctor Seabury, who'd scarcely said a thing since making his introductions and apologies, raised an interesting question. "You said he sent you a letter, some kind of response. Is there any chance you possess it still?"

I shook my head. "Oh no. I destroy all such correspondence within a week or so, or someone might come and find me out."

The inspector said, "That sounds like a shame."

"Well, it isn't. And I don't have it anymore, and I can't *imagine* what on earth a strange biology sample has to do with him going daft. And just look at this." I flipped the paper up and tapped the pertinent paragraph with my finger. "He thinks I might be mad, too—and he believes our conditions are rooted in that April sample. Or that's the sound of it, if one could be so bold as to assign meaning to this . . . message."

"But you're fully possessed of your senses," Wolf said politely. "Undoubtedly, there's no true connection to be found . . . but it may not matter. When a lunatic decides upon a fact, no evidence to the contrary can sway him. He's coming here, looking for you. He has your address, if you've been corresponding— or some portion of it, I should think."

"He knows the town where I reside, but I've always had him send his letters care of my sister, who he knows as 'L. B. Andrew,' via the general post. Mr. Katz has always delivered such mail without asking questions, and if he has any suspicions, I'd be stunned."

"You've taken great lengths to preserve your privacy, but if Zollicoffer knows the town and knows even this much about your situation . . . he's likely to find you." The inspector's face was grim and concerned, a set of expressions almost comical on the face of one so plump and pink.

Lizzie returned his expression, and put a sharp edge on it

when she said, "I assure you, we can fend for ourselves. Better than you might expect."

The doctor added, "And I'm at their disposal as well, should they require added assistance. It's been some years since the war, but I'm a good shot—and there's life in these old bones yet."

"I don't doubt it, but perhaps some police presence should be added."

Lizzie snorted. "If you can talk them into it, but I wouldn't get my hopes up. The local authorities think I've gotten away with something . . . and anything that befalls me henceforth must be richly deserved."

"You give them so little credit?"

She and the doctor exchanged a look. Seabury answered for her. "The trial made them look bad. Like they hadn't done their jobs, perhaps because they didn't know how. There is plenty of bitter blood to go around. That said, I've often wondered why you stayed here," he said to her. "Utter anonymity might elude you, but there are other places, farther away, that might have proved more welcoming."

"Fall River is my home," she said, as if that explained everything.

She did not add that my health had been a large concern. At the time, it was suggested that I might not survive such a strenuous undertaking as a cross-country move. This was part of it, yes—but also, by then we knew of the creatures and the threat to the town. She was determined to save it, though sometimes I can't say why.

And obviously, we couldn't share that with Inspector Wolf. He knew enough already, but we didn't know him—and our weird little coterie of three was intact, in that regard. Seabury had not betrayed Maplecroft. He'd only betrayed me, and only a little bit at that.

That's what I told myself, over and over.

Later, after the strange little inspector had left us, I told it to the doctor, too.

He disagreed, bless him, but I couldn't shake the sting of him knowing something so private, and sharing it.

"I only told him the truth," he said, "because if he's right— a spree killer is on his way to Fall River, and *you* are his intended target. You never know; the inspector might be in a position to help us, when the killer arrives. And if nothing else, we're now one step ahead of the fiend. We're waiting for him, and we won't be surprised by him."

"A killer," I echoed. "Dear Doctor Zollicoffer. I can hardly imagine it. He was such a . . . an intense, and bookish fellow. How that translates to murdering madman, well, I'm at a loss. And all this over a sample, just some weird specimen I found on the beach."

Lizzie's feet clomped slowly down the stairs. She'd been up there, checking on Nance. I assumed there was no news on the girl's condition, or else she would've told us about it. Instead, she pointed out something so obvious that it hadn't yet sprung to my mind.

She said, "The specimen and the murders. The creatures who come, and the people in town who are likewise losing their battles with madness. They're all connected. They're all pieces in one large, awful puzzle."

Seabury quickly agreed. "The deaths Wolf described had much in common with those I've seen in Fall River. We'd be daft if we ignored the possibility that they're related."

"But how?" Lizzie asked, with such exhaustion and desperation that my heart nearly broke for her.

"Perhaps the monsters are causing it . . . ?" Seabury suggested.

Lizzie didn't think so. "We don't know what we're fighting, not really. The creatures that come around after dark . . . they must be a symptom of something, not a cause. I can't shake that feeling, and I don't think any of this new information contradicts the possibility."

"Symptoms . . . ," the doctor mused. "Yes. We may be thinking about this the wrong way, or . . . or I don't know if there's a *right* way, but we ought to think about it *another* way."

My sister settled into the settee at the far end from Doctor Seabury. She leaned her head back and closed her eyes. "I've tried everything, but all this time I've been fighting blind. The creatures and the murders—we can think of them as symptoms, pieces of a bigger whole, but at the moment I'll be damned if I can figure out what that bigger whole might look like."

Seabury held out his hands, using them to gesture while he talked—explaining on top of his explanations. He had an idea, and he was getting excited.

"Here at Maplecroft, you've been treating all this as if it were supernatural—and reasonably enough, might I add. There's nothing natural about what's occurring, but let us approach it as science. Or more particularly, let us call it *medicine*," he said with emphasis. "If we were to examine this town as if it had contracted an illness, where would we begin? How would the first symptoms present themselves?"

Lizzie opened her eyes, and at first she stared off into the distance. Then she said, "Changes in behavior. Of ordinary people, I mean."

"All right," he said with something perilously akin to cheer. "One moment, let me find my way to some paper and a pencil . . ." And when these things were acquired, he used the coffee table for a writing desk. "Yes. So. Changes. Can you be more precise? I assume you didn't wake up one morning and find yourself in need of an axe."

Not his most delicate handling of a subject, but she didn't seem to take it amiss. She only answered, "Sleeping more."

"Sensitivity to light," I added, recalling a day when our father screamed at me to close the curtains, for the sunlight was killing him. His wife had done similar, and by the time the end came 'round, we were all living in the dark.

He echoed me as he composed. Then he said, "Now, not everyone will have all these exact same symptoms. Nance did not, is that correct? She simply fell into the catatonic state?"

"She had . . . *some* symptoms," Lizzie qualified. "She became obsessed with the basement, obsessed to distraction. She'd stare at the door so long, so hard, that it was as if she'd become a somnambulist overnight."

"Father had taken to sleepwalking, too," I pointed out. "I caught him once, in the middle of the night. I thought he was planning to jump out a window, and crawl for the ocean." That might have been a strange way to phrase it, but it's what sprang to mind.

"Somnambulism." He added that to the list.

"Changes in diet," Lizzie supplied. "That's another one. No one cooked anything anymore. Only cold food. That part happened gradually. God, I wish I'd kept some sort of journal at the time. I could've traced this better, in retrospect."

"You had no way of knowing," he told her, without taking his eyes away from the growing list of issues. And when we couldn't think of anything else, he said, "Very well, let's move on to the more demonstrable, physical symptoms in the afflicted. Tell me more about your parents."

"The eyes," Lizzie and I said at once, startling ourselves.

Then I amended the thought. "A certain dullness to them. A constantly dilated pupil . . . but then again, it's as I said—we were living in the dark."

"And eventually, they stopped blinking," my sister concluded.

Seabury paused, his pencil hovering over the sheet. "Yes. I've seen that symptom, too. In Matthew," he murmured. "I noticed it, but didn't know what it meant."

"And then the slowness comes . . . ," Lizzie said as well. The closer we came to the details of death, the more quietly all of us spoke.

"Slowness," he jotted.

I added, "Their skin—it changed, became paler. They took on a bloated appearance."

He swallowed hard, licked his lower lip, and said, "I saw it. In your stepmother. Not in time to do anything about it, but I know precisely what you mean."

"And toward the very end, they moved oddly," Lizzie said. "Jerkily, like they had difficulty with their joints. It was different from the clumsiness of moving slowly, as if half asleep—this next stage, it was violent, almost. Their arms and legs shot out, knocking things over, breaking things, hitting things . . . hitting people. Sometimes Mrs. Borden would spasm so hard that her back would arch up, and it looked like she was trying to bend herself in half. Once I thought I heard a crack, as if her ribs would not withstand the strain."

Her voice was fading, and her eyes were drifting . . . so I tried to bring her back, away from those last days, with another detail, one I'd only just remembered. "But before that, there was all that . . . well, *spit*, Doctor. Like they couldn't or wouldn't swallow anymore."

"Excessive saliva, perhaps?"

"Perhaps. All in all, I'd say it was as if they'd stopped paying attention to their bodies entirely."

"Toward the end," Lizzie went on, "they had trouble breathing. That wheezing noise . . . you must've heard it when you met the creature outside the other night. They make that sound, too. It's a sound that scrapes against your very soul."

She might have continued, but upstairs I heard Nance awaken and begin to moan.

There was a heavy thump, and a rattling sound, and a cry. Lizzie excused herself, but not before I saw the tears in her eyes.

The doctor and I gave one another pained looks, but without my sister we were out of things to talk about, so I pleaded exhaustion and asked him to see himself out. It was better that way. I would've only accused him, and been cross with him . . . for doing what he thought was best for us. But he shouldn't have done it anyway, damn him.

He should've left it up to me.

Owen Seabury, M.D.

❦

APRIL 29, 1894

The condition of Nance O'Neil is little changed as far as I can tell.

We keep watching her for signs of improvement, but all I see are signs of fever and delirium, and a grown woman who must be managed like a babe. Her hostess cares for her accordingly. Dutifully. Lovingly, I might suggest, but I'll suggest nothing further. It's no business of mine.

Speaking of cases—Inspector Wolf has retired to Boston, or to somewhere else; I'm not sure. He took his leave, at any rate, with a vow to remain in strict correspondence through telegrams, as necessary. He wishes to summon a force from his home district, or at least rouse a few curious, courageous men to keep watch over the house where the women reside. There's really no telling who would show up, should he provide such protection. I still don't even know what kind of inspector he really is.

And anyway, how he'll manage all of this without undoing Emma's carefully constructed alias, I do not know. He promised to try, and I must trust him to do his best. He's a man of principle—I'm confident enough to declare that much.

But if any men *can* be persuaded to come, what bizarre misfortune will await them? Will they see any of the creatures? Engage them? Fight them? Or will these poor fellows fall prey to them, or to the sickness which must (I will henceforth assume) accompany their presence? Should we issue them all axes when they arrive on the property, with vague instructions like "Keep these close, and you'll know when to use them"?

Maplecroft will have much explaining to do, and precious little credibility to stand upon while doing so. It is a precarious position in which these women live, and I wish I could be more help to them both. To all three, now that Nance is tied up in the situation—as completely as I am, if not more so.

I think, though the ladies resist the idea, that having a protective guard outside would be a good thing for everyone. If this professor is coming, with bizarre murders on his mind, then at least they would have some first line of defense. Other than me, that is. For it's not as if I can simply move in, and camp out in a spare bedroom.

Or is it? I'm not sure.

It may come to that, eventually. I'd be willing, if they'd be willing to have me. This house of mine has gone cold, filthy, and quiet these last few months. I miss my wife. I miss the cat we used to keep, the one that disappeared a few weeks after its mistress died. I miss having a fire in the hearth, one that I did not start myself, at the end of a long day.

But is this enough reason to impose on the Maplecroft women? Probably not.

Still, I feel that we are getting closer, together—the three of us, making progress on this terrible affliction that seems to be spread farther and wider than I'd previously expected. At the northern end of the state there have been other cases, as I described . . . and the incidents are closing in on us. Coming at us from above and below, or from the north and from the ocean beside us, too—crushing us in the middle.

Here's a stray thought, one that's been jangling around between my ears: What does this all have to do with the water?

The sample Emma sent Doctor Zollicoffer . . . it came from the ocean. And now he seems to be coming *back* toward the ocean, back to the place from whence it originated. Back to Fall River, and to the woman who picked it off the rocks and mailed it to him.

What if this is some sort of homecoming for the poor deranged fool?

Or a more horrible question still: What if he is not deranged? What if he knows precisely what he intends, and is bent toward it with precision and malice, and (what is reported to be) a keen intellect?

Surely, I am asking the wrong questions. No one could commit such acts of atrocity and still be deemed sane, regardless of his apparent clarity. But I'm finding my way toward the *right* questions.

Maybe. I think.

Courtesy of the Maplecroft crew, as I'm coming to think of us collectively . . . I have compiled a list of symptoms and cross-referenced them with my own notes, from the cases I've seen about town. I've also noted that in my recollections of these cases (in the previous weeks) one could almost make the case that my own mind has been slipping, too.

I worry myself, when I read those entries. I sound like a man on a precipice.

But no longer. I am returned, restored, and ready to solve this mystery. I hope we can solve it in time to save Nance, or if not her, then the rest of the town. Maybe the rest of the world, for all I know.

We must at least *begin* with Nance.

She's within easy reach, being held and cared for by my only full and knowing allies, and if she *does* continue to deteriorate, well, I'll have a firsthand case study that will ultimately surpass the usefulness of the Bordens, and their sad demises. At the risk of sounding morbid, they fell victim to the ailment and became violent, and eventually were killed . . . but all the while, Lizzie had no inkling that it was anything other than an isolated case. She told me herself that she hadn't paid close enough attention (a fault that makes two of us, I fear), and hadn't recorded their downfall in any useful fashion. With nothing to rely on but her memory, several years old at this point, the details have become muddled and the progress unclear.

But now we have Nance, and *she* will be my subject. I do not mean to suggest I'd experiment on the poor dear. That's not my intention at all; but I have no earthly idea how to treat her—and I can only cross my fingers that I'll stumble across some pattern of symptoms that might give me insight into her condition.

If I can figure out what's wrong with her, I can devise a system to address the problem.

I say that as if it's fact. I know it isn't. People die from known causes every day, and this isn't merely an unknown cause—it might be a supernatural one. Little wonder the Maplecroft ladies have discovered so little with any certainty.

. . .

J now describe the general progression of symptoms, compiled from my own notes previously recorded, and from a conversation with the ladies last night. Below is a general flow, not a positive timeline of events. Different people manifest the symptoms in different orders, though the general arc seems more or less the same across the board.

1. Distraction, accompanied by obsession.
2. A change in appetite, followed by a significant decline thereof.
3. Skin takes on a strange pallor, bloated appearance.
4. Dilated pupils, and the cessation of blinking.
5. Excess saliva, sometimes accompanied by digestive issues.
6. Fever (Sometimes. This one is by no means consistent.)
7. Slowness of movement, speech.
8. Cessation of talking, except certain words or phrases, which are repeated at length.
9. Difficulty controlling the limbs and joints, resulting in jerky, violent movements.
10. Difficulty breathing, resulting in a distinctive rasping sound.
11. Full-fledged madness, manifesting in self-harm or harm to others.

Lizbeth suggests that it's possible . . . God help us . . . that the final stage in this affliction might be a transformation into the wretched, twisted, shuddering, glass-toothed creatures that have been making themselves known at Maplecroft. But I'll not yet write that down in the list of symptoms, because I have my doubts. The anatomy was all wrong—not merely a warping of human physiology, but a different form altogether, some different species. It's always possible that I'm off the mark, but I think not.

Whatever these things are, I am positive they're related to the Fall River Madness; but I don't think they are victims of any illness, supernatural or otherwise. More likely, they're a vector.

Lizbeth does not seem to think so, but she's not a medical professional—she's a research enthusiast, coming at the problem with Bibles, tomes, and texts of ancient magic. I do not record this to demean her efforts, for she's accomplished such great things that I dare not call her an amateur—indeed, if there's any expert on earth with regard to this Problem, it's her.

But I wish she'd confided in me sooner. I wish she'd invited some third party to lend perspective, or at least approach the matter from another angle or two. We might have saved some of those who've fallen. Or then again, we might not. And to be clear, I understand why it's taken her this long to admit someone into her strange little circle. It took great courage—and no small measure of Emma's prompting, I suspect—for her to do so.

So, we've become a team late in the game, but now we're coming at the Problem as a united front. We must make the best of it. We must pool our resources—Lizbeth's copious research, and my education—and find some set of overlapping details, some recognizable pattern, however peculiar or unlikely.

We must save Nance O'Neil, and then Maplecroft, and then Fall River. Then Massachusetts, and the nation, and the world if it should come to that, and I fear that it *might*. The thought is so huge, it makes me choke. But if I choke, and the ladies are overcome by the terrible professor on his insane, inhuman errands . . . what hope is left?

𝔍'𝔳𝔢 spent over an hour staring at the list of symptoms, compiled above. I'm seeing something, yet I'm missing something, too. I feel like there's a thread flowing between them, and I'm not catching it.

I'm either looking too hard, or not looking hard enough.

I'm reminded of something, but reminded so barely, so faintly, that I can't lure the memory to my mind's surface. I refuse to believe that it's mere desperation or false hope bubbling up to taunt me.

There's something here. And I will find it.

Lizzie Andrew Borden

❧

APRIL 30, 1894

It's been a day of hope, and a day of misery. I'm tempted to say
that on the balance, it evens out . . . but with Nance's life and
sanity in some kind of suspension, it's difficult to lend too much
weight to what scant hope did manage to appear.

She's been thirsty. Gasping, as if for air—but not satisfied
unless it's water. She isn't passing much of it, I shudder to say,
and I do not think it's my imagination that she's taking on something of the bloated appearance of my father and stepmother.
She's not so bad yet, but I can see it coming. It's barreling down
on me like a train, and there's nothing I can do. No action I can
take to prevent or stall the matter, and it's killing me more certainly than it's killing her. After all, it might be argued that it's
only *changing* her.

But I'll begin with the hope. It came earlier in the day, after all, so I might as well present things chronologically.

Doctor Seabury beat on the door sometime right after breakfast. Emma was upstairs, and Nance was upstairs, too—in the extra room, tied down to the bed lest she wander, roam, and prove some danger to anyone. Therefore, I was alone so far as capable adults went, so I was delighted to see our visitor. I was lonely, and I hadn't even realized it.

He arrived with a wild look in his eyes, but not an unpleasant one—he had achieved some great idea! Or so he told me, as I bid him come inside and offered him coffee or tea. He picked coffee, and we both went into the kitchen while I set the percolator in motion. Without waiting for a cup, he began to speak.

"I've been looking at the symptoms, the list we made together, you and I and your sister—and I've been considering the other factors, things we may have known to serve a pattern, but not in the same way as the physical changes have presented themselves."

"I'm not certain I understand," I confessed.

"Neither do I. Not precisely, but that's all right for now. Patterns aren't always precise, and there's an exception to every rule. But we can learn something, even from the exceptions. The exceptions can show us plenty. That's what I mean—it's the exceptions that are revealing a whole picture, even if it's a picture with holes in it."

I was frankly concerned. He was talking in circles, and the line between madness and normalcy as I knew it had grown so narrow in this past year.

"Doctor, I do pray you'll explain yourself. You're beginning to worry me." Might as well be honest. After all, we were veritable partners in madness these days.

He shook his head, accepted a porcelain cup and a pitcher of cream, and offered his apologies. "I'm very sorry, though I know what you mean. There's been some shift, hasn't there been? And here, on the other side, it's difficult to retain perspective. But no, let me assure you, there's no madness or affliction to be found in me. Not *yet*."

Until just then, I hadn't noticed that he'd brought a satchel with him, but now he lifted it onto his lap and extricated a medical textbook, one which was intended as a basic introduction to common diseases and their causes. A freshman's book, I should think. He flipped it open before I had a chance to note the title or author.

A page was dog-eared, and he turned to it swiftly. "I spent all of yesterday afternoon and evening mulling the question, staring at it from every possible direction, hoping to figure out what the pattern might be. Then this morning, I shot awake with an idea. *This* idea," he told me, slapping his index finger onto a heading titled "Tetanus: Generalized, Local, and Other Manifestations."

"Lockjaw?" He couldn't be serious.

"The overlap is not one hundred percent, but I think you'll agree there's enough similarity that it warrants further investigation."

I wasn't prepared to agree to anything yet. "Convince me."

Just the invitation he was looking for. His face was positively alight. "Very well. Here's our list of symptoms, presented in and around Fall River—in various combinations and severities. Now watch the correlation: difficulty swallowing, resulting in excess salivation; fever, seizures, and spasms. All of it, right here. Symptomatic of tetanus.

"You mentioned seeing your stepmother's body arching backward—there's a term for that, you see? *Opisthotonos.* It's every bit as violent as you reported, and often results in broken bones and muscle tears. The difficulty of controlling one's body, see, it's right here in black and white. Tetanus. And in the later stages, sufferers have terrible difficulty breathing, resulting in something like the rasping we heard the other night."

"You think . . . you think the Bordens had somehow contracted tetanus?" My mind was prepared to reel, but it wasn't spinning yet. He had drawn some interesting parallels, but it wasn't enough to make me drop my wariness. It was too ordinary an explanation. It couldn't be that simple. Not when monsters walked the grounds of Maplecroft.

No. It *wasn't* that simple.

"I'm saying that what we're dealing with, this Problem we have in Fall River . . ." I almost heard the capital letter he used to start the word "Problem." "It shares some similarity in its presentation. There's a *pattern*, Lizbeth. Not a perfect one, but if we stand far enough back . . ."

Yes, imperfect to say the least. "But the eyes, the pallid skin, the bloating . . . and what of the acute and dangerous madness?"

"Well . . . pronounced irritability is a known symptom."

"That isn't the same thing, and you know it. You've seen it yourself."

He was losing his steam, and becoming frustrated with me, but he did his best to keep from showing it too harshly. "No, not exactly the same thing. It's as I said, they share a . . . a general shape, if not a clearly delineated match."

I granted him that much. "Very well, I see." It was an

overstatement to say even that much, but I didn't want to dampen his enthusiasm altogether. If there was any link between the two, any link at all, it was worth discussing—all my caution and concerns aside. Or at least tempered. "So explain it to me. Tell me everything there is to know about tetanus."

"How much do you know already?" he asked, scanning the paragraphs from the book, hunting for highlights.

"Tetanus is . . . often fatal. And caused by wounds, isn't it? Some kind of infection?"

"Yes and no," he said. "It's caused by a bacterium, *Clostridium tetani*—typically found in soil and animal feces, or the one contaminated by the other, as it were."

And then he said something that sent a spark of recognition crackling between my ears.

"It's often acquired from dirty wounds, yes, but it may also be carried in rust. At least that's the going speculation. Injuries caused by old metal seem particularly prone to—"

I cut him off there. "Rust?" I blurted out.

He lifted his eyes from the textbook. "Yes. Rust. Did I say something helpful?"

"Maybe . . . ?" I went around the corner and retrieved my axe. I held it up close, so I could see it in detail—its blocky head and smooth cutting edge, sharp enough to trim paper. I honed it almost daily, but even if it'd seen no use there was always something, always a little grime to be filed away. Always a tiny smattering of rust, there at the corners.

"Lizbeth?"

"Here," I said, returning with the weapon and placing it upon the table, beside the book. "Rust and iron . . . it's another piece of your pattern puzzle. The same puzzle, I think—though it might not look that way at a glance. In my own studies, the arcane books and clandestine tomes that I keep downstairs . . . they routinely describe how iron wards against various kinds of evil."

"And you've told me before that your axe is the only thing that truly fells them!" He was getting excited again, and I hated to admit it, but I was, too.

"It works better than anything else, though I've only tried shooting them once, to limited effect. We have Father's old war weapons, but they're a measure of last resort."

"Not half so quiet as an axe," he observed. "A wise course of action, considering."

"Well, you know . . . we wouldn't want to wake the neighbors. So if you ever hear gunshots at Maplecroft, you may assume that the end is nigh indeed. I always leave the guns with Emma," I added, though I wasn't sure why I was telling him this. It was true, but felt almost too personal to share. I shared it anyway. "That's what I mean. If there's shooting, it means they're finished with me and they're coming for her."

This grim note gave us pause, but only for a moment. "Let's not borrow trouble," he gently urged. "Instead, let's consider the possibilities. I say we should absolutely write down the axe and its attendant properties as part of the tetanus pattern, although . . ." His voice trailed off.

"Although?"

"It begs the question of whether the creatures are *infected* with the bacterium, or simply susceptible it. They do seem to . . . Hm."

"Please stop doing that. Think aloud, I beg you. I'm a terrible mind reader."

"My apologies. I was only considering that if the creatures suffer from some form of tetanus already, it seems unlikely that an added blow with a contaminated weapon would make the matter worse. Or perhaps it would." He sighed, and closed the book. "It's as I said—the pattern is far from perfect."

"But it might be worth something, after all." I pushed, a new idea working its insidious way into my mind. "What sort of treatments might one use to combat tetanus? I'm afraid this isn't my area of expertise."

"Ah, well. There are some fascinating studies on the subject overseas, with talks of vaccine prophylactics and antibody treatments."

"Is there any chance we could . . . I don't know, create these antibodies ourselves? Or import some from elsewhere? A hospital or . . . or a university, perhaps?"

"I don't see why not."

"Do you think there's any chance they may have some positive effect on Nance?"

"I have no idea. Speaking of, how is she doing?"

"No better."

He made encouraging noises that didn't do anything but annoy me, bless him. "Stick with her, Lizbeth. Keep trying, keep watching. I'll do my best to procure some of the necessary antibodies, and we'll try that approach. It can't hurt, and might help."

I asked, "Are you sure?"

"Of which point?" he countered. "Nothing's certain, and I won't insult you by suggesting otherwise."

I refused to nurture the hope that threatened to bloom in my breast. I'd come close to solutions before, and watched the mirages turn to sand as I approached. I would not let myself be disappointed so harshly again. I braced myself against further failure by asking the inevitable questions. "But wouldn't it be too late? Vaccines are preventatives, and whatever's happened to Nance, we surely have failed to prevent it."

"Tetanus is *treatable*," he insisted. "And not by any means a death sentence. All is not lost, and we have . . . it's hardly a plan, but it's a starting point."

"And if you're wrong?"

"If I'm wrong, I'm wrong. We'll try something else."

"What?" I asked, and I hated myself for the note of despair that crept into the word.

"I don't know, but we'll think of something. You and I, and Emma. And maybe this Inspector Wolf—you never know. He might turn over some rock and discover another useful path to direct us down. All is not lost," he said again. Maybe he hadn't heard himself the first time, or maybe he needed convincing as badly as I did.

I did not reply, because the words were stuck in my throat. But Nance is my all, and if she's lost, then yes. So's everything.

Emma wouldn't like the look of those last lines, but what can I do?

Emma is only dying of normal things, so far as anyone can prove. Emma has all of her faculties, and some autonomy of her own—whether she'd act upon it or not. Some days she maneuvers the stairs just fine, and others she needs waiting upon, hand and foot. I shouldn't doubt her, but so help me God, on those days I *do*.

Look at the state we're in.

Maybe it's all her fault, anyway. Maybe that stupid, stinking, putrid sample she forced me to box up and mail . . . if that's where this began . . .

If that's where it all began, and I lose Nance because of it.

If that's what it comes to. I don't know that I will ever be able to forgive her. I am strong, but I am not resilient. When my heart is manhandled it does not bounce; it shatters.

So the doctor left me with much to think about, and two women upstairs who need me all the time. He didn't look in on either of them. He offered to, but I told him not to bother. Emma was fine, and napping . . . and Nance was not fine, but there was nothing new for him to address.

I didn't tell him about the breathing trouble. I had planned to, but when he got to the part about how it's a symptom of the later stages of tetanus poisoning . . . I couldn't bring myself to say it out loud. He could be wrong. We're all throwing stones in the dark, after all.

Tetanus. So logical. So down-to-earth, quite literally. It *cannot* be that easy. If it were that easy, science would've saved us by now. There is some dark agency at work, and we would pretend otherwise at our peril.

I couldn't bear the futility of it all. That's why I told him that all was as before, and she needed no attention from him.

In short, I'm a coward who lies to herself.

And now, the rest.

The bit I've written around, and struggled to keep from writing.

It happened long after Seabury left. After supper, after bedtime. After Emma had been tucked in and Nance was sleeping, or doing a fair impersonation of sleeping; I don't know.

As for me, I was sleeping on the chaise in Nance's room. I wanted to be near her if she needed me. I wanted to know if anything changed, even if it changed for the worse. If anything changed, if anything happened . . . or let me be honest with myself, just this once: If she were to die, at least I would know.

(I grow more fatalistic by the day.)

Somehow, I fell asleep. I say "somehow" because it's never come easy to me, I don't think; I've always slept lightly, especially since Emma has required a caretaker. It's as if I stay just barely unconscious, suspended just beneath the surface, so I can listen for any calls, cries, or bells that might summon me; and if I let myself fall too deeply, I might not be able to come when I'm needed.

And the matter of the creatures, of the madness, of the Problem (as Seabury put it) has only made things worse. And so has Nance's treachery, for it fulfilled the worst of these nightmare fears.

But somehow, I slept.

It was pure exhaustion, I suppose. I could only brace myself against it for so long, and the recent weeks had taken a toll too great for me to withstand. So there, on the chaise, I closed my eyes. At least this time it wasn't Nance's treachery, but treachery from my own body that put me under so soundly. Unless there are worse forces at work than Mrs. Winslow and her numbing tinctures.

Regardless, I did not hear Nance rise.

I do not know how she undid the ties that held her to the bed. I did not see her escape. I did not watch her tiptoe across the floor. I do not know if she saw me, or if she paused to look down upon me, or offer some kiss of affection—but I know how likely that last part is, so I'll put it from my mind. It only makes me feel worse.

I do not know how I slept through it, and I'm surprised that Emma did.

But Nance arose; I'm not sure when.

She extricated herself; I'm not sure how.

She found her way to the washroom, a large, modern one here on the second floor. It has always been one of my favorite things about this house—with its wide dimensions, elevated iron tub on lion's feet, and all the lovely pipes feeding back and forth, in and out of the wall. I have always loved that room.

I awoke to the sound of dripping water, so soft but so near, I thought it must've begun to rain. And in my half-sleep state, I wondered at the nighttime shower raining down outside, pattering against the windowsills. Rainstorms are such soothing things. So pleasant for sleeping through.

But the drip, drip, drip, was not the last of April's showers, and something in the back of my mind insisted that I must collect myself and investigate.

I did so unwillingly. I was so tired, and so heavily asleep. Reluctantly, with awful slowness, my mind dragged itself up to alertness, or something like it. The effort to lift my head was herculean, and unkind.

Drip, drip, drip.

Coming from the washroom down the hall. There was no other water source so close by. Had I left a tap loose?

I rubbed my eyes. I forced them to focus.

And on the floor beside the bed, I saw the ties I'd used to keep Nance secure. Tangled but unknotted, lying in a loose heap.

My heart stopped.

It started again, banging like a hammer, and I threw myself from the settee—flying forth from my blanket and discarding it into some corner, somewhere. I ran to the bed, where the imprint of her body remained. There was no sign of how she'd undone the ties, but I did not have time to wonder about it—not when the water was there in the bathroom, drip, drip, *dripping*, and I knew where she must have gone.

Any minute I expected to hear the clang of Emma's bell, but I didn't, and for a tiny, horrible moment I wondered if she was even alive anymore. She might have died in the night, expiring from her persistent illness; or no, I'm lying again—because it crossed my mind that Nance might've gone on a spree like the rest of the maddened victims, or like so many of them have.

But surely not. Surely she would've started with *me*. (I deserve that much, don't I?)

I dashed to the corridor. Washroom to my left. Emma's room to my right. One ringing with the delicate patter of water on water. One silent as a tomb.

I went to the left.

In the washroom, the light was not on but I could see enough to know what I was up against. The tub was filled to overflowing, and a thin trickle of water spilled slowly, dripping over the lip, splashing down to the white hexagonal tiles, into a puddle that covered half the floor. My feet were soaked before I noticed. The water was spreading, pooling, creeping out into the hallway and the floors might be ruined but I hardly noticed, and did not care.

I stood half paralyzed in the doorway, until I shook myself lucid enough to fumble for the gaslight switch. When the hiss came and the light sparked it was too much—entirely too much—and I winced against the sudden brightness, but I could not look away.

I knew what was in the tub, so full of water, with a placid

surface unbroken by anything except the coiling tendrils of Nance's hair. Moving languidly. Stirred only by the persistent stream that still trickled from the tap.

I wondered what it meant, that the tap was mostly off. Either she'd been there an hour or more to fill it, at that rate, or she'd thought to turn it off when she was finished filling the tub. I told myself that must be it—it must have been a deliberate act, and she was still alive, still herself inside that muttering shell of skin.

Honestly, I had no idea. I still don't know. Perhaps I never will.

But there she was. Wholly submerged, unmoving.

I moved, but I did it slowly, sluggishly. The whole moment was dreamlike in its stickiness, like I could walk toward the tub forever and ever and never reach it. Except that I *did* reach it, and I looked down, and I saw her wearing the oversized nightdress of mine that positively swam on me, as my stepmother would have put it—and I hated the phrase, because yes, it swam and billowed, and it was almost translucent. I could see every nook and curve of her skin through the light white cotton, pouring around her body, floating there, suspended just beneath the surface. Eyes wide-open, staring up toward me, but not at me. Mouth slightly parted. Wholly submerged. Unmoving. Ophelia drowned, needing only the flowers in her hair to make it uncanny.

There were no flowers. Only the body, almost as pale as the nightdress, almost as translucent. Serene, I wanted to say.

My throat was full of fear, full of my heart—which had leaped there and stuck like the inconstant bastard it truly was.

I didn't know what to do.

I should pull her out. That's what I thought. I should lay her on the floor, roll her over and over, push the water from her lungs, and command her to breathe, *breathe*, goddammit. I should send immediately for Seabury, and order him to revive her if I could not, because there was no chance she was dead—it simply was not an option, for this motionless, cold, empty thing to be my Nance, who had come to an end in this manner.

I was shaking so hard that I could scarcely control myself, teeth audibly chattering though it was not so very cold. It was only the water that slipped between my toes. It was only the sight of Nance, calm at last, cocooned and finished.

I reached out with one quivering hand and touched the water's edge, where one long lock of her hair had crept over the side of the tub, drawn there by some unseen, unfelt eddy, dangling damply.

I touched it.

Her eyes jerked toward me, and I screamed.

I screamed first with shock and then with hope, and the sound of it broke whatever spell I'd wound around myself, around her, the washroom, Maplecroft, Fall River.

I shoved my hands into the water and seized her, tried to haul her out in one fell swoop, but she was too heavy for that—even bone-dry, and even when she didn't fight me, I didn't know if I could lift her up over the side, but I tried—I flung my entire being into the effort. Bringing her up into the air, like a baptism.

She wanted the reverse. She fought me.

Her hands moved swift as minnows, shoving me back and shoving herself deeper. The whole tub rocked, heavy as it was. The whole room was soaked, and I was soaked, too. Nance writhed, demanding wordlessly to be left where she was, but I was not leaving her there. She was not drowning right in front of me.

. . .

No. She was not drowning.

Even in the violence and water that moved us both I could see it, how she wasn't choking or bubbling, and she didn't gasp or gurgle under the water. She simply did not breathe, and it didn't bother her in the slightest as far as I could see.

Well, it bothered the hell out of *me*.

Emma's bell was ringing, ringing, ringing, off in the background someplace, like the water had been dripping in the back of my awareness not five minutes previously. She was alive, then. I'd like to say that relief washed over me, but here while I'm being honest, the only thing that washed over me was the tepid bathwater that Nance splashed out in vast, violent arcs as she rallied her resistance.

But Emma was alive, yes. And that was good, a good thing to know, there in the back of my awareness. I would not worry about her. I had more pressing problems. Frantic, coiling, flailing problems, for Nance was running out of water and there was less and less for her to cling to, barely a foot's worth to hold her, and she was determined to remain there.

Her foot shot out for the handle and to my great surprise, she grazed it—and water burbled out from the tap.

"No!" I shrieked at her, reached one arm over and wrenched it off.

Her hands pushed against my face, not clawing exactly but not showing any tender gentleness, either. I blocked them, left and right. I used my hands to stop hers, and to hold her wrists when I could catch them—but it was like grasping buttered eels, and I was getting tired.

At first I thought that she was getting stronger, drawing

some resilience from our struggles, as if it fed her to fight me; then in a moment's instinct . . . some weird little snap of connection, I had an idea: I reached for the drain plug and pulled it.

She shrieked, there under what water remained. I could barely hear it, just a wet warble that could've come from the middle of the ocean. I halfway thought that her cry would become an earsplitting wail when the water was gone, like that liquid buffer was all that stood between me and her wrath.

She twisted in the tub, feeling for the drain, trying to cover it with her feet, her hands, her shoulders; but I pulled her back, away, and when the water spilled down it wound itself in a circle, and then it was gone, and she wasn't shrieking anymore.

She was gasping, but not for air. She was gasping for water— I could see it in her eyes, where there was terror if not recognition. Bathwater gushed in coughed-up waves over her chin, down her cheeks, into her hair, and her body convulsed as I ripped it from the tub.

(Not a baptism but a birth, and a terrible birth at that.)

She fell on top of me, knocking the wind from my lungs, but only briefly. I locked my arms around her and rolled until I was atop her, able to pin her in place and holler her name, over and over, demanding that she look at me and remember me, and understand that I loved her and was calling for her. I had to call louder than whatever else was calling her; I had to make myself heard over this maelstrom in the washroom, in her head, in my house.

I do not know if she heard me or not.

When she weakened enough to allow it, I let go of her arms and shoved at her chest, determined to force the last of the water free. She would breathe again. I would *make* her breathe again.

She cried and cried and cried, and the sobs became drier and drier.

I considered that I might've made a mistake. She was weakening, failing right there on the floor beneath my well-intentioned ministrations, though she'd been vigorous in the water. But no—in the water, that was not Nance. That was something else, whatever had overtaken her. And I meant to banish it. Cast it out, like Christ with the Legion, if I might dare to be so bold. And why shouldn't I? Fortune favors the bold. Maybe Christ does, too.

Her head rolled to the side, and she panted like a nervous dog—that swift, shallow breathing through the mouth that's one part plea and one part self-comfort. And still she breathed, even after I'd stopped pressing on her chest and belly. Even after I tried to take her face in my hands, but she closed her eyes and I let her go. Back and forth her head lolled. Back and forth, until I stopped it with a firm hand on her chin. I grabbed her with surprise and urgency, and I held her face immobile.

I'd seen something.

I wanted to see it again.

"What was that . . . ?" I asked quietly, holding her chin aside, stretching her neck. There: a small slit of skin, fluttering. As light as if it'd been cut with a razor, a tiny fillet of flesh that wrinkled when I touched it. I felt the two more horizontal flaps before I saw them. That made three altogether, with the start of a fourth, not quite as long. Not quite as defined.

All of them sucked shut against her throat, lying so flat that if I hadn't known they were present, I would've never noticed them. I tried to touch them again, but felt almost nothing. The faint texture of paper cuts, or maybe the delicate, almost not-even-there-ness of a small fish's fins.

Her lungs were working again, heaving and hauling air in and out of her chest. It was a ragged, damp sound and I hated it, even though I'd been fighting for it all this time. She was breathing, and she still was not herself—no more so than when she'd been below the surface, taking oxygen through what must have been gills.

I write the word again: gills.

Nance had grown gills, or been granted them, or acquired them as part of her affliction—I don't know. But she *had* them, and I am not such a great liar that I could pretend otherwise.

Whatever had happened, however she was being changed, she wasn't changed all the way *yet*. I'd pulled her out in time, even if doing so had still failed her in some awful way I did not understand. Her body still functioned, if reluctantly, the way it ought to—and not through some unnatural mechanism that ought to be left to the fish in the sea.

"Nance—" I begged her, and it sounded like I was crying, too, but I wasn't. My eyes were the only thing dry in the entire room, and I don't know why. Maybe it'd finally happened: I was all cried out.

Nance didn't respond, except with that awful wheeze that had become the sound of her breath.

From down the hall came the never-ending ringing of Emma's bell, but I scarcely heard it. It'd become just another noise, like the dripping of the faucet or the hissing fuss of something that struggles to breathe air. Just another sign of horror, another note of impending awfulness that I was no doubt powerless to stop.

Over my shoulder I shouted, "Emma, I hear you—*shut up!*"

The ringing stopped, from surprise or satisfaction I cannot say. But it stopped, and that was all I wanted. That, and for Nance to breathe and open her eyes and look at me.

Might as well have wished for the moon.

Owen Seabury, M.D.

APRIL 30, 1894

LETTER TO CHRISTOFF DANE, c/o UNIVERSITY OF
RHODE ISLAND, KINGSTON

Hello there, Christoff—and I hope all is well at that wonderful
new university of yours. Not quite ten years on, is it? You must
be very proud; I've heard only exceptional things about you and
your research programs, particularly with regard to that very
fine agricultural experiment station; and although I realize it's
been some time since last we spoke, it is because of that station
(and its general subject matter) that I write you today.

To be more specific, I'm interested in your progress and prac-
tice concerning a vaccine against *Clostridium tetani*—a vaccine
which I'm led to understand you've developed with some degree
of success. Or if not you, personally, then I seem to recall that
you're performing further development and refinement upon it. I

hope you'll forgive my lack of clarity on the matter, as it's been a trying series of months, and I'm not at my sharpest right now.

I suppose you think my request must come out of the clear blue, but I must impress upon you the dire nature of my inquiry: Here in Fall River, just a handful of miles to your east, we find ourselves afflicted with a particularly virulent strain—one that's striking willy-nilly throughout the town. I can't say how it's evolved in its present aggressive state, only that I'm somewhat confident that this is indeed the bacterial foe we face.

I had considered taking the morning to ride out and visit you in person, so that we might have this conversation over coffee or breakfast, but I pray you'll understand why I've decided against it. My reasons are many and varied—not least of all because I have a sudden new wave of desperately ill people suffering from the condition, and to the last man, woman, and child, they seek my guidance. And besides that, what if it turns out Fall River is inadvertently incubating some terrible strain that might spread? I could not live with myself if I were to carry it with me, against my knowing, and pass it along to you or your students.

I realize that this must sound paranoid, but I ask you to trust me. I would also ask you to remain where you are, and to speak of this to no one. I do not wish to cause any panic. I only wish to contain the situation before it grows wholly out of control.

Ours is a little place, close-knit and quiet. Our people prefer their privacy, even in the face of danger. Please allow me to make some serious effort toward solving the crisis quietly, before we take the next obvious step and involve more public authorities.

I honestly believe that we can solve this problem. If I did not, I would've summoned higher assistance already.

To this end, I was hoping I could impose upon you for any

literary works you may have on hand—any lesson plans, research notes, or the sort—that you could share with me. I have access to a very good laboratory, and there's a chance I can generate a vaccine or treatment of my own if I could only learn what is required; but I do not know how many days that is likely to take, and we seem to be short even on hours. So if there's any chance you have any serums already made, I would beg of you to send whatever you can spare with all haste.

It's a peculiar request, I know—and I'm giving you few enough details that you must wonder at my sanity. You could absolutely be forgiven for doing so! I'm exhausted and frightened, and overwhelmed, if you want the truth. I fear that I'm standing on the brink of some tipping point, between this town and wholesale peril . . . and it terrifies me to feel such responsibility.

But I know what I'm looking at. The connections between the affliction are clear—there are very sharp parallels between what I'm seeing, and an advanced strain of tetanus, so I have been shown a direction and a pattern, and I will extrapolate the rest with cunning and science.

(It is not my imagination that leads me to this conclusion; it is research and observation, and consultation with another great scientist who lives quietly here in town.)

I will with all haste reimburse you for any expense you may incur through the university, should you opt to assist me. Likewise, I shall send this missive by expedited courier from the contents of my own pockets—and anyone you send with a speedy response will surely be compensated in kind.

This is an emergency, Dane. But it is also an opportunity to do something great, to resolve a frightful mystery, and contribute to the annals of scientific knowledge. And on a more personal note, it might well save the lives of my neighbors and friends, who fall one by one to this sickness that I can't thwart with my own limited, conventional devices.

If there is any aid you could lend me, I would be forever grateful. The whole town will be in your debt eternally, and I will see to it that should we succeed in our lifesaving interventions, the papers will give all credit and praise to you and your department. Fall River may serve as your case study, and you may build your department upon its salvation . . . or if not, then you may rest assured that no mention of your involvement will ever become known.

I would not ask you to gamble your reputation on my inconstant hunches. I am prepared to absorb all the risk, and all the guilt should I fail. I am only offering you the chance for public approval and, I should think, a fine endowment for your program—that your research may continue, better funded, with better equipment.

Please, Dane. I am begging you.

Send word with haste?

Sincerely,
Owen Seabury, M.D.
Fall River, Massachusetts

Phillip Zollicoffer. *Physalia Zollicoffris.*

❦

Doctor E. A. Jackson is a slippery soul, but I'll find him yet. I feel him, his general presence, his life pulsing somewhere yet to the south—but I knew that much already, so it might only be a psychosomatic sense (in addition to an address on a package) that draws me toward Fall River, origin of his missives.

To the origin of the sample.

For some weeks, the sample has been diminishing.

It was not my imagination, though that's what I told myself at first. At first, what was there to mention? Precious little. An added space inside the jar where she lived, a greater presence of fluid and a lesser presence of her amorphous bulk. In time, I could see the sun's rays through the glass if I held it to the light, so little of her remained.

But that was before I moved at night. Before the sun became too much for my eyes, now so sensitive that I can see every line of every blade of grass . . . in the darkest night without a moon. And now I am reminded of the strange, small things that live in caves and go white, for there is no illumination by which they might compare their colors. I recall small crawling things with eyes that look like milk inside a cup, yet still they *see*—for all they are called blind.

Physalia has left me, even as she has come to me. I knew it when I rose one dusk and dressed myself, counted out the slim contents of my earthly lot, and saw that what remained of her could've fit in the palm of my hand. Not dead, not dying. Living stronger than before, and needing less of herself to do so. That which was left, fit easily in my mouth.

And I do not carry her jar anymore.

I buried it beneath the floorboards of a house, one perhaps forty miles from my goal. The house burned behind me, so I do not think it's likely to be discovered anytime soon. Not unless she decides that it ought to be found.

She might. She is a mystery to me, beloved in all her uncertainty.

I can imagine a day, some months from now when the weather begins to cool, when all the charred beams and all the black cinders and all the white ash that pooled in the corners, dusting the remains like sand dunes or snowdrifts . . . I can see the foundations being cleared. I can see workers prepared to build anew on the old spot, undeterred by anything that happened there.

Brave men. Or ridiculous ones. Doomed ones, I should think, regardless.

But who among us isn't?

For a while I dithered, considering how I ought to dispose of her carriage, that ridiculous jar with the ghost of an old jam advertisement on the side, and the residual fluids of her body left within. I ought to take it to the ocean, perhaps? I ought to bury it in some holy spot, some aquarium or castle? Some church? Some intersection between two streets where no men ever walk, but the night creatures pass back and forth—knowing one another and saying nothing, exchanging only glances and signs . . . ?

She did not express an opinion.

If I am forced to speculate, I might conclude that she does not care, and it does not matter. Regardless, I cannot shake the feeling that whatever she leaves behind is too holy to discard, and too powerful to remain hidden. I am only an acolyte, but a devout one.

So I did not bury it deep, and I did not hide it well. I only left it there for later, in case she should find some use for it—or have some interest on another day. I know where it is. I will retrieve it upon her request, should she make one.

Sometimes she speaks to me so clearly. Sometimes her silence shames and worries me, though she tells me it should not. All I can offer her is my service, and my best execution of her will, as I understand it.

She says that we are right, and we are pleasing unto her. She says we are doing Her work, and that our journey will be completed soon enough.

I trust her, and I trust Her.

. . .

(I have only recently come to understand that there is not one, but many. Likewise, there are many, and there is One. The many I have become, having taken her into myself—having been blessed with that task, a better vessel than a jar. And the One who waits for us, *Physalia zollicoffris* and Doctor Jackson alike, on the other side of this strip of dirt, where the ocean meets the rocks, and we will walk upon the sand. But briefly.)

She tells me—not she who lives within me, but She who calls from without—She tells me that we are not alone together, the doctor and I. Through Her mind I sense another set of many, pinpoints of light that cluster together for warmth or comfort. I see them flickering as individuals, operating as one.

I know how this feels, but I do not know what this means . . . unless the doctor has become as I have become (this I have long suspected), and has taken on others with his form. Yet my gut suggests it isn't quite so, that the small swarm of lights I feel at Fall River are too distinct to operate on one directive—but what do I know of the Mother's wants? Perhaps the doctor has some greater favor in Her eyes, having found *Physalia* first, and shared her so kindly with me. It might be the proximity to the ocean. It might be anything.

It feels like a woman. Or if not a woman, than a womanlike thing—a creature or creatures who birth and bleed, and so it is fitting. So it is right, I have no doubt. I have only questions, and they are not important questions.

All will become clear in time. And not much time, at that. Only as much time as it takes me to make these last few miles into town, and inquire more precisely if I cannot follow the beacons She lays out before me, but I do not think it will come to that.

I do believe that the nearer I draw to the water, the louder Her voice will ring. And if I am wrong, I will only be a little wrong. If I am wrong, I will wear my professor skin and ask polite questions of polite people, who will politely provide the information I require; and if She tells me they should be left, I will leave them. If She tells me they are to return to dust, I will grant that, too. I will grant Her anything in my power, for I have no power except what She sees fit to lend me.

I owe Her all.

I will give Her all. I will be Her humble servant on land, a lamp unto the feet and a light unto the path of those whose ways have grown dark. And when She calls me back to the water, back to Her arms, I will sing hallelujah and praise Her name.

For all the rest of my days.

Forever and ever. Amen.

Christoff Dane, M.D., Ph.D.,
University of Rhode Island, Kingston

❧

MAY 2, 1894

Hello in return, my long-lost colleague—and though I'm glad to hear from you, of course, I do find myself appalled at the circumstance, and I hope this response is timely enough to be some benefit to you. I'm including what samples I have on hand, and which I can afford to lose without compromising our ongoing experiments, so you will find included in this package, the following:

Three vials of tetanus immune globulin, which is not strictly a vaccine—but a preparation made from the serum of an infected horse. The antibodies ought to provide immediate short-term treatment and protection to any very recently afflicted (or potentially afflicted) person, but it is not a long-term prophylactic.

Three vials of tetanus toxoid, which is to say, a volume of the bacteria itself, treated with formaldehyde.

I'm also sending a sample batch of the live bacteria, carefully enclosed—though it should be noted, it cannot survive or grow for long without a steady supply of air. Handle it with the utmost care—I am trusting you to do so!—and see to it that it does not fall into the hands of any unsavory persons, as it is a dire poison. I would hate to see it transformed by some unsavory whim into a weapon.

But should you need to manufacture more treatments, you'll find that having the live bacteria (separated from fecal and soil samples) will make your production faster and easier. Otherwise, the process is a great rigmarole of back-and-forth between infected hosts, and hosts with successful antibodies. (The process is time-consuming and it sounds like you don't have time to start from scratch.) If you have access to a good laboratory, as you say, then the accompanying notes ought to help you get a fresh supply under way more or less immediately. Or within an afternoon, I should say instead.

The rest of what follows in this letter is an aside—should you feel like you lack the time to read or appreciate it, then put this note away and return to it later, and you'll hurt no feelings of mine.

The vaccine for tetanus is only recently derived, in the Koch laboratories—by a German named Behring, and a Japanese colleague named Kitasato. Together, they were seeking a solution to not only tetanus, but diphtheria as well. They developed their antitoxin in much the same way we do here, at our facility—by infecting a small research animal, collecting the blood, and then passing it along to a stronger animal, such as a horse. From the horse's blood, the antibodies are extracted, processed, and developed into the vaccine.

For all of that back-and-forth, it's still brilliant in its simplicity, I would argue, and by all reports it is highly effective. Here at the university, we are building on their research, but cannot take the credit for spawning it; and it comes thirty years too late for men like you and me to really run it through its paces.

Can you imagine if we'd had access to such a thing during the war? How many lives we could've saved?

Maybe not the worst of them, but there will always be an outlying case or two that can't be cracked with conventional methods. For example, I do not know if the Behring-Kitasato antitoxin would have much effect if deployed against cephalic tetanus, for the bacteria digs in and holds down tight, when it settles into the inner ear. (And there were so many head wounds, you'll recall. Or perhaps you'd prefer not to. I know I'd sleep better at night not remembering the lion's share of what I witnessed on those fields.)

Ah, well.

There's little we can do about the past, but to do it honor, we must turn all our efforts to the present and the future—and save what lives we can, using what knowledge we may glean and assemble between us.

You're still doing God's work, Seabury. I'm proud to call you a friend and colleague, and I wish you the very best with your efforts there in Fall River. If there's anything else I can do, any assistance I can provide—or advice, or supplies—please do not hesitate to ask.

Yours,
Christoff

Emma L. Borden

❧

I can't rely on anyone anymore.

Lizzie may as well have gone deaf to the bell; I suppose if I fired a warning shot or two into the ceiling, she might grow curious enough to come check on me. Maybe a shot in my own temple would be warning enough to bring her around. Maybe it would take her days to notice.

Doctor Seabury's a lost cause, too, given that he couldn't keep the one secret I most needed kept, or *wanted* kept at any rate. His heart was in the right place, but mine is not—mine is trapped here, and has so little in the way of escape . . . what am I to do? What if the inspector, that pink-faced baby in a suit, makes my alias known? I'd lose even this one little tie to the world beyond Maplecroft, when I need it now more than ever.

I say that . . . but the truth is, it's been weeks since I wrote or researched.

I too have become lost in this Problem, and I don't know the way out. No one does, unless it's Doctor Zollicoffer, maddened and lost in his own private way.

Or that's what I believe. I do not consider for a moment that he was always a maniac. He was a decent, gentle man. A nervous one, and even a fussy one, after a fashion, but a good one. Not a killer, bent on a spree. Not a murdering bandit, but my *friend.*

Anyway, if he's no longer my friend (and indeed has become everything that everyone accuses him of) . . . there's precious little I can do about it. I can't run. I can't hide. I can only hole up and wait, with Father's gun by my nightstand and enough bullets to defend myself for ninety seconds, if I'm lucky.

I should not be forced to beg for my sister's aid.

I am fully aware that she's given it freely, and for years now. (Has it been years? Dear God. Years indeed.) But I did not choose my condition, and I have no other recourse. No husband or lover of my own to prop me up and carry me onward toward the grave, like Lizzie will carry Nance any day now.

Is that too harsh? Well. It must be harsher still to pretend otherwise. No one benefits from such deception.

Contrary to Lizzie's denials and insistence, the girl grows worse by the day, by the hour. The other night's adventure in the washroom was not some climax; it was only the logical progression of whatever afflicts her, as it afflicts this town—and the end result will be one of two things: She'll die, or she'll kill us all.

She's changing. Turning into something piscine, or you could make the case for it. The gills she's developed are small and unsatisfactory for oxygen, not for a creature of her stature; but they will grow if given the chance. Before long, she won't be able to breathe air anymore. That's my suspicion. And when that happens, what will Lizzie do? Put the damned wretch in an aquarium? Turn her loose at the ocean's edge? Leave her in the tub, close off the washroom, and keep her as an exotic pet?

Really, I am at my wits' end.

If it were up to me, I'd see her finished already. It'd be a kindness, and I think Seabury would agree with me there. Or perhaps he wouldn't. He bears no specific love for the girl, but he's fascinated by her. Quietly, he confessed to me that he does not expect her to survive any more than I do, but in seeing how she dies, we might learn how to save everyone else.

He's a grim fellow, but I suppose he has every right to be. If the war hadn't made him so already, surely our company would've done the trick.

I wish I still liked and trusted him. I *want* to like and trust him, but the affection isn't there anymore—even though he now tries to confide in me, as if he has a secret large enough to trade for the one he broke.

Even so, he's virtually all I have.

Lizzie still sees to it that I'm bathed and dressed and fed, but otherwise ignores me in favor of watching Nance struggle to breathe.

She's torturing herself, and I can't stop her, but I can't help her, either. Except for my correspondents, she's been my only companion since Father and Mrs. Borden died—and we are sisters, after all. The age difference notwithstanding, the bond should be greater than this, shouldn't it? I should not have to grovel, should I?

If I were the sort to look on the bright side, I might smile piously and thank God for the time we've had together thus far, and the care with which she's provided me. I'm fortunate for that, and also for the inheritance that would keep me convalescing in relative comfort even if she were to decide she's done with me, and have me sent away.

But it bites. It feels like betrayal, every time she walks past my room and I call her name, and she pauses only to reply over her shoulder that she'll check on me in a minute. I don't always want to be checked on. Sometimes I'd only like a word, or someone with whom to confer about the matters at hand. The Problem.

I'm not helpless. Not like she thinks. But I do need help, and I need a friend. I need my sister, and she feels more greatly needed by some tart she pulled off a stage and into her lap. They carried on like fools together, and now Lizzie carries on like a fool alone, while the girl languishes, transforms, and dies.

I hope she dies quickly.

Oh, that looks awful on paper! But it's not the first time I've said it, and it's still true. I hope she goes sooner rather than later, not entirely for selfish reasons—though I have those reasons in plentiful measure. I must also hope she passes in peace, and with speed. While there's any dignity left.

That's another conversation I must have with Lizzie, then. As soon as I can get her attention for five minutes. If the Problem comes for me, I want her to finish me with her axe before it ever comes to this. That's what I want. I will write it down more formally, on some official-looking paper and present it to her, in case she needs the reminder.

Should the time come.

I hope it does not. But if it does, I don't want to be the burden Nance is . . . not to Lizzie, and not to myself. I'm heavy enough on my sister's life as it is. As she reminds me, daily, even without words.

And now Doctor Phillip Zollicoffer is coming here, for me.

That's its own kind of burden, isn't it? If I'm the lure that draws him, and he homes in on me like a pigeon, then the responsibility for this Problem is *mine*. It's my burden, the only one I'm fit to bear, even if it proves to be the greatest yet . . . all because of that stupid sample. All because of our address, or at least our town—scrawled loosely on a package and sent upstate.

I wonder if Lizzie's thought about it like that. I wonder if she blames me, and this neglect is how she penalizes me for bringing this down upon our heads. Who knows? She's folded so tightly into her own box of sorrow that these things may well not have occurred to her.

I hope it hasn't. I hope she's only preoccupied, and not hateful. I don't want her to hate me, like I hate her lover—as if I'm some interloper in need of constant care, and unable to contribute anything except chaos, by accident if not design. I want her to love me and comb my hair, and read the newspaper to me at night beside my bed, like she once did.

I want my sister back. Or maybe I only want Nance gone.

Either way, I'm a horrible person. I deserve whatever becomes of me.

On second thought, to hell with it. I've only been devoted, only been her supporter and companion when *she* had no one else, either. Let us spiral down together, then, because neither one of us can go it alone. I've been her captive audience and her character witness all this time, and if she wants to blame me for things beyond my control, then she deserves whatever becomes of her, too.

We all do, I guess.

I hear the door downstairs. The doctor's here, I think. If it isn't him, then God only knows. Tonight I haven't the strength to go find out.

Owen Seabury, M.D.

❦

The Maplecroft laboratory is a strange place, if clean, well stocked, and well lit. Any university or hospital would be proud to have such a variety of tools and equipment, and indeed, I'm inordinately fortunate that she trusts me enough to leave me here, to my own devices. Especially considering what has become of Nance after her foray downstairs.

I wonder why it changed her so, and yet it leaves my mind more or less intact.

I wonder if I'm wrong about the latter.

Well, I'm not *completely* wrong. That much is obvious, for I have the willpower and acumen and clarity of thought to follow Christoff's notes and sort the samples he has provided me. I've also begun to incubate the live bacteria, for I'll need more of it down the road. I'm developing my theory, fleshing it out by degrees. It might be a bad one; it might lead nowhere at all, but it's more than I had a week ago, so I will pursue it all the same.

Lizzie has been helping some, for she's intrigued by my speculation and sees at least enough merit to show an interest. She's such a sharp woman; it's such a pity what's become of her life, and her sister. Speaking of the sister, I do wish Emma would join us; but between her health and her general aversion to me these days, she remains upstairs. I do not know if she's capable of descending the basement steps.

But I shouldn't underestimate her.

In truth, I have no idea what she is or isn't capable of. I thought I did, at one time. I thought I knew a lot of things, but I've been proven wrong about so much . . . now I'd rather steer clear of assumptions. I think Wolf would be pleased to hear me say it. He doesn't like assumptions, either.

Though still I assume Emma's mad at me for sharing her secret. I don't understand why she was so angry. I only told Wolf about her pen name in order to protect her. To protect everyone here. She knows this. She's admitted this. So why harbor the grudge?

Women. I'll never understand them. It's a wonder any of them understand one another.

But Lizzie and Nance, *they* certainly had an understanding. No sense in pretending that the arrangement was sisterly or otherwise; I know how the world works. I also know how to politely pretend the contrary, for although I find it troublesome, when all is said and done it's (as I've said here before, and as I continue to try to convince myself) no business of mine—except for how it complicates things at Maplecroft.

And really, I don't think this would be any less complex if

Nance were a sister or beloved friend. Regardless of their relationship, Lizzie feels such guilt for what's happened. She owns it. She
feeds it, and it grows.

(For that is the way of all things richly nourished.)

Nance remains upstairs, tethered to the bed, her body shifting
around—her organs and bones wrestling for some new arrangement within her skin. It's a fright to behold, but Lizzie insists on
beholding it. She spends most of her hours seated at that bedside, reading newspapers or books aloud, holding Nance's hand
when she remains still long enough for that kind of contact.
This is Lizzie's penance. I think she sees it that way. It's a punishment she deserves, not assistance she provides. Nance will
recover with or without her. She'll die with or without her.

I just wish Lizzie could look away for longer periods of time,
for if I could drag her away more frequently from her self-
imposed exile on the second floor, she might be more use to me
as an assistant.

That might be unfair. She observes the test case of Nance,
and that is helpful. She writes everything down, every bead
of sweat, every spasm, every murmur. God, if that isn't self-
punishment, I don't know what is. Maybe she'd call it devotion,
or madness.

Whatever it is, it keeps her from the laboratory, and that
means I'm largely left alone down here.

As a precautionary measure (on the off chance there's any
measure that might hold water), we've moved every stray scrap
of iron on the premises to this place in the basement, and stacked
it upon the cupboard beneath the floorboards. It's not an elegant
solution, and it's created a pile of rusting detritus that I must

occasionally navigate around during my activities . . . but I do think it has somewhat muted the call of the weird green stones stashed therein.

Most of the time, I can work without thinking about them. Most of the time, I am only aware of them as a very dull hum somewhere beneath the pile of buckets, horseshoes, fireplace implements, railroad spikes, part of an old bed frame, several skillets, a pie pan, and whatever else Lizzie was able to scare up. (My only contribution was part of a decorative garden trellis and a shovel head.)

It's nice to have this laboratory, even if it's haunted, and even if it isn't mine. It's good to have a clean, quiet place to work, and all the necessary components to see a job through.

I gave Nance a dose of the globulin sample the day I received it, and noted no change. I gave her another dose yesterday, and will give her a third today—which will exhaust the supply that Christoff sent. It would've lasted longer, had I not already taken the step of inoculating myself, Lizzie, and Emma. I didn't tell them that this was all we had, because I knew Lizzie would fight to keep every drop for Nance. But I wanted to make sure we all had a chance at protection. Frankly, it's likely to be more use to us than her.

As for the live bacteria, I'm busy culturing it, trying to bolster the supply. I think we might need more—if my theory holds up, that is. If it doesn't, we're all damned regardless.

But if it *does*, we might stand a chance against the darkness.

Next, I will try the toxoid on Nance.

I have a feeling that if anything is likely to produce a strong response, the dead and treated bacteria will be more likely to prompt it than the serum, which has previously developed antibodies that have reacted to the bacteria. The toxoid should force her to create her own antibodies, or that's what I'd like to see.

If that makes any sense.

I am throwing darts at a wall, and I'm running out of darts.

3 told Lizzie about my plan to give Nance the toxoid, and she balked at the prospect. I'm not sure why; at this point the girl will either live or die, and if we do nothing, the outcome is guaranteed so far as I'm concerned. Why not apply the potential remedies at our disposal, in case we might get lucky?

"But you've given her the other doses already, and she hasn't responded."

"She's not responded *much*," I admitted. "But *some*, I think. Her fever is down from yesterday, and her breathing appears more normal to me."

"Do you think?"

"I do," I assured her.

"Please, don't lie to me, Doctor. I don't want to play games with myself, or fool myself into thinking there's some improvement if there's none to observe—and I watch her so closely, I know her body more thoroughly than my own. I'm not arguing with you; it's just that I prefer no hope at all, if the only other option is false hope."

"That's brave of you, and reasonable, too." I then explained why the toxoid might provoke a more vigorous reaction, and did my best to reassure her without being cruel. "It may help her, or at the very worst, it will have no effect."

"It won't infect her with tetanus? I've heard infection is a concern with some inoculations, but I know almost nothing about this one."

"It will *not*," I promised, uncertain of whether or not I was lying. But it's as I said: the girl is dying anyway. Our best hope is to see her improved, or passed away before she can harm anyone else.

Lizzie accepted my promises, and I felt a twinge of guilt—but nothing I couldn't ignore. This was for the best. And for all I knew, I was telling the truth.

It's a hard line to take, but I've taken it before.

During the war, every day was a hundred such choices, a hundred opportunities to kill or save, and a hundred spins of the roulette wheel—tempted and tilted with nothing but our prayers.

And here I am again. Throwing prayers at pathogens, invocations against monsters.

No. I have more than that, this time. Or I will, given time.

Dear God, give us *time*.

Emma L. Borden

❦

MAY 5, 1894

Soon.

Very soon. It's not that I can "feel" him, as the doctor keeps asking me; it's not that I can sense the tug of him, like Lizzie senses the green stones. (And as I have sensed them before, to a lesser degree.) It's simple math that leads me to my conclusion. He's been approaching long enough, and this is no Greek paradox. Eventually, the monster must arrive.

Lizzie asked if I was afraid. I told her no.

Seabury asked if I was feeling well. I told him yes.

Some days I am afraid. Some days I feel weak. Nothing is really untrue anymore, much as nothing really makes sense. Seabury can go on and on about his patterns, and I don't think he's strictly mistaken; but likewise, he surely is not strictly correct. He tries to engage me with his theories, and I try to listen.

It's not that I don't understand them; it's that I find his efforts toward companionship difficult to reconcile, given his betrayal, and now his trust—as if I'm some partner. Or no, that's not it. Not exactly. He does not view me as a peer. He treats me like a student, and I have little patience for it.

He would not have shown such casual, well-meaning disrespect to E. A. Jackson. No, of course not. That's why I guarded my other name, my other self so closely. And there you see the fissure between us now.

He thinks he's mending a fence, but he's digging a trench.

I let him inoculate me against tetanus, because it seemed to make him happy. He wants so badly to help, and we all so badly *need* the help, that it would've been silly to refuse. Just like it was silly for Lizzie to initially fight about dosing Nance with the *tetani* samples. It was ridiculous of her, given how long and loudly she's complained about having no action to take, no hopeful means of bringing her lover back around.

But eventually Lizzie acquiesced, and from the sounds of things, there's been some slight, barely perceptible change in the right direction for our bed-bound guest. An improvement in her respiration, a decline in the fever that has left her sweating through the sheets, soaking great yellow stains down to the mattress.

But for all we know, these are only the signs of an imminent end.

We can't really control her—that much has been established. We tie her to the bed, but at night, when no one watches, she frees herself and wanders down to the cellar, or throws herself into the tub, or whatever else her somnambulistic brain finds appropriate. Now, I suppose, we insist upon the ties for the insurance of having done so, should anyone learn of our plight and ask us why we didn't do anything.

Well, we *did*. That's what we'll tell them. We tried everything. And we stuck to it, even when it didn't really work. The times, they were desperate indeed.

But I doubt anyone will ever inquire.

We've proceeded this far into darkness largely because no one wants to be seen talking to us, or visiting us, or otherwise providing any ordinary human interaction. We're starved for it, prevented from it except for our new old friend the doctor—whose presence no longer gives me any joy at all—and we've been starved for years.

That's our punishment, I guess. Since they couldn't convict my sister, and they couldn't banish us to memory. Since she went free, and we stayed here. They will ignore us . . . and in that way, they get what they want. They get to behave as if nothing ever happened.

To hell with Fall River.

Things happened.

And things are happening still, so many things that even the blind, bored, petty, avoidant people of this godforsaken little burg are being forced to sit up and notice. This time they cannot blame any strangeness on my sister.

They might blame it on me, if they knew how—but they'd be wrong.

In part. I summoned Zollicoffer with the sample; that's my cross to bear, and I'll carry it with these withered shoulders because apparently I have no choice. It was an accident, a simple act of friendliness that somehow warped into one of evil summoning, and I do not understand *how*. But I understand and accept my place in this otherworldly passion play.

Likewise, I do not understand what happened to Abigail and our father. They changed before the sample was sent, and before anyone else began to show signs of the creeping madness and violence. They were the first to go insane, and the first to become deadly and turn on their loved ones.

Father was, anyway. Abigail didn't care about us one way or another, so it could scarcely be argued that she "turned" on us. But the sentiment stands.

Lizzie believes it has to do with that pendant Father gave her for their anniversary that year, a few months before their deaths. The pendant is under our floorboards now, under our house; I think it first came from a pretty bit of sea glass Abigail found while down at the shore one day.

Or maybe I'm only filling in that part. Maybe I never knew, and I only want to apply some symmetry to the horror. Let us say that it all came from the sea: the glass pendant, the sample, the creatures with the needle-glass teeth that hound Maplecroft when the air is right and the call goes out. My sister holds to her speculations, that the monsters are transformed people, or they rise from the earth. She hasn't gone so far as to suggest that they fall from the sky, but she's curiously averse to admitting the obvious: They come from the ocean, too.

The webbed fingers, translucent eyes and skin. The teeth that remind me not of sharks or piranhas, but those you'll find in the mouths of Lophiiformes. Yes, it's very much like the anglerfishes and their kind—a jumble of pins and needles, protruding more than they're concealed.

All of it comes from the water. Everything, at the start. Didn't Darwin suggest as much? That life itself came from the ocean, in some roundabout way? Well, if not him, then his followers and subsequent researchers have certainly posited it, and with great vigor.

Life and death.

Our mother and grave, and the only thing between us is the shore.

FAMILY SLAIN IN MAYFIELD

❧

Parkridge Gazette, May 7, 1894
Reporting by Alfred Hanson

In the wee hours of Tuesday, May 2, four family members were gruesomely slain as they slept in their beds, on a farm three miles outside Mayfield. Authorities are withholding details in advance of a formal investigation, and pending the visit of an inspector from Boston, arriving to help manage the difficult case.

At this time, very little is known for certain, and that which is certainly known does not make the very best of sense. The victims are a husband and wife, Bradford and Margaret Moore, and two of their three children, four year old Christian, and two year old Beverly. One child survived the attack, and miraculously uninjured—according to the woman who discovered the scene, Daisy Rogers, a young widow who had joined the family recently in order to help with spring demands.

Miss Rogers was instructed to avoid speaking with the press, but so terribly has she been rattled by the incident that bits and pieces have found their way to our type-writers nonetheless.

According to her report, there were pools of bloody water all across the floors, soaking the furniture, and splattered across the windows—and the bodies were gruesomely mutilated, as if they'd been struck repeatedly by a hatchet or some other heavy blade. Furthermore, they had been propped up around the dinner table, in some weird tableau of horror.

Perhaps worst of all comes from the lone survivor, eight year old Constance. Constance was found lying in a dry bathtub, crying because she could not work the pump or carry the water to fill it. Despite her distress, she was not injured in any way, and in fact spoke wistfully of the handsome man of the sea. This detail is chilling, for the child has been blind since birth—and has no way of knowing whether or not the killer was handsome or horrible. Yet she insists that she saw him, and that he smiled at her, and told her to wait.

At present, the child is in the care of her aunt and uncle, who watch her carefully for clues beyond what she's stated about the event. If she's upset by the loss of her family, she does not show it. But then, according to her new guardians, she's always been peculiar. It has been suggested that she's an imbecile, or something close to it.

At this time, there is no further, formal word on her condition, or the state of the investigation; but officials are recommending that all citizens in the region should keep watch for strangers, and take reasonable precautions to guard themselves during this unusual time of creative violence, perpetrated against innocents.

Owen Seabury, M.D.

❧

MAY 7, 1894

Nance is gone, but I'll explain this part first: I found the newspaper article in an envelope, stuck inside my door with a brief
telegram—explaining that it'd been sent via express, courtesy
of Inspector Wolf. I don't know how he knew about it so soon,
much less how he got it to me with such alacrity (all the way
from Boston), but here it is, and here the monster comes. Ready
or not, as the children say.

Mayfield. That's not five miles out. He's drawn this near,
and he'll draw nearer still. He could walk the distance in a short
afternoon. One must assume that he will do so.

Assuming it, and being able to plan against it . . . those are
different things.

I've been terribly busy as it is, for let's take off the rosy glasses—Fall River is going to hell, one man at a time. One woman. One child. Mad and sick and dead, with anyone caught in the middle babbling to the authorities and being sent away. People are finally beginning to talk in earnest, sensing a pattern beyond the sensational Hamilton deaths—the most sensational in town since Lizzie Borden took her axe and inspired school-yard rope-skipping—but there's too little and too late, and this is a fine show of both.

I've heard talk of calling in the government for assistance, but what help could soldiers be? Then we'd have armed murderous madmen in our streets, as opposed to the armed murderous madmen who stay in their homes or fling themselves into the ocean.

Chatter goes around regarding some plague, unidentified and untreatable; and there are worries that specialists from the city will be called for, and we shall all be trapped in our homes, as in older times, when people knew nothing of cholera or anything bubonic. There are whispers that men in masks and official jackets will patrol the streets, and the calls of yesteryear, "Bring out your dead!" will ring through the town. We shall all be cut off, from our loved ones and the rest of the world alike. We shall die alone and in infamy, victims of things we do not understand and cannot fight. Fall River will go down in history as a place where people die in awful, unexplained ways. It'll be a ghost town in a year. The government will burn it to the ground as a public health hazard.

Not the worst idea I've ever heard.

So anyway, there's talk.

And there's plenty of fear to go around, even though the denizens of Fall River know nothing about what's coming, or who's coming. They have no idea what they're up against.

Neither do I, but knowing what little I do . . . somehow that's worse. It'd be better, easier, I think, if I only worried about what germ or contagion we fought. It'd be simpler if I did not know that it had a name, and that it wore a man's face, and it killed more viciously (if more swiftly) than any microbe.

Whatever it is, it comes from the water. I'm confident of that now—as confident as I am that the tetanus pattern is a pattern in fact, and not in theory. Not a perfect one, but a recognizable one. I will cling to that which I recognize. But regardless of what Emma thinks, I do not cling to it without reason or clarity, without evidence. It is *there*. I *know* it's there. I can see it.

That's why I cling. It gives me a direction, and reinforces my sense of purpose.

Especially now that Nance is gone. Especially now that this Zollicoffer comes closer.

Nance is gone, but that wasn't the first thing I knew this morning.

The first thing was the express package from Wolf, and the second was that Mrs. Easley down at the dry goods store has taken a pair of scissors and shut herself in the storeroom, and no one has been able to speak with her or open the door—but there was water pouring from underneath it. No pipes had burst, for there were no pipes to fail; no pump was within the store, and no one could explain the flood that poured out from under the doors, and the mist that steamed the windows from within.

I learned this when a neighborhood boy came charging up the steps, right as I was finished reading the news clipping, standing there on my own stoop in a dressing robe and bare feet, stunned and full of questions.

The boy's name is Arnold, or Arthur, or Allan, or something along those lines. He gasped out that I had to come to

Granston's quick, because Mrs. Easley was infected and she had holed up in the store with a set of shears.

Infected. They now speak of it in terms of illness. As they damned well ought to.

I thanked the boy for the information, told him I'd be on my way as soon as I could find some shoes, and shut the door in his face. Too abruptly, I'm confident. He must've thought he'd angered me, or that I was a jackass; I don't know. But I spent a moment leaning my back against the closed door, wondering if I should bother to go address the situation. I was thinking of Ebenezer Hamilton, and that terrible scene, and knowing that whatever awaited at Granston's Dry Goods would surely be no better.

Then I wondered if she was alone. I hadn't given the boy time to say one way or another. There might be other victims within. There might still be someone to save. Not too little, not too late, for one person or more.

It was a stupid hope, but I held it aloft regardless as I found proper clothes and dressed myself; it took longer than it should have—yes, I know. My house is filling with detritus, with nonsense. I'm entombing myself and even I can see it, plain as day.

I have stopped seeing patients in my home, and will only make house calls—and every day, more do clamor for my attention. I've canceled what appointments I can, and spent those hours in Lizbeth's laboratory.

It's a good laboratory she's built. She's done a fine job. I've lost what feels like days there; down in that space, the time doesn't pass the same way, I don't think. Something about the stones she keeps in the box beneath the floor. I know where they are, under what floorboards the cabinet lies, but I do not even stand atop it. I walk around that place on the floor, lest the temptation to open it become too great.

It will not become too great.

I know too well what became of Nance before we lost her. It cannot happen to me, too. If it happens to the rest of the Maplecroft crew, then truly the world is done for.

As I said, or as I tried to say and lost track of myself . . . we lost Nance.

I mean to write about that, and I will. It happened the day after I gave her the heavy dose of the toxoid, so I suppose we know that, at least. Or do we? Correlation and causation . . . *post hoc, ergo proper hoc*. It's bad science, but it's all we have time for.

So I'll say it then: The toxoid brought about a change in her.

But first I went to the dry goods store, and I was too late, thank God.

(If He exists to receive any appreciation. I remain ever the filthy atheist, but He's crept into my language, and it's just as well. It keeps people fooled. So thank God, I say.)

By that, I mean that I did not have to intervene in anything. No one else was involved, and the woman was dead before I arrived, the scissors opened just enough to stab through both her eyes. Self-inflicted. I saw it in a moment.

I saw it in the gory fingerprints, and the bloody messages she'd scrawled across the floor, the walls, the windows. Using her blood for ink.

They were hardest to read on the windows, for they were runny and almost washed clean with water. Like everywhere else I'd seen the phenomenon so far, the water came from nowhere and smelled terrible. It drained out through the store, and seeped through the floorboards to soak the foundations. It was gone by the time I got there, just like the life of the woman whose troubles had summoned me.

(As for the message—mostly it was one word, written again and again: *out*. And perhaps even more oddly, the handwriting did not appear to belong to one person alone. It came in script, in print, and in combinations of the two. It was smeared in angular lines, and smoothly composed with a flowing hand. I do not know what this means, but I'm writing it down as I write everything down, and for the same reason. It might be useful. To someone. Eventually.)

I told the officer on the scene that I'd send for Inspector Wolf, and whoever the young man was, he looked relieved—for this was out of his hands at last. Thank heaven there was someone more qualified to manage these unmanageable acts.

It isn't true, really. To the best of my immediate knowledge, Wolf is no more qualified than anyone else. Certainly no more qualified than Lizzie or myself, and if we are the best informed of mankind, then there are dire times ahead indeed.

Or . . . no. I might be wrong.

It could be, Wolf is looking at patterns just like we are—but he's seeing different ones, that's all. He's seen the crimes as they connect, even if he cannot draw the lines precisely between them. And I call him "inspector"—everyone refers to him thusly—but now that I pause to consider it, I have no idea what force or office employs him. Is he a policeman? A federal agent? Some kind of marshal?

I wonder whether I ought to call him and tell him to join us at the spinsters' house, that he may wait with us. He did offer to deploy security men, didn't he? I'd prefer if he came himself, alone. He might be able to help.

Or he might be one more body when the smoke clears.

I don't know what to do. Well, he's the one who sent me the

article, so he knows already how near at hand is our peril. The decision is his. He can come if he wants, or leave us if he doesn't.

𝕴 walked around the scene of the crime, if suicide by gruesome means can be considered a crime. Is it? Surely not. If suicide is illegal, then nothing in the world makes sense.

At any rate, Mrs. Easley harmed no one but herself, however violently she might have done so. I did not want to investigate it. There was nothing I could tell the earnest, frightened policemen. Nothing to ease their worry or reassure them that this was an isolated incident. They already knew it wasn't. They already knew about the Hamiltons; and they knew about the Davids, the Jessups. They knew about Mr. Winters and Miss Angeline Frye. They were aware of the situation with Harlan Sykes.

They know they might be next. Oh, those poor boys. They are so afraid.

I am jealous of them, because they do not know how afraid they *ought* to be.

𝕴 left the scene without taking notes. I did not mention the waterlogged floor, the damp-damaged walls, or the scissor handles protruding from the woman's face, like a demented pair of spectacles. I made no commentary on the blood—they thought it must be too much for one corpse to hold, but they were mistaken. The water made it look worse, having diluted and spread the gore around; if you don't know the viscosity of blood, you wouldn't know the difference. Besides, those boys had no idea how much fluid a body can hold. They'd never seen one drained before. I have. In the war, but that wasn't quite the same thing. Those were bodies broken apart, smashed and incomplete, oozing rather than gushing or spilling. So little left inside them that nothing pumped, ticked, or flowed.

I didn't tell them any of that. I only told them that they knew where to find me, and I said I would send Inspector Wolf a wire.

I couldn't if I wanted to. He's never given me any contact information, or any office where a telegram might be received. I still have no idea who he works for, or why.

All day, the knowledge that the monster was so close, and coming closer, weighed on me. All through those hours, I carried the weight of Zollicoffer's impending arrival.

I shouldn't have bothered to visit the late, lamented Mrs. Easley. I'd known already what I would find, and I contributed nothing to the conversation as to her demise. It would've served no purpose to tell the young officers that she'd been driven mad and committed suicide because there was a monster who had been transformed by something pulled from the ocean last year. It would've done nothing to help, if I'd added that the monster was on his way, and the nearer he drew, the more events like this we ought to expect.

On the other hand, he's almost made it to town—and the worst he can do is kill us all, and then it'd all be over.

I laughed at the thought. Alone in my cluttered, increasingly musty, and foul-smelling parlor, I laughed out loud and then sobered quickly, because laughing aloud, alone, in dirty rooms is what madmen do. I had this much awareness about me, still. I thought of my scissors, and then I wondered where my scissors were located in this jumbled wreck of a house. Couldn't think of where they might be. At first I was angry with myself, for having allowed my living circumstances to come to this. But then I found this thought reassuring, for if I couldn't find them, then I couldn't stab myself in the eyes, now could I?

You see? Madness, creeping in around the edges.

So soft, so subtle, that it goes unnoticed until you try to speak the process aloud. For now, when I hear my own words pronounced in my own voice, I recognize the insanity for what it surely is. For now, I am able to draw myself back from that precipice.

"I was angry because I did not know where I had placed my scissors, because I might need them. I might be required to stab myself in the eyes."

I suppose the next step will be more difficult. Next, I will need to hear someone else speak aloud before I recognize how strange I have become. I need to spend more time at Maplecroft. I need to visit with the ladies there, for they are the only ones who will know when I go mad—and who will know the difference between confused and afflicted, and gone beyond all hope of retrieval.

Or perhaps I ought to avoid them altogether. At this rate, I do not know how much longer I will be a help to them, and how soon the transition might make me a danger to them.

Ah, you see? I just read that last short paragraph aloud, and it made sense. I am still here. I am still sane. I am still a knight of this place, this town, that house. Not prisoner, but sentry. Though I didn't do much to preserve or protect Nance.

Since we lost her, and all.

I should've skipped the viewing of the soggy and departed Mrs. Easley. I should've gone directly to Maplecroft, but I didn't. After leaving that scene I should've proceeded straight to that marvelous mansion wherein I might find kindred spirits, but something had sent me home first, instead—a niggling worry that Wolf might send some kind of word, and then I'd miss it.

He'd sent no word.

And I laughed alone in my parlor, and then headed to Maplecroft. On the way there, I met the Bordens' neighbor boy. He was out of breath, running full speed, his pockets much enriched by how many messages he'd passed between us over these last few weeks.

He wheezed, "Miss Borden sends for you, sir. A change in your patient, she says."

I didn't know if he meant Emma or Nance, but either way, it probably wasn't good. I hoped it was Nance, and I felt briefly bad for doing so. But I know Emma better, and I find her more useful. Ever since her descent into a fugue state, Nance had become useful only as a specimen, which must sound cold; but the whole world is cold, and how else am I to learn, except to observe?

I hoped that Nance hadn't experienced some catastrophic change since the afternoon before, when last I'd seen her, but the boy's frantic presence suggested otherwise. I hoped Lizzie or Emma could provide me with strictly accurate details about any changes I'd missed, assuming still that we were not speaking of Emma.

Lizzie could enlighten me with regard to all I'd missed, or so I comforted myself as I made the dash to her home.

On the way, the sky began to spit intermittent gobs of rain. The air felt like tepid bathwater, and everyone sweated and shined, despite the lack of excessive heat. I hated running in the thick, wet air, but I ran anyway—never pausing to respond to greetings, short queries, or other inane interruptions hurled at me from the sidewalks and doorways.

By the time I arrived, I was soaked.

Lizzie had been watching for me; she flung the door open before I could knock, and she drew me inside with surprising vigor for such a small woman. "In here," she said breathlessly, pulling me by my arm through the parlor. A loud clap of thunder sounded outside, lending an ominous air to something already so ominous that I shuddered to consider what awaited me . . . but sometimes the weather knows things, and we would all be ill-advised to ignore its warnings.

The house was dark, though it was only late afternoon. Or was it later? It *felt* later. How long had I stood alone in my house, laughing at myself? At the gods?

The clouds had closed like curtains, and there was no sun at all. But in Maplecroft, the lights were not yet switched on.

"She's in the basement. Oh God," she continued.

"I thought you'd barred it."

"I *did*."

I believed her, but the door was open now—kicked inward, or bashed that way. A great dent sank the middle of it, and the hinges were crooked, barely clutching the frame. "Did *she* do that?" I asked.

"She must have. But I didn't see. I only heard."

"Where's Emma?"

"I don't know," she said offhandedly, and that worried me—or it would have, if I had any further room for worry. If Lizzie wasn't concerned, I couldn't afford to be concerned, either. "Here, down here, you see?"

And I did see.

The laboratory was lit up, not quite bright but at least some of the lights were burning, unlike the upstairs. The illumination had a sickly, greenish glow to it—one I'd never seen before, or had never noticed, at any rate. Was it ordinary for gaslights to cast such a shade? Probably not. Probably nothing was ordinary anymore, and this was the veritable nexus for all the extraordinary things for miles and miles around.

The walls were wet; rivulets of water cascaded here and there, pooling on the floor and draining through the boards. The water smelled like brine and death, like low tide after some great mammal has beached itself and expired. Just as Ebenezer Hamilton had told me.

All the tables were overturned, which inexplicably annoyed me; all the floorboards at one side of the room had been lifted up—for Nance had been searching for something again, but not the stones. Not this time.

She stood barefoot and naked, staring down into a hole.

Watery light washed over her, and her skin looked like the hide of a dolphin, slick and neither dark nor pale, but muted. She was the wrong color. Her body was not quite the wrong shape, but there was something wrong about it all the same. She didn't turn to look at me, and she didn't respond when Lizzie called her name.

She didn't move at all except to wiggle her toes at the edge of that precipice, where I realized with a sudden jolt of horror that the cooker was waiting for her.

Its lid was open. Its dials and buttons were alight, and its contents hummed and smelled terrible. Of course they did. The cooker was ready to cook. It'd been primed and warmed, full of lye and whatever else might turn flesh and bone into syrup, and Nance was staring down into it, as if she were prepared to make a swan dive into that shallow contraption.

"Nance," I tried.

She didn't answer me, any more than she'd answered her lover.

Lizzie tried again, and then reached for her—but the girl's arm lashed out and threw the other woman backward, crashing into a fallen table. It was too light a gesture for such a magnificent blow, too quick and flippant to have cast her across the room, but there it was. Lizzie gasped and clutched her stomach, but I could see she was not badly hurt. She was stunned, and this was not the first time Nance had cast her aside. I could see that, too.

"Nance, what are you doing?" I asked, thinking a question might prompt more response than a mere call of her name.

I was right.

"Fighting," she whispered.

"You're . . . you're fighting? Fighting what?"

"Him."

Lizzie climbed to her feet; I heard her behind me, gathering her wits and hauling herself upright. But my eyes were fixed on this girl, bare as the day she was born. Tall, and I don't suppose I'd ever really noticed it. Sturdy, like she'd grown up with manual labor. Had they mentioned something about it? A farm girl, I wanted to say, but wouldn't have sworn to it.

"Nance, don't listen to him," Lizzie pleaded. "Stay here, for the love of God!"

"I'm trying," she replied.

Lizzie began to cry. Not a delicate cry that could be conquered with a handkerchief, but more of a manly, racking sob that was so full of rage and sorrow that I felt it like a wave, pushing me forward.

I let it push me one step, then another. I was not within arm's reach of Nance, no—not quite that close. But I was closer, and she hadn't moved to evade me, or attack me. "Lizzie's right," I told her. "You mustn't listen to him."

"I know," she said. It came out bubbly, like she'd said it underwater, or perhaps her lungs were full of slime.

I commanded her, "Back away from that cooker. It'll be the death of you, and you know it."

She agreed, and seemed curiously at peace. "That's what he says. He says it will kill me."

"Then *back away*."

Her head turned, slowly, a slick pivot on her neck that made all the bones look loose beneath her dolphin-wet skin. She looked me in the eye, and for a span of seconds, I saw her wrestling with something. It flickered back and forth, a white milkiness behind her pupils—and the sharp knowledge of the woman whose soul must somehow remain inside.

She was fighting, yes. Just as she'd said.

I said it again: "Step away from the cooker."

She sneered, but it was not contempt. It was a twisting of her mouth that she couldn't quite control—more of a spasm than an expression. And she said, "I should save you. I should jump. But he says . . ." She struggled to line up every word, I could hear it in the precision with which she pronounced each individual letter.

"I don't understand," I told her.

"I know." She nodded, and again it looked like her joints were fastening and unfastening, her bones sliding around, rearranging themselves.

Lizzie swallowed a sob and screamed, "Stay with me!"

Then, with a sharp flicker of sorrow, Nance made her decision—or had it made for her. "He won't let me save you. Won't let me jump." She looked at Lizzie now, directly and without blinking. Like the others, she wasn't blinking anymore. Calm and level, but so unhappy I could feel it in my own bones, when she said, "Or stay."

Nance shook her head and withdrew, stepping away.

More thunder rollicked through the clouds. It climaxed with a crack so loud that when the lightning came, it was bright enough to illuminate the whole house. Some of it even trickled downstairs, to us. Some of it set the room on fire, and for half a second—maybe less—everything was so clear, so bright.

Nance looked up when the lightning flashed again upstairs, though this time I hadn't heard the thunder that preceded it. It flashed and sizzled, and Maplecroft smelled like ozone and fire. It crackled through the house, the loudest white you've ever seen.

The lights went out. The lights came on again.

The cooker was empty. And Nance was gone.

Lizzie Andrew Borden

❧

Nance was gone, and I stood there—wondering if my eyes had deceived me, or if I'd finally succumbed to the madness of Fall River, or if perhaps I was simply mistaken about what had occurred.

I tumbled forward—nearly toppling into the cooker myself—but I found no sign of her. The lye and its accompanying chemicals did not simmer or writhe with bubbles as if they'd been disturbed, they only swirled and hummed with the motion of the motor, spinning and whirring, ready to devour anything that might fall. This flytrap of a machine. There in my floor. It was empty, except for the liquids that do its job.

Nance had gone somewhere else.

I flung myself toward the far wall, where the switch

controlled the gaslights—and I twisted it hard enough to break the knob, but the light didn't brighten and Nance was still gone.

Corner to corner I scanned the room and saw only the usual bits of equipment, paraphernalia, tables, stools, glass vials, books, burners, measuring cups and spoons, scraps of notepaper, lists of trials and errors. In the corner, a broom. Against the wall, my axe. No, not the axe after all, for it was upstairs. I hadn't known she'd be coming down here again, so I hadn't brought it.

I'd been so afraid for her that I'd forgotten to arm myself.

"Lizbeth." Doctor Seabury called to me, and I was startled— I'd looked right past him. He was there, but I hadn't noticed him. You see? Such things are possible after all.

"She *can't* be gone," I insisted to him, not answering his summons except to give him some indication that yes, I was still in possession of my senses. "There's no way out of the basement except up the stairs, and out the exterior cellar doors, but they're locked." I could see the barred fastener from where I stood. It had not been disturbed. "Did she . . . did you . . . did she push past you? Shove you aside?" It didn't hurt to ask.

"No," he told me gently. "No, Lizbeth. We lost her."

Exasperated, I spit—"Through the walls? Like some kind of ghost?"

"Through the walls, past them—I surely don't know and can't say. But she's left this place."

I clapped my hands over my mouth, then changed my mind and pressed them over my breasts instead. Holding myself down. Holding my horror inside, so I did not scream it out. Quietly, with only what little whispered breath I could spare—lest it all fly forth at once—I said, "He was telling her to do something awful to us. To you, me, and Emma. She was fighting him. That's what she meant."

"That's one reading of the situation," he replied, more coldly than necessary, in my opinion.

"It's the only thing that makes sense!" I shouted back at him. Not shouting was too hard.

"Sense has long ago gone out the window here, my dear. She's gone. That's the main thing. She neither did anything awful to us, nor did she fling herself into the cooker—that's all we know for certain."

"Then we have to go looking for her!"

Now he was exasperated with me; it showed in his eyes. He tried to steady his voice, to lend at least one of us some sense of calm or control. "Lizbeth, if she is trying to protect you by leaving . . . would you undo her efforts by chasing her?"

"Yes!" He was right. Sense had gone out the window, or perhaps out through the walls, like a ghost.

I pushed past him, since she had not. I ran up the stairs, two at a time, noisy as a horse on a boardwalk.

She *had* to be out there somewhere. I ignored Emma, who did her best to get my attention, wondering what was going on; I saw her standing by the landing in the foyer, holding the stair rail for support. Amazing how she can stand, walk, and even yell when she feels motivated enough. Amazing how that's always when I'm in the middle of something important.

I left her where she was.

The doctor could fill her in, or help her out, or whatever it was she required on that occasion. I had problems of my own. I had to go find Nance.

I grabbed my axe as I dashed out the door, and I carried it around the side of the house in the dark—no, in the intermittent light, flashed from above, cracking the clouds apart like eggs.

It was almost enough to see quite clearly, tumbling from corner to corner across the sky. Flickering, sometimes, unlike the flash one automatically thinks of when one considers lightning. Farther south, I think they call it "heat lightning," though what that means—and what difference there might be—I haven't any idea.

Behind the house I went, determined to see if the cellar door had been breached, and to double-check that I had not been distracted by madness downstairs—but no. It remained stubbornly affixed, and locked from within as I knew it must be.

My heart no longer beat; it clenched and unclenched behind my ribs, so tightly, so forcefully, that I almost felt I couldn't breathe.

Something was wrong. Everything was wrong. Not just the hot-sparkle chasing and crashing of the light in the clouds, or the roll of thunder—one minute hesitant and shaky, the next a clattering godlike gong that shook the whole town. No, not just that. *Everything.*

Nance was gone, and I had to find her.

My lover was alive again, running again. Moving and speaking, as I'd begun to fear I'd never see again. She was herself again, if somewhat changed—not hideously, no. Not like the other people so afflicted with the sickness and insanity. No, she was still her own beautiful self: tall and strong, capable and kind, quick and funny, and sharp and loving.

I stood still and panted, making some halfhearted effort to stop gasping and start breathing normally, despite the cinch of my undergarments objecting to every deeply drawn lungful of air. Where was there to go? Fall River sat between the ocean and the woods.

Between the two, she'd go find the ocean.

I knew it in my soul, and the knowing made me weak with dread. It's as Emma and her Darwinian colleagues suggest, isn't it? All life emerging, cell by cell, fin to foot, from the ocean—to form a bipedal ape that walks and talks and breathes, and creates poetry and cities and gods.

Can it be that ugly and easy?

We crawled primordial from the water, our grand-ancestors times a million generations; we escaped the tides, the sharks, and the leviathans of the deep, only to find ourselves on land—where we became the things we'd sought to escape, and we invented gods to blame. Not gods of the ocean, for we'd been to the ocean, and seen that the water was empty of the divine. Not gods of the earth, for we have walked upon the dirt, and we are alone here.

So we install our gods in the sky, because we haven't yet eliminated the firmament as a possibility.

Next, I suppose, we'll send them into space—where I expect they will live a very long time indeed, for it shall take us another million generations of descendants to reach them, and learn that they are projections of light and story, cast into the heavens by us alone. And we will be alone again (unless by then, we discover some more distant place in which to hide our image).

Over and over again, we lift God out of our reach. Over and over, push Him beyond our grasp, yet still we stretch out our fingers and seek to touch Him.

But find nothing.

If Nance had gone to the ocean, I would go to the ocean, too.

I would chase her there, to the shore. To the pier, I supposed—though why I would leap to this conclusion, I do not know. Call it instinct, or call it that bond that joins humans when they have shared flesh, and held one another's bones. Call it dumb luck if you like.

If there are no gods, there should be luck, at least.

And if there are gods after all, perhaps we should not strug-gle so hard to get their attention, if this is the attention they would lavish upon us.

To the shore, then.

I ran the whole way, clutching my axe by the middle of its handle to keep it from swinging; I pushed my feet forward, run-ning below the ever-churning, ever-rolling, ever-noisy sky and wondering if there would be any rain at all—for none had fallen yet. No sprinkles, no deluge. Only the whisper-sharp tang of lightning, that scorched electrical smell that comes before a strike.

But none of the lightning touched me. It only showed me the way, all the way down to the water where the pier was lo-cated, and where the Hamilton family once had a shop, and where I would push my sister in her wheeled chair, so that she could climb out and sit or lie on the rocks and warm her body on the sunnier days. Pretending we were taking a holiday some-place nice, where no one knew who we were. Chatting about the tide pools. Poking sticks into holes in the sand, and finding strange samples there—specimens to discuss or to send by post to monsters in other towns.

A hard, sharp shout of light—and I saw her, or I thought I did. More importantly, I *believed* I did—and I screamed her name at the top of my lungs, even though nothing could've heard me over the celestial furor, the thunder coming so fast, one roll after another. It'd come to sound like a low, magnificent hum not merely above me, but around me. Inside me.

I almost stopped hearing it.

I almost couldn't hear my own voice, crying for Nance.

But *she* did. I'm certain she did—and I'm certain it was her, too. I saw her in silhouette, and then in a too-white flicker when she faced me, and her skin was as bright as a shark's belly. Her face was flat and featureless, and it's true that I was some distance away, but I could not make out so much as a pair of dark holes where her eyes must have been, or the horizontal slash of her mouth. She faced me, but didn't see me. She was being erased.

I tried her name again, but this time the phantasm turned its head and vanished—or rather, when the next stroke of lightning cut the darkness a moment later, it was gone. *She* was gone.

I ran toward the spot where last I saw her; I was still carrying the axe, though I scarcely felt the weight of it. I felt only the wind, tearing at my dress and dragging at my hair; I felt only the misery and fear of knowing Nance was there, but not there.

I reached the edge of the street, and there was nowhere left to go except for the pier immediately before me, or onto the naked, jutting rocks that flanked it on either side. They clustered between the water and the sand, monuments of basalt and granite or whatever stony barriers the ocean best prefers when it throws up walls to keep us out.

I did not shriek for Nance again, because it was clear now that even if she caught my voice, even if she remembered her name and recognized it—and recognized me, and knew that I loved her—it was not enough to hold her here. My voice was not enough to make her stay.

I scanned the pier, the large rows of rocks that stood huddled like soldiers in poor formation. I checked the street behind me and the trees, houses, and merchant stalls back behind that.

Nothing. No one.

For all I knew, I was the only person alive in Fall River.

The light-frosted sky told me nothing, until I heard some strange new sound, a howling not drawn from the wind scraping against the unsettled waves. Whatever storm battered Fall River, it did not make this cry—this unearthly, inhuman, unlikely, and unbelievable wail that came from . . . below or maybe *beyond* the water, I think. It came from the ocean, off in the distance—this high-pitched groan that carried on the storm the undercurrents of a creak, a squeal, like a great door opening or a lion's mouth stretching into a yawn.

It was a living cry; that's what I mean to say. Not the insensate noise of a ship leaning or a tree beginning to break; it was a sound made on purpose, by something that wished to be heard. Yet it must also be said that this sound was mechanical in nature—or its underpinnings seemed that way to me. I heard chains, unspooling. Metal on metal. Rusted cogs objecting to the thought of being turned, but turning nonetheless.

I did not have long to muse about the sound's nature or origins, for I saw her again.

Only for a flicker, for the briefest shaved moment of a second.

On the rocks, to the left. On the tumbled boulders worn smooth and treacherous by the tide, moving across them as easily as Christ must have walked upon the sea. She moved steadily, but the motion of her limbs was not natural—her bare skin gleaming and wet; she looked like she had too many limbs, clinging and rattling, crablike, across the stones. (She had a center that did not move, only dangled between clicking, clattering, clawing appendages that gripped the uneven terrain and navigated it soundly, for all their strangeness.)

I tried her name again, but without any force this time. She wasn't listening to me. She was listening to the cry that rose up out of the waves, and I wondered if this was the cry of Zollicoffer— of the monster who hounded us, and who must have surely arrived in Fall River by now.

Had he met us here? Now? Finally?

But no, that couldn't be right. The mad professor would be coming by land. Whatever wet god summoned Nance from the Atlantic, this must be what called to him, too. The monster that calls to monster. The evil so great that it draws all other evil like a lodestone.

(Is this what we fled, when we left the ocean? Did we grow legs so we could run away?)

Somewhere in the back of my head, I wondered if Zollicoffer hadn't already arrived at Maplecroft. He would stop there first, wouldn't he? He might be there already.

But there was no turning around now. I'd picked my path, and this is where it led me—after Nance, down to the water. Onto the immense, uneven boulders that keep watch over the place where the water meets the shore.

I slipped and stumbled, for my shoes were not made to prance across boulders wet with tide and the ocean spray. I was not dressed for beachcombing or swimming; I was not ready to fight the slick stones for handholds, so I crawled gracelessly across them, between them, through them—always toward Nance, who was moving toward the waves.

I lost my footing, or my handing. I lost something, anyway.

I tumbled down into a small valley, a damp, sandy stretch between two stones, and the spot was filled with water up to my knees. My feet sank and struggled, and I shoved my hands against the boulders on either side of me. I dragged myself forward.

The sky above me still flickered violently with the lightning that never struck, and only scattered.

I had no idea where I was, or how I'd find my way past the rocks and out to the open water. I didn't know where Nance was, and she was my guiding light. Perhaps I'd die down there between the stones, and turn up bleached and dead when the waves went back out again.

It would not have been the worst of all outcomes.

But that wasn't what happened.

I dredged my shoes out of the sandy muck one after another, hefting them up and forcing my feet forward. I braced my hands on the stones beside me, and I moved incrementally toward the ocean—even as the water level rose past my knees, to my thighs, to my hips—and I wondered if the tide was coming in, or if I was only making progress. I didn't know, and couldn't remember what the schedule was that day. The timetables would've been in the paper, but I hadn't read it. It'd seemed such a small and unimportant thing, so irrelevant . . . but now I was wishing I'd taken a glance, so that I'd know for certain whether or not I was charging toward my death.

Nance was somewhere above and beyond me, and I was waist-deep in water, half swimming and half clambering past the last of the rocks before I knocked my leg against something like a step. Not a stair, exactly, but a place where the grade changed—and I could draw myself up out of the water.

Hand over hand, foot over foot, and soaked to the bone, I rose.

I dropped myself atop the nearest, flattest boulder and stayed there on all fours. I couldn't imagine standing in that wind; I couldn't stagger upright against the waves that hurtled around me, crashing and spraying, dousing me in splash after splash.

Open water was much closer now. I'd covered more ground than I'd thought, and most of the rocks were behind me. I was exhausted, but I didn't notice it any more than I noticed the cold. I only felt it; I didn't believe it. I didn't let it stop me. I scanned the water and the nearest rocks; she'd been moving so much faster. She must've gotten away from me. She must've made it to the water by now.

While I hunted, squinting against the night, that unearthly call continued, booming and banging, and I thought I sensed some rhythm to it. Not quite a drumbeat. Not quite a heartbeat. Something lower and not quite so fast. Some vibration, slowed down until it no longer hummed, but moaned instead.

(I recalled some old lesson about the music of the spheres, about monks and their chants trying to re-create the tones of the universe—to sing the song of creation. This was not that. Or else it *was*, and I have misunderstood everything, for my whole life.)

Then I saw her again.

Not a flash, but a prolonged, static moment wherein she did not move—she did not even appear to breathe—she stood like a statue, tall and beautiful as always. White as the moon, her hair as wet as mine, spilling down her shoulders and back. All of it whipped by the wind, like a flag on a pole.

I did not scream her name this time. She would not have heard a scream. I whispered instead, "Nance?"

And she turned to look at me, but I did not see her face. The wild ocean and the vivid black sky kept her shadowed, lit from behind, and blank, and again I was struck by the sensation that she was being erased in front of me. A stupid thing to feel, but there it was. That's what I believed.

I gazed at her as if I could draw her back to me by sheer force of will.

She looked away. She did not whisper back.

She jumped. Neat as a sea lion. If she made a splash, I did not see it. I did not hear it. I heard only the ocean and the demented, incessant cry of whatever waited beneath it.

I leaped awkwardly to my feet and cast myself forward, sliding and fumbling, meeting so much resistance from the wind, the water, the rocks; but I reached the place where I'd seen her and I looked down, and saw nothing but the churning froth of the tide coming in, or going out. It was ink and inscrutable. I did not care whether it came or went.

I jumped, too.

If I couldn't save her, then I couldn't save anybody. And maybe it didn't matter if I did. From exhaustion, or madness, or despair—I could not say—I threw myself into the open ocean.

Wherever she'd gone, I would go. Whatever strange god she now served, I would serve it, too. It could have me, too. It could have anything, as long as it would let us be together. If it wanted a soul, it could take mine. If it wanted a priestess or confidante, I would sing its worship until the end of time. If it wanted a meal, I would offer it my bones and beg it to stop there. I would plead and pray: *I will be your sacrifice. Just leave the rest of the town, the rest of the world . . . in peace.*

I hit the water hard, and hit something else while I was at it.

Another stone, a bit of driftwood? Perhaps one of the pilings, underneath the pier. I might've been close enough. I don't know, but it stunned me. I tried to swim anyway, but the currents around me were erratic and powerful.

I kicked back and forth but found no purchase to anchor me; the water was too deep, and the waves were too insistent. They splashed over me. I dove beneath the surface and opened my eyes—which hurt, but told me nothing. I saw nothing at all, so I flailed with my hands and legs, taking up as much room as I could. If only I could touch her . . . grab her, draw her back to me or at least let us go down together, if that's what it came to. I would die alone for her, if that's what needed to happen; but I'd rather die in her arms, if I could be granted that one final grace.

I spun and bobbed, taking air only when I had no other choice. I was never a strong swimmer, and I was already half-dead from the run, the rocks, and the waves. I could feel the last of my strength bleeding away, and except for the fact that I'd not found Nance, I could not force myself to care.

Under the water the voice sounded different. The Leviathan cry was peculiarly clear, and it sounded like music played by a mad-man on an instrument found in hell.

Stars sparkled across my vision. I did not know if my eyes were open or closed anymore. I could not tell the difference between water and sky. I felt nothing. No, that is not true. I felt despair, but even that was leaving me. At least the end was in sight. That was something, wasn't it?

No. That was not true, either. Nothing was.

A hand reached me—strong as iron, fingers tangled them-selves in my hair and pulled me. It did not hurt. It felt like un-familiar pressure; I was aware of it, but I didn't understand it. I wondered if this was Nance, if she'd changed her mind and come back for me. But it wasn't her hand. (I never really thought it was.)

A second hand joined the first and I was hauled out, bodily. Dredged from the deep like an insensate lobster, confused to find myself in the open air.

On the pier. On its very edge, after a short trip up a ladder that I remember only vaguely . . . some lunge, some jerking pull, as I was brought up rung by rung. By force. I was dropped to the boards, and below them I heard the waves, swearing in thunderous rushes. They hadn't quite been finished with me yet.

More's the pity.

Emma L. Borden

❧

MAY 7, 1894

They left me here. Abandoned without second thought, I should think.

Left behind at a full run, one of them after the other, chasing after that warped phantom of a girl who isn't a girl anymore. It was plain as day that she wasn't coming back; she would never be talked away from the edge of whatever precipice she'd found, even if she was talked away from the cooker, at the end.

I stood beside the stairs, still clinging to the rail for the strength to stand. This was not one of my good days, only a desperate day—where the last vestiges of endurance must be rallied and brought to arms. I could scarcely hold myself upright, and my lungs felt as if I'd been breathing fire.

In fact, I had only been breathing my own blood. I realized

this when a cough surprised me, sneaking up before I could pull a handkerchief from the pocket of my dress. I hacked and spit, and my eyes watered; and when they cleared again I saw blood across the floor, against the painted white of the banister, and splattered on the nearby divan. It was more blood than usual. Too much. Enough to remind me that this was not a strong day but a weak one, but it didn't matter how I felt or what I wanted.

Especially not today.

Not when the town was under celestial assault, if the light show and the thunder were any indication . . . but no matter how hard I peered through the windows, I saw no sign of rain. All the water was staying in the ocean tonight, so there was one small mercy granted. At least I could see outside, for the night was uncannily bright—albeit loud—and at least I could stand upright, whether my body truly wanted to, or not.

I considered my father's gun. In the cabinet, a handful of yards away.

I ought to get it, I decided.

It would be better than nothing, against whatever was likely to come—and something was definitely coming. We'd felt it for days, and now I knew it in my soul: Zollicoffer was imminent. Even if I couldn't do the math to predict his route . . . the whole sky was shouting his arrival.

Maybe it was the noise, or the lightning, or just the timing that made every move feel so urgent, so necessary.

They were all small moves, the only motions I could manage, but I *did* manage them: one hand off the rail, one hand *on* the rail; use my free hand to grasp the divan; release the rail altogether, lean on the divan; make sure both feet follow, not just the one; hand over hand, foot beside foot, walk the length of the divan and then use one hand to grasp the low table beside it; steady self on the table, which rocks a little from that one leg being not quite the right length; extend one foot to the middle of the floor, to the empty space between me and the liquor cabinet drawer where the gun rested these days; feel the edge of the rug's hem with my toe, and stretch for it.

Not too fast, now.

Pause. Pull myself together.

Another coughing fit. I hung my head between my hands, and flung more blood, this time on the tilting table and onto the floor; only a little splash reached the divan.

This was a bad one. None of them were good, but this was very bad—one of the worst. I should've been in bed. I should have been sitting down at the very least.

I should rest on the floor and wait for my sister or the doctor to return. They would return, surely. Eventually.

But I was within perhaps ten feet of the cabinet, and the gun. I would feel less helpless with the gun, assuming I had the power to lift and wield it, when I barely had the power to lift and wield myself. And outside, a new sound urged me onward, reassuring me that this was a night when I could not afford to be helpless. It was not a keening, precisely . . . it was lower than that. I thought it must be louder than the thunder, though it seemed to come from farther away, from out in the ocean.

It was not the cry of any creature I'd ever heard, and anyway, what throat could produce such a bellow? Nothing smaller than Fall River itself. Nothing smaller than Boston, perhaps. It was as if a whole city screamed in pain or longing.

I listened, but listening told me nothing—except that something huge cried out somewhere far away, and I heard it, and I didn't know what it meant. I looked out the window. It was a stupid gesture, for I rationally knew that I wouldn't be able to see a great marauding monster rearing up out of the ocean—or anything of that sort, despite what damage had been done to rational knowledge these recent months. But I looked anyway, and I saw the sky still wild, the wind thrashing the trees. The light showing me the yard, the neighbors' houses, the street outside which had only been paved last year.

The man.

I froze.

I'd say that our eyes locked, except that I couldn't see his eyes. Everything about him was left in shadow, and I saw little to distinguish him. A hat, tall enough to be a little out of fashion. Shoulders that implied a good tailor with a fondness for sharp cuts. A cane in his left hand, or a stick of some sort. He didn't lean on it. He held it, like it anchored him.

I wiped my mouth with the sleeve of my dress. I left a smudge of vivid crimson there—the kind of red you see when blood comes straight from the lungs. I know it means that I'm dying. That's what it's always meant.

I looked to the front door. Seabury had the good sense to close it and lock it as he left, trailing behind my sister. Maybe he had only abandoned me without a first thought, and spared me a second one after all. But how long would the lock hold? A few minutes? A few seconds?

I looked again to the cabinet, and the drawer where waited the gun.

I could reach it. I could use what willpower and effort I had left in my reserves to seize it and brandish it, probably before the man outside (it wasn't a man, but you understand my meaning) could reach the door, open it, and accost me in whatever gruesome fashion he undoubtedly had planned.

I had seen the news articles. I had spoken to Seabury when he was flush with brandy, and sharing more than he intended about what was coming across the state, barreling down upon us like a train, only so much worse.

I looked at the man (who wasn't a man) and I waited for the lightning to flare just right, at the precise angle needed to see him more fully.

He did not move, and that flare did not come.

So it must have been by design—surely no accident—that the wonder-filled sky roared and complained, and illuminated the whole world except for the one man I most wished to see. (I know, I know. Not a man. But shaped like one.)

And if the weather itself worked against me . . . if he was the one who compelled the lightning (not lightning, but shaped like it) . . . what good would a single revolver be against that kind of might?

I was afraid to look away from the shadow on the lawn. If I looked away, he might vanish—only to reappear nearer. If I looked away, he could do anything. Be anything. Become anything. But not while I watched. So long as I fixed him with my gaze, he would not move; I felt it like a superstition. It was a fiction I invented on the spot, and when he moved . . . it wasn't a grand motion, just an adjustment of his hand upon the head of the cane, but it shocked me.

It positively *undid* me.

It shouldn't have. I know exactly how useless superstition is.

I whipped my eyes over to the cabinet again, and dismissed

the gun as being too much trouble. What good is a gun against something like him?

(It. This was no longer a *him*.)

"Zollicoffer." I said his name, because the oldest stories of all make it clear that names have power. God named Adam, and Adam named the animals. This is how we know who has power over whom. Witches, warlocks, and servants of gods keep their names to themselves, lest they be used in magic against them.

Well, I didn't give him his name, but I knew it. (Its name.)

"Zollicoffer," I said again. "Come and get me, if that's what you're here for."

He would come anyway, whether invited or not. I knew it as well as he did, but I'd made the challenge, and now the terms were mine. I would not die on any other.

I turned to the end of the divan, and shuffled down its length at a quicker pace than before. This threat was no theory, no potential hazard. Now this was a monster, and it was here. (He was here.) My chest ached, and it might have only been some morbid fancy on my part, but I swear I felt the blood sloshing back and forth in my lungs. Let it slosh, I thought. Just let me reach the cellar.

I'd never attempted the cellar stairs before.

It'd been too dangerous, too ludicrous to attempt it, which often made me sad and a bit jealous. Between the two of us, Lizzie was not the scientist; the vials, burners, and tubes were not her passion or pastime. *I* should have been the one to take the notes and watch the results. It should have been *me*, measuring carefully and plotting experiments. I would not have experimented with legend and lore. I would have put to bed her insistence on myth and mystery, and the nuggets of truth therein. She wasted her time looking for them. She crawled too far up her own hypothesis, and could not be lured back to reality. She could not be lured up the stairs, or convinced to bring me down them.

Oh, she claimed that this was for the best, and besides, the experiments she performed were gruesome. So she said.

Her idea of gruesome and mine have never matched up very well. Zollicoffer outside could've told her that, and maybe—had the sample I sent him been a benign, smelly thing—he would've had the chance.

Not now. We were all out of chances.

But down in the cellar there were toxins and globulins, every bit as risky as any magic potion. Untried, untested, unstudied—except on ordinary men and women, ordinary animals through the university. So it showed some progress against tetanus. Fine. So these creatures seem to be infected with some weird strain of tetanus. All right. The connection was tenuous . . . more tenuous than I'd wanted to let Lizzie know, not while she still held out some hope for Nance. But we were past that now, and I had nothing else at my disposal with which to fight—nothing else with even the vague peddler's promise of a weapon.

So when there is nothing left but magic, we start learning spells—and I'd rather take a chance on Seabury's scientific spells than on Lizzie's ancient songs.

My sister's judgment could not be trusted. Nance was proof of that. Seabury's behavior could not be trusted. His betrayal of my secret made that clear; but I might yet trust his training and his instincts. If not that, then perhaps I could trust his friend in Rhode Island. Perhaps I could trust a poison concocted by bright men in white coats, in clean, cold laboratories where things too small to see are grown and harvested.

These were the straws I grasped, one by one, all in a row. I followed them like bread crumbs.

Around the divan, to the stair rail again; along the wall, where I clung to the kitchen's entryway; my breathing was wretched and forced; I fell to my hands and knees, and while I was down there I crawled because there was nothing I could use to pull myself up. I reached the cellar door and I turned the knob, and at that very moment I heard a knocking at the front door.

Such a peculiar pleasantry. Can't imagine why he bothered. (Why it would've cared.)

I pushed the door open and nearly tumbled inward right down the stairs—a faster way down, to be sure, but not my goal. I caught myself, and it wasn't so bad. I had been sitting on the floor to start with; now I was only sprawled across it, half on the cellar landing and half in the kitchen. I drew myself onward with my hands, to the edge of the landing and to the step beyond it. I turned on my hip and thigh, so that I faced the right direction. Should I fall, I could at least fall productively, and in a somewhat controlled fashion.

I pulled my feet over the edge, and felt for the next step; I grasped the handrail and gave it a tug, knowing it might not hold me. I went sideways, almost, using my bottom to catch myself. One step. Caught with my toes, my knees, my rear end. Another step, navigated painstakingly in the same way. A third. How many? Eleven more to go.

Another knock behind me, more impatient and less precise, less polite.

Let him knock.

I did not stop my downward progression, painful though it might have been. I coughed, and wiped with my arm. I spread more phlegm and gore before me; I dragged it after me, smeared it with my dress and my hands. Everywhere I went, everything I touched . . . I left it looking like the scene of a terrible crime.

When I thought about it that way, it was almost funny—or I almost thought so, in one moment of insane hilarity. I was creating my own murder evidence, wasn't I? Just as well I make a big mess of it. It might be my last creative act.

In my head, I performed calculations. Seven to twelve seconds per step. Another ten steps. Nine steps. A minute or so left, depending on how my strength held up. Less than that if I slipped and fell, meaning no strength left at the bottom. (I was reasonably certain.) Less time also if I were to tuck my head down, release the handrail above me, and roll forward. Perhaps some strength left at the bottom, perhaps a broken neck.

Was it worth the risk? The thing at the door was knocking again, erratically now, without the rhythm of a visitor.

Five more stairs. I would not fling myself headlong. I would need my strength at the bottom, for I would need to stand again. From my elevated position on the incline, I could see where Seabury's satchel was placed, beside a packet of letters which he'd already read to me. And knowing their contents, I knew what to do with the contents of that satchel, if I could reach them.

First I had to reach them.

Three more stairs, and my body ached at every joint. The knocking upstairs had become constant and was coming harder, more like the pounding demands of a policeman or a burglar.

Why didn't it just come inside? If Nance could vanish from the basement, never mind the doors, walls, or anything else . . . why couldn't Zollicoffer appear in my presence, and frighten me in person?

Last stair.

My feet were finally on the floor, planted beside each other.

I leaned forward, hoping to leverage myself up off the step with my own momentum—but I went light-headed, and I swooned instead. I heard the sound of something dripping, and I wiped at my mouth again but found nothing new.

It was only blood. I watched a droplet fall from my face to the floor . . . but it was coming from my nose. I don't know why. That had never happened before.

I wiped my nose, then, and I looked back to see a trail of smudged blood behind me. It was all over my dress, all over the floor. All over everything upstairs, too. How much blood could I possibly have left?

No wonder my vision swam, and my head felt like it was stuffed with cotton.

I sniffed hard, and tasted the tang of filthy coins—which set me to coughing again, but what of it? I always coughed. If I didn't cough now, it'd be strange.

Upstairs, the front door broke.

I heard it shatter, and I heard bits of splintered wood bursting into the foyer. Glass was breaking, too, but I didn't know what or where. The china? The mirrors? The windows? Had Zollicoffer come alone, or had he brought minions?

I considered the corpses of the needle-teethed monsters Lizzie had carted indoors, into the cooker. She tried to prevent me from seeing them, but I saw them. She tried to protect me, I suppose, but she's never protected me from the right things. Not even when I told her what the right things were.

More breaking upstairs. Glass again, and something else. I couldn't imagine what, and didn't have time to—I knew that now. I was out of time for fancies and prayers, that was for damn sure. I only had time for action.

I hauled myself to my feet, and I felt the flimsy banister crack beneath my weight. I pushed myself off from it, and caught myself on the corner of the nearest table. This was not the table I needed. I needed the next one back. That's where Seabury's gift awaited. That's where he and Lizzie had been mixing up the treatments that did nothing to treat Nance.

(Or perhaps they did. Perhaps that's why she woke up at all. Maybe it gave her just enough strength to open her eyes and not kill everyone in the house. I doubt I'll ever know, and to be indelicate, *I do not care*.)

One more table back.

God, the whole room was full of them, a gauntlet of tables covered in delicate equipment. And there, in the middle of the floor, I spied the cooker. I'd never actually set eyes on it before, though obviously I knew its job and I knew about its installation. Lizzie had the whole thing brought in through the cellar entrance, so no one would see it. Even me.

(I know she did not mean to exclude me, but it's difficult to keep from feeling excluded.)

The cooker was bigger than I'd guessed; it looked menacing and awful—open wide and faintly bubbling, its corrosive agents always working, always cooking . . . even when there was nothing fresh to feed it.

I tiptoed around it, and when I was past it, I paused to heave the cabinet door closed.

It winded me something awful, but I couldn't chance leaving the thing opened like a trap—ready to swallow me up if I were frightened or careless.

More frightened than I was already, I mean.

I reached the satchel, and pulled it toward me by the strap—dragging it across the table and almost spilling the vials within it. (This was not careless. This was hasty by necessity, and those two things are not the same.) I sorted them quickly, for my knees were weak and I was horribly aware that they could fail me at any moment.

I did not know how long I had.

Globulin *here*, in these glass tubes—labeled on white paper with blue ink. Toxins *here*, in these tiny jars with the wax-sealed stoppers and warnings written in red ink. Simple enough.

There was less globulin to go around than toxins, for we'd been sampling those ourselves (and giving them to Nance), but it was too late for those anymore. If I was not immune by now, I never would be—and if those globulins had not been enough, more would be meaningless.

I had a theory. Or rather, Seabury had a theory.

It might be the last sane, intelligent thing he ever constructed, because if we are all to be honest with ourselves, and therefore with everyone else: The man is going mad. I don't know how much more time we'll have with him, before he is too far gone.

Upstairs, I heard footsteps. One, two, three, four. Pressed heavily into the floorboards, each with a musical creak. Each announcing something much larger than a man, or much heavier than a man ought to be, though I had seen its shape and it did not appear uncannily huge. And between the steps, the slow, inexorable motion of the thing drawing forward through our parlor, I heard the dull punctuation of his cane, tapping alongside his feet.

My brain raced. I would have given anything for more time.

There were so many things I could have done, should have

done, if only I'd had the strength and foresight. There might be time yet if I hadn't been left behind, ignored and abandoned like a baby bird having fallen from the nest, left for the cats.

It paused, and tapped its cane. Thoughtfully? Impatiently? I could not say.

And then it crossed the threshold into the kitchen. The timbre of its footsteps became more muffled when it reached the linoleum.

Had Lizzie taken her axe? She sometimes left it upstairs, and sometimes down here in the laboratory. I didn't see it. Not that I could've necessarily lifted it, but like the gun I did not have, it might've made me feel (or at least look) somewhat less defenseless. I'm not sure how long it'd fool anyone, but again, I did not know how much time I had.

My knees were quivering, and I knew they wouldn't remain locked for long. I grabbed the toxin vials and pocketed them all, a half dozen or more. Into my pockets they went, except for one—which I clutched as, yes, my legs gave way and I folded to the ground.

I withdrew as far as I could, scrambling slowly backward, with great difficulty. My whole body ached, and felt like it was not precisely mine. My bones felt like rubber, or something softer. Darkness scattered across my vision, and I struggled to see through it, to focus on the little vial full of awfulness in my hand—and its careful wax seal around the stopper.

I picked at it with my nails, and I looked up at the landing.

The gaslights were on, but they were not working correctly . . . unless that was some aggravating trick of the blood loss. The laboratory was not alight, but it glowed strangely, partly from the fixtures and partly from something I couldn't put my finger on. Around me the walls had a greenish tint, or maybe bluish from another angle. It was like being underwater. It was like holding your breath.

I looked up at the landing.

I didn't hear the footsteps anymore, because Zollicoffer had stopped walking. He was paused at the edge, not quite venturing onto the stairs. His feet and the tip of his cane. I could see nothing more. The light upstairs was brighter, and it illuminated him from behind; from my vantage point he was nothing but a pair of shoes and a walking stick, planted against the seam between my house and my cellar.

I did not move, not even to wipe my nose. I was bleeding again, and I could taste it all the more strongly—leaking down into my mouth as I gasped for air.

I'd overexerted myself, stretched myself so far beyond my ordinary limits that I thought I might be dying. I might not even live to see Zollicoffer come down the stairs. If he ever came down the stairs.

His disinclination to do so was driving me insane.

I wanted to scream at him—to tell him to come on down and do his worst, for heaven's sake! Or go away, if he'd rather. Go away, and wreak his preternatural destruction on some other town, some other house, some other woman. But I did not have the breath, and my lungs would not have let me speak above a whisper. (It would have been a wet whisper, and the words would've come out covered in blood.)

Zollicoffer, whether he was man or monster, ran the tip of his cane along the slim bit of wood into which the closed cellar door should sit. And he began to speak.

"What a funny superstition." The words poured down the stairs like boiled tar. "All these nails, beaten into place. An old ward. Something about the fey, or goblins, or whatever else you'd prefer to prohibit from your home."

I'd forgotten entirely. Lizzie and her nails, in the middle of the night. Every doorway, every windowsill.

"It is an old rule. I do not know how much truth it holds, or why. But I will confess, I can . . . *feel* them. The sharp spikes of iron, driven through the wood . . . I can feel them through my shoes. It is unpleasant, but by no means insurmountable. For *me,*" the man-shaped thing added quickly. "Though the smaller things that walk with me . . . they've elected to remain outside."

One by one, the ideas lined up neatly in my head. The nails, the rust. The tetanus.

There was a pattern after all. Seabury was right, in some fashion or another. And so was Lizzie.

I wondered where he was. I wondered if he'd caught up to my sister, or if he'd been captured by the smaller things Zollicoffer spoke of . . . torn apart by the needle-mouthed monsters that stalked Maplecroft in the wee hours, when we'd rather sleep than wage war.

Then I wondered about my sister.

The tip of the cane passed over the nails, each one pounded into the floor in a haphazard line. Then the left foot, and the right. `

"You see? It's only a peculiar sensation, that's all."

It descended the stairs with great deliberation, moving from the brightness upstairs to the cold, muted light here below. It did so with grace, and with the countenance of a curious man who is delighted by all the wonder he surveys.

It was of average height and a slender build, with a face that seemed very lean and sharp. That face cast strange shadows when it moved, those cheekbones, that high forehead, the cut of those rather full lips and devilishly arched brow. If I'd seen him on the street and mistaken him for a man, I would not have said he was handsome . . . not at first. But I would have looked at him twice, and on a second look, I might have revised my estimation.

I should say instead that it was *compelling.*

It wore a suit that had been finely tailored, perhaps for someone else. An expensive suit, and worn with rigid confidence . . . but I believe it was likely stolen. All of it, black and gray. From the shiny black shoes with the pointed toes, to the gray felt hat with the sweeping curves and lofty height.

It looked so very human, until it smiled at me.

I was cornered, pressed up against the wall, holding the vial of toxin between my fingers, behind my folded-up knees so he couldn't see what I was doing as I worried at the wax, picking at it without looking at it. I met his eyes instead. They were cold, not like a serpent's but like a shark's. Dead and hungry.

Slowly, deliberately, with profound and devilish malice, the thing walked toward me. It stopped less than ten feet away, and planted its cane down hard. Right atop the cooker, whose cabinet door I'd closed.

(I wondered if I should've left it open after all. If I could have found some way to push the creature inside, in case that might've killed it. Surely nothing could survive a bath in the cooker, could it? Not even this bony shark of a thing? Regardless, it was too late. I'd made my decision, and I would have to live with it. Or die by it, as the case may be.)

In that low, odd, smoother-than-oil voice, he said, "Doctor Jackson?"

I was startled by how unstartled it appeared. "Doctor

Zollicoffer?" I replied in a whisper, not because I was afraid of him (although I was), but because my strength was almost gone—and a whisper was the most I could manage. A whisper, and a frantic wheedling with my thumbnail, struggling to remove the stopper on my vial of toxin.

"I was." It confessed more than I'd asked it. "Now we are different, and we have you to thank."

"We . . . ?"

It came closer and crouched down, knees cracking as it bent nearer to my eye level. It left one hand atop the cane and regarded me with curiosity. "*We,*" it confirmed. "We are not what you expected. But then, you are not what we expected, either."

"I am a woman," I breathed.

"You are weak," it countered, as if I'd missed the point entirely. "But we can help."

"I don't want your help."

"Are you sure?" it asked, cocking its head and giving me an odious smile.

"I want you to leave."

"Yet you scarcely have the breath to say so. I was weak once, too."

"We aren't the same, you and I," I assured it.

It agreed. "No, not the same. But there is some sameness about us. We both see things more clearly than the rest. That's why you sent me the jar, isn't it?"

"I sent it because . . ." White sparks fizzled before my eyes, and I struggled to compose myself. I realized that I'd stopped picking at the wax cork, and I began again—adjusting myself to sit up straighter, hoping to mask the tiny motions of my subterfuge. "I thought you would find it . . . interesting."

It nodded vigorously. Earnestly. And for a moment I glimpsed, or I thought I glimpsed, some spark of the humanity he once had possessed—the eagerness for knowledge, for novelty. A fondness for discovery.

"Life-changing, really. And not just mine. Your small act of kindness will change the world." It turned that long, sharp nose to the right and its eyes closed halfway. It smiled again, lips pressed together. "Do you hear that?"

"Hear . . . what?"

"She's calling. She knows we are close. You and I," it clarified. "She's leading us home."

I wondered who she was, or *what* she was. But yes, I heard her. If "she" was the thing with the bellowing, wailing, moaning cry that overtook the storm outside. I shuddered to consider the possibility of it. "I hear her, but she does not . . . I do not feel . . . *called*," I tried to explain.

"You will," it insisted, and the two small words sent shivers down to my soul. "I will help you. I will bring you to her, and you will believe—and you will be strong."

Strong.

The word tugged at me, like I tugged on the cork—still wedged into place, but loosening with each passing second. I was running out of seconds, but in case it bought me more, I murmured, "I would like to be strong again."

I had pleased it. It smiled that eerie smile, the one that did not reach its eyes (and showed no teeth). Smoothly, it stretched out a hand in welcome.

The cork came loose.

Owen Seabury, M.D.

I refused to believe that Lizzie had drowned, though she looked drowned enough when I hauled her onto the pier. She's a little thing, but even little things are heavy as stones when wet, even when they don't fight you.

I have always been a good swimmer—and I've always enjoyed it—but I am older now, and not as strong as I once was.

I do not know what she saw, when she leaped off the tall rocks and went headlong into the water. Nance, I must assume. I didn't see her, but that doesn't mean she wasn't there.

I wished for more light and more time, but all I had was the thundering sky and the flashing, inconstant illumination of the lightning that never quite struck; and all I had was the time it took Lizzie to be sucked out away from the rocks, to the edge of the pier. I pulled off my coat as I ran, kicked off my shoes before I jumped, dove into the ocean, and drew myself toward the last place I'd seen her.

She hadn't gone far. I felt her before I saw her.

I caught her by the head—my fingers brushing what felt like seaweed. I wrenched her upright by a great tangle of her hair, out of the water, and I towed her back to the ladder, then hauled her up it.

She was so full of water.

The ocean poured out from her nose and mouth, and when I thought she couldn't possibly give up another drop, I sat her upright and squeezed her from behind. My arms were better leverage that way; and then, yes, more fluid spilled out from her mouth, so it must have been the right thing to do. Finally, I laid her back down again and checked her eyes. They had rolled back, showing too much white . . . but her lashes flickered, bucking against my probing fingers, and I was encouraged.

"Lizbeth!" I shouted her preferred name, and I slapped at her cheeks and gave up on the preferred nonsense and went for the more familiar. "Lizzie, answer me! You must answer me!"

She did answer—with a terrific intake of breath that transformed into ferocious coughing. She pulled away from me, and on her hands and knees she coughed up more, and then vomited, and then finally breathed. It was uneven, damaged breathing; the air raked back and forth out of her chest, but she was *breathing*.

"Where's . . ." She gargled the word.

"Nance is gone," I told her bluntly. Now was not the time for false reassurances or platitudes. "And Zollicoffer is coming. He's coming to Maplecroft, coming for your sister," I added, uncertain if that would spur her to action or give her pause. Their relationship had so clearly become . . . complicated. The

Problem complicated it. Nance complicated it. For that matter, maybe I did, too.

(As I'd fled the house, I wondered if I was making the wrong choice—picking the wrong sister to save, if I had to choose just one. What a terrible choice, not even spur of the moment. Not even a second to split, and I was forced to decide, regardless.

What was I to do?

Well, Lizzie ran, so I chased her. As useless and direct as a dog running after a cart, that's what I did.)

The sky was positively screaming, announcing the mad doctor's imminent visit . . . and the ocean howled it, too. I heard the water moaning, chanting a soulful tune. There was music to it, I swear. Music so slow and loud that it takes a long stretch of listening before you'd even recognize it as such. At first you'd think it was something like wind, roaring through a jagged cave. At first you'd think it might be a shout, offered over the ocean, its message garbled and lost. But if you listened, you'd know. Even if you didn't listen, it'd occur to you eventually . . . you couldn't escape it. You couldn't *not* hear it.

I held Lizzie by the shoulders as she hacked up the last of everything she'd swallowed. "Do you hear me?" I asked.

She nodded without looking at me, her hair spilling down to the ground, tangled and wet. "Emma," she said.

I was surprised. I'd expected her lover's name first, but maybe she believed me when I said the girl was gone; or maybe she knew something I didn't. Maybe she caught whatever she'd been chasing, and now she knew the loss for certain.

"Help me up," she said.

I did.

She used both hands to smooth her hair away from her face. "My axe," she said.

"I don't know where it is. I'm sorry. I didn't see where you dropped it."

But she pointed, back at the ground near the edge of the rocks. Yes, there it was—the oft-polished blade glittered in the light of the frantic sky. "I need it," she said, and she began to stagger toward it. Her strength was waning; small wonder, considering the mile-long run to the rocky shore, and her subsequent swim.

But she picked up speed as she stomped down the pier, her footsteps echoing loudly even against the thunder, and the cry of the ocean (if indeed it was the ocean, and not something worse). I followed her, not because I couldn't outpace her—she was still weak from her ordeal, or weaker than usual, if I must degrade her strength—but because I was ready to catch her if she stumbled or fell. I'd saved her; now I had to protect her. Now I was responsible for her. Isn't that the way of philosophy?

I patted at my chest for my gun, but it was gone. I'd lost it in the water, or somewhere along the way. "My gun!" I exclaimed, almost tripping at the end of the wooden walkway. I collected myself and arrived at Lizzie's side as she retrieved her weapon of choice. So one of us was armed, and there was that much on our side.

"When we get back to Maplecroft," she wheezed, "you can have my father's."

"Your father's?"

"His gun. Liquor cabinet, in the parlor. Top drawer," she said. She picked up the axe and flipped it expertly, feeling for the familiar move and sway of its weight with more grace and better precision than the most experienced of lumberjacks. It was almost lovely, the way she turned it between her hands—almost divine, how the light sparked off it and bounded back into the sky.

I was wrong. She wasn't weakened at all.

I do not know what fueled her beyond that point of near death, into vigorous rebellion. Pure willpower? Terror? Curiosity? Oh, but I hoped it was that simple.

She turned to me, and stepped so close that I could feel her breath in the hollow of my throat. Her gaze was dark and deadly, even though her eyes were rheumy and bloodshot, and vomit-water clouded the front of her dress.

She said, "He's here."

I nodded. "Let's go."

Together, we set off—not at top speed, but at a steady pace. Did I say it was a mile to Maplecroft? A little less than that, I think; but in the dark, after such an evening of exertion, an outright run was more than either of us could manage.

(It's more than I could've managed. I do not know about her, since I do not know what kept her moving. I did not want to consider that she was tainted somehow, too, granted extra strength, or a touch of madness, like the rest of them. I wonder if she wondered it about me. Fine then. We're all mad, maybe. No one will escape the Problem. Nothing but consensus will have the final say.)

Anyway we hurried as best we could, and as we retreated to the big house I tried to formulate some plan. "When we get there," I gasped, timing my words between footfalls, trying to lay them down between the crackling, fracturing heavens and all their requisite chatter. "We should . . ."

"Yes?" she said, not looking back. She still outpaced me. She was younger, after all. And I was glad she looked steadier now than when I'd first pulled her from the water; I was no longer certain I could catch her if she fell. I wasn't sure from one step to the next, for the exhaustion and confusion were at war with my excitement, and I was light-headed from the turbulence of it all.

"The toxins," I told her. "Use the toxins against the professor."

"You still think it will help?"

"It can't hurt to try," I insisted, my chest burning from the running and talking in tandem. This was what old age felt like. Old age and death: remembering how it felt to run without pain and the tightening lungs, but unable to do so anymore.

"The globulins . . . they worked on Nance." She nodded, but not to me. Still facing forward, toward the house, toward our fate—whatever it might turn out to be. "She did not go mad. She awoke. She did not kill us all."

A rather loose definition of success, but she wasn't wrong— and given the circumstances, I'd cling to anything, even a margin so slim as that one. Perhaps *someone* would make it out alive.

"But the toxins, not the globulins, they are . . ." I struggled to catch my breath. "Deadly. To us, maybe to them."

"I know. You told me."

I honestly could not recall having done so. I remembered *thinking* about telling her, and sorting out the facts, and working to assemble the loose pieces of this terrible puzzle. I remembered telling Emma. Or I thought I remembered. I might well have been wrong.

I am slipping.

The thought whisked through my mind. My feet were still sound. My footing was sound. The ground was not wet, for it had not actually rained at all—the sky's noisy protests be damned, it was only the squishing of my wet socks in wet shoes. I was running, and we were nearly upon Maplecroft, and my legs felt weak but I was still upright, still determined. But I was slipping all the same, and cursed to be aware of it. A stupider man might not have noticed. Someone more inclined to self-deception might never have considered it.

Regardless, there it was. A loosening grasp on sanity. One finger at a time giving up, letting go.

But I had no time to confront it, not then and there, when the house loomed up out of the darkness before us.

I say "loomed" as if it were a monster, and it wasn't; but the jagged, pretty, gingerbready shape loomed despite itself. A large, lovely place, broad and welcoming. A beautiful house, shrouded in darkness . . . and then, in flashes of light that wasn't lightning—illuminated and awful. The brilliant flickers showed the whole thing in stark shadow, black against white, and then the reverse . . . so quickly that the impression was burned on my retinas, making the effect all the stranger, every time I blinked.

"Doctor!" The word was strong and sharp, fired like a bullet.

Immediately, I knew why.

I announced, "I see them!" For I saw them, and it was enough to stop my hammering heart.

Crawling around the house like spiders, their spindly white hands clutching at the windowsills, the stairs, the bricks, the shrubs. Tramping on the roses, marching through the bushes. I saw half a dozen at a hasty count, but there must have been more around the rear of the house, or the sides we could not see. They were battering the place, but not entering it . . . as if some strange boundary or supernatural order prevented them.

One by one they looked away from the house, and they stared at us with hateful, hungry eyes that were pale and white. Fish eyes. Watery eyes. Eyes with hate, but not intelligence—not the clever, conniving eyes of a cephalopod, or the serious squint of a seal. These eyes were cold and flat like a shark's, but that is unfair. A shark's eyes were only black and hungry. They were not shrouded, and full of malice.

One by one the creatures peeled themselves away from the mansion, their attention drawn to us. Moths, and we were the flame. All but two, who remained at the front door on all fours, padding back and forth, their backs arched and their fingers pointed, they slathered and stalked.

The front door was open. It took me a few seconds to notice. It was open, but still they paced before it, unable or unwilling to enter.

I was confident that I had closed and locked the door behind me. It was the last sane, deliberate act I performed before leaving the house, in fierce pursuit of the younger Borden sister—leaving the elder one behind. Therefore, something or someone had opened it. Something or someone had gone inside, for surely Emma lacked the strength or the stupidity to leave it ajar.

"Lizzie," I breathed, drawing up to a halt.

She slowed to a sure-footed walk but did not stop. She adjusted her axe, twisting it back and forth between her hands. She said, "Stay with me."

Stay with her? I supposed there wasn't much choice.

She was armed and I was not—though I spent a frantic moment wondering if I shouldn't take the axe away from her and wield it myself. But no, that would not do, if for no other reason than that I probably couldn't. She might not leave me my hands. Or my life.

She was as single-minded as the creatures that stalked her porch.

I stayed close behind her as commanded, but I remained far

enough back that she was unlikely to strike me—which was good, because the first creature reached her and she whipped the axe around, catching it in the head. Splitting it like a melon. Not even looking at it, not even checking to see if it was down and would stay that way . . . she moved onward, keeping her eyes on the front door.

"They'll follow us inside . . . ?" I meant to suggest, and ended up asking, with a pitiful question mark affixed to the end.

"They won't."

She knew something that I didn't. And not for the first time, either.

We were drawing nearer and nearer to the house. More and more of the things were crawling into the yard, drawn by us. Having seen the one thing, the one time, all those nights ago when I first came to understand the mystery of this place . . . that was bad enough. This was a nightmare in motion, and God help me, we were all of us awake.

"Have you ever seen this many?" I asked her.

"No."

"They come from the water, don't they?" I was jogging again to keep up with her, and my breathing was raspy, not quite in her ear.

"I think so."

"That's why . . . that's why the toxin . . . the tetanus . . . your axe," I tried to tell her, but I could no longer talk and run at the same time. I had not enough strength to do both.

This is what I meant to tell her: the *tetani* bacteria cannot survive in the water—it needs open air to thrive. These creatures that she fells with her axe like so many trees . . . they never encounter the infection in their native environment, only on the land, here, where it lives so abundantly in the soil and in the flesh of our land-dwelling creatures, and heaven knows where else (or maybe heaven doesn't). They are vulnerable here. They are vulnerable to her axe. To us. They are not indomitable. (But neither are we.)

"The gun," she said. We had almost reached the porch. "Better than nothing."

"The cabinet?" I whispered harshly. It was the only voice I had left.

"Just inside. The near wall of the parlor," she gasped back. "I'll take care of these things."

She swung hard to the right and caught one of the brutes through the neck—fully beheading it, so great was her momentum. She reached the stairs and with one fast sweep she stunned the first sentinel at the door, and grievously wounded the other. Blood that looked like bile splattered across the paneling and across her dress, and the glittering shards of crystalline teeth sparkled across her nightdress. She swung again, and struck the creature again, pushing it aside.

She swept the way clear and faced the yard, where the bad things gathered. She braced herself and readied the axe.

Without looking at me, she said, "The cabinet. *Go.*"

"Yes," I said. Her plan was simple and clear, but I was thickheaded with fright, too tired to argue.

I jumped sideways past her, through the open door. Inside, it was dark. Or as dark as the night outside anyway—for Maplecroft's interior flickered and flashed between daylight-sharp and midnight-inscrutable.

I was disoriented.

I looked around and saw mostly black stripes of shadow cast by the windowpanes and curtains. I saw the outlines of fixtures and furniture, small statues and a pair of matching vases, the lacy shapes of doilies and shawls tossed across the divan, candlesticks they didn't need (now that the house had gas), and shards of broken glass. I do not know where it came from—if it was windows or picture frames or art glass from the shelves and cabinets.

My feet crunched upon it, announcing my presence as I dithered, unsure of myself.

I'd been in the parlor a hundred times. A thousand times. More than that, I knew . . . Where was the cabinet? I'd seen it. I'd leaned against it. I'd served myself a drink from it, when invited to do so. Suddenly I couldn't picture it to save my life; I stuttered on the entryway rug, then staggered to the hallway runner and then, yes, the parlor.

There it was.

I ripped the drawer open so hard I pulled it right off its rails and the gun toppled to the floor—along with a box of bullets that burst open, scattering its contents across the carpet. I dropped to my knees, scavenged a handful, and grabbed the gun, a service revolver. Its weight told me it was loaded.

(**funny**, the things you remember, from the old days in service. Old habits, old memories. My hands recalled the feel, the balance. The shape of the handle. It was similar to my own, the one I'd lost in the water. I think I lost it in the water. Might have lost it somewhere else. Likely, I'll never know.)

By the time I got to my feet, I could see Lizzie on the move outside.

Her dress billowed and she looked like a vengeful ghost, she moved so swiftly and with such grace—the wind tearing her hair and her clothes as she parried, struck, and swung with the axe she'd sharpened each night with deadly precision. She seemed bigger, wilder. Positively preternatural, though I saw her efforts only in fits and starts through the narrow frame of the doorway.

I was mesmerized for the moment.

She called my name. Not "Doctor," but "Owen!"

It was the first time I'd ever heard her say it. The informality worked. It roused me from my stupor, and surprised me into motion. I ran outside, ducking past her and narrowly missing the pendulum swing of the axe, sweeping in a terrible arc. It was a pure coincidence of timing that she missed me. I surely wasn't paying enough attention to have dodged the blow on purpose.

But I came out shooting.

I took her place on the porch, and I opened fire.

She ducked behind me, and disappeared inside.

I stood my ground, and I guarded the front door.

To my left, two dead creatures—one of them in pieces. To my right, a third dead thing, oozing gore. Its corpse was shifting; it wasn't moving, exactly. It was decomposing too fast, collapsing in upon itself. I don't know why. I didn't have time to investigate, though the question nagged at me. Fourth and fifth corpses were on the foot of the stairs or just beyond them. She'd killed them on the way inside, I dimly recalled.

A shriek rose up, and it was joined by other voices. They came from beside me, in front of me. From farther away—behind the house? Elsewhere in the neighborhood?—they sang out, meeting in a weird pitch that made my ears hum. Somewhere, more glass was breaking. I could barely hear it, but I knew the sound.

And here they came. A rickety wave of arms and legs with too many joints, mouths with too many teeth, eyes without enough pigment. The light storm showed me five, but I'd heard more than that. I knew there were more. I didn't have to see them to be confident of their presence, and I didn't have to count the bullets in my pocket, in my hand, in my gun, to know that there weren't enough.

I cocked the revolver and shot the first one between the eyes. Its head exploded in a mass of tissue and gristle, and whatever fluid filled those bulbous orbs it used to gaze out at the world. If in fact the things could see at all.

If there was blood, it didn't look like blood. If there was brain matter, I didn't see it . . . just the spongy, scrambled-egg leavings speckled with bone. They scattered across the porch and another creature came up behind it, slipped in the mess, and fell down.

I fired twice. It struggled, but did not stop coming so I fired again. It fell backward, off the steps, but I saw it moving.

Lizzie was right. She'd told me long ago that the axe worked better than bullets. But I didn't have an axe. I had bullets, maybe one or two left in the gun and a pocketful after that. I looked out across the lawn and counted seven, eight, maybe more. All of them coming for me.

The injured creature with the needle-glass teeth came crawling up the steps again. I kicked it back down. I shoved my boot into the center of its face, where a nose ought to go, but didn't.

It toppled backward again, but there were more. So many more.

Seconds away.

With a flick of my wrist, and that old muscle-memory from the war and from all the days after it, I reloaded on the fly and fired again. I aimed for their heads. If one shot could take them down, that was the shot that would do it. The dead thing beside me, added to Lizzie's pile, suggested as much.

But a glance down at the thing told me it twitched still, a jerk of the knee, a shift of the elbow. Its head was exploded, and still it struggled to rise.

I put my boot against this one, too. I stomped as hard as I could, catching its skull between the oak slat boards and my heel, and I crushed it down to pulp. Then I raised my gun. The rest of them were coming.

They were at the steps, fumbling up the bottom, grasping toward my feet.

I fired, and fired, and fired, and reloaded from my pocket until there were no more bullets left—and then I rushed inside the hall and slammed the door shut behind myself. I would have locked it, but the lock had ripped away, or blown away; it was gone, and I had nothing to barricade it with except for a nearby plant stand. I pulled it down and used it to brace the door in its frame—poorly, I'll grant, but better than nothing. I pulled up the carpet runner behind me, rolled it up, shoved it up against the door; I pulled down curtains and threw them into the pile along with their rods; I dragged a small end table into the mix and then a tall-backed chair from the parlor.

Outside, they cried . . . and they beat their hands against the badly shut door, but they did not push it open. Outside, they hovered and complained, as Lizzie promised they would. She knew something I didn't. Outside, they stayed.

(I was inside, where I'd chosen to make my stand—or been forced to make it, if I were being truthful in this record, which I will leave behind somewhere, for someone, in the event that I go fully mad. Let this remind Fall River that I was not always insane, and that I fought for my home. I fought for my life, my soul, my sanity. And for everyone else's.

Then again, maybe I'll destroy everything. This could be my last gift: that the world should never know the lengths we went to, when we stood between Fall River and the ocean . . . armed with little more than an old axe.)

𝕴 was forced to come inside. I could not have taken them all.

I went to the cabinet and found the rest of the bullets, scattered on the floor. I gathered them up carefully, quickly. I pocketed every last one, except for the six I thumbed into the chambers. My fingers shook. I dropped two bullets, and collected them again.

From below, far downstairs—in the cellar laboratory where I knew that Lizzie and Emma were not alone—I heard an inhuman, unearthly howl.

I cradled the gun. I leaned against the wall and fought for courage—any courage I might have left. I gathered it like bullets, and I feared that, like the bullets, it would not be enough.

Lizzie Andrew Borden

MAY 7, 1894

I left Seabury to hold the front door as long as he could, not because I thought he could defend us all against the peril outside, but because it might thin the ranks out there. We couldn't have those things running amok in the neighborhood, making Fall River an even greater hell than it'd already become. Killing them while they were gathered in one spot would be easier, in the long run, then hunting them all down later.

And it might buy me time.

I already knew that the nails were working, though why they worked, I still had no idea—and I still did not care. Tetanus poisoning, magic, some other mechanism . . . it did not matter. The barrier held true. The creatures had not come inside, and that was reassuring. It meant there was a pattern after all, and maybe

the pattern was broad enough to include the toxins and the globulins, because why not?

The front door had been opened, burst inward—its lock destroyed. *Something* had come inside. Not the minions, but their
master. He was strong enough to ignore my precautions. He
might well be strong enough to withstand the toxins, or bullets,
or my axe, or any other weapon at my disposal.

Then what would it take to kill him?

Once inside, I dithered but a moment—trying to figure out
what had happened to Emma. We'd left her sitting in the parlor; she couldn't have gone very far. Did the mad professor ab-
scond with her? Did she manage to move herself to safety?

No. There was no such thing.

Seabury was still shooting on the front porch. The repeated
percussions battered my ears, they were so very close, as I skit-
tered from room to room, looking for my sister. I slipped on
some bullets that had rolled across the foyer; Seabury must've
spilled them. I saw the opened drawer, dangling from its hole in
the cabinet. So we were all uncoordinated and frightened, and
not so alone after all. I had my axe. He had my father's old gun,
and that was good. Let it serve some purpose after all, and after
all these years. One last hurrah from the thing, and one more
hurrah for the old soldier who fired it into the night.

I hoped it was not his last. Or mine.

A wicked flash of illumination revealed a scene of bloody
carnage, bloody handprints. My sister's, I believed—but she
might not be injured. She might be coughing; this might be terrible, but not supernatural. Another stroke of lightning. More
blood, in smears and spatters. Well, if all that blood came from her
lungs and not some grievous wound, it was still bad enough. I'd

never known her to lose so much at once, in so many directions. It was everywhere. The floors, the banisters, the doorjambs.

I gave up on Emma. I had to.

Either she'd found a hiding spot, or she was gone—and either way, something had come inside. *Something* was here, even if she was not. If she was dead, there was nothing I could (or should) do for her. If she was alive, somewhere else, then I would do my best to keep her that way.

Wherever she was. Whatever had come inside.

I cut through the parlor, skidded into the kitchen, and saw the cellar door open. A damp, yellowish light spilled up into the first-floor space, gleaming on the linoleum—but everything was otherwise dark. I spent a moment confused . . . but how did it take me so long to notice the gas was off, or none of the lights were on? I don't know, but everything was dark except for the flickering sky, and maybe that was it. It flickered with such great constancy that it almost felt like midmorning, between the hard cuts of night.

And down below in the cellar, something else gave off its own peculiar light.

Whatever the light was, it hummed. It buzzed. It shifted from a sickly lemon color to a putrid soft green, and back again.

I heard the low tones of Emma's voice, too far away to pick out any of the words.

She was down *there*? In the laboratory? Having traversed all those steps? But *how*? The monster must have carried her there, or dragged her.

(**An** ungenerous thought streaked through my head: Perhaps he only invited her, and helped her along. She's always wanted to see the laboratory. I don't think it would require much persuasion on his part, or anyone else's.)

Another voice answered her.

Yes, there it was. A man's voice. Deep and very smooth—an educated voice, persuasive and almost warm. It carried a New England accent, highborn enough to sound like Old England, almost. It hummed, like the light downstairs. He must have brought the light with him. It must have been part of him, part of the unnatural madness he courted and spread like a disease.

The stairs were sharp and steep, and the light glowing from below made them disappear.

I stepped forward down into a black pit. My foot found the second step by memory, and the rest by force. I shuffled down them, my skirts snagging on the splinters, my free hand running along the rail for guidance.

My feet tripped over themselves; I only remained upright by virtue of momentum and the counterbalance of the axe.

I gripped it for my life.

I reached the bottom with a sharp gasp. It was hard beneath my feet, which wore only the tatters of my house slippers; I don't know how they'd even stayed on this long. Through the water and the running, it was nothing short of a miracle; but they were as wet and thin as old socks. They left damp footprints trailing behind me as I stepped forward into the grim yellow light . . . into my laboratory, where I was not alone.

Emma was there, and she was a terrible sight: covered in gore of her own making, spilled down her chin and matting her hair, staining her clothes. Her eyes were wild, and her body shook. She saw me. She tried to speak, but only coughed.

The man turned around, to see what she was looking at.

Oh, but he wasn't a man at all. I could see that in an instant. A dark, awful instant that I'd prefer to forget.

The not-a-man was slender and dressed well enough, in clothes that didn't quite fit him—he must have taken them from his victims, but he'd arranged them nicely. His shoulders were narrow, his hands long and delicate, like a pianist's. I met his eyes because I could not refuse them . . . they were the color of a storm clashing with a setting sun. Gray and blue marbles, with amber threads—but that makes them sound alive, doesn't it? And they weren't. They were utterly lifeless, though his face lit up at the sight of me . . . like he was pleased to see an old friend, long lost and thought forgotten. It turned my stomach.

"Elizabeth," he said.

"That's not my name."

"And your sister's name is not Edward, nor Edwin. Not Edgar, Ethan, Ellis, or Emerson. *Emma*," he said without looking at her. "You're Emma and Elizabeth."

"That has *never* been my name. Contrary to popular belief."

He ignored me, as if I had no idea what I was talking about. He would hear only what he wished to hear. It might be to my advantage—or that's what I told myself, even as the delirious slip and sweetness of his voice was confusing my brain. It was a spell of some kind, or if not a spell then something more scientific. But who cares about that? He was enchanting me, and I wanted to kill him for it.

"What do you want?" I asked him, knowing how little the answer meant. He would take what he wanted. He'd fight for it, or he'd charm it free. He stood and spoke and moved like a man (or something else) that knew he'd have his way eventually.

"I came here to visit my friend and colleague, the inestimable Doctor Jackson. Much to my sincere pleasure, I have found her . . . though I admit, I'm a bit stung. She could have told me the truth, and I would not have cared. Things might have gone differently, but by no means badly." He returned his attention to her. He wasn't really speaking to me when he continued.

"Once, I was a lonely man, and I looked forward to your letters. I might have appreciated them all the more, had I known they came from someone as beautiful . . ." He reached out and touched her tousled, bloodied hair, streaked with the wisps of silver. He caressed it almost lovingly. "And only a few years my senior . . . not more than a handful, I shouldn't think. Not scandalous in the slightest.

"But now you see, things are different. Not *perfectly* different, but different all the same. I believed that you and I shared the same goals. I thought we understood one another. Mother implied as much." He added that last part beneath his breath. He had doubts, and I was glad. Not everything was set in stone or water.

Not yet.

I pressed at his doubts, feeling for their edges. "I don't know who your mother is, and neither does Emma."

"You're not as wrong as you think. Not so incorrect as you fear."

(He was right, I think. I knew more than I understood. I knew when he spoke of his Mother that he meant the howling, hungry thing out in the ocean with a voice like chains grinding together, hauling something heavy out of the tide. Hers was the voice of salvage, of dredging. Of something larger and more terrible than a mountain, drawn out of the water foot by foot, by this thing in front of me. I knew Who She was. I knew that's Who called him. That's Who was calling us, calling for Her children.

But I was not Her child. Emma was not Her child, either. Nor the doctor, nor anyone else in Fall River, so help me *God*.)

𝕷𝖔𝖚𝖉𝖊𝖗, I complained, "That doesn't make any sense." I wanted his attention returned to me. I needed to take his eyes off my sister, to draw his attention elsewhere. He was creeping so very close . . . hovering in the very air she breathed. Close enough to kiss her.

"Sense is relative."

"Many things are relative," I agreed, stepping closer—against every instinct in my body. I wanted to flee, I wanted to scream for Seabury, but he was upstairs. I heard him moving furniture, barricading the door like a fool. Would he trap us all inside? With the monster himself? He must have gone madder than I'd considered, and I had a sickening moment of worry that this was deliberate on his part, that he was working in tandem with the monster now—completely overtaken.

I could not entertain the possibility. I forced it from my mind. If it was true, there was nothing I could do about it anyway.

"Why are you here? Who is your mother? Why can't you leave us alone?"

He fixated on Emma's face. A snake, charmed by the flute. Or was it the reverse? "*Our* Mother," he asserted.

"Our mother is dead," I countered.

"Not *that* one."

I looked down and saw the cooker's cupboard. The door was shut. I reached with my foot and opened it . . . quietly. Whether he heard or not, I couldn't tell. Maybe he did hear me, and didn't care. He didn't believe I was any threat to him, or his mysterious mother.

I tiptoed around the cooker and tried not to gaze down to

the rumbling, fizzing liquid within it. He was still a dozen feet away, with a heavy wood table between us. Could I move him a dozen feet? Could Emma?

He faced me again, that chilly, sharp face that was so white it was almost blue.

"You can hear Her, can't you? She calls us, Emma and me. Just as She spoke to your Nancy."

I swallowed hard. I breathed, "That isn't her name."

"You're very particular about such things, aren't you?" He viewed me quizzically.

I nodded hard, and I locked my eyes to his. If I hadn't, I might have watched Emma ratcheting herself to her feet. She used the wall to brace herself, used her knees to propel herself up, all the way. To the table's edge, which she grasped with one hand while the other hand felt quietly for a series of vials that were scattered across the top. She was already holding one; she was showing me what it was.

A tiny glass container tinkled when she knocked it over.

Trying to cover the sound, I said quickly: "Names mean things. You changed your own name, didn't you?"

He appeared confused, but only for a flash. He mouthed a word without speaking it. *Zollicoffris*, I think. "My name has always been . . ."

"Phillip Zollicoffer," I prompted. Emma was shaky on her feet. She shot me a look that I wished to God I knew how to read—but I couldn't watch her too closely. I didn't want him to see that she was upright behind him.

His lips twisted, miming what I'd said. I believe it honestly confused him; he toyed with the shape of it, uncertain of whether it was familiar or foreign in his mouth. He came to a decision. "Close enough," he said. And then he sounded more sure of himself as he looked over his shoulder and said to Emma: "You must come with me, you know. She wants to have us both. You were the one who found the specimen; you were the one who saved it from the sun." He looked back to me and said, "You see? Look, she is standing. Already she is stronger. She is ready and willing, little sister. You must not stand in her way."

Ready and willing?

When I looked at Emma's face, her posture, her fierce grip on the vial in her hand . . . it was not readiness or willingness I saw there. It was anger, red-hot and raw. She looked swiftly back and forth between the madman and myself, and for one blazing, awful instant I could not tell who she hated the most.

But I couldn't watch her, or interrogate her. I had to watch *him*, and while I had his attention, I said, "I won't let you leave with her. I won't let you take her away. She's all I have left. She's my whole world."

"It's not my fault that the feeling isn't mutual," he said, and I don't think he meant to be unkind. If anything, I heard some small note of apology in the observation.

Even so, his words bit me with their truth. He was charming me again . . . not to win my affection, but to keep me from interfering. That charming, charming voice, with those charming, charming eyes . . . except they weren't charming at all. They were dead inside, just like him.

I shook my head, and water sloshed roughly in my ears. I realized I was still holding my axe, but I'd let it sink. Its head was set upon the floor, and my fingers held it so loosely that I was in danger of dropping it altogether.

No.

I tightened my knuckles to clutch its reassuring handle, and lifted it up.

Emma lifted something up, too. The vial in her hand. She nodded at me, but I frowned at her—I still didn't understand! What did she want me to do? Was that the toxin? Were those the vials she fiddled and fumbled with? Yes, I thought so. What else could they be?

"I won't . . . go . . . with you," she told him.

Zollicoffer was not confused or angry, only insistent when he looked back to her and said, "You will. You must. I would not compel you of my own regard, but Mother compels *me*. This is the order, now. And you will see, it is for the best."

"To hell with you and your Mother."

She threw the vial. It hit him without hurting him that I could see, but the stopper had been removed and the contents splashed against his neck—splattering him from chest to cheekbones.

He winced, blinked, and regarded her with bemused astonishment. "What sad little trick have you played, Doctor Jackson?" He reached for his shirt buttons and tugged them, opening the fabric to expose his chest as if to examine it.

"The only one I had," she spit, and crumpled back to the floor.

He looked to me, as if I might explain.

So I did. In two steps I was past the table, and very near to him. I swung the axe.

He lifted an arm fast enough to deflect the blow, but the axe was heavy and my arm was strong; I caught him across the shoulder, missing most of the dampness she'd spilled upon him. He caught the iron head with his hand. It cut down, not too deep . . .

. . . but he withdrew, clutching at his fingers. The metal had burned him, or shocked him. He let go of the axe and pushed it away, trying to push me with it.

I ducked back, leaned to the side, and took another swing—not a great one, for I was off balance and we were in closer quarters now: between my sister and the table behind me, between the walls and the cooker with its opened cupboard and foul-smelling contents.

My next blow took him closer to the collarbone. It left a hard red dent in his flesh, but it did not cut him. What was he made of, now that he was no longer a man? His skin was tougher than leather!

He laughed at me, and pushed me back when I struck again. He grabbed at the handle this time; he was learning, you see. And he nearly jerked the weapon free, but I held on tightly and I would not let him shake me loose.

I kicked him and the leverage pushed me back, onto the floor on my rear, sliding and picking up splinters, picking up bruises.

"You can't hurt me, little sister."

"Yes, she can . . . *now*," Emma panted.

He ignored her, and tended to me instead. He loomed over me, not quite close enough to hit. It was the most open target I was likely to have . . . his shirt was still open, wet with the contents of Emma's vial. He was close enough that I could see the skin begin to bubble there, a tiny sizzling frisson that told me he could be hurt after all. That's what it said, that raw little patch of burning skin: *We have hurt him.* The toxins—Seabury had inoculated us against their deadly effects, but this creature before me, *he* was vulnerable. Why, I did not precisely know. Patterns, I supposed.

But I could kill him. I only needed the strength (and luck, and timing, and divine assistance, surely) to make it happen.

I crawled up to a crouch, braced myself, and I hurled the axe as hard as I could, straight at his head.

My aim wasn't perfect.

I caught him in the neck, and there—where the toxin was eating away at him, ever so slowly—his skin split beneath the blade.

No one was more astonished than I was, except possibly Emma.

No, not Emma after all. Emma did not see my blow, for she was unconscious. She'd slipped down to the floor, folded over like a ragdoll cast aside. Beneath her face, a dribble of blood and saliva pooled. Her gore-soaked hair was sticking to the floorboards, and her eyes were not quite closed.

But I couldn't rush to her side. Not yet.

I was transfixed by the axe, even as he pulled it free of his skull and tossed it out of my immediate reach. He clutched the wound it left behind, and blood the color of tar squeezed out from between his fingers.

I grabbed at the table and used it to pull myself up, knocking it over in the process.

But then I lunged at Doctor Phillip Zollicoffer, who had once sent us friendly notes about crustaceans and cephalopods, and had mailed us a box of chocolates shaped like seashells at Christmas, and had murdered countless people, lost his mind, his humanity, his soul—if I could bring myself to believe in souls anymore.

I lunged for him because somehow, he had killed Nance, and in some way he'd killed me, too. What on earth was left for me without her? A sister who loathed me, and a daft doctor who only wanted to help? There was nothing left worth counting.

I lunged for him, and I caught him in the torso, where his skin was peeling, crackling, and turning black. The toxin was still working, still weakening him. I took it as encouragement. I needed some. I needed something other than the press of his horrible body, and the stink of his skin corroding before my eyes.

Still holding on to his broken head, he pushed back with his shoulder, absorbing some of my momentum—but I shoved him again, with all my weight. Together we fell over the upended table—him backward, me atop him—and he tried to catch himself. He extended his free hand, and landed on it. Not half an inch beside the cooker.

He teetered. The edge so close he must've been able to smell the lye and the heat.

He leaned, and tried to roll away.

He released his grip on his head wound, and blood gushed forth . . . or if not blood, then something thicker than that. Whatever weird oil went through his veins, it splattered the room, the table, the floor, and the cooker.

Hastily he scrambled, the long pianist fingers clawing at the floor. The nails breaking, splitting. The fingers bleeding, dragging themselves up and down against the table, which lay on its side and blocked his escape. He scuttled on the floor, half-blinded by the fluids that drained from his head.

He was trapped between the table and the cooker. Between me, and the precious few weapons at my disposal. (The devil and the deep blue sea.)

I braced myself behind the table, planting my shoulder and my knee against it. (My laboratory. My table. My sword, my shield.) I threw all my weight against it, and it scooted—not even a foot. Not even another foot, when I pushed it again.

But it was *enough.*

I forced Zollicoffer back against the cooker's precipice, and past it, and over the edge.

Hip-first he splashed down, and the lye solution cascaded—

eroding and consuming, sizzling against his skin. It splashed and frothed wildly as he wrestled to escape, but I was behind the table, pushing it atop him, hounding him, hiding from the worst of the deadly acid spray.

Even as he bathed in the cooker, he was not finished yet. With a burst of strength, he seized the table and broke it—more by accident than design, I think. He was flailing; these were his death throes.

(But they were formidable, violent throes, and I knew all too well that I might not survive them.)

Lye sloshed onto the floor, and spattered the room. Without the table's protective barrier, I got spattered, too, though I scarcely felt it at first.

His hand seized my ankle, and he nearly pulled me into the cooker alongside him. But his energy waned. He only pulled me down, only to the edge, with those bony hands that had lost most of their skin—and were reduced to knuckles and tendons and twiggy phalanges exposed to the air.

He only brought me within kicking range.

I shoved my foot against his face and tried not to see how that face was melting, and how my foot scraped off a rag of skin from his forehead.

He released me. He leaned back, his mouth open to scream. His tongue withered, and writhed.

I dove for the cupboard door, refusing to look back—refusing to watch what I was doing—and I lifted it up, so I could close it down on top of him.

Or I *tried* to close it.

One of his arms and one leg refused to be contained, though the rest of his body thrashed in the cooker's belly; still, even as it ate him alive, he sought to drown me, too, in the depths of the machine, if not in the ocean, where he would take Emma. Where somehow he'd taken Nance.

Where we all came from. Where we all were going.

I climbed atop the cupboard door and held it upon him, using what little leverage I had to offer; and when Seabury finally appeared at the top of the steps, crying my name and Emma's . . . I screamed for him to join me.

(He did not attempt to rescue the madman, thank God. He did not try to feed me to the cooker. He was not mad after all. Not that mad, anyway. Not that *kind* of mad, at least. Not so mad that he did not know himself, and who his friends were.)

Together the good doctor and I held him down, and in time, there was not enough left of Zollicoffer to move those stray appendages.

He stopped fighting.

The only thrashing came from the chemicals, given so much work to do. The only protests came from the floorboards, all of them near the cooker ruined by the acids. The only burns and stains left were on my arms, and my knees where I'd knelt in the puddles.

We opened the lid, just enough to shove the rest of him inside, and the straggling scraps of his corpse disappeared, sank, and began their dissolution into liquid.

Seabury and I laid ourselves down on the cupboard door, holding it down with our bodies, not believing it was enough. Not until we stopped panting and caught our breath, and realized that there was no more thunder. There were no more cries from beneath the ocean, crashing over the land, rumbling across the sky. The house was dark. The basement was darker still, or it would've been, except for the pitiful sizzle of one lone gas lamp that struggled against the shadows.

Seabury carried Emma upstairs and tended to her while I bathed, discovering new injuries, new burns, with every swipe of the washcloth.

The water made me scream, and I chewed through my bottom lip trying to contain myself, to hold in all the pain. My blood tasted like pocket change. The burns and welts blistered, and seared, and stung like brimstone on my forearms and ankles.

My skin rose, and puckered.

I soaked myself in the tub where Nance had drowned but did not die, and I did not think of her floating hair and her waterlogged skin. I did not remember the touch of her lips on mine, her hands on mine, her body on mine. I held the soap and I held the rag, and I washed and washed and washed until my fingers were prunes and the water had gone cold.

Nothing was clean.

Nothing was finished. Everything was merely *over*.

Inspector Simon Wolf

July 4, 1895

Boston, Massachusetts—Eighth Street Office

Post-field report

It is true that my initial reports were sparse; but given the deaths across the state prior to the Fall River Event, my attention and my resources were stretched perilously thin. Even a man of my size can't reach from the northern boundary to the ocean—not when scores of grisly murders lingered on the docket, each incident demanding investigation and assessment. If I had been allowed to proceed directly to Fall River, once it became clear that this was the locus of whatever occurred, I might have been able to offer a better understanding of how and why so many have died in the stretch between August of 1892 and May of 1894.

As things stand, all I could do was send warning to my contacts there. I gave them all the time to ready themselves that I could. If you'd allowed me to raise a few good men to assist at Maplecroft, they might have been readier still.

Maybe a small force would've changed the outcome there, and maybe not. But it was cruel of you to prevent me from giving it a try.

I realize that some of my superiors would quarrel with my dates, but I will insist with my dying breath that Abigail and Andrew Borden were the start of this. Perhaps not the center of it, no, but a catalyst of some kind. Somehow, they were the first.

I cannot say for certain, as I was not present for their murders or the subsequent trial—though I've studied the court transcripts forward and backward. I've found nothing to contradict my conclusions, and plenty to support them. I know the captain calls the details "circumstantial," but he's mistaken, and I believe he might've been behind the sincere and deliberate effort to keep me away from that setting, even in the wake of the Hamilton case.

He thought I was on the wrong track, and wasting resources. He was mistaken about that, too. Now, I suppose, he's making an effort to save face.

I won't have it.

I was forced to lobby *vehemently* to address Ebenezer Hamilton with any specific authority, and this should not have been the case. No permission ought to have been required. I should have set off without questions or bureaucracy standing between myself and the answers we needed.

The present hierarchy is worse than inconvenient: It is *incompetent*. I can scarcely believe the organization took so long to classify these crimes as falling within our jurisdiction, when they were so *clearly* beyond the understood geometry of mankind.

Due to our consistent, solid, reproducible results, we have enjoyed the indulgence of the Boston law enforcement for this long—but the day may come when they realize what we are, and what we do. If we delay too long (as in this Fall River catastrophe), or fail too much (and *greatly* did we fail in this particular matter) . . . then the day may come when we are revealed as being too strange for them. They will blame us for the very horrors we seek to solve and remedy. They will cast us out like witches—and that's if we're lucky.

But I digress.

Something tells me you'll stop reading there and begin swearing aloud, calling for Miss Ellen to seek me out and fire me on the spot . . . but you really shouldn't. After all, I'm about to answer the laundry list of questions you put forth, in the wake of my initial response—wherein you called my research "incomplete" and my notes "full of holes." Of course it was incomplete and aerated; I was given neither the time nor the support to provide the fuller picture you ostensibly desired. If you actually wanted to see the scope of this thing, you should've left me to my own devices.

I have always performed best that way, and you damned well know it.

𝖂ith regard to Nance O'Neil, actress and woman of dubious moral fiber: No trace has yet been found, and I'd be astonished if that ever changes. I know her manager does not wish to hear my recommendation, but he can get in a very long line, I suppose—because here it is: She ought to be declared dead, and perhaps have a memorial plaque installed upon some theater house, somewhere, if people really cannot let it go.

The girl is gone. Whatever came for her, took her—and won't likely be persuaded to give her back.

According to the Borden sisters, she'd been ailing for some time before she vanished. Sleepwalking! That was their feeble explanation, and they had no plans to tell me the truth; that much was clear. And what could I possibly do about it? Argue? Threaten? Hardly a gentleman's response to the younger Borden's clear and authentic anguish. Besides, she may not really know. Being a witness to something and fully understanding it are hardly the same thing.

For that matter, it wouldn't be a chivalrous response to the elder sister, either, though Emma lends the impression that she's almost glad to be rid of Miss O'Neil. Whatever happened in that house, to that girl, wherever she's gone . . . Emma knows as much of the answer as anyone (however little that may be), but she'll speak of it no sooner than Lizzie.

Regardless of this bond of silence, Emma has no further interest in remaining in her sister's care. When last I spoke with her, she was in the process of moving out . . . undertaking the endeavor despite (or because of) a precipitous decline in her already meager strength. Apparently, she's made arrangements for herself at a health care facility in Providence. She offered no explanation for this, and Lizzie declined to supplement my understanding beyond a vague suggestion that Emma required more intensive care than she could provide at Maplecroft.

Something has happened between them, and maybe that something was Miss O'Neil, or maybe it was something else. Maybe the Fall River Event was more than their bond could stand. Maybe it was never a very tight bond to begin with. The age difference between them is something like ten or eleven years; their relationship was probably always a bit odd for siblings.

I overheard Emma curtly inform Lizzie that she intends to send letters. I guess we'll see how their future works out. Sometimes, a bit of distance can help. Sometimes, it's easier to write things down and mail them than to have the most difficult conversations in person.

I hope they *do* correspond, given the obvious sorrow and loneliness of the notorious Lizzie Borden, or Andrew, or whatever she's calling herself these days. (Sometimes she appropriates some version of her father's name, for the sake of anonymity—or something like it.) I do believe the woman is guilty of her parents' murders, but there's no proving it now . . . and if I could, I might not be inclined to. She isn't just hiding something. She's protecting something, perhaps with very good reason.

Something or someone. Herself? The town? Doctor Seabury? You tell me.

Speaking of Seabury, since you asked about his state as well, I wish I had better news. I noted previously that his mind was slipping, and that I had concerns about his continued involvement in these events—not that there was any good way to remove him from the situation. The ladies of Maplecroft took him into their confidence at the start of this affair, and could not (or would not) extricate him from it. If anything, he's been their sole friend and confidant these last couple of years.

But when I asked after him, Emma could scarcely bring herself to say his name. When she did, it was with a bitter gleam in her eyes. That woman is leaving town, and she's not looking back. I'm not sure I blame her.

(Do what you must; that's what I say. But then, I rather liked her. I wish her well, for all that my wishing can do for her.)

But Seabury. His state. When I finally caught up to him for coffee, it was clear that he's slipping yet further, and I'm not sure how it'll end.

He's unlikely to recover from whatever ailment plagues his mind—experience has taught us that, if little else. He remains mostly sequestered in his own home, rearranging the furniture and muttering to himself, pretending that all is well and he's cleaning house, or searching for some long-lost documents belonging to his late wife, or . . . or whatever excuse he reaches most easily these days. The man is building a fort, and he means to live the rest of his days barricaded inside it.

Lizzie makes a routine effort to engage him, visiting with cooked meals or merely companionship; but from what I saw, it's almost entirely one-sided. Only once in a while will Seabury rouse himself and notice she's present—at which point he'll begin to chatter wildly about all the preparations and warnings yet to be made before "mother" arrives.

God only knows what he's talking about. His mother's been dead for decades.

Well, God and Lizzie Borden, perhaps. She's patient with him, gentle and kind. Especially now that her sister is leaving, she has no one else to interact with, really. I suppose it's him or nobody.

Apart from her routine visits to the doctor in his makeshift fortress, she rarely leaves Maplecroft. She sits on her porch, which has been customized all the better to hide her—that she can rest outside in the fresh ocean air without being seen. She feeds and watches the birds, and she feeds and watches the stray cats—that the cats might leave the birds in peace. She reads the newspapers, and whatever books she orders from the library. She waits for Nance O'Neil, who will not return, and she waits on Owen Seabury, who will never leave.

If anyone knows the true shape and scope of what occurred in Fall River, it's her—but she doesn't know or trust me well enough to share that burden. She carries it around instead, as if it's more than ill cargo: it's a duty. *Her* duty. Her penance, maybe, for her transgressions carried out since the axe first hit her father. (Or was it her mother—stepmother—she struck first? I'll be damned if I can recall. At any rate, you know what I mean.)

I am satisfied that I know some vague outline of what's taken place, and I know it better than you ever might—not because I'm unwilling to give you the information, but because you're unwilling to receive it. You asked me to investigate, and I investigated. I can't help it if you don't like the results. The facts are the facts, warped and strange and uncertain though they might be. I'd know more of them if you had given me room to find them.

But I'm finished complaining about that. I'm finished complaining about you, and the organization, and the lack of support combined with the rise in demands. I'm done, do you hear me? Give me the freedom and resources to do my job, or cut me loose.

Perhaps I can be of greater service to mankind without you.

Yrs,
SW